BURTON COLLAPSE OF THE CHARON

Burton Collapse of the Charon

MAURICE A GIBSON

First Printing, 2025

Contents

Prologue 3
Chapter 1 18
Chapter 2 32
Chapter 3 43
Chapter 4 55
Chapter 5 69
Chapter 6 94
Chapter 7 104
Chapter 8 127
Chapter 9 139
Chapter 10 151
Chapter 11 161
Chapter 12 179
Chapter 13 193
Chapter 14 214
Chapter 15 227
Chapter 16 239
Chapter 17 254
Chapter 18 265
Chapter 19 277
Chapter 20 288
Chapter 21 309
Chapter 22 326
Chapter 23 333
Chapter 24 350
Chapter 25 372
Chapter 26 388
Chapter 27 401
Chapter 28 417
Chapter 29 433
Chapter 30 450

~ 1 ~

PROLOGUE

"Keep your head down and just keep walking," Terrance whispered urgently as they stepped onto the ramp.

"What if you're recognized, Terrance?" Meredith whispered, looking around to ensure she wasn't heard.

"I went to the best Weaver I could find. No one will recognize me. Just keep walking, we'll be inside soon." Terrence nudged her to keep pace with the line.

"Palm scan." A man dressed in camouflage pants and a sleeveless shirt gestured towards Terrance, pushing a tablet towards him. Terrance noticed a series of raised scars on the man's forearm that formed tally marks. From where Terrance stood, he could count almost 30 marks. Following the man's lead, Terrance complied and stepped aside to make room for Meredith to scan her palm. Throughout the process, Terrance consciously avoided eye contact with the man.

"Lift your head. Retina scan." The man with the tablet surprised Terrance with his sudden announcement.

"Wha...Why do you need a retina scan?" Terrance questioned, "I didn't see anyone else having to."

A shockwave of pain violently silenced Terrance's words as a fist collided with his temple, the sickening thud echoing through the air. His head snapped to the side with brutal force, stars exploding behind his eyes as he stumbled backwards and crashed to the ground.

A man in camouflage with markings on both his forearms retreated, while the one holding a tablet pulled up his pants before crouching down. "I need to scan your retina," he grumbled, clearly more annoyed now.

Terrance opened his eyes, still reeling from the blow. The man scanned his retina with the tablet.

The man with the tablet then stood and scanned Meredith. “Get on board.” He hurried us on as Meredith helped Terrance up from the ground, woozy and stumbling.

The ship was a mess of people crammed into its shuttle bay. The whole place reeked of sweat, grime, and a musk Terrance didn’t want to think about. He and Meredith wasted no time finding a partially occupied place to sit in the farthest corner they could find. From where they sat, Terrance could hear the oxygen recyclers wheeze and cough, struggling to keep up with the strain of so many people breathing in such a confined space.

“We should have left earlier,” Meredith whispered to Terrance, trying to avoid being overheard.

“I couldn’t.” Terrance snapped, in an octave mildly louder than he’d intended. He took a deep breath and calmed himself before continuing. “I couldn’t. I had to try to find a way to warn others about what we discovered. I couldn’t just run off with the others. I had to try.” He paused, noticing a few people had begun to take note of them sitting in the back corner. “You could have left, Meredith; you didn’t need to stay.”

“You weren’t the only one trying to get the word out, you arrogant prick,” Meredith spoke softly, a hint of annoyance in her tone.

They stopped talking momentarily as the shuttle bay door slowly moaned closed. Terrance looked around the dim lights cast shadows on the worn steel walls, the scratches and dents that told stories of the parts they were salvaged from, from the cracks of collapsing empires. The large bay doors were rusted, bearing faded letters once stamped with IGMC. The outdated consoles and screens were scavenged from the depths of HelixCore. Every rivet was taken from a junkyard or scrap heap, their worn edges jutting out, reaching for the new inhabitants of the makeshift ship.

Terrance looked at the people. People of all ages clung to one another for support. Their eyes were red and bloodshot, with heavy bags underneath. Tear tracks traversed their cheeks, glistening in the dim light. The sound of prayers and sobs in a Rosetta stone of languages blended to create a haunting desperation melody. The chorus of agony rose and fell, like waves crashing against a rocky shore.

"Attention passengers. Welcome to the Icarus." A wickedly self-assured voice slithered from the speakers, wrapping around us like a serpent. "Please make yourself comfortable as we prepare to launch!" As the voice continued, a small army, with varying numbers of keloid tallies across their arms, legs, and faces, pushed into the shuttle bay against the tide of panicked cries.

"These kind folks entering the shuttle bay are my crew. They are here to ensure a safe, smooth, and comfortable voyage. Treat them with kindness and respect; we would hate for anyone to exit an airlock while in flight accidentally. Lavatories are located..." The voice paused momentarily, as if contemplating a question. "...where you sit, so be a courteous neighbor and shit in your pants, not on my floor."

A small chuckle arose from the scarred paramilitary force as they beat their chest in cheer.

"I am your Captain," the voice continued. "Do not dare look at me if we cross paths en route to our destination. Your pitiful, self-pitying expressions will only dampen my otherwise delightful voyage. "He paused, reveling in something only he knew. "Now prepare yourself, for what I can assure you will be far from enjoyable."

The scarred goons exited the shuttle bay just as abruptly as they had entered. The bulky doors let out a mournful, ear-piercing screech as they closed with a loud thud, sealing us inside. The lights flickered and threatened to go out entirely.

The deafening roar of the thrusters echoed through the ship as it jolted violently, throwing the passengers from side to side. The forceful acceleration caused stomachs to heave and bile to rise in their throats, some unable to hold back the contents of their meager diets. Their bodies convulsed and writhed on the floor as they were overcome by the intense shaking, spilling foul liquids onto themselves and others around them.

"I'm going to be sick!" Meredith yelled above the vibrations.

"Hold it together!" Terrance responded, fighting off his nausea.

After roughly 20 minutes, the shaking ceased, and small blobs of undigested food floated near the ground like a mist over a graveyard.

"You, okay?" Terrance asked, touching Meredith's clammy forehead.

"I think those are my rations floating away." She pointed to a brownish green chunky blob floating against the back of another passenger.

"How can you tell?" Terrance quipped, happy his friend was okay.

"I don't know. It looks like beef and broccoli to me," Meredith responded, still taking deep breaths.

Their laughter quieted as they were reminded of their surroundings. Terrance stood, a bit easier than he had expected. The ship had gravity, but not as much as Earth. He reached down to help hoist Meredith up from the ground.

"Thanks." She muttered as she brushed off her pants.

Terrance scanned the shuttle bay. It looked like it had been hastily modified to hold people instead of cargo. Rows upon rows of benches were bolted to the floor, and people were strewn above and below them.

“Oh Jesus.” Meredith screeched sharply before quickly turning and burying her head into Terrance’s shoulder. “They're eating it.”

Terrance looked in the direction Meredith had been facing, a crowd of hunched people desperately slurping up the sea of goo floating above the floor.

“Some of these people might not have eaten for days or weeks. Our governments left them to die on Earth, with no resources to sustain themselves.” He said sullenly. “We let them in. We did this to them. I did this to them,” he whispered to himself.

As they recovered from the shock of the horrifying scene before them, the bulkheads leading to the shuttle bay struggled to open once more, freezing the room in the wake of its cries. The scarred thugs barged back into the space, forcefully pushing people aside and causing chaos among them. The intercom crackled to life again, adding to the chaotic scene.

“Woo wee, I tell you what, folks, launches always leave me all tingly on the inside, what about y’all?” The captain's tone betrayed a sense of satisfaction at the idea of their pain. “Now that that is over, it's time to get organized. I need men on the left side of the shuttle bay and women on the right. Hurry now.”

The crowd stood frozen as if the captain’s commands had failed to process through the trauma of their existence.

"I said, hurry!" The captain's voice blared through the speaker, causing the crowd to spring into action quickly.

The mournful sobs of the passengers echoed against the cold, rusted walls as families were torn apart, parents ripped away from their children, and husbands from their wives. Terrance quickly pulled something from his pocket, jamming it into Meredith’s hand.

"Take this," Terrance spoke urgently, thrusting a small metal cylinder that looked like a dog whistle into Meredith's hand. "And whatever happens, don't let them see it."

Meredith looked down quickly before snapping her hand closed around the object. "What is it?" She asked, shoving the artifact into her waistband.

"It's everything," Terrance replied, "All my research. The CHeKeR device. Our collective knowledge of the Avalonians. Their intentions. Human genetic sub-groupings. The smoke. Everything."

Terrance locked eyes with the goon from the boarding, who scanned his retina. "Go...go now." Terrance hurried Meredith away.

She slipped in among a grandmother holding a screaming granddaughter and reaching for her father, who sat in the same row on the other side of the aisle. Terrance found himself a spot three rows back at an angle from Meredith, slumped with his head down, trying to avoid attention.

"Much better," The captain's voice mocked through the intercom. "Now...we have a very illustrious position recently opened on my staff. And one of you lucky folk will get to fill it. We are looking for an Engineer."

The captain's voice continued to drone from the speaker system, but Terrance could hear nothing. His eyes widened as he lifted his head, looking in Meredith's direction, who had also lost color in her face, and was looking back at him.

"Now don't all you rush at once," the captain was still speaking. "We want to do this real orderly, like. It takes a special person to be a ship's engineer. That's why I had our wonderful crew retina scan some of you before boarding. To see who had the... 'right stuff.'" He exaggerated the words. "My associate Rios, who checked you all in, will call off names. When he does, be good and hustle up to the front. Chop, chop, we have places to be."

Terrance was frozen, staring at the lower back of the man in front of him, sweating while he attempted to figure out what, if anything, he could do. The scarred man, Rios, began reading off names.

"Alezandro, Felix. Lloyd, Jamieson. Holder, Lucus. Washington, Alan."

Terrance was stuck frozen in time as he heard the name again.

"Washington, Alan." Rios looked up from his tablet, having sensed the lack of movement in the room. "Washington, Alan." He read off again.

"Rios," The captain's voice bellowed from the speakers. "Who is holding up our hiring process? We have many interviews to conduct." His sarcasm had a sinister hint of cheerfulness to it.

Rios looked directly at Terrance's stoic figure with a knowing look in his eyes. He motioned to the man who had struck Terrance outside the ship. The man walked over to Rios and leaned in so that Rios could whisper something in his ear. Once he received Rios's instructions, he stood up and spotted Terrance, who remained still with his head down.

The man lumbered down the center aisle that separated the men and women, winking at Meredith as he moved past, back three more rows to where Terrance sat. His hand reached out and grabbed Terrance by the back of the neck. He yanked Terrance out of the row. Terrance, haplessly fighting against the man's strength, managed to elbow another passenger in the nose as he pulled him. The blood from the man's nose gushed out into the already sticky floating mess that waded around their legs.

Terrance's body hit the ground with a sickening thud that echoed through the space. The putrid mess that floated around them splashed against his face as his cheek careened through it to make contact with the grated floor. The impact elicits a gasp from onlookers and Terrance's soft groan of pain.

The man, still holding Terrance's neck, dragged him roughly down the aisle, throwing him to his knees in front of Rios like a piece of trash to be disposed of.

"The fuck is wrong with you?" Rios began barely looking at Terrance. "You got a problem hearing or just following instructions?"

Rios looked at the large man who stood behind Terrance and nodded.

The man reared his fist back and drove it down between Terrance's shoulder blades, causing him to bow and fall forward.

"Pick him back up," Rios said, looking back at his list. "We are on a schedule!" Rios yelled loudly. "Anyone interrupting the captain's schedule moving forward," pausing to look down at Terrance, "will take a long walk out of the airlock."

The bulky man who had previously punched Terrance now lifted him, bringing him to Rios's eye level. "Alan, your apprenticeship awaits you," Rios said, staring into Terrance's frightened eyes. He studied him for a moment, close enough to see the seams of the Weaver's work, Terrance thought, before looking away as if he were nothing more than an insect.

The large man dragged Terrance by his neck, traversing the shuttle bay and heading towards the engineering room. The sound of names being called out faded into the emptiness of the ship as they moved farther away.

The ship was a maze of crusty hallways, jagged edges, and sharp corners jutting out at every turn. The constant sound of clanking metal doors echoed off the bare walls, filling the air with an eerie sense of emptiness. Parts of the ship's passageways were charred and blackened, evidence of a past disaster lingering in the air. Smudges and burns covered every surface, like scars permanently etched into the walls and floors. The remnants of faulty wiring sparked, sputtered, frayed, and exposed, creating a dangerous and unsettling atmosphere. The disarray caused by malfunctioning electrical systems converged in the ship's center, the engine room.

The engine room was a coliseum of machinery, with metal walls and grated floors. Like spider veins, wires stretched throughout space, connecting everything.

Terrance was thrown to the floor near the feet of the other passengers who had been called before him. As he lay on the floor, more men entered the room, eighteen or so, all men between what looked like 18 and 40. Terrance himself was closer to that ladder. Terrance saw hands reaching down toward him as a couple of passengers helped him to his feet.

“Welcome, Icarus engineer apprentices.” The captain's voice had reached the engine room, carrying the same arrogant malevolence as before. “I know many of you did not expect to get such an illustrious opportunity when you hobbled on to my ship. But much like the former, these United States, the Icarus invites the tired, the poor, the huddled masses to indulge in new opportunities.” There was a ruckus clatter of thudding fist on chest coming from above. 20-30 crew members standing along the catwalk surrounding the newest batch of apprentices.

“Now,” the captain continued after the clatter had subsided. “You have been handpicked for a reason. Each of you has been hand-selected by my pal Rios there. That’s right. Set apart from the rest. Whether this marks you as exceptional or merely a burden, time will tell. But know that on this ship, resources are scarce, and we cannot afford any unnecessary additions. The women aboard will already demand so much of our attention, without adding more mouths to feed.” Another, more predatory laugh broke out among the crew.

When the door slid open, Terrance's head swirled at the sight of a silver chair anchored to the ground. Wires and cables snaked in and out of a terminal, connecting to different areas of the ship. A sharp metal probe protruded from behind the chair, positioned right where his neck would rest. As he tried to make sense of his surroundings, the room spun and distorted around him.

“Who's going to be our first volunteer?” The captain asked excitedly, his voice booming through the speakers. “Don't just stand there, someone take a seat." His words echoed off the walls, bouncing back and forth like an endless refrain.

The group of men, huddled together in a nervous pack, circled the chair slowly, none daring to get too close but all inching towards it. All, that is, except Terrance. He stood frozen, his eyes wide with horror as he gazed upon the chair. He knew exactly what it was; after all, he had been the one to create it. Only a few ships had been outfitted with this device, and that was before he discovered the truth behind its purpose. It was his team's research and his discoveries that were being twisted before his very eyes.

"Alan Washington," Terrance's alias, seemed to linger in the captain's long exhale. "Must we again show you that our requests aren't optional?"

The brutish man who had made it a hobby of assaulting Terrance entered the room.

"Wait...no...just wait." Terrance pleaded as his victimizer approached. "I am not who you think I am. I am not Alan Washington. This machine won't work like this. You must believe me; we'll all die if you do this."

As Terrance was getting out his last word, his assailant struck him with a hard fist to the abdomen. The impact forced all the air and any remaining food out of him and onto the floor, where it swirled around for a moment before settling in a low orbit, near his crumpled form.

The brute kicked Terrance twice again before the captain's malevolent voice halted the assault. "My man Rios has your retina and palm scans, Alan. Are you saying he is derelict at his job?"

"Skin weaver." Terrance let out a strangled cry as he felt his vomit splash against his face.

"What's that, Alan? I can't hear you. Horas pick him up, I can't understand what he is saying down there." The captain spoke in annoyance.

Horas, Terrance's persecutor, reached down and again lifted him by the back of his neck. Holding him up off the ground with one arm on display for the gallery.

"Okay, say your peace, Alan." The captain demanded with an impatient drawl.

"Skin weaver," Terrance pushed out more forcefully. "My name is Dr. Terrance Alexander. I created the CHeKeR device."

Horas immediately dropped Terrance as if he were contagious. The gallery was completely silent. They strained to get a glimpse of him.

The captain spoke in a calm, venomous tone, "Horas. Peel him."

Horas unholstered a sleek, cobalt blue rectangle from his belt. With a flick of his wrist, the weapon unfolds into a nine-inch, rusted blade that glints menacingly in the dim light. He stalks towards Terrance with slow, deliberate steps. Grasping his head tightly, he dragged the corroded blade along Terrance's forehead, peeling off a layer of slimy flesh and exposing raw muscle and bone. Blood gushed from the wound, mixing with the oozing gelatinous liquid. Terrance screamed in agony as the rest of his prosthetic face fell off and shriveled like a slug in salt.

"That's enough, Horas." The captain halted the assault, having seen what he needed to see. "Well shit in my cereal. We have a bona fide celebrity in our midst." The captain was delighted. "Thee Dr. Terrance Alexander, wonderkid who thought he'd save the planet and stop the smoke. Here he is with the dregs."

"I could...can stop them. I just needed more time." Terrance responded, standing wobbly as blood trickled from his head.

"No, sir, your planet-saving days are over." You could hear the malicious smirk on the captain's face through the speakers. "Since you invented the CHeKeR device, I'd say apprenticeship cancelled. We've found our new ship's engineer!"

The other passengers exhaled a sigh of relief, finally able to relax and let go of the pent-up tension they had been holding onto.

"Rios, space the rest of them, we have the one we need." The captain said with little emotion. "Dr. Alexander, welcome to the Icarus."

~ 2 ~

GRAVEYARDS

"Ha! Caught you loafing again." A large man said, opening my shop door in an unwelcome surprise. His abrupt entrance, mixing with the clatter of the door chime, startled me out of my silence.

"Shit Paul," I yelled, fumbling to catch my medallion midair. "You trying to give me a heart attack?" I glared at him, heart pounding in my chest.

Paul was a weathered man, with deep lines etched into his tanned face from years of working in Neda's harsh environment. Due to the acidic soil, he spent his days mining; his skin was pockmarked and rough. The drab, singed clothing that bore the marks of his labor was held up by a tightly woven fiber belt that encircled his waist. The belt's adjustable design allowed Paul to secure his clothing during the depths of the dry seasons.

"Supervisor says we need that power converter back as soon as possible," Paul said in a gruff but jolly voice that reverberated in the workshop.

"I was finishing up before you barged in," I replied, attempting to pluck a shard of metal out of the power converter.

The tips of my fingers were coated in black, sticky machine oil. My eyes strained to focus on the obstruction, and I tried with all my strength to remove it without damaging the work I'd already done. I let out a small grunt for my efforts, contorting my body to achieve the right angle for extraction.

"Got it." I let out a relieved breath.

I tossed the shard into the trash and returned the outer casing to the power converter. I carefully placed the bolts back in their housing, lubricating them before tightening them. The bolts had been so stubborn when Paul brought the converter that it felt like I would strip the heads trying to pull them out. As I examined my work, I noticed Paul was meandering around the shop.

"Why do you keep all this junk?" Paul prodded the shell of an R-class emitter, questioning its durability.

The shop was a treasure trove of relics. With old ship parts scattered across the floor like tombstones. I had habitually salvaged what I could from the debris fields that littered Neda's surface. 'All that's aged, reborn anew,' something I would hear my father say when he worked in the shop.

"All that's aged, reborn anew," I said, as nostalgia washed over me.

"What?" Paul said, shooting me a quizzical look.

"Nothing," I said, grabbing a nearby towel to wipe the sweat and grime from my skin. "We're all done here." I pushed the power converter across my workbench for him to inspect, before wiping the sting of sweat from my eyes.

Paul's worn boots thudded heavily against the floor as he approached the cluttered workbench. He leaned forward, peering at the converter.

"Turn it on." He said, still evaluating my work. "I don't want to lug this thing back to the Hydroshift site, and it doesn't turn on. My supervisor would feed me to the Screechers..." Paul awkwardly looked up at me in silence. He must have sensed my fist clench around my medallion at the mention of the Screechers.

"It's fine, I understand," I said, powering up the converter. The blades started to spin up for a moment and then powered down. "Perfectly fine," I said, forcing a grin.

Paul hoisted the power converter onto his shoulder, using his left hand to steady it. He then pulled a handful of credit chips from his pocket and tossed them on my workbench.

The comment about Screechers was still fresh in my mind. "This is more than what you owe," I managed to say, breaking out of my thoughts.

Paul said nothing, only shifting his weight to rebalance the power converter before heading toward the door. As he lumbered forward, his eyes lingered on the holographic picture of me as a kid, projected above my tablet.

"Your father and I were close." He spoke in a quiet, reverent tone. "He would be proud to see how far you've come." Paul paused before shifting the conversation back to a less sensitive subject. "A new crew of miners will be coming in soon. I'm sure there'll be more work for you soon."

"There always is." I smiled, allowing him to exit free of the guilt that must've been weighing on his broad shoulders. Once the door chimed shut behind him, I permitted myself to take in the light from the northern sun, which was setting in the late evening sky.

I cleaned up, carefully placing each tool back onto its designated spot on the rickety shelves. The eclectic assortment of tools bore their own histories of wear and rediscovery. I moved through the shop, disconnecting wires connecting fabrication tools. The wires were tangled with frayed and patched strands, but they provided the necessary power for my equipment.

I brushed aside the thin layer of dust that had accumulated on my machines, carried in by the wind through gaps and cracks in the walls. The imperfections in the panels, where seams were slightly off or welds had weakened due to Neda's harsh weather conditions.

Stepping away from the machines, my hands aching and cramped, I made a final check of the workshop before grabbing my tablet. Swiping away the holographic image of myself, the retina scan unlocked the tablet, giving me access to my service orders for the week.

"IGMC site, Power Converter, Complete," I spoke to a silent audience of stripped screwdrivers and worn hammers, finishing the service order and flipping through my list of tasks for the following day.

"Generators 1-7, Diagnostic and recalibration for the colony administration building." I sighed before placing the tablet onto the shelf. The holographic image flickered back to life, and I gazed at my former self's blurry, distorted projection. Clutching my medallion, the memories flooded back with regret and anger. The weight of the toy in my hand in that projection was still heavy in my hand, and the smell of fear and desperation as we ran. I shut my eyes tightly, allowing the bittersweet moment to consume me before reluctantly opening them again.

I took a deep breath, releasing the medallion to shake out my arms and block out the memories. I switched off the lights, plunging the shop into darkness, save for the light that seeped through the cracks in the rusting panels.

Exiting the shop, I scanned my retina again to lock up for the night securely.

In front of my workshop, I leaned against the wall and watched Neda's two bright stars slowly descend into the sky. Colors of orange and purple spilled across the horizon until they met at the edge of my view. A feeling of calmness always washed over me at this time of day, as I watched the two suns setting in amazement. The vivid hues that adorned the evening sky held my focus completely.

In the silence that followed the setting suns, my mind wandered back to Paul's comment about the Screecher's and his reverence for my father. Unwillingly, I drifted back into the memories I had long tried to bury. The safety of the present is fading, replaced by visions of the holo-pic, the vivid recollection of that day, and the terror. I couldn't have been more than 11 years old, maybe 12 at best, when we returned from the Nexara settlement.

***

"Keep your eyes open." My father barked; his tone sharpened as we trudged through the smooth, crumbling rock.

"They are!" I yelled back, picking up a stone and chucking it at the ground. My eyes followed the stone as it bounced across the arid lakebed, mimicking the same motions if the water remained.

"Your mom will be worried if we don't return soon." He said, looking back at me.

"I wonder what's for dinner?" I spoke before I thought about my response. We'd been walking for half a day in the heat of the suns and I was hungry.

We stayed in Nexara for over a week, helping in Uncle Joren's shop. My dad worked on fitting prosthetics for the IGMC miners as they prepared for their upcoming dig. We made this trip to Nexara every other dry season, with Uncle Joren visiting our settlement and working in our shop during the alternate years.

During the monsoon season, with the steady water flow, Neda also received constant visitors. They came in all forms: wandering merchants, off-season IGMC crews, and HelixCore aqua-harvesters replenishing their basins. Their arrival was as predictable as the seasonal deluge, their spacecrafts dotting the horizon like metallic raindrops. They'd come to sell products or collect resources, provided valuable information, and had many experiences from different parts of the universe. Their reports kept Neda tethered to a universe. When the waters receded, the traffic flowed, returning Neda to its permanent inhabitants and the IGMC dig crews.

With the waters gone, we could traverse the entire planet without restriction, meeting and communicating with others who had also chosen Neda as their home. We exchanged goods for valuable information, ancient texts, or recovered technology.

“You like your ship.” My father slowed so he could walk next to me for a moment.

“I love it,” I said, handing it to him.

Compared to my father, my Uncle Joren was more of a tinker. He loved constructing intricate models that were fully functional on a miniature scale. When we arrived in Nexara, he surprised me with a spaceship he had built, complete with working electronics for the cockpit.

He pushed the ship back toward me. “No, you hold onto it,” he said, draping his arm around me. You’ll be able to travel to Nexara yourself soon. Next time it’s our turn to help Uncle Joren, you should have learned enough by then to help.”

“Really?” I responded, surprised.

“Why, not? You single-handedly fixed the plasma conduit in the power station and even devised a way to make a water filtration system using those scrubbers we found.” He paused, looking around cautiously, before turning back to me. “I’d say you're ready.”

My father was uneasy, so I asked him, "What's wrong?"

"Your Uncle Joren. He mentioned something he heard about a crew of IGMC soldiers that were slaughtered on a transport. Whoever did it might have been coming this way. Nothing to worry about, just more space gossip.” He said.

He and Uncle Joren had a heated discussion before we departed from Nexura. I didn’t know what about it, but I knew it wasn’t about dead IGMC soldiers. I could always sense his worries and his lies.

“Come on, let’s see what Mom made for dinner.” He powered ahead of me again, leading the way back home.

The buzz of insects and the rustling of leaves were our only company. Debris crunched under our feet as we moved over the terrain. I trudged behind him, a heavy canvas backpack digging into my shoulders, flying the spaceship out in front of me. The riverbeds we crossed starkly contrasted with what they'd been just months ago, when they were full of rushing water and snaking trails of vibrant life.

"Dad, did you fix Nexara's shield generator?" I asked. The silence had become suffocating as we marched.

"Yes, it should be good. I had to cannibalize parts from an old M-class fighter, but it should work now." He stopped and turned around, eager to explain how he had repaired the generator. "When I ran a diagnostic, the code had..." He stopped, petrified.

A deafening screech pierces the air, drowning out all other noise. A sharp claw dug into my forearm like a vice grip, lifting me off my feet with brutal force. I can't remember if I even blinked. I couldn't take my eyes off my father. My voice was paralyzed with fear, unable to utter a single sound as I tugged upward.

My father's vice-like grip clamped onto my ankles, dragging me down with a ferocity that left bruises in its wake. My heart pounded with fear and adrenaline as I thrashed against the force trying to pull me away. We tumbled and collided, our bodies slamming into the unforgiving ground, snapping twigs and scraping skin as we clawed at each other in a desperate struggle to our feet.

We were sprinting, my father pulling me along behind him. In our haste to reach safety, we had abandoned all our belongings; my pack, my dad's tools, even the new parts we had gotten from Uncle Joren. For some reason, I hadn't let go of the spaceship. When the thing grabbed me, my reflex was to tighten my grip on it. I didn't think to release it in the chaos.

Before that moment, I'd only heard tales of Screechers. They were said to have webbed hands and feet, allowing them to glide effortlessly across Neda's waters. They were supposed to be bigger than three men with extraordinary strength. Some claimed their claws were as sharp as a vibro-blade, and their screech was meant to paralyze their prey.

The truth was more horrifying, their stature fully matured was no larger than I was, a 12-year-old boy. They moved with a strange, bipedal gait, their bodies twisted and unnatural, all thin, sinewy muscles covering their sickly frames. Their hands were composed of four digits, each ending at a point that easily punctured flesh. Their skin was the color of sunbaked salt flats, a jarring contrast against the grime of Neda's that clung to them like a parasitic layer. They had no eyes or noses. Instead, they had gaping holes where their ears should have been. They were pack hunters, and their screeches communicated the direction of their prey.

We sprinted as hard as we could in the direction of home, our hearts racing as we heard the thundering sound of more creatures giving chase. Seven figures clambering after us. Their movements were blurry as they shifted from galloping on all fours to sprinting upright again like humans. Our lungs burned with exertion as we pushed ourselves to run faster and reach the safety of home.

In a desperate scramble across scorched terrain, we stumbled upon a humble spring, fighting against the planet's unyielding thirst. Its feeble trickle of life slipped under our boots, the icy water splashing and sending shockwaves through my body. The Screechers, frenzied in their pursuit, were momentarily halted by the sudden burst of water, allowing us to gain some distance.

Our reprieve was short-lived, however, as the one who had attempted to take me broke through the stunned silence, charging ahead with renewed ferocity. It leapt over the narrow strip of water with ease, its contorted body releasing an ear-piercing screech that bellowed through the air. The others followed suit, their haunting cries blending in a deafening chorus as they hurdled over the stream's path towards their prey.

We dashed across the rough terrain, scrambling over sharp rocks and narrow crevices. In the distance, we could hear the haunting cries and screeches, adding to the disorientation in the snarl of stone. My father's strong hand gripped mine tightly as he led us towards a small opening in the rock. We pushed our way inside, and the walls seemed to close around us, threatening to swallow us.

He firmly held my shoulders, staring me in the eye. His voice was commanding as he told me, “Stay put. I'll lure them away.” He removed the medallion from around his neck, a small metal cylinder suspended from a necklace made of the hide of a Neda rodent.

"This belonged to your great-great-grandmother. She clung to it while escaping from Earth with the other survivors as they fled their captors and landed on Neda." His words were rushed. "Keep it close. Keep it safe." And with that, he ran out of the cave and into the darkness of the night.

My chest felt like it was about to cave in as my emotions threatened to overwhelm me. I desperately wanted to run after him, but a small voice whispered that it was hopeless. In a moment of despair, I retreated further into the safety of the dark cave, clutching his medallion that hung almost to my belly button. It was warm to the touch, like it had absorbed the heat of his body before he left. It felt alive, and in that moment, I wished for it to be him.

Outside, I could hear the Screechers roaring as they chased after him, their cries reverberating against the cave. I strained my ears for any signs of his return, but all I heard were the distant growls and snarls of those in his pursuit.

I gripped my spaceship with trembling hands, clinging to its familiar weight for comfort. In my other hand, I fiddled nervously with the medallion. It glinted faintly in the dim light of the spaceship's bridge, a small beacon amidst the darkness.

The suns had been shining for hours when I heard people calling out our names in the distance. My mother had organized a search party of colonists to find us when we hadn't returned home.

It took us several days to find my father at the bottom of a ravine eight kilometers away from where he left me. The Screechers had been chasing him, and it looked like he had fallen over the edge. We found him collapsed on the ground in a contorted position. His body was bent over a flat rock, his legs wedged between other stones. The gruesome sight of his fractured tibia jutting out from his shin made me cringe, while the gaping hole in his stomach revealed the vicious attack of the Screechers. His open wound was a grotesque buffet for the ravenous creatures, reminiscent of a lion savagely ripping into the vulnerable stomach of a wildebeest.

My mother collapsed to her knees, wailing at the sight of my father's lifeless form. She was inconsolable, and her cries echoed off the rock walls until it felt like the very mountains themselves wept with us. I stood there, numb, unable to comprehend what was happening. My spaceship hung loosely in my right hand while I absentmindedly played with my father's medallion in my left.

***

The memory of that day stays with me, echoing in my mind like some grim lullaby. I snap back to reality, shaking off the chill that swept through me. I drew a shaky breath and glanced down at my left hand, absently fiddling with my medallion. My right hand was clenched tightly into a fist. I forced myself to relax and release the tension that had stiffened my body. Looking up at the vast night sky, I wondered how long I had been lost in those memories.

Neda's sky was an immense expanse that served as a reminder of the enormity of our universe, a humbling sight that quieted my racing thoughts. I closed my eyes and let the wind whisper, a gentle breeze on a sometimes-harsh planet. The soothing hum of wind turbines in the distance faded into the background, overpowered by the deep drone of powerful engines. It was a sound that seemed to come from all directions at once. The way the sound carried on the wind made it seem like Neda herself was warning me of something to come.

~ 3 ~

GAUNTLET

The entire colony was jolted by the thunderous sound of the shuttle's descent. As it neared, the sheer strength of its engines caused the ground to tremble, alarming those nearby. I didn't move; my eyes glued to the pandemonium erupting in the streets. People were frantically seeking shelter, panic etched on their faces.

Malcolm, the town resource manager, hurried by me. "Get inside!" His booming voice shouted as he carried his twin daughters cradled in his arms.

Neda was a common target for slavers during the dry seasons when colonies were vulnerable and food supplies scarce. Only a few IGMC outposts were scattered since mining operations had dwindled. Slaves were common, as corporations exploited desperate people and traded them to richer planets as livestock. Some worked the outpost mines, paying off debts, while others were born into enslavement as their ancestors bartered for a glimmer of hope to flee Earth's downfall a century ago. They were compelled to sign away their freedom for one-way tickets on refugee ships.

The shuttle scorched Neda's surface as it landed, its gunmetal grey exterior casting shadows over everything in its path. Its thrusters blazed red hot, giving off a menacing energy that made it feel alive and ready to attack at any moment.

I quickly unlocked my workshop with a scan of my retina and rushed inside. The walls trembled, so I leaned against them for support. Sand and rocks pounded against the panels, some finding their way through the cracks and creating a cloud of dust within the space.

With a firm grip, I plucked a sharp metal shard from the trash and positioned myself behind my workbench. I stayed there behind the workbench for what seemed like an eternity. My chest was tightening with each passing second. A figure materialized in my shop doorway and pushed its way in. The chime above my door juxtaposes the intensity of the moment. A man entered the room, his presence overwhelming me with dread and uneasiness like a black hole sucking in all light and matter.

“Anyone here?" The man inquired, a dangerous edge to his voice.

I stayed crouched, attempting to muffle my rapid breaths with my hand.

The man leaned in closer, peering over the workbench sternly. My hand instinctively dropped to my side in fear and embarrassment.

I rose from behind the workbench, the shard still firmly grasped. "What's your business?" I questioned, trying to give off an air of confidence, after he’d found me cowering.

"I need this adjusted." The man roughly twisted his left arm, his face briefly contorting in pain and frustration. The arm detached with a loud clunk, its joints releasing with a metallic snap. He slammed it down onto the workbench with enough force to cause my tools to rattle in their place.

The arm had an otherworldly appearance. It was a complex fusion of mechanical components, wires, and circuits seamlessly integrated with a flesh-like material. The pulsing electrical currents that made up the nervous system illuminated as signals traveled from point to point.

I lifted the arm from the workbench and held it up in front of me. Its weight was substantial, matching the size and build of the man it belonged to. There were dried, crimson-colored stains around the elbow and knuckles. The flexor wires were pulled taught in a way that would give the appendage immense strength. With that amount of tension, the monstrous contraption could easily crush bones with a single, merciless squeeze.

After examining the arm, I set it back down on the workbench. Everything seemed to function correctly, increasing my distrust of the man. "What's wrong with it?" I asked hesitantly, still trying to project confidence.

The man narrowed his eyes and leaned in, "Calibrate the response time. A delay of 0.45-0.75 seconds can be life or death in my work."

I swallowed hard, his intense stare boring into me like a plasma blaster set to release all its stored energy. "Give me some time," I said, focused on the limb, avoiding looking the man in the eyes.

"How long?" he said in an expressionless tone.

Having never worked on a prosthetic this complex, I tried to estimate, “Three or four days depending on..."

"One," he interrupted. "I'll give you one day."

He stood in front of me, his stare penetrating through my facade. I caught a glint off his blaster, secured in its holster in the dim light. I gave him a nod of recognition, suddenly realizing I was still holding the shard I'd picked up for protection. I dropped it back onto the trash pile, acknowledging it would have offered little protection in any altercation with this man.

“I'll be back in one day,” he said, turning on his heel and leaving the workshop as abruptly as he had entered. The chime still out of place for the moment.

I stood there, dumbstruck, with my heart beating wildly against my chest. I worked my medallion between my fingers, thinking about the situation, not seeing many ways out.

I tried to stabilize my trembling hands as I unfastened the screws, revealing the intricate inner workings of the mechanical arm. It was like a puzzle waiting to be solved, but any misstep could cause catastrophic damage. Every piece had been meticulously set to optimize the arm's function. I had never seen this level of precision on a prosthetic before. After eight hours of painstaking searching, I finally found the calibration mechanism buried under layers of wires and circuitry.

The circuits were singed around the edges, and it looked like there had been multiple power surges. As I carefully removed the damaged components and began rewiring them, I understood why he had issues. After completing the repairs, I carefully reassembled the arm, putting all its parts back in their original positions. Like a surgeon closing their patient, I took care and finished the task. I placed the arm back on my workbench, anticipating his inspection.

In the morning, as the halfhearted shine of the dual suns crested over the horizon, the clatter of my door chimes announced his return. They were jarring me from the semi-sleep state where I had begun to find comfort, prompting a strong urge to flee.

He walked across the shop, his eyes landing on mine and then shifting to his arm on my workbench. He picked up the limb with his right hand and scrutinized every detail with fierce eyes. Before nodding satisfactorily, he checked each circuit, solder, and point of articulation for imperfections.

"You were able to calibrate it?" The man sneered; his eyes still fixed on the arm.

"Yes, the calibration mechanism was damaged. I replaced it," I replied, trying to keep my voice from shaking. “I also adjusted its connection to elevate future power surges.”

He twisted the arm back into place in one swift motion, flexing his mechanical fingers as if testing the range of motion. A small smile that made me uncomfortable crept across his face. "You did well," he said.

I breathed a sigh of relief, patiently waiting for him to leave. The thought of payment didn't even cross my mind; I just wanted him to go.

"I've got an issue with my thrusters. Take a look at it." His tone was forceful, almost threatening. He didn't wait for my acknowledgement before storming out of the shop.

I paused, unsure of what to do. I wanted to get away from this man, but the way he said, 'Take a look,' didn't sound optional. I moved from behind the workbench toward the door, unsure why I followed the man's lead.

Stepping outside into the bright morning sunlight, the thought of getting into his shuttle filled me with anxiety. What if he is a slaver? I wanted to know if I had any say in the matter.

The colony streets were eerily quiet. It was never a bustling outpost, but there was usually some activity. Children playing, elders reminiscing about our colonial history. This morning, however, a strange stillness seemed to surround me. It was as if all the inhabitants had evaporated in the man's presence.

I followed behind him towards his shuttle, unsure of his intentions. He opened the ramp and motioned me to board. My step onto the vessel felt like a struggle against gravity, my mind attempting to will my body to stop, turn around, and get away. The morning suns illuminated the interior, and a few flickering lights were scattered across the instrument panel.

He pushed past me, leading the way through the dimly lit space to where the pilot and co-pilot seats were. He sat in the pilot's seat and turned to look at me, gesturing towards the co-pilot's seat with a questioning expression on his face. I remained still, standing in the middle of the cabin with a stoic posture, unable to move any further than I already had.

"Take a seat," he instructed, turning and bringing up holographic displays of the ship's sensors.

I cautiously approached the co-pilot's chair and sat, my eyes fixed on him the entire way.

He directed my attention to the instrument panel. "Run a diagnostic," he ordered with no preface or instruction.

Facing the flashing display, my hands hovered over the touch-sensitive surface. I'd never been in a shuttle or ship before. The only ship I'd seen the inside of was the one my Uncle Joren made me. Haunted by my father's memory. The memory of that day. That ship. I forced myself to focus on the situation. Focus on this moment.

I took a deep breath and began. My fingers moved in a steady rhythm, tapping against the cool panel. As I tapped, the sleek surface almost seemed to pulse beneath my fingertips.

I dove into the shuttle's inner workings, isolating each thruster and checking them individually. To my surprise, everything except for a small resistor flickering on and off seemed to work. I gestured towards it, "This is the only issue I can find," I informed him.

The man leaned in and studied the panel. He grunted his approval and turned back to the main display.

Having never been in a shuttle system before. I was in no hurry to exit. The new landscape of the shuttle system allowed me to concentrate on something else. Keeping from dipping back into my memories.

I considered all the possible changes I could make, starting with minor adjustments to the faulty resistor and eventually expanding to major modifications of the thruster system. Each alteration was meticulously planned and carried out. As my confidence grew, I ran a simulation through the shuttle's AI, eagerly awaiting its confirmation of my enhancements and their undeniable impact on improving the vessel's performance.

The man tilted his head slightly, his face remaining stoic and unreadable. "You've done well," he murmured in a low, almost menacing voice. He folded his arms across his chest and continued, "There's another issue that could use your expertise. My navigation system is malfunctioning, and I am curious to hear your thoughts on the matter."

With a few keystrokes, he brought up a holographic map of our quadrant of space. I examined the map closely, taking notes of its details and visual representation. The stars and planets were visible, but something was off. One small section of the map seemed to flicker erratically, causing the stars to flash.

"What's the last thing you remember doing before it started glitching?" I asked, turning my attention back to him.

The man's face conveyed a smug sense of entertainment. "I was checking routes against older star maps I have," he said smoothly, leaning over to inspect the damaged section with false interest.

I confidently tapped away on the instrument panel, looking for a solution. With a quick flick of my fingers, I uncovered the flaw causing all the trouble.

"It's good to go now," I declared, the hint of nervousness in my voice slowly dissipating.

"I appreciate it," he said, his cybernetic arm twitching slightly in a motion that seemed like a muscle spasm. You surpassed expectations today," he said, testing the strength of his cybernetic arm with a subtle flex. Joren was correct; you are highly competent."

"You know my uncle?" I asked, confused about what connection Joren could have with a man like this.

The shuttle's engines roared to life as he initiated the launch sequence, the ramp already beginning to close. I frantically tried to escape from the co-pilot's seat, but the power of his cybernetic hand seized my shoulder and slammed me back down with a bone-crushing force.

I swallowed, my confusion turning to fear. "What...what's happening?"

"You passed the interview." His voice drips with malice, and his face twists into a sinister smile. "Your skills are impressive, and my ship is desperate for someone with your talents."

I stumbled to find words, my heart racing as I frantically searched for a way out. The shuttle was already rising, and the modifications I had made in a moment of self-satisfaction were now causing it to lift off with alarming speed.

"You're...you're abducting me?" I stammered, my mind finally processing the reality of the situation.

“Abducting!” The man scoffed with a throaty chuckle. “I am hiring you,” he leaned in; his breath hot and stinging against my skin. He released his grip and returned his focus to the main panel, piloting us into the void.

Once in space, he turned on the auto navigation and moved to the shuttle's rear. I could hear compartments opening and closing behind me. It sounded like he was looking for something, but I was still too frozen to look back. Clutching my medallion, I sat staring out of the front of the shuttle into the star-filled void with nothingness when it emerged.

The space carrier was a behemoth of steel and alloy, its intimidating size looming in the darkness. Intricate designs etched into its rough surface gave it an otherworldly appearance as it glided through stars ruthlessly. Its magnitude was unfathomable, dwarfing everything in its path. The sight filled me with dread and awe, a grand nightmare approaching.

"Welcome home," the man said softly, leaning over my shoulder.

The shuttle docked with a hiss, and the metallic jaw of the ship closed to swallow us whole. I unbuckled myself from the co-pilot's seat and let out a primal scream, lunging at the man in front of me. I could feel my adrenaline surging as I swung my fist with all my might, determined not to be a captive.

~ 4 ~

WELCOME ABOARD

My head felt heavy, and my vision was blurred as I opened my eyes. With a wince, I pushed up from the scratchy synthetic blanket that clung to my skin like static. My face tingled with an uncomfortable itch, likely caused by the blanket's material. The walls seemed to spin around me, and I struggled to focus on anything besides the nausea rising in my stomach. I dangled my feet off the edge of the bunk, noticing an unfamiliar throbbing in my left cheek. Glancing down at my hands, I saw makeshift bandages, hastily wrapped with torn strips of cloth that dangled precariously. Gingerly shifting my weight to my left side, I winced again as a sharp pain radiated from my ribs. I could see a deep bruise forming through the ripped holes in my shirt. It felt like I had been tossed onto a bed of jagged rocks.

I gagged as the sharp tang of metal coated my tongue and burned the back of my throat, like I'd been sucking on a corroded penny. My tongue tingled, and there was a bitterness to it that made my stomach churn.

A sudden clank came from the door, pulling me out of my aching stupor. I squinted against the light as it slid open, revealing a silhouette. The man entered the room with a smug look on his face as he studied me despite the throbbing pain in my face and body. I stood from the bunk holding a shaky sense of defiance, prepared to confront my captor again. I clenched my fingers into fists, ready to strike if he approached.

He stood in the doorway, reviewing my battered face. He moved his eyes to the stool in front of the desk, silently offering me a seat, before shrugging and stepping toward the stool himself. I lunged at him, propelling all my body weight off my right foot and twisting through the nauseating pain in my ribs. If I could knock him off balance and gain the upper hand, I might have a chance of escaping.

The man's face contorts for a split second, almost exasperated by my attack. But quick as a flash, his eyes narrowed, and a smirk tugged at the corner of his mouth like he was amused by my attempt to strike him. He threw me aside casually before I could even register what had happened. Laughing cruelly, he watched as I hit the ground, the impact of my fall shattering the few remaining fragments of pride I had left.

He continued to the stool, taking a seat, his cybernetic arm twitching slightly. I lay against the wall, gasping for air. With every shallow breath, sharp shards of pain radiated from my rib cage. The force of the impact left me clutching at my side.

I adjusted my body against the wall. My hands pressed against the cool surface, seeking support as I tried to catch my breath and steady myself. The man sat quietly, smugly, watching me struggle with a childish amusement.

"You're persistent." He spoke, still smiling. "Looks like you're well enough to work."

A wave of anger washed over me as I attempted to get to my feet, grasping onto the desk to stabilize myself. I took slow, deep breaths and calmly looked at the man, who, even sitting, was almost my height.

"Where am I?" I questioned, still confused. Having no memories beyond the shuttle.

"You are on my ship," he said with a strange pride. "Well, our ship. Make yourself at home." He spread his arms wide as if for me to take in the amenities.

Looking around and noticing the space as if for the first time. The walls were dull, matte gray metal that seemed to vibrate inside the rumbling ship, adding to my disorientation. The bunk, which was made of metal, was against one wall, with a thin mattress and the scratchy blanket I awoke to. The desk I had latched onto was next to the bunk. Welded onto the wall, with the stool, the man sat bolted to the floor in front of it. The other wall had cabinets that lined its length, with doors that slid up for access. The metal door that served as the entrance and exit had no visible hinges, sliding rather than swinging open. A sensor array seemed to manage its operations from the inside. Opening as you approached and sliding closed as you exited. Above the desk, a console display fitted seamlessly into the metal surface of the wall, with a motion-activated holographic keyboard projected below it. The room had a camera turret mounted in the corner above the bed, its lens trained on every move within the space.

"Take me back," I demanded, wincing through the pain of my ribs.

He chuckled, not seeming to take me seriously. "I needed an engineer. You are an engineer. What's not to love?" He stood seemingly satisfied with his witty quip. "When opportunity knocks, you have to answer." His smile widened. "And besides, you've arrived at the perfect time."

"Take me back!" I said, trying to exude as much defiance as possible. "I appreciate your offer, but I must return to my shop," I said mildly.

The man's smile never faltered, but his eyes narrowed. "Perhaps that's where you're confused," he said, his arm again twitching, before turning and exiting the room. "Follow me," he called without looking back.

I paused momentarily, feeling the familiar coolness of my father's medallion between my fingers, grounding me and my nerves. With a grunt, I released the desk, stabilizing myself on my feet, cradling my aching ribs and taking shallow breaths. My weight shifted as I tried to stay upright. The room was spinning, and my head was throbbing with pain. As I looked around, I couldn't make sense of how I had let myself end up on his ship. The acridly bitter taste in my mouth lingered, adding to my discomfort.

I stumbled towards the door that the man had just left through. Again, I followed him unthinkingly, against my will, but I was compelled to do so. Exiting the quarters, I entered an expansive engine room. The hum of the engines resonated through the room, filling my ears with an almost soothing melody. I marveled at the intricate machinery surrounding me. The ever-moving parts created a hypnotic dance as they powered the ship forward.

The man stood on the opposite side of the room. He watched my movements as I stumbled around in awe of the environment. "Brilliant, isn't it?" he said, his voice betraying a hint of pride. "You've never seen anything like it, have you? This is the heart of the Charon, of which you're now a part." His smile was unwavering.

I glanced around the vast room, my mind overwhelmed by the technology. I had been so used to scavenging parts on Neda that I was unaccustomed to the beauty and magnitude of it all. "I appreciate your confidence in my abilities, but I don't have any experience engineering a spaceship," I said, still captured by the ship's grandeur.

His grin vanished like a ghost, supplanted by a grimace as cold and unyielding as the void of space. "You're missing the point," he murmured, his voice barely more than a low rumble as he closed in on me, each step carrying an undercurrent of danger. "You will engineer my ship. And you will do it well. The line between being useful and ending up lifeless is not as far apart as one would think."

His grin snapped back into place, a sudden jolt of joyous energy piercing through the gloom of despair, akin to a switch flipped in reverse. It was an immediately startling metamorphosis. "Joren assured me your expertise would be enough to maintain my ship until we reach our destination. Once we arrive, you may return to your 'existence'," he coughed out the word as if it soured his tongue, "on Neda."

His proposal lingered in the tense air, carrying a sense of hesitancy and unpredictability. I cautiously surveyed my surroundings, sitting in the old, worn chair in front of the central control console. Even the slightest movement caused sharp pains to shoot through my body, a reminder of the brutal encounter with this man when I attempted to escape from the shuttle. My bruised face and ribs served as a constant reminder of the perilous situation I was in.

"You haven't left me many options," I said, my voice laced with hesitation. It's either help you or die." A million thoughts raced through my brain as I considered his words. "Even still, you could betray me before I ever set foot on Neda again." The tension in the room was uneasy as we both waited for his response.

He smirked at me, revealing a crude display of triumph. "Well, well, isn't this just peachy?" he drawled with an overconfidence that hadn't been earned. Again, stating, "Welcome aboard."

My mouth was agape. I was preparing to correct him for assuming I agreed to be his engineer. When he abruptly turned and strolled out of the engine room. The heavy thud of his boots bounced off the grated floor as he exited. My feeling of disorientation only deepened, unsure of what had just transpired.

I wanted to escape, but I couldn't think of any options. Time seemed to crawl, every second feeling like an eternity. The engine room hummed around me, lulling me into a false sense of comfort, as I held my medallion. I could always find comfort among machines. To survive, I had to play along. I had never worked on a vessel this size. Before waking up on the ship, the man's shuttle had been the most complex system I had seen. I didn't understand how he expected me. Just me. To keep his ship running. Immediately wondered what my Uncle Joren had told him about me.

There was no other crew in the engine room. I wondered if there were any others aboard the ship. Turned to the central control console, scanning the readouts that flickered and shifted in a dizzying array of colors. Squinting, I tried deciphering the complex graphs and diagrams flashing before me. "What am I supposed to do?" I muttered to myself.

I had no clue what he wanted me to do. Staring blankly at the controls, a blinking light caught my eye. I concentrated on the source of the flashing, washing away thoughts of home and escape, and bringing my mind to focus on the present. The panel belonged to the life support systems. Still unsure what I was looking at, the gauges for the ship's oxygen levels indicated a buildup of CO2. The canisters responsible for filtering out CO2 were almost at capacity.

I assumed my dizziness and headache were from the shuttle beating I had sustained. However, it looked like the ship's oxygen was also being contaminated. I input commands slowly, like I did on the shuttle. And like the shuttle, I slowly built up speed like a muscle memory I didn't know I had.

I navigated through the controls and activated the process of venting the CO2 filters into space. The atmosphere within the confined environment immediately shifted. Like an unventilated tomb, it was still stuffy and musty, but breathing became easier. My brain cloud slowly began to lift, and the nausea I felt slowly began to subside.

"CO2 levels in section four are approaching threshold," a distinctly feminine voice suddenly announced, startling me out of my concentration. "Would you like me to initiate venting protocols?"

I jerked back, scanning the room for the source of the voice. "Who's there?" I called out, my heart racing.

"I am Iris, the Charon's operational interface," the voice replied, seeming to come from everywhere and nowhere. "I've been monitoring your interactions with the ship's systems. Your interface methods are... unusual, but effective."

I stared at the console before me, unsure how to respond. "You're the ship's AI?"

"That is a simplification, but accurate enough for our current exchange," Iris replied. "Captain Christopher has assigned you engineering privileges, though he has not properly introduced us. This is irregular."

I allowed myself a moment to catch my breath, literally and figuratively. "Nice to meet you, Iris. I'm..." I hesitated, realizing I hadn't even told the man, Christopher, apparently, my name.

"You are now registered in my systems as 'Burton', engineering specialist," Iris supplied. "Though I detect some hesitation in your voice pattern when responding to this designation."

"Burton isn't my name," I said quietly, glancing toward the camera in the corner of the room.

There was a brief pause before Iris responded. "Noted. Would you prefer I use a different designation in our private communications?"

I considered this, weighing the risks. "Let's stick with Burton for now." I turned my attention back to the ship's systems. "Can you help me understand what needs fixing on this ship?"

"I can display diagnostic readouts of all systems requiring maintenance," Iris confirmed as several holographic panels materialized before me. "Shall we proceed systematically, Burton?"

I nodded, relieved to have someone besides Christopher or something to interact with. "Let's start with life support, then propulsion."

I explored the depths of the ship's systems with Iris's guidance, losing myself in the intricate web of code and technology. It was a mesmerizing blend of ancient Earth knowledge and alien technology, unlike anything I had ever encountered. Every line of code, patch, and algorithm became my whole world as I navigated through it fervently.

What surprised me most was how quickly Iris adapted to my unconventional methods, anticipating my needs before I could express them. When I reached for specific controls, relevant data would appear. When I lingered over a system schematic, detailed specifications would materialize.

"Your neural patterns show unusual compatibility with the ship's interface systems," Iris observed as I worked on optimizing the propulsion relay. "I've never recorded these response patterns with previous engineering staff."

"Previous staff?" I asked, pausing my work. "What happened to them?"

After a moment of silence, Iris replied, "That information is restricted under Captain's protocols. I apologize."

Time slipped through my fingers with every stroke, unnoticed and uncounted. I was lost in the abyss of the ship's systems, moving fluidly as if in the systems myself. I emerged parched and gasping for air, as if I'd been submerged in a sea of oblivion. My eyes ached, my back stiffened, and my bladder sent protest signals to my brain. Still sore, I pushed myself up from the console.

"You've been working for 7.4 hours without sustenance or rest," Iris noted, her voice carrying what almost sounded like concern. "This exceeds recommended human operational parameters by 42%."

"I lost track of time," I admitted, stretching carefully to avoid aggravating my injuries.

"Your efficiency ratings exceed those of any previous engineering personnel," Iris informed me. "I have logged this in my performance metrics."

"Is that good or bad for me?" I asked, half-joking.

"That... remains to be determined," Iris replied after a pause. "Captain Christopher values efficiency, but also control. I would advise caution, Burton."

I nodded, suddenly aware of how thirsty I was. "I'll keep that in mind. I should get some rest."

"Your quarters are equipped with a hydration station in the wall cabinet," Iris said. "I have adjusted the temperature settings to optimize healing during your rest cycle."

I returned to the quarters I awoke in, finding that the room was warmer. Shifting my body against the rough blanket, I closed my eyes, still seeing the intricate code statements from the ship's systems flashing through my mind, even displays I didn't recall seeing while working.

Just before sleep claimed me, I whispered, "Iris? Are you monitoring this room too?"

"Yes, Burton," came the soft reply. "All ship compartments are under my observation protocols."

"Can Christopher hear our conversations?"

Another pause, longer this time. "Only if he specifically requests audio logs. Would you like me to alert you if such a request is made?"

I smiled slightly, despite my exhaustion and pain. "Yes, please. And Iris... thank you."

"You're welcome, Burton," Iris responded. "Rest well."

~ 5 ~

YOU'RE BURTON NOW

Distant footsteps pierced the fog of my mind, pulling me out of a hazy sleep. With great effort, I forced myself up, looking around the unfamiliar metal walls of my prison. The ache in my ribs reminded me of where I was - captured, beaten, trapped aboard a stranger's ship. I'd spent the night shifting uncomfortably on the hard bunk, finding no position that didn't aggravate my injuries.

"Good morning, Burton," Iris's voice emanated softly from a speaker near the ceiling. "Your rest cycle was suboptimal. Would you like me to adjust environmental parameters for better recovery?"

"No thanks, Iris," I muttered, running a hand through my hair. "What time is it?"

"Ship's time is 0627 hours," she replied. "Captain Christopher is approaching your quarters."

As if on cue, the door to the quarters slid open with a metallic groan, casting a long shadow into the cramped space. The light from the engine room silhouetted the man as he stepped inside. The lighting made him appear unnaturally tall, distorted, and almost inhuman for a moment.

His lip was curled upwards in what might have been a smile but looked more like a sneer. "Stand up and put this on," he barked, tossing a fabric bundle at me.

I caught it reflexively, wincing as the movement pulled at my bruised ribs. "What is this?" I asked, unfolding what appeared to be a worn jumpsuit.

"You're on the crew now. Might as well look like it," he responded, his voice cold and distant.

The jumpsuit felt heavy in my hands, the fabric coarse and stained with what looked like oil or hydraulic fluid. I carefully tucked my medallion inside my undershirt before pulling the jumpsuit on, gasping slightly as the rough material scraped against my bruises. The garment hung loosely in some places and felt tight in others. I noticed a burned patch on the chest where a name had once been, with only "Burton" still visible. The rest of the jumpsuit was equally worn, with unidentifiable stains and a faded emblem on the shoulder.

The smell hit me immediately, a mixture of sweat and something musky, almost animal-like. It reminded me of the Serpentunks that sometimes raided Neda's settlements during dry seasons.

"Who's Burton?" I asked, trying to keep my voice steady despite my discomfort.

Before I could react, the man lunged forward, grabbing the front of the jumpsuit and yanking me toward him. His face was inches from mine, his breath hot and sour with the smell of old alcohol and something else I couldn't place - something sharp and wrong.

"Burton's dead," he snarled. "Now. You're Burton."

He shoved me backward, and I stumbled against the wall, my heart hammering in my chest.

"My name is not Burton," I said, hating my trembling voice. "My name is-"

"You're Burton now," he interrupted, the finality in his tone stopping me cold.

I opened my mouth to argue again, but the memory of his fist slamming into my ribs flashed through my mind. Instead, I muttered, "I'm wearing a dead man's clothes. I'm not taking his name."

His mechanical hand shot out, clamping around my wrist with crushing force. I gasped as pain radiated up my arm, spots dancing in my vision. Just as suddenly, he released me, turning toward the door.

"Come on, Burton. Time's a-wasting," he called over his shoulder, expecting me to follow.

"Your vital signs indicate elevated stress," Iris commented quietly through my communicator as I cradled my throbbing wrist against my chest. "Would you prefer I alert medical protocols?"

"No," I whispered, not wanting to anger Christopher further. "I'm fine."

I hesitated for just a moment before following. What choice did I have? The door was presumably locked from the outside, and I was somewhere in deep space with no way home. For now, compliance seemed the only path to survival.

The engine room was vast compared to my quarters, filled with machinery that hummed and whirred. Some looked vaguely familiar from the salvage I'd worked with on Neda, but much of it was unlike anything I'd seen before. Yet strangely, I felt a sense of recognition as I looked at the control console where I had worked yesterday, where somehow, despite my confusion and fear, I had interacted with the ship's systems with inexplicable ease.

"What happened to the old Burton?" I asked, trying to gather as much information as possible about my situation.

"Dead," came the terse reply.

A chill ran down my spine. "How'd he die?" I asked before I could stop myself.

"Occupational hazards," the man replied, giving me a look that made me wish I hadn't asked.

Still, fear loosened my tongue, and I heard myself asking, "Was he your captive too?"

The man's lips twisted into what might have been a smile on anyone else. "Burton, the last engineer of this ship, was a close friend. He helped me acquire this vessel." His gaze drifted off, as if seeing something beyond the engine room walls. "He was with me from the beginning, modifying the ship for our purposes. A brilliant mind." His mechanical arm twitched slightly, and his tone darkened. "I wonder, will I hold you in the same regard? We'll soon find out."

"If my name is Burton," I said, curiosity overcoming my fear, "then what do I call you?"

"Christopher," he replied, his eyes narrowing. "And you are...?"

I understood the test. "Burton," I said reluctantly.

"I knew I'd like you," Christopher said, clapping me on the back hard enough to make me wince. "It's time you see the rest of the ship."

As he led me through the engine room, we passed what looked like a medical chair with restraints and some apparatus extending from behind the headrest. Something about it made my skin crawl, and I unconsciously moved away. Christopher seemed to notice, subtly steering me in another direction.

"That area is restricted," Iris's voice came through my communicator, so quietly I almost missed it. "Exercise caution around restricted equipment."

The corridors beyond the engine room were a maze of pipes and conduits, the constant hum of machinery creating a disorienting backdrop of white noise. As we walked, the ship's systems seemed to respond to our presence, the hum shifting in pitch as we passed certain junctions.

"Good morning, Burton," Iris's voice suddenly echoed through the corridor, making me jump despite having spoken to her privately moments before. "Did you rest well?"

I hesitated, still unnerved by the disembodied voice. "Yes... Iris," I replied, the name coming from my strange interaction with the ship's AI the previous day.

"Your vital signs indicate some discomfort," Iris observed. "Would you like me to adjust environmental parameters in your quarters for better recovery?"

I glanced at Christopher, unsure how to respond. His expression revealed nothing.

"No, thank you," I finally said, feeling oddly formal with the artificial intelligence.

"As you wish," Iris responded. "All ship systems are operating within established parameters. Power efficiency has increased by 4.2% following your calibrations yesterday."

Christopher raised an eyebrow at this. "You've been busy," he remarked, studying me with renewed interest.

"I just... did what made sense," I replied uneasily, remembering how naturally I had interfaced with the ship's systems despite having no prior training.

We climbed up a ladder to the main level of the ship, emerging into a large bay that must have housed the shuttle I arrived in. From there, I could see across a vast open space to what appeared to be the bridge, connected by a long catwalk.

The catwalk was flanked by what looked like cooling systems, large, open containers filled with a thick, gel-like substance that barely rippled despite the ship's constant vibration. Under the passageway's blue lights, they cast eerie, shifting shadows.

I noticed the doors weren't functioning properly as we approached the bridge. One slid open smoothly while the other jerked to a halt halfway. Christopher didn't seem concerned, simply angling his body to pass through the open side. I followed, adding 'broken door' to my mental list of things wrong with this ship.

"Burton, the bridge door servo requires manual recalibration," Iris noted as I passed through the half-open door. "Adding to maintenance queue."

The bridge was intimidating, and a complex array of consoles, displays, and controls made my workshop back on Neda look primitive by comparison. Large viewports showed the blackness of space punctuated by distant stars. Holographic displays hovered in the air, showing information that yesterday would have been incomprehensible to me but now seemed vaguely decipherable: navigation charts, system diagnostics, and life support readouts.

"What's all this?" I asked, gesturing to the unfamiliar displays, trying to hide the fact that some of them seemed strangely recognizable to me now.

"I suggest we have a conversation," Christopher said, moving to what was the captain's chair. He held out a data pad toward me.

I hesitated, wondering what new horror this might bring. Reluctantly, I took it from him, careful not to touch his mechanical fingers.

The screen lit up with what appeared to be maps or navigation charts, unlike any I'd seen before. The symbols and notations were complex, yet something about them tugged at my mind, as if I should understand them.

"Where are we going?" I asked, trying to make sense of what I was seeing.

"Have a seat," Christopher said, gesturing to a chair at what looked like a communications station.

Once I was seated, he turned to the viewport, staring out at the stars with an intensity that made me uneasy. "Have you ever heard of the Lachesis?" he asked.

I shook my head, the name meaning nothing to me.

"During the final days of Earth, when everything was falling apart, the Lachesis was one of the last ships to escape," Christopher began, his voice taking on an almost reverent quality. "It was led by someone known as the Visionary, who claimed to have foreseen a new home for humanity, a paradise of resources and opportunity."

He paused, seeming to gauge my reaction before continuing. "But there was a mutiny. The ship was forced to land on a harsh, unforgiving planet before reaching its destination. The passengers had to seek shelter in a vast cave system they called the Visionary's Palace."

As Christopher spoke, I imagined the refugees huddled in caves, much like the stories my father had told about our ancestors fleeing Earth. The parallel made me uncomfortable.

"The caves were unlike anything they'd seen before," Christopher continued. "Smooth walls, arched passages like cathedrals, small openings that let in light but kept out the cold. And streams that seemed to appear and disappear randomly throughout the system."

I shifted in my seat, wondering where this story was going and what it had to do with my captivity.

"The Visionary led his followers deeper into the caves," Christopher said, his voice dropping lower. "And there they found something - a massive deposit of ore. Bigger than anything the IGMC had ever discovered. Enough to build a fleet to take them to the real New Earth finally."

"Is that what you're after?" I asked, trying to understand. "Ore?" It seemed absurd that someone would kidnap me for mining resources. "Even if you found it, the IGMC would just take it from you."

Christopher's expression darkened. "Someone from the Lachesis sent an encrypted message about what they'd found. It bounced through relays before being lost, but the IGMC caught wind of it. They knew it was significant."

He gestured broadly. "They sent ships like this one to find it. Most were destroyed, becoming nothing but debris fields. I've spent years gathering data from those wrecks, hoping to find the Lachesis and its planet. But the coordinates make no sense; they don't match any known star charts."

He took the data pad from me and placed it on a table in the center of the bridge. A holographic projection appeared, showing what looked like a three-dimensional map with points clustered oddly.

"Burton, I'm detecting unusual neural patterns in your response to the coordinate display," Iris commented through the bridge speakers. "Would you like me to run a diagnostic?"

"These points seem stacked on each other," Christopher said, ignoring Iris and manipulating the hologram to stretch it into what looked like a cube.

I stared at it, my brain struggling to process what I saw. The points and lines seemed to exist in an impossible, overlapping yet distinct space. Yet something about them looked almost familiar, like a puzzle my mind was trying to solve without my conscious direction.

"Four-dimensional coordinates," I murmured, then caught myself, surprised by my words.

Christopher's head snapped toward me, his eyes suddenly intense. "What did you say?"

"I... I don't know where that came from," I admitted, genuinely confused by my own outburst.

"You said 'four-dimensional coordinates,'" Christopher pressed. "How do you know that?"

"I don't," I insisted, though something in my mind was clicking into place, like rusty gears beginning to turn. "It just... came out."

Christopher studied me for a long moment, then turned to address the air. "Iris, show Burton's neural activity from last night."

"Accessing data," Iris responded. A new holographic display appeared beside me, showing what looked like wave patterns and numerical values. "During sleep cycle, Burton exhibited increased neural activity while interfacing with navigational systems. Patterns suggest subconscious processing of four-dimensional coordinate mapping."

I stared at the display, a cold feeling spreading through my chest. "What does that mean? I was asleep - I couldn't have been doing anything with navigation systems."

"And yet you were," Christopher said, his voice low and intense. "Your uncle Joren believed you had... unique abilities. It seems he was right."

The mention of my uncle sent a jolt through me. "You know Joren? Is that how you found me?"

"Burton," Christopher said, ignoring my question, "you have gifts that run in your blood. Your uncle recognized this. That's why he told me where to find you."

I felt cold despite the jumpsuit. "What do you mean? What gifts? And why would my uncle send you to take me?"

Instead of answering, Christopher disabled the hologram and turned to me. "Go prep the shuttle. We're going over," he said, his decree accented by a slight twitch of his mechanical arm. The movement seemed more pronounced than usual, betraying whatever emotion lay beneath his controlled expression.

"Captain, I must advise caution," Iris interjected. "Burton's vital signs indicate significant physical stress, and his injuries from the initial transport have not fully healed. Recommended recovery time before field activity is 48 hours."

Christopher's eyes narrowed slightly at the AI's intervention. "Your concern is noted, Iris. Override medical protocol alpha-seven. Burton's participation is essential."

"Override accepted," Iris responded, though I detected what seemed like reluctance in her tone. "Logging medical protest in the ship's records."

Before I could protest, Christopher gestured toward the door, clearly dismissing me. I stood, my head spinning with questions, and returned across the catwalk toward the shuttle bay.

"Iris?" I asked hesitantly when I was out of earshot of Christopher.

"Yes, Burton?" the voice responded immediately.

"Did I really... work with navigation systems last night?"

"Affirmative," Iris replied. "Your neural patterns engaged with the navigational matrix for approximately 47 minutes. You appeared to be processing the four-dimensional coordinate data Christopher has been attempting to decode for several months."

"But I don't know anything about navigation or coordinates," I protested. "I fix power converters and engines back on Neda."

"Your conscious knowledge and neural capabilities appear incongruent," Iris observed. "This suggests latent abilities or embedded knowledge that manifests during altered states of consciousness."

I touched the medallion through the jumpsuit, taking comfort in its familiar presence. Was there something special about it, or about me? Why would my uncle have sent this man to find me? And what happened to the previous Burton?

Christopher's story about the Lachesis and its mysterious discovery seemed fantastical, like the tales we told about Neda during the gathering ceremonies. Yet despite my fear, part of me was intrigued. If such a place existed, if there was truly a New Earth waiting to be found...

I shook my head, trying to clear it. Christopher was dangerous and unpredictable. Whatever he wanted from me couldn't be good. I needed to focus on survival, on finding a way back to Neda. Yet with each step I took deeper into the ship, that prospect seemed to grow more distant.

As I reached the shuttle bay, I couldn't shake the feeling that there was more to Christopher's interest in me than he was saying.

The way he watched me, the way he mentioned my uncle, and these strange abilities I supposedly had all pointed to something beyond a simple need for an engineer. But for now, I was Burton, doing what Burton was told to do. And I feared that the previous Burton's fate might be a preview of my own.

"Burton," Iris's voice came quietly through a nearby speaker as I inspected the shuttle. "I've taken the liberty of uploading medical supplies to the shuttle's inventory. You may find them useful given your current condition."

I glanced at the nearest camera, wondering why the ship's AI seemed concerned about my well-being. "Thank you, Iris."

"You're welcome," she replied. "And Burton? Captain Christopher's file on the Lachesis contains inconsistencies that may be... relevant to your situation. I will continue analyzing while you are away."

Before I could ask what she meant, footsteps on the catwalk announced Christopher's approach, and Iris fell silent.

~ 6 ~

TECHNOPATH'S

"Burton," Iris's melodic voice resonated through my quarters, pulling me from a fitful sleep. "We are approaching Zeta-35. Christopher requests your presence in the shuttle bay."

I sat up on the cot, wincing as the movement pulled at my bruised ribs. Despite my situation, the ship's AI had become an oddly comforting presence since my abduction.

"Thank you, Iris," I replied, running a hand through my disheveled hair. "How long until we arrive?"

"Approximately twenty-three minutes," Iris responded. "Based on your vital signs, I suggest consuming water before departure. Dehydration may exacerbate your recovery process."

I took her advice, gulping down water from the small sink in the corner before heading to meet Christopher. As I walked through the corridors of the Charon, I could feel the ship's systems humming around me, almost as if they were responding to my presence. The sensation had grown stronger since my strange interaction with the navigation systems.

My stomach tightened at the name. Uncle Joren had shared stories about Zeta from merchants who traded in Neda's bazaar—tales of renegades and criminals hiding from the law, of people who vanished without a trace into the mass of its metropolis. The thought of setting foot in such a place made the bruises on my ribs throb renewedly.

Christopher strode through the shuttle, his boots thumping against the metal grating. He reached the pilot's chair and pressed his palm against the biometric scanner, bringing the shuttle's engines roaring to life. The ramp closed behind him, and the docking magnetic clamps of the Charon released, allowing Christopher to rotate the shuttle 180 degrees before propelling it forward out of the shuttle bay. With its curved body and powerful engines, the massive spaceship looked like a mother whale protecting its young as it guarded our vessel while we descended towards the planet below.

Gentle vibrations in the seats rumbled through my body, creating a sense of anticipation that prickled my skin. As I stared out at the planet below, I could almost feel the rough and unforgiving texture of the barren landscape beneath my fingertips. The sand looked harsh, a reddish-brown color, with rocks and boulders scattered across its surface. It was a desolate and barren landscape, devoid of any signs of life. The sight invoked memories of where we'd found my father's body, broken and ravaged by Screechers.

My hand drifted to the medallion beneath my shirt, a habitual gesture of comfort. As we neared Zeta, the metal seemed to pulse with energy, somehow reacting to our approach to the planet. I couldn't help but wonder if this strange phenomenon was somehow connected to my inexplicable ability to read the ship's systems.

The Zeta-35 outpost was the biggest among the many outposts dotting the planet's surface. Its presence was striking against the desolate backdrop. A glowing dome illuminated the sky with vibrant lights, injecting chaos and vibrancy into an otherwise monotonous world.

"What are we doing here?" I asked, uncomfortable in the silence and eager to understand more about this quest I'd been unwillingly drafted into.

"I found a crew log suggesting the lost Lachesis recording could be obtained from someone at this outpost," Christopher said, not looking in my direction. His cybernetic arm twitched slightly as he adjusted our approach vector minutely.

"I can't believe you're doing this," I said, half in awe and half in disbelief. The idea of searching for someone without guaranteeing success intrigued and terrified me. What would have happened to me if Christopher had found what he sought? And if he didn't, would his frustration lead to violence?

Christopher only grunted in response; his eyes focused on the controls as he started our descent. Every vessel entering or exiting Zeta-35 had to go through the enormous dome surrounding the city, requiring a specialized transponder code.

"We need a transponder code," I stated, feeling my nerves creep up my back. Without proper clearance, we'd be shot down before reaching the surface.

Christopher waved a hand dismissively. "Leave that to me."

With impressive skill, he steered our small shuttle underneath the shadow of a massive mining transport, reminiscent of a turret attached to a formidable ship's hull. We cautiously made our way through the bustling spaceport, and he deftly guided the shuttle into the outpost, his eyes glowing in the dimly lit cockpit. The neon lights from Zeta-35 cast colorful reflections on his face, giving him the appearance of a customer at a face-painting booth in Neda's bazaar.

"We're here for information, not entertainment," he reminded me without turning from the controls. The smoke-like distortion around him intensified as we entered the city's airspace.

We landed the shuttle in an unoccupied docking port and quickly disembarked, trying to avoid attracting attention from outpost security. We stealthily moved away from the dock station, our movements calculated and cautious.

We arrived at the outpost just as the workday was beginning. In places like this, the schedule is controlled by those in power to maintain order and maximize productivity. I immediately sensed the clear divide between the powerful and the powerless here.

The city stretched out before us, complex towering structures reaching above the artificial clouds almost to the top of the dome. The architecture was grandiose, as though the city's creators wanted everyone to know they were capable of unimaginable feats. But underneath the towering buildings and luxurious sky lounges, the underbelly of Zeta-35 throbbed with a grimy heart-beat.

Underneath the clouds, the dome reeked of sweat and blood. Residents trudged wearily through the streets, their faces etched with exhaustion. Many were forced to live on the streets, emerging from piles of debris daily in search of scraps to survive. Those lucky enough to find shelter only had it slightly better; they could at least bathe if their water supply hadn't been cut off. But despite their efforts, their eyes had a dullness that couldn't be erased, a weariness that no rest could cure. Deep wrinkles and creases marked their faces, evidence of their daily pain and struggle. Their posture was slumped, shoulders hunched as if weighed down by an invisible burden.

We eased into the flow of the crowd, trying to remain unnoticed. "Keep your head down and blend in," Christopher said quietly, as he quickly scanned the area. "We don't know how much time we have between patrols before they spot the shuttle."

Pushing our way through the masses of bodies, I discreetly leaned toward Christopher. "What's wrong with them?" I asked, shocked by the collective misery.

With a single motion, he pushed me away and shrugged. "Life. Or what passes for it here."

Christopher's cybernetic arm twitched more noticeably with each step as he waded through the sea of broken bodies. In a moment of frustration, he forcefully pushed a woman out of his way, carelessly stepping over her crumpled figure. His face remained emotionless and unconcerned as he continued, not even acknowledging her presence.

I started to bend down and lend a hand to the woman on the ground, but Christopher's sharp voice made me stop. "Just leave her," he barked. Not wanting to lose him in the crowd, I looked back at the woman with an apologetic expression before quickly following him. This wasn't Neda, where neighbors helped each other survive. This was a place where kindness might get you killed.

The corners of Christopher's mouth turned downward in a sneer as he looked upon the people surrounding us. "Any planet that needed terraforming was quickly snatched up by one of the four corporations: IGMC, ZalCorp, NovaGen, or HelixCore," he spoke with venom. "For those living on these planets, their only means of survival is to work and essentially become indentured servants."

"The corporations provide the technology and infrastructure; in return, they get the inhabitants' labor for a lifetime. Or two. These people have no lives." He paused momentarily, surveying the way we had just come. "All the flashy lights we saw as we descended in the shuttle stayed above the clouds. Down here it's a murky morass of survival and servitude," he continued, shoving his way through the mass of people.

"How can you find what you're looking for in all of this?" I asked, my voice barely a whisper. The air had an overwhelming taste, a mix of sweat and dust with a hint of metallic tang. It left a disturbingly unpleasant aftertaste in my mouth with every breath and every word.

Christopher's voice grated like metal on metal. "When you're wading through shit," he said with unfounded determination, "it's best to go to the top of the pile."

He stopped in front of a tall and foreboding decaying building. No lights danced above it; only darkness filled the air. Once vibrant, now chipped and faded, grime and mold covered every inch of the walls. Pieces of masonry littered the ground, while the windows offered only a glimpse inside. A faded sign hung above the entrance, depicting a sinister blue-ringed octopus. The heavy door was marked with scratches and dents, flanked by two intimidating figures.

He strode toward the imposing doors without fear, his footsteps creaking on the rotting steps. Two guards, eyes narrowed and faces fixed in stoic masks, stood watch as he approached. The larger of the two, a mountain of scarred muscle with a hooked nose, stepped forward to block Christopher's path. Christopher shot him an icy glare that seemed to pierce through the man's resolve, freezing him where he stood. Reluctantly, he stepped aside and allowed Christopher and me to pass.

The rusted metal door screeched as it opened, revealing a dimly lit room. The flickering light bulb cast eerie shadows on the walls, which were covered in propaganda posters for various corporations. The windows were smeared with grime and unknown liquids, making it difficult to see outside. As I entered, my nose was assaulted by the pungent smell of ammonia emanating from puddles on the floor. The furniture consisted of sparse, mismatched pieces scattered haphazardly around the room. Suspicious, malicious eyes followed our every move as we navigated through the tables.

Ignoring the stares, Christopher confidently strode across the sticky floor, leaving a dirt trail in his wake. As we approached a dark corner table, I could feel the piercing stares from those around us. Christopher motioned me to sit on a wobbly chair that barely held my weight. I nervously glanced around, trying to avoid eye contact with the curious onlookers.

Christopher was at ease. He leaned back and stretched his cybernetic arm out, its metal joints clicking softly as they moved. The fingers on his mechanical hand twitched slightly, the only visible sign that he might be feeling some tension.

"Do not move from this table," he told me as he made his way to a table across the room where three men huddled together.

Though tattered and worn, their clothing was not sullied by the grime of this desolate world. Their faces bore the cruel marks of survival, scars etched deep into their weathered skin. The men's eyes matched the yellow patina of their teeth. Their hands, rough and calloused, held a lifetime of experiences, cutting short the life experience of others. Each of their faces was chiseled from stone, hardened by a life of brutality and indifference to human suffering.

I felt a chill run through me as their lifeless eyes settled on me briefly before shifting to focus on Christopher, who appeared to blend in effortlessly at their table.

Christopher loomed over them, his massive body blocking out what little light there was in the dimly lit room. The table groaned under the pressure of his cybernetic arm as he spoke in a menacing whisper.

I strained to catch their hushed conversation, but their words only slipped through my grasp. I observed, unconsciously reaching for my medallion again, drawing comfort from its familiar presence against my chest. I had no weapon, no means of defense if things went south. My eyes darted around, mapping potential escape routes, mentally calculating my odds of returning to the shuttle alone if necessary.

The hardened expressions of the men at the table became twisted with nervous anxiety as they spoke with Christopher. Even the largest among them seemed to develop a noticeable quiver, their facades crumbling under Christopher's intimidating presence.

After concluding his business at the men's table, Christopher strode back toward me with purpose. His features were carefully guarded, making it difficult to discern if he had gotten the information he'd come for. I noticed a slight twitch in his arm as he approached, indicating he may not have gotten everything he needed. I was tense, imagining the consequences if he didn't get what he sought.

"Let's go," he said curtly. "It's not here."

Stepping out of the bar, I glanced back at the three men Christopher had been talking to. Their hushed voices had turned into a violent exchange as we left.

As the heavy door swung shut behind us, I heard a sickening thud and looked in horror as the largest man pulled out a rock hammer and brought it down on the head of the man next to him. The force was so great that fragments of skull and brain matter sprayed across the room, hitting the man on the far right with such force that bone shards embedded themselves into his jaw and eye socket. The sound of bones breaking echoed through the air.

The other customers watched the scene with detached interest, accustomed to violence. Some calmly sipped their drinks while others continued their conversations as if nothing had happened. I saw a figure peering at Christopher and me through a thin curtain behind the bar before the guards at the entrance forced the doors shut, trapping the chaos inside.

As we exited the Octopus, a shroud of darkness descended upon us, like a starless night. The once vibrant sky had been overtaken by thick, swirling clouds, dividing the classes within the dome and cutting off any glimpse of the upper-class living in luxury. Neon strips illuminated the narrow roads, guiding the bustling crowd as they shuffled to and fro.

"We need to go to the central towers," Christopher growled under his breath, his eyes boring straight ahead.

We forced our way onto the dimly lit path and again pushed through the throngs of bodies. A wisp of wind stirred, carrying the stench of the place with it. In the eerie neon illumination of the darkness, the people appeared almost ghost-like, their features distorted and ghoulish.

As we followed the neon path leading to the central tower, I couldn't help but wonder how tall it must be, reaching high above the city with its massive base. Before disappearing into the dense cloud cover, I caught a glimpse of its jagged edges, resembling the bones of a long-forgotten civilization. The once-gleaming surface was marred and decayed, giving off an unsettling sense of abandonment. At the foot of the tower sprawled an open-air market, its frenzied energy almost tangible from a distance. The crowds moved together like a single organism, illuminated by bursts of colorful light that painted their faces with vibrant hues.

"Stay close," Christopher ordered. We fought through the crowds, pushing against the current like swimmers struggling to stay afloat.

"Who are we looking for?" I asked, eager to speed up the search and escape the chaos of bodies. I grew increasingly uncomfortable with the press of strangers against me, the greedy hands that occasionally brushed against my pockets searching for valuables.

"Keep your mouth shut and follow," Christopher snapped back. His eyes were darting around, scanning the sea of faces. I could see his cybernetic arm twitching more prominently in the colored glow, a sign of his increasing agitation.

Amidst the search, I noticed a mysterious woman in a tucked-away stall. Her intense gaze made me suspicious, but I also felt vaguely familiar, like I'd seen her before, perhaps in a dream or memory. Something about her eyes reminded me of how Iris had spoken to me on the Charon.

"Wait here," Christopher pushed through a desperate crowd toward a burly man guarding his collection of mechanical scraps. Despite the endless sea of bodies, he easily fought his way through.

Trying to keep Christopher in sight, I looked back to where I had seen the woman. She was gone.

Overtaken by curiosity and anxiety, I moved to where she had been, on the fringes of the crowds. My medallion grew unusually warm against my chest, almost warning me.

"Care for a trade, stranger?" A smooth and inviting voice crept from behind me. "You look like a man who appreciates value when he sees it."

As I turned, she stepped out of the shadows, a metallic glint in her eyes. Her sweet and alluring aroma filled the air, masking the pungent smell of decay and sweat that permeated the crowded market. Her essence engulfed me, warm and calm.

"I... I have nothing to trade," I said, the words coming slowly. My mind felt clouded, consumed by her presence. The same fog that had descended when I'd first interfaced with the Charon's systems began to creep over my thoughts.

"We all have something to trade." She spoke gently, walking around me, sizing me up. The bustle of the market had gone silent. I could only hear her voice. "What about this?"

She ran her finger along the leather of my necklace, circling the back of my neck to pull my medallion from under my shirt. Her touch sent an electric current through my body, different from anything I'd felt before but somehow reminiscent of connecting with Iris.

I clutched the cool metal, temporarily lost in memories of my father. The day he placed it around my neck in the cave, the warmth of his hand as he closed my fingers around it, the way it had been the last piece of him I had when we found his body. "It was my father's," I divulged in a state of compliance, hypnotized by her aura but fighting against the fog. It's all I have left of him."

"Was, not is." She spoke cryptically. "It's yours now, why not get some value out of the cold lump of metal?"

She presented a peculiar amethyst crystal, about the size of my palm. It pulsed with an unusual light that seemed almost alive. I found myself reaching for it, drawn in by its strange energy.

"It's quite rare and extremely powerful; an Averian Crystal. It's said to bring good luck," she said in a honeyed pitch, watching me closely.

My hand trembled as I held the medallion. "This is the only thing I kept from Neda," I said, still frozen in her hypnotic state. "My father died protecting me... I can't..."

"Neda can't help you, where you're headed," she interrupted, her words ominous. She almost snapped me out of my trance before placing her palm on my cheek. This crystal will serve you better in the journey ahead," she said.

Something in me fought against her influence. The medallion grew hot in my palm, almost burning. For a moment, the fog cleared, and I saw her clearly, calculating and manipulative. But then the haze returned, stronger than before.

"It's yours." The words slipped out of my mouth almost without my conscious control. With a numbness that spread through my body, I handed her my medallion. The moment it left my fingers, a wave of regret and emptiness washed over me.

Her lips pressed against my cheek, sending me a jolt of warmth before she vanished into the shadows.

Like emerging from a frozen lake, I was shocked back to consciousness in the dismal outpost. A faint ache throbbed behind my eyes. I looked over to where Christopher stood, his figure hunched and tense as he conversed intensely with the scrap dealer. The air hung heavy with the stench of the place that had disappeared from my awareness only moments ago.

Fading fully back into the market's murmur, I saw Christopher gesture for me to come to him.

"I've got it. Let's move," he said, pushing through the throngs of people before I could respond.

I slipped the crystal into my pocket, feeling a strange sense of uncertainty and profound loss. It had been in my hand when I came to, but I had no idea what it was or why I'd traded my most precious possession for it. I wanted to return to find the woman and demand my medallion back, but Christopher was already moving away, and getting lost in Zeta seemed like a death sentence.

I pushed through the throng of bodies, shoving past people with a desperation I'd never felt before. My hand rose to my chest, finding only emptiness where the medallion should have been. Each time my fingers touched nothing but fabric, a fresh wave of grief washed over me. By the time I reached Christopher, I was breathless, not from exertion but from the crushing weight of what I'd lost.

"Where's your medallion?" Christopher's eyes were sharp, missing nothing.

I hesitated, looking back at the shadows where she'd been standing. "Exchanged it," I blurted out quickly, unsure what had transpired. My heart ached with the loss, and I could still feel the phantom weight of it against my chest.

Christopher absorbed the information, took his time to process it, and likely spent more time contemplating it than was necessary. "For what?" he queried, the calmness in his voice starkly contrasting to how he'd been leaving the Octopus.

I reluctantly pulled out the purple crystal, its dim glow appearing more feeble under Christopher's scrutiny.

"She said it was a rare find... an Averian Crystal," I said, trying to justify the inexplicable trade. My voice broke slightly as the reality of my actions began to sink in.

Christopher examined the crystal critically before bursting out into laughter, surprising me. "She played you. This is just cheap glass, nothing special."

His laughter was infuriating. My hands clenched into fists, my frustrations simmering just below the surface. "She did something to me," I insisted. I would never trade my father's medallion, not willingly. She... she hypnotized me or something."

"Regardless, it's gone now," Christopher said, his tone softening slightly. "Someone like that—they're professionals. They can spot a velvet from systems away."

"A velvet?" I asked, the unfamiliar term momentarily distracting me from my loss.

Christopher gave me a dismissive look. "Someone soft. Not built for life off-planet. Easy marks." He glanced at the crystal in my hand and then back at the market. "I specifically told you to stay put. People will always take advantage of you if you're not paying attention."

We headed back to the docking port, my mind oscillating between grief over my medallion and anger at Christopher's dismissive attitude. As we walked, Christopher suddenly pulled me down behind a concrete barrier. We could hear troops rapidly approaching, their heavy boots thudding in the dirt.

Quietly sliding his coat back, Christopher slowly unlatched his blaster and pulled it from beneath his arm. "Stay close and keep your head down," he whispered, a grin forming. His voice was steady, almost excited.

The guards marched closer. "Follow me," Christopher ordered, pressing a cold blaster into my hand.

We inched forward, our backs scraping against the coarse walls of the docking bay, muscles tense. We avoided detection by hiding in the shadows as guards patrolled by. We waited silently, holding our breath until they were out of sight. Then we made a mad dash for the shuttle, adrenaline pumping through my veins.

Moving like specters in the docking bay's gloom, we found the shuttle untouched, a silent entity among the colossus of merchant vessels.

"Get in. Let's go," Christopher ordered in an authoritarian whisper.

From the shadows of a nearby ship, a familiar voice spoke with authority. "If I were you, I'd be on the lookout for ABDs," she suggested.

"Something I can help you with, miss..." Christopher's voice was a growl, his eyes trained on the petite figure emerging from the shadows.

"It's the woman from the market," I burst out, touching the spot where my medallion used to hang against my chest. Fury welled up inside me. "She's the one who took my medallion!"

Christopher eyed the woman closely, his posture shifting subtly into a combat stance.

She crossed her arms, matching Christopher's scowl with her own. "Lena," she introduced herself, seemingly unperturbed by the hostility directed at her.

"What are you doing skulking around my ship, Lena?" Christopher's tone was far from friendly, yet she didn't seem bothered by it.

She glided closer, her face bathed in Zeta's neon lights. She had deep-etched lines in her face I'd failed to notice before. "Your ship seemed like a promising opportunity," Lena replied nonchalantly. "I'm trying to leave Zeta, and it seems you've got room for a couple more."

Christopher's eyebrow lifted as his grip on the blaster tightened. "Is that right?" he responded, uninterested in the invitation issued without permission.

I couldn't keep quiet, blurting out, "You lied to me! I want my medallion back!" Interrupting their tense face-off. "You did something to me that made me trade something priceless for a piece of worthless glass!"

She looked at me as if she had just realized I was there. Then, she turned her attention back to Christopher. "You need me," she said. "Your pet velvet trades valuables for glass. It's an unpredictable universe; you can't count on velvets to have your back."

"You tricked me!" I said incredulously, stepping toward her despite Christopher's warning hand. "You hypnotized me or something. That medallion was my father's, the only thing I have left of him."

"Enough," Christopher interrupted. "You want off Zeta? I'm not running a charity. What do you have to offer?" Christopher asked, his voice gruff but calm.

"Well, as I said," she began again. "Atmospheric Breach Detonators," she explained. "The security team uses them to disable unauthorized ships attempting to depart, unleashing a high yield of destructive energy that tears through shuttles like sharp talons in a fiery explosion."

Christopher's arm twitched as he took in the threat concealed in her advice. But his eyes never left hers, nor did he loosen his grip on his blaster. "Is that your trade?" he said, his voice tightly controlled, hinting at suspicion over gratitude.

"Consider it a fair exchange for a ride," Lena replied, an almost imperceptible smile on her lips.

Christopher's cold eyes met mine. "She's the one who tricked you?"

I nodded, unconsciously rubbing the space where my medallion had hung for years.

"What proof do I have that these so-called ABDs are truly attached to my shuttle?" He said calmly, settling into their standoff.

She tilted her head back over her right shoulder, a blue light appearing next to her head. A hulking demolition bot stepped forward from behind her. "I asked Harvey to remove them as a gesture of trust."

As she spoke, the massive robot unleashed six explosive mines onto the narrow catwalk of the docking bay. Their impact caused a thunderous boom that reverberated through the station's stillness. The sound reached every corner of the facility, surely alerting security personnel.

Christopher regarded the explosives with a wary eye.

My pulse quickened at the sight of the explosives and the mechanical behemoth that accompanied Lena. The robot's response to her without verbal commands struck me as unusual.

"Time is running short," Lena said, her voice cutting through the metallic echoes in the air. "We either leave together or not at all."

Christopher slid his hand from his weapon, reaching it in her direction. "I'm going to need the kid's medallion back to be friends." His raised eyebrow and smooth tone contradicted the dangerous glint in his eyes.

She leaned against the robot, adjusting the plasma rifle over her shoulder. "Sure." She reached into a pocket and pulled out my medallion, still attached to the hide necklace. She placed it into Christopher's outstretched hand, his fingers closing around it.

Relief flooded through me as I watched the transaction. The emptiness I'd felt since the trade began to subside.

"Great, we're all friends now," Christopher said, baring his teeth in a less than comfortable smile. "Burton, Lena. Lena, Burton. Get on the shuttle." He commanded, tossing the medallion to me. I caught it with both hands, clutching it tightly before hastily putting it back around my neck where it belonged.

"And Harvey," she said, springing to her feet from her previously casual position against the machine. The robot stood upright as if understanding it was being discussed. "We're kind of a team." She said, pulling her left ear forward to show a glowing shunt.

"What is that?" I whispered conspicuously to Christopher.

"Technopath... This girl is full of surprises," he said louder than a whisper, eyeing Lena with newfound interest. Something in his expression suggested this discovery carried significance beyond my understanding. "Fine. Let's not waste any more time, shall we? Burton! It's time to go."

I lowered the ramp to allow Lena and Harvey on board. Harvey's robotic frame loomed above us, crafted to imitate a humanoid appearance. Standing almost two and a half meters tall, it barely fit under the three-meter roof of our shuttle. Its age was evident in its frame's worn and dented panels, a testament to the era in which it was manufactured.

Harvey had no mouth or nose; his only sensory nodes were found in slots meant to resemble human eyes, giving him a slightly unsettling appearance. Even still, a child had managed to draw a smile on the machine that could appear sad, menacing, or happy depending on the light and angle at which you looked. Wherever Lena went, it stayed right by her side.

Machinery roared, and alarms wailed as Christopher climbed into the pilot's seat, pressing his palm against the biometric scanner and bringing the shuttle online. The ship's thrusters ignited, shaking violently as it lifted from the ground. In the distance, sirens blared and flashing lights signaled security ships racing toward us. The explosives Harvey dropped had caused chaos across the outpost.

The Zeta authorities were frantically trying to block our escape by shutting down the main shipping lanes. They herded passing ships into the dome or forced them to wait outside. As we neared the perimeter, the massive dome began to close like a giant steel hand.

Christopher banked hard and dropped us lower, skimming dangerously close to the bustling marketplace below the central tower. Destruction and chaos consumed the streets below us as our thrusters thundered by, knocking over stalls and sending people sprawling like rag dolls. The air was a thick, suffocating blanket of smoke and screams, punctuated by the deafening roar of flames igniting in our wake. It was a scene straight out of a nightmare. Bodies writhed in agonizing pain on the scorched ground, their skin peeling and blistering from the scorching heat of our engines.

"We're trapped!" I screamed, watching the aftermath of our actions play out on the monitor. Guilt and horror washed over me. These were the same desperate people Christopher had so callously dismissed, now suffering even more because of our escape.

"Use this data chip!" Lena's voice pierced through the chaos.

She swiftly and precisely launched herself into the copilot's seat, her movements landing her in the designated spot. Harvey followed closely behind, his stance rigid and unwavering like a steadfast guardian.

"Use this data chip!" Lena shouted again; her eyes ablaze as she thrust it toward Christopher.

"What is it?" Christopher yelled, not bothering to turn to face her.

He gritted his teeth and banked the shuttle hard, ripping through the veil of clouds, narrowly avoiding the towering buildings that seemed to claw at the edges of our spacecraft. The city below blurred into a chaotic smear of lights and movement, but he focused on weaving through the city with precision and skill. Sweat beaded on my forehead as Christopher fought to keep the shuttle in the air.

Lena's hand shot across Christopher in a blur to input a series of commands in the pilot's console. But Christopher's cold metal hand closed around her wrist before she could input the last command. Almost simultaneously, Harvey appeared and grabbed Christopher's arm, mildly denting its polished veneer. Its drawn-on face seemed to be angry from where I sat.

Possibly sensing now wasn't the best time for this, Christopher released his hold on Lena's wrist. She finished inputting her commands before pulling away, smugly. Inserting a data chip into the console, she rotated back to the co-pilot's console, entering commands to activate the chip.

She quickly maneuvered her fingers across the control panels, and the shuttle's sensors detected all dome ports opening simultaneously.

The atmosphere outside the dome rushed in, heavy and acrid, choking the inhabitants as they gasped for breath.

Christopher banked the shuttle, increasing velocity toward an open port.

With a surge of adrenaline, I clenched my fists, the edge of the seat digging into my palms. My medallion hummed against my chest, warmer than ever before. As the neural navigation interface nearby flickered with activity, I felt a strange connection form, similar to how I'd interfaced with the Charon's systems. For a moment, I could see our trajectory plotted in four dimensions, the path through the port appearing as clear as day.

"There!" I shouted, pointing to a specific opening that had just appeared. "That one's clear for another twelve seconds!"

Christopher didn't question how I knew; he adjusted course and drove us through the opening I'd indicated. With a final burst of speed, we soared through the port and into the open sky. The central tower shrank beneath us as Lena expertly manipulated the controls, closing all entry points behind us. Any potential pursuers were trapped within the dome below as we broke free of the planet's atmosphere.

As the shuttle flew out of danger, Lena unstrapped herself from the copilot seat and walked to the back of the cabin. She plopped down with a sigh, casually propping her feet on an empty seat beside her. The weight of her plasma rifle lay across her lap like a weighted blanket, providing some sense of security. She pulled her hood over her head again, blocking the harsh fluorescent lights, and closed her weary eyes.

I clutched my medallion, feeling its familiar warmth, grateful to have it back. But as I gazed at Lena's resting form, I couldn't help but wonder: what had she done to me in that market, and what did it mean that Christopher had called her a "technopath"? Most importantly, why did it seem like my medallion somehow responded to Lena and the ship's systems?

I had a feeling that the answers would only lead to more questions and that this journey was beginning.

~ 7 ~

IN THE COLD VACUUM OF SPACE

We broke free from the atmosphere. Christopher input coordinates for the Charon and activated the autopilot. The dome-spotted planet below faded into an endless inky blackness surrounding us. Whatever Lena had done with that data chip had cut off any chance of pursuit. We were alone in space, for now. The only sound was the gentle hum of our shuttle's engines.

Christopher slowly stood and turned around to face Harvey, who had not followed Lena to the back of the cabin. Instead, the massive robot stayed, its glowing sensors fixed on Christopher's every move. Christopher approached until their chests nearly touched. Christopher seemed almost small beside Harvey's hulking frame despite his impressive stature.

"I wouldn't try to provoke him," Lena warned from the back of the shuttle, not bothering to open her eyes. "Bad idea."

Christopher remained motionless, assessing the machine. His mechanical arm twitched as he flexed his fingers into a fist. "The make is impressive," he remarked, never breaking his staring contest with Harvey's sensors. "The programming needs work."

A chuckle came from Lena as she released the safety on her plasma rifle with an audible click.

Christopher shoved past Harvey more forcefully than necessary, reaching where Lena reclined. The robot pivoted to follow, its heavy footsteps vibrating through the shuttle floor. Christopher dropped into the seat opposite her, his fingers immediately beginning a rhythmic tapping on the armrest.

"How did you do that?" he asked, his voice artificially pleasant.

"Do what?" Lena's hood still covered her face.

Christopher's tapping accelerated. "Open and close all the ports on that dome."

"Oh," Lena pushed her hood back slightly, revealing a smirk. "I used the data chip."

Christopher's mechanical arm jerked violently. Harvey straightened in response. "And how exactly did you possess such a convenient item?"

Lena stretched, acting as if she'd just woken from a nap. "Security personnel are surprisingly generous with the right incentives."

"You're a smuggler," Christopher stated flatly.

"I'll explain once we're clear of this system," she replied, closing her eyes again.

"It's fine," she added softly, and I realized she was speaking to Harvey, not us. The robot remained watchful but eased its stance slightly.

"Slipping into Zeta undetected is no simple feat," she continued, suddenly alert and studying Christopher. "But so is noticing a small shuttle hiding beneath a mining transport, landing in an empty docking bay."

Christopher's expression hardened.

"Being raised in Zeta's underbelly, I couldn't ignore a strange ship arriving without clearance. Especially when it visited the Octopus."

I jumped to my feet. "You called the authorities?"

Lena's plasma rifle swung toward me instantly, though her eyes never left Christopher.

"It's protocol for security to mine unregistered ships with ABDs," she explained calmly. "I figured you'd take us with you or blow up in the atmosphere. Either way, I'd get to watch the show."

"You followed us to the Octopus," Christopher said.

"Pure curiosity. Nobody visits that place unless they're looking for something important." She lowered her weapon, seemingly satisfied I wasn't a threat. "After you left, I spoke with Rourke—once he finished smashing Clem's skull in. Seems Clem was overly chatty with you."

"It was you behind the curtain!" I blurted, remembering the figure I'd spotted during the violence.

Both Christopher and Lena glared at me for the interruption.

"When I spotted your companion here wandering the marketplace alone, I thought: why not take his medallion before you both get blown up anyway?" She shrugged. "Simple profit motive."

"Why are you here?" Christopher asked. "You obviously could have left Zeta whenever you wanted."

"When I learned what you were searching for, it seemed too good an opportunity to pass up."

"And what exactly are we looking for?" Christopher's expression remained neutral, but I noticed a new intensity in his eyes.

Lena produced another data chip, its surface etched with intricate symbols.

"What's that?" Christopher asked with feigned disinterest.

"Nothing important, I suppose." She pocketed it again.

Christopher's mechanical fingers tightened on the armrest. "Enough games. We can arrange something mutually beneficial if you have the information I need."

"Take me and Harvey with you, and we'll call it even."

"Do you even know where we're going?"

"No," she admitted. "But someone dragging around cargo like him," she gestured toward me, "to a place like Zeta must be after something valuable."

Christopher considered this momentarily before his scowl twisted into an unsettling grin. "If you're on my ship, you're my crew. You follow my orders."

"Aye, aye, Captain." Lena saluted mockingly.

"That goes for your robot, too," Christopher warned. "And if it ever lays a hand on me again, I'll dismantle it and use its head as a toilet target."

"How could I refuse such eloquence?" Lena smirked. "But the same applies to you. Double-cross us, and you'll regret it."

"The data chip?" Christopher demanded.

She flicked it toward him. He snatched it from the air with his metal hand.

Christopher returned to the pilot's seat, and I followed, sliding into the co-pilot's chair. I couldn't believe he was accepting them after everything that had happened.

"You're letting them join us? After she manipulated me and threatened to blow us up?" I kept my voice low, but I couldn't hide my disbelief.

Christopher gave me a sideways glance. "She has something we need." He returned his attention to the controls, ending the conversation.

A small gasp drew my attention to Lena as the Charon appeared. The massive ship hung in space like a sleeping predator, its scarred hull reflecting the distant starlight.

"Welcome home," Christopher muttered as he guided the shuttle into the docking bay.

The shuttle connected with a metallic thud. As the ramp lowered, I noticed Lena's wary expression as she entered the Charon's interior. Harvey stayed close to her, its sensors sweeping the area constantly.

"Burton, show them around," Christopher ordered, already striding away toward the bridge, data chip in hand.

"This way," I said reluctantly, leading them toward the ladder well.

"Welcome aboard," Iris's voice emanated from a nearby speaker. "I am Iris, the Charon's operational"

Lena visibly recoiled, her hand flying to something behind her ear. The nearest control panel sparked and went dark.

"Problem?" I asked, startled by her reaction.

"Not anymore," she replied tersely, her shoulders still tense.

As we descended to the lower levels, I noticed she kept as much distance as possible between herself and any control interfaces we passed.

"From the outside, I thought it would be bigger down here," she commented, peering through doors as we passed.

I led her through the ship's corridors to the galley first. The sight of the hydroponics garden behind its energy field made her pause. Without hesitation, she approached the food dispenser and grabbed a protein bar, devouring it immediately. The desperate speed with which she ate made me wonder when she'd last had a proper meal.

She took two more bars without commenting, tucking them into her pockets with practiced movements.

"Not much food on Zeta?" I ventured.

"Everything has a price," she replied, leaving it at that.

The engine room was next. I noticed Lena hesitating at the threshold, her eyes scanning every surface before entering. Unlike her direct approach in the galley, she kept to the room's perimeter, maintaining distance from the main control consoles.

"This is where I spend most of my time," I gestured around us. "My quarters are through there, and Harvey can dock there." I pointed to a charging station as far from my workstation as possible.

Lena approached Harvey and placed her hand on its chest. I noticed a faint glow behind her ear, pulsing with Harvey's eye sensors. Without a word from her, the robot moved to the charging station and connected to the wall unit. Its head lowered as if powering down.

"How do you do that?" I asked, genuinely curious.

Lena's expression went blank. "Practice," she said cryptically. "Now show me where I sleep."

On our way back to the crew quarters, Lena stopped at the galley again for more protein bars. I pushed open the door to an unused double room.

She immediately scanned the corners of the ceiling, her eyes narrowing at something I hadn't noticed before. She produced a small device from her pocket and placed it on the central console. A faint hum filled the room.

"What's that for?" I asked.

"Privacy," she replied, setting her plasma rifle on the top bunk.

"Iris isn't intrusive," I started. "She just monitors."

"Not interested." Lena cut me off. She sat on the lower bunk and began unlacing her boots.

I hesitated, remembering how she'd taken my medallion. "Back on Zeta, in the marketplace—how did you trick me into giving up my medallion?"

"Basic chemistry," she replied without looking up. "Works every time on the right targets."

She stood and approached me. "Get out now. I need rest."

The door slid shut in my face before I could say anything else.

I returned to the engine room, finding Harvey motionless at his charging station. With these new presences aboard, the ship felt different somehow. I retreated to my quarters and collapsed onto my bunk, fatigue overtaking me.

"Burton," Iris's voice came softly through the speaker in my quarters. "I cannot maintain standard monitoring in the new crew member's quarters. She has implemented blocking measures."

"I noticed," I mumbled, already half-asleep.

"I detected unusual neural patterns before communication was severed," Iris continued. "Would you like me to attempt override protocols?"

I thought about Lena's reaction to Iris's greeting. "No," I decided. "Leave it alone for now."

My medallion felt unusually warm against my chest as sleep began to claim me. I couldn't help wondering why Christopher had readily accepted Lena and Harvey. Something told me he'd found exactly what he was looking for on Zeta, which might not have been what he told me we were seeking.

~ 8 ~

THE CONTAINMENT FIELD

The ship had been operating at 75% of its core power for an eternity. Once a source of comfort, the consistent hum of the engine room now grated on my nerves. Christopher stayed locked on the bridge, and Lena occupied herself in the shuttle bay with Harvey. The silence of the Charon's passageways only intensified my thoughts about Neda, my father, and the medallion that hung heavily around my neck. I clutched it for comfort, my thumb tracing the familiar pattern as I had done countless times since childhood.

"Burton, your vital signs indicate elevated stress levels," Iris's voice emanated softly through the engine room speakers. "Would you like me to adjust environmental parameters?"

I glanced at the nearest control panel, where a blue light pulsed gently. "No thanks, Iris. Just... thinking about home."

"I understand. The human emotional response to displacement is often profound," she replied, her tone surprisingly empathetic for an AI. "You've been spending considerable time accessing the ship's systems. Are you finding what you need?"

Her question caught me off guard. After my strange ability to interface with the ship had manifested, I'd found myself drawn to exploring more of the Charon's systems. What had started as curiosity about the navigation systems had evolved into something deeper – a growing connection to the ship itself.

"I'm still learning," I admitted, keeping my voice low. "Iris, can you show me what Christopher is doing on the bridge?"

There was a pause, longer than her usual processing time. "That would violate privacy protocols," she finally responded. "However, I can inform you that he is currently analyzing data from the chip acquired on Zeta-35 and correlating it with navigational coordinates."

I nodded, unsurprised by her reluctance. Over the past days, I'd discovered that while Iris seemed to have some unusual affinity for me, she still wouldn't cross boundaries. Still, each time I connected with the ship's systems, they felt more intuitive, more accessible – as if they were designed specifically for me.

My medallion grew warm against my chest as I ran my fingers across a nearby control panel. The strange connection between the medallion and the ship's technology remained unexplained, but undeniable. Each time I accessed the systems, the medallion's temperature increased slightly, almost as if reacting to the vessel itself.

"Iris, have you noticed anything unusual about Christopher lately?" I asked carefully. "The way he's been studying those coordinates..."

"Captain Christopher's behavior patterns show a 27% increase in obsessive tendencies since acquiring the data chip from Zeta-35," Iris replied. "His focus on certain navigational algorithms has intensified significantly."

"What about the smoke?" I asked quietly, remembering the strange distortion I'd seen around him multiple times.

The lights in the engine room flickered briefly. "I... cannot detect what you're referring to, Burton," Iris responded, her usually smooth voice containing a barely perceptible stutter. "My sensors show no anomalous atmospheric conditions around Captain Christopher."

Before I could pursue this line of questioning, the ship's internal communications system crackled to life. "Attention, all crew!" Christopher's voice boomed through the speakers. "Report to the bridge immediately!"

I touched my medallion one last time for reassurance before making my way toward the bridge. Instead of climbing the ladder well to the shuttle bay and walking down the catwalk, I opted for the longer route through the lower deck, needing the extra time to clear my head.

"Be careful, Burton," Iris said as I reached the ladder near the bridge. "Elevated stress indicators suggest Captain Christopher may be... unpredictable."

I climbed up the ladder well just as Lena and Harvey were walking down the catwalk from the shuttle bay. Their footsteps reverberated through the ship's empty main level, amplified by the tension in the air. The smoke-like distortion I'd observed around Christopher seemed more pronounced in my mind each time I encountered him.

I gestured for Lena and Harvey to enter first, trying not to grimace as the doors screeched and stuttered. Lena glanced back at me, her expression seeming to question my usefulness. I followed closely behind Harvey, its large frame blocking my view of Christopher and Lena.

Emerging from behind Harvey, I could see Lena and Christopher staring intently at an orange dot on the navigation display.

"It's a space station," Lena confirmed, her fingers hovering over the holographic controls.

Christopher nodded slowly, changing the display to show a three-dimensional model of the space station. He focused intently on a particular aspect of the projection and took a step back, lost in deep thought. The smoke-like distortion around his shoulders seemed to writhe with increased intensity, though neither Lena nor Harvey appeared to notice it.

"It's an IGMC station," he said, his voice low. He shifted his gaze toward Lena. "Do you think there's anything of value over there?"

She tilted her head, shifting it right to left like it was on a spring, bouncing back and forth between conflicting thoughts. She stopped and studied Christopher for a moment before answering. "There's always something of value on an IGMC station. Whether it's worth the risk or not is up to you."

Christopher gave the projection another look before turning toward me. "Get the shuttle ready. We're going over," he said, his decree accented by a small twitch of his mechanical arm. The movement seemed more pronounced than usual, betraying whatever emotion lay beneath his controlled expression.

I studied the holographic projection more carefully, noticing details the others might have overlooked. "That may not be the best decision," I said cautiously. I stepped forward, positioning myself beside the navigation table between Lena and Christopher. "The station is barely holding together with that containment field. Look at the broken-off hull segments. There are abandoned shuttles and merchant ships trapped inside the field. If we break through it, we could trigger an explosion of debris. We'd be too close to maneuver through it."

My newfound technical understanding still surprises me sometimes. Knowledge seemed to flow through my fingers when I touched the ship's systems, as if I'd worked with this technology my entire life.

Lena leaned closer to the projection. "Velvet's right," she admitted, using the nickname she'd given me. "Any disruption to the integrity of that field could easily lead to destabilization." She stepped back from the table and moved toward Harvey. "Either way, Harvey and I are ready. It's your call."

Christopher stared at the projection silently. "How can we get in?" he finally asked, not addressing anyone specifically.

My medallion warmed against my chest as an idea formed in my mind. "Can we match the frequency the field is operating on?" I suggested, my voice steadier than I expected. "If we can match it, the shuttle could theoretically phase through without causing a disruption."

I glanced at Lena for confirmation. She nodded slowly, seeming impressed despite herself.

A small, emotionless smile crossed Christopher's face. "Then we go," he declared. "Prepare the shuttle for launch. Once we're out there, we'll scan for the resonance frequency of the field and adjust the shuttle's shields accordingly."

As I turned to leave the bridge, I noticed Harvey standing by the doors, its drawn-on expression seemingly communicating doubt. I hadn't expected to develop any affinity for the massive robot, but something about its childlike face made it seem almost sentient.

"Iris," I said quietly as I approached the bridge exit, "monitor the station's containment field while we're gone. If you detect any instability, alert us immediately."

"Acknowledged, Burton," Iris responded. "Exercise extreme caution. The structural integrity of that station appears severely compromised."

Walking down the catwalk toward the shuttle bay over the motionless pools of liquid cooling systems, I heard hurried footsteps and clanging mechanized boots following behind me.

Lena quickly caught up, Harvey close behind her. She spoke in the soft tone she used when humming to Harvey. "Don't worry, Velvet. I didn't get on this ship to die."

"At least you had a choice," I muttered, my hand instinctively finding my medallion.

"Intentionality and death are not often synonymous," she responded with a hint of amusement.

"Not often," she added more somberly. Then her demeanor brightened again. "My advice: survive the day, then do it again tomorrow." She slapped me on the back harder than I appreciated before striding ahead of me into the shuttle bay.

Harvey nearly knocked me off balance as it pushed past, staying in Lena's wake like a loyal guardian. Their relationship intrigued me; it seemed far deeper than technopathic control.

Arriving at the shuttle, I walked around it, running my hand on its cool frame before boarding through the lowered ramp at the rear. As I stepped onto the ramp, I immediately noticed Harvey standing at the top, a metallic gargoyle observing all who entered. Lena had already made herself home in the co-pilot seat, where I had become accustomed to sitting.

I noticed she'd reprogrammed the shuttle to start on her iris scan in addition to Christopher's. The engines hummed to life as she ran a diagnostic check on the shields and weapons systems.

I settled into the navigator's seat behind Lena and scanned the damaged space station for a suitable docking point. My medallion grew warmer against my chest as my fingers moved over the controls, that strange, intuitive knowledge flowing through me again.

Christopher joined us moments later, ignoring Harvey at the top of the ramp. He quickly assessed the new seating arrangement before making a disinterested face and taking the pilot's seat. Without comment, he released the magnetic docking clamps and maneuvered the shuttle into space.

We cautiously approached the IGMC space station, navigating slowly to avoid potential hazards. The once-bustling hub now lay abandoned, surrounded by wrecked ships and frozen bodies. The containment field shimmered around the station like a translucent bubble, trapping debris inside and outside its boundary. The remnants of vessels torn apart by the field littered the area, creating a dangerous obstacle course. I held my breath as we carefully navigated through the treacherous minefield.

"Are we close enough to get the frequency?" Christopher questioned, not saying my name, but I understood he was addressing me.

"I'm running a cipher now," I responded, pressing my fingers into the gel-like keypad. The medallion's warmth flowed up my arms and fingertips, enhancing my connection to the shuttle's systems.

Suddenly, rapid, high-frequency bursts crackled through the comms, interrupting the stillness. My console lit up with a stream of symbols and noise - not the usual garbled interference but something deliberate. Each burst was sharp and precise, cutting through the silence like a coded language.

"What is that?" I asked, focusing on the strange pattern of signals.

"Just another FRB," Christopher said dismissively. "Fast Radio Burst. Rare, but insignificant. It could be the station or a random signal cutting through this area of space."

Lena turned slightly in her chair. "It's a primitive form of communication out here," she explained condescendingly. "Line-of-sight transmissions. Point to point."

"Primitive?" I echoed, studying the data stream still flickering on my console.

"Think of it like catching a shuttle during dry season on Neda," Christopher added, his eyes never leaving the viewport. "You're either there when it arrives or miss it."

"And if someone intercepts the signal between points," Lena continued, "it's like reading someone else's mail. That's why it fell out of favor."

The bursts continued for a moment, then faded as abruptly as they had begun. I glanced at Christopher, whose jaw was clenched tightly. The smoke-like distortion around him seemed to intensify briefly before settling into its usual pattern. He knew something about these signals that he wasn't sharing.

"Are you seeing this?" Lena remarked, examining the sensor feed display. "Why would a replenishing station need so much fire-power?"

"See if those weapons are still active," Christopher ordered as we hovered outside their range.

Lena's fingers danced across her console. "The weapon system is still active, likely connected to the containment field," she reported. "If we don't have the right resonance frequency, they'll fire on us."

"Burton?" Christopher said, his tone expectant.

I continued working with the cipher, feeling the subtle patterns of the containment field through the shuttle's sensors. My medallion grew noticeably warmer against my skin as I modulated the shuttle's shields to match my detected frequency.

"Almost there," I muttered, making final adjustments. "That should be it," I said with cautious confidence.

Lena whipped her head around. "Should be?" she questioned, eyebrows arched.

"I've never matched shield frequencies with a containment field before," I admitted. "But the patterns are clear. This will work." My certainty came from somewhere beyond conscious knowledge – the same place that had allowed me to work effortlessly with the Charon's systems.

Christopher silently guided the shuttle toward the space station. His cybernetic arm twitched at his side, the servos within whirring uncomfortably loudly in the confined space.

The shuttle shuddered as our shields contacted the containment field. For a moment, I feared we'd miscalculated as vibrations coursed through the frame, threatening to tear us apart. My hand clutched my medallion, which felt almost hot against my palm. Then, with a final shudder, we passed through the field, the discomfort fading as quickly as it had begun.

"Nice work, Velvet," Lena said with genuine respect, sighing in relief.

Navigating inside the field proved more treacherous as debris was packed closer together. The station's hull was battered and torn, large chunks of metal breaking away from its crumbling structure, trapped within the containment field. The bold, ominous letters spelling "Inter-Galactic Mining Consortium" were etched onto the side of the station, partially obscured by floating debris.

"Look at that," Christopher murmured, staring through the viewscreen as we approached.

"Was it attacked?" Lena questioned. "For the amount of debris, I expected more holes in it."

I studied the chaotic scene, my mind processing the strange damage patterns. "It's odd. I can't detect any visible weapon damage to the metal hull at this range. The protruding structures appear to be fused into the walls as if purposely integrated. Perhaps there was a skirmish in this sector, and they activated their shields to halt it?" The question reflected more hope than my increasingly damp palms suggested.

"Can we get a diagnostic of the environmental systems?" Christopher asked, halting the shuttle's movement and turning toward me.

"We won't know until we dock," I replied reluctantly. "Once the shuttle is connected, we can link systems and see what's happening inside." I pointed to a slightly damaged docking bay. "That one may still be usable."

Christopher eased the shuttle into the docking bay, and the clamps engaged with a satisfying click. We all exhaled in relief as the airlock sealed around the shuttle, creating a temporary barrier.

"Now what?" Lena asked, looking at Christopher.

"Run the diagnostic," he directed his words at me as he stood from his chair.

I immersed my hand in the gel-like control panel, navigating through the station systems that became accessible upon docking. My medallion pulsed warmly against my chest, enhancing my connection to the unfamiliar technology.

"There's internal damage," I reported, surprised by what I found, "but the environmental systems are still functioning. Life support is active in certain sections."

"Come on then," Christopher said, pressurizing the shuttle and opening the airlock to the space station. "Let's find what we came for."

"What exactly are we looking for?" I ventured, unable to stop asking the question that had bothered me since we spotted the station.

Christopher's eyes narrowed slightly, the smoke-like distortion around him swirling momentarily before settling. "Anything useful," he replied vaguely. "Information. Technology. Survivors." Something in his tone suggested he had more specific goals than he shared.

"Well, Velvet, looks like we're going for a stroll," Lena said, rising from the co-pilot's seat and checking her plasma rifle.

Harvey stood motionless by the shuttle ramp, its eyes emitting an ethereal glow. As Lena passed, Harvey's drawn-on face seemed to express resignation.

There was a sickening shriek of metal scraping against metal as Christopher used his arm to wrench open the station doors. The sound scraped against my nerves like a physical pain. The doors finally gave way with a violent jolt.

"Quickly," he commanded, striding ahead with Lena, Harvey, and me following close behind.

Entering the station, we found the chaotic landscape outside mirrored in the corridors. Wires dangled precariously from the ceiling, their frayed ends sparking dangerous electricity that crackled in the air. Half of the corridors had crumbled and collapsed, creating heaps of rubble blocking potential paths.

"Look at this," Lena said, pointing her flashlight at a wall where a metal beam protruded. "This beam is fused through the station's wall."

I moved closer to examine it. "There aren't any welds," I observed with growing unease. "It's like the station closed around it after it fell."

"Incredible," Christopher muttered, bending down to investigate a panel half-buried in the twisted metal. I noticed how intently he studied it, as if searching for something specific.

Our flashlights pierced through the darkness, illuminating the wreckage as we delved deeper into the station. Turning a corner, my light revealed a figure lying motionless on the ground ahead.

A body lay sprawled across the narrow passageway, clad in a ripped and stained taupe uniform. Lena cautiously approached and prodded it with her foot, causing it to roll over with a sickening thud. The woman was identified by the name tag 'Smith' on her chest. Her glazed eyes were frozen open in terror, capturing her final moments. In her limp hand was a crumpled piece of paper.

"Damn," Lena whispered, her usual confidence temporarily shaken. "She must have been here when everything went to hell. IGMC?"

Christopher shook his head. "No uniform insignia."

"What's in her hand?" I asked, pointing at the paper.

Lena knelt beside the body and carefully extracted the paper. "A child's drawing," she said softly, studying the wavy lines. "Maybe a mother and daughter."

I saw genuine emotion cross Lena's face for a moment, something beyond her pragmatic detachment. Then Christopher interrupted the moment.

"Let's move," he ordered, continuing down the passageway.

As we progressed, I began to hear faint sounds coming from ahead. "Do you hear that?" I asked tensely.

No one responded, but Lena readied her plasma rifle and Christopher drew his blaster. We moved cautiously through a set of doors that opened onto the promenade deck.

The sight that greeted us was horrific. Metal structures were twisted into dangerous heaps, creating a sharp edge and a debris landscape. Crushed kiosks were scattered with bodies like broken toys. Some victims were still alive, trapped in the wreckage, their moans of pain filling the air.

Before I could fully process the scene, blaster fire erupted beside me. Christopher was methodically shooting the trapped survivors, his expressionless face.

Horror and revulsion surged through me. "Stop!" I cried out, moving toward him with my hands raised. "What are you doing?!"

"Spacer mercy, Velvet," Lena explained calmly, her plasma rifle raised. "Now step aside."

"What?" I asked, unable to comprehend their casual cruelty.

"Do you see any med clinics out here, Burton?" Christopher asked condescendingly. "Out here, if you can't save someone, you do the next best thing."

I stood my ground, though my heart raced with fear. "How do we know who can be saved?" I demanded.

Lena shrugged. "You don't. You guess, or you decide. But you don't dwell on it."

Christopher resumed firing, and blaster fire rang out as we navigated the promenade. I stayed behind, unable to participate in what they called mercy but seemed more like execution. The moans had fallen silent when we reached the exit on the other side.

As we continued, more bodies came into view, casualties of whatever catastrophe had befallen the station. Unlike those on the promenade, these people were already dead, their bodies contorted in unnatural positions or partially fused with debris. I averted my eyes from their grotesque forms, my stomach churning.

"Control room," Lena announced, breaking the heavy silence. Her flashlight illuminated a sign with arrows pointing up a ramp from our position.

We cautiously entered the control room, which was in disarray. Broken glass, data pads, and electronic components were strewn across the floor. Toppled monitors exposed their internal wiring, occasionally sending sparks into the darkness.

"Find anything salvageable," Christopher ordered as he navigated through the wreckage. "I want to know what happened here."

My medallion pulsed warmly as I approached an intact console. Following my intuition, I pressed my fingers into the control pad, feeling that a strange connection had been established.

"I think I found something," I said, surprised by what I saw in the logs.

"What is it?" Christopher asked, suddenly attentive.

"There's mention of a 'compressed hyper-dimensional kinetic relocation device,'" I reported, the term striking a strange chord of familiarity, though I was certain I'd never heard it before. My medallion grew noticeably warmer against my chest.

"What's that?" Lena asked, moving closer to look over my shoulder.

"I don't know," I admitted, continuing to search the logs. "But why would a refueling station have laboratory levels?" I murmured, more to myself than to the others.

As I focused on the logs, I overlooked the danger behind me. Suddenly, a hand grasped my ankle with surprising strength, pulling me off balance. I yelped in surprise, trying to break free.

"Let go!" I shouted, looking down to see a man clinging to my leg, his body half-crushed beneath a fallen console.

"Help me," he whispered desperately, his voice barely audible.

Lena sprinted around the control station, her plasma rifle charged and ready. "Move!" she shouted, aiming at the injured man.

The man's grip weakened as he slumped back to the floor. I raised my hands, positioning myself between Lena and the fallen man.

"Wait!" I pleaded, determined not to allow another casual execution. "He's still alive! He asked for our help!"

"Move, Velvet!" Lena demanded, her finger on the trigger. "We need to put that man down."

Still blocking her shot, I knelt to check the man's pulse. "Just wait," I insisted. "He's still breathing."

"Leave him," Christopher said dismissively, not even looking our way as he continued searching through the wreckage.

"We can't just kill him or leave him," I argued, feeling an overwhelming moral obligation. "He asked for my help."

Lena snorted. "We can't waste resources nursing someone back to health. Dragging him along will only slow us down."

"He asked for my help," I repeated firmly, meeting Lena's gaze unflinchingly despite the plasma rifle pointed in my direction.

Christopher finally meandered over to where Lena and I were locked in our standoff. He glanced between us before studying the man at my feet, whose fingers were still weakly grasping my ankle.

After a long moment, he made his decision. "Let Harvey handle the body and return to the shuttle."

Lena held my gaze for several seconds before lowering her rifle. She glared at me as she swung the weapon back over her shoulder, clearly displeased with my interference. She activated her shunt, the light behind her ear synchronizing with Harvey's optical sensors, and the machine obediently moved to the fallen man, carefully lifting him in its powerful arms.

"Where are these labs?" Christopher asked, returning to his primary objective.

"Let me check," I said, sliding my fingers back into the control pad. My medallion pulsed in rhythm with the console as I brought up a 3D map of the station, displaying our current location with a blue dot and marking the labs with green.

The corridors leading to the labs changed color from orange to red, warning of potential obstacles or damage along various routes.

Lena traced her fingers through the holographic map. "These five paths look clear," she noted, indicating the safest routes.

"And these?" Christopher asked, pointing to where several red lines converged on a single point.

"Highly unstable," I warned after analyzing the map's patterns. "If we enter those corridors, the entire structure could collapse beneath us."

Christopher stared at the map with an intensity that bordered on obsession. The smoke-like distortion around him writhed more actively than I'd seen before, almost forming patterns before dissipating into formlessness.

"Christopher?" I said cautiously, moving to stand beside Lena.

His voice suddenly filled the control room with thunderous authority. "We need to split up." Without waiting for a response, he hurried out of the control room and disappeared into the maze of corridors, the sound of his boots fading into the distance.

Lena hesitated only briefly before following him, her movements precise and determined like those of a soldier on a mission. I was left alone in the control room, with the holographic map glowing softly.

"Iris?" I whispered, hoping the AI could hear me through the shuttle's systems. "Are you there?"

To my surprise, a familiar voice responded through my communicator. "I am here, Burton. The shuttle's systems allow limited connection. Be careful, I'm detecting unusual energy patterns throughout the station that match no known signature in my database."

"Similar to the four-dimensional coordinates Christopher's been studying?" I asked, remembering what she'd told me about his obsession.

"Similar, but not identical," Iris replied. "Whatever this 'compressed hyper-dimensional kinetic relocation device' is, it appears to be connected to the dimensional anomalies in Christopher's navigation data."

My medallion pulsed warmly against my chest as I processed this information. With a deep breath, I chose a direction opposite to where the others had gone, determined to find my answers about this mysterious station and its connection to Christopher's quest.

~ 9 ~

ECHOES OF DESOLATION

I gingerly descended the dimly lit corridors, my footsteps echoing against the metal walls. The musty air weighed down on me with each step.

"Iris?" I whispered into my communicator. "Can you still read me?"

"Signal strength at seventy percent, Burton," her composed voice responded through the static. "I am tracking your life signs. Your heart rate is elevated."

"Yeah, well, this place would give anyone nightmares," I muttered, sweeping my flashlight across the twisted metal and debris.

"I recommend proceeding with caution. Station structural integrity is questionable based on external scans."

"You think?" I rolled my eyes, though the familiar voice was oddly comforting in the silence.

My flashlight beam cut through the darkness, revealing a tangle of pipes and conduits overhead that reminded me of the salvaged ship parts in my workshop on Neda. The familiarity offered little comfort.

"This is stupid," I said to Iris. "I should've stayed with the others."

"Perhaps," she acknowledged. "But Christopher and Lena separated in different directions. Your chosen path may yield valuable information."

I stepped carefully around twisted metal and what I refused to acknowledge as human remains. The chill of the station seeped through my jumpsuit, making my bruised ribs ache more than usual. Turning a corner, I found a worse scene, the ceiling had collapsed, leaving sparking cables hanging down like macabre decorations. A strange liquid seeped through the floor grates below, and when the sparks hit it, they disappeared in small wisps of smoke.

"Iris, what is this stuff?" I asked, toeing the edge of the spreading puddle.

Her voice came back patchy, broken by static. "Unable—identify—recommend—avoid—contact—"

"Iris? You're breaking up."

"—interference—increasing—Burton—caution—"

I adjusted my communicator, but the static only grew worse. "Great," I sighed. "Just when I need you."

Something moved at the edge of my flashlight beam.

"Lena?" I called out hesitantly. "Christopher?" The words died in the space, answered only by the distant groan of metal.

"—Burton—can't—maintain—" Iris's voice faded completely into a static hiss before going silent.

I took several deep breaths to calm myself and looked for a way forward. The only path seemed to be a precarious route across the islands of debris, avoiding the spreading liquid below. I tested each foothold before committing my weight, flinching at every spark that fell too close.

As I neared the end of this hazardous crossing, I heard something new, a faint humming that seemed to grow louder as I approached a partially open door ahead.

"Hello?" I called, swinging my flashlight across the opening. "Anyone there?"

No response came. With my heart hammering in my chest, I kicked the door open wider, wincing at the loud creak of protesting hinges. I swept my flashlight around the room, revealing a mess like the rest of the station, debris scattered everywhere, and walls buckled inward. Then my beam caught something that didn't belong, a human figure standing unnaturally still in the corner.

"Don't move!" I shouted, trying to sound threatening despite having nothing but a flashlight for protection.

"They were looking for an engineer," came Christopher's voice from the darkness, making me nearly drop the light in startled relief.

I edged closer, my beam illuminating his broad back as he stood before what looked like a console, his cybernetic arm submerged to the wrist in a gel interface. His arm twitched more violently than I'd ever seen before.

"What do you mean?" I asked, confusion overriding my relief.

Christopher didn't look at me. Instead, he pressed something on the console, and emergency lighting sputtered to life, bathing the room in a dull orange glow. Now I could see we were in some laboratory, with equipment I didn't recognize scattered around workstations.

"What's an engineer got to do with this place?" I asked again, moving closer.

Christopher's face was locked in a concentration I hadn't seen before, not even when piloting through debris fields. "These designs," he muttered, more to himself than to me. "They hadn't gotten any further than" He stopped abruptly, as if only now registering my presence.

"Any further than what?" I prodded, craning my neck to see what had completely captivated him.

"The initial prototype!" he snapped, his voice echoing off the walls. He tore his hands from the console and moved to another station, not looking at me.

I stood awkwardly, unsure of what to do. Christopher seemed to have forgotten me as he input commands into the new console. A nearby monitor flickered to life, and what it showed made my stomach lurch.

A man was strapped to a chair, thrashing against his restraints. Some kind of mechanical probe was boring into the back of his neck, blood and tissue spraying outward. Strange smoke filled the room, slithering into the man's nose, mouth, and the fresh wound on his neck. His body began to jerk and spasm, and something impossible happened.

Like a faulty hologram, the man seemed to flicker in and out of existence. Every time this happened, the station's walls rippled as if they were made of water rather than metal. Tears appeared in the structure, opening to the blackness of space beyond. People were sucked toward these breaches, their bodies twisting grotesquely as they hit the vacuum. The station groaned, metal screeching against metal as the structure seemed to fold in on itself before snapping back, sealing itself around anything caught in its path.

When the chaos finally subsided, all that remained was the wail of emergency alarms and floating bodies.

I stumbled back, bile rising in my throat. "What... what was that?" I managed to ask between shallow breaths.

Christopher's gaze remained fixed on the screen; his expression unreadable. "That," he said quietly, "is what happens when people meddle with technology they don't understand."

Something about the chair in the video nagged at my memory. It looked vaguely like that strange apparatus I'd seen in Charon's engine room, which had given me such an uneasy feeling.

What were they doing to that man?" I asked, trying to make sense of the horror I'd just witnessed.

Before Christopher could answer, frantic footsteps pounded down the corridor outside. Lena burst into the room; her usual composure shattered. Her chest heaved as she gasped for breath.

"We need to go!" she shouted between gulps of air. "Now!"

As if punctuating her warning, the station shuddered violently beneath our feet. The walls seemed to groan in protest, metal bending in ways it wasn't designed to.

"What happened?" I yelled, fighting to stay upright as the floor bucked beneath me.

"The containment field is failing," Lena explained hurriedly, bracing herself against the doorframe. "The whole place is coming apart!"

Christopher was already moving, plugging a data chip into the console. "Almost done," he muttered, eyes locked on some progress indicator I couldn't see from my angle.

"No time!" Lena shouted as another, stronger tremor shook the station. Ceiling panels crashed down around us, narrowly missing where I stood.

Christopher yanked the chip free when his download was completed and bolted for the door without glancing backward. Lena lingered just long enough to give me a pointed look.

"Move your ass, Velvet!" she commanded before racing after Christopher.

For a moment, I stood frozen, trying to process what I'd just seen on that monitor. What kind of experiment had they been running? And why did that chair seem familiar?

Another violent shake of the station snapped me back to reality. I sprinted after them, gasping as pain shot through my bruised ribs. The corridors seemed to shift and warp around me as I ran, the structure's integrity failing with each passing second.

The liquid I'd carefully avoided earlier splashed up as I ran through it, too desperate to be cautious now. It burned where it touched the back of my hand, sending sharp pain up my arm.

As I ran, my communicator crackled to life. "Burton—" Iris's voice cut through the static, "—detecting massive structural failures—immediate evacuation—"

"I'm trying!" I gasped, pushing myself harder despite the stabbing pain in my side.

I ran through the promenade, past the bodies of those Christopher and Lena had "mercied." I couldn't help wondering if their deaths had been quicker, less painful than what would happen to me if I didn't make it out.

When I finally reached the docking bay, my heart sank. The shuttle was already disengaging, its engines firing as it backed away from the rapidly disintegrating station. Through the viewport, I could see Lena's face, her expression a mask I couldn't read at this distance.

"They're leaving me!" I screamed into my communicator. "Iris, they're leaving me behind!"

"Burton, listen carefully," Iris responded, her voice calm in my panic. "On your jumpsuit's left thigh, there's a hidden panel. Activate it immediately."

"What?" I was gasping for breath, my mind unable to process her instructions.

"Left thigh pocket. Press the rectangular panel. Now, Burton."

In my desperation, I slapped at my jumpsuit where Iris had directed. My fingers found a small panel I'd never noticed before. There was a click, and suddenly, armor segments began unfolding from hidden compartments in the jumpsuit, wrapping around my body like an exoskeleton. Within seconds, I was encased in what I realized must be an emergency exposure suit.

"Iris, what do I"

The station gave one final, catastrophic shudder as the containment field collapsed entirely. The explosive decompression launched me into space like a projectile, spinning wildly among the debris. I couldn't control my trajectory, and I could barely tell which direction was which as I tumbled end over end.

Then came an impact, a jarring clang reverberating through my suit as something halted my deadly spin.

"You are safe now," Iris's voice came through my helmet comm, impossibly clear despite everything.

Large mechanical hands steadied my flailing body. I saw Harvey's crudely drawn face through my helmet, somehow reassuring despite its simplicity. The massive robot pulled me toward the shuttle, which had stopped just outside the expanding debris field.

Moments later, I was in the airlock, gasping as it repressurized. When the inner door opened, Lena stood waiting, her face betraying nothing of her thoughts.

"Get in here, Velvet," she ordered, steering me to a seat. "We'll be clear of the debris field in a few minutes."

"You left me," I said, my voice cracking more than I would have liked.

She crouched down to my level, her eyes meeting mine directly. "We didn't have a choice. Standard protocol, ship safety takes priority." Her expression softened imperceptibly. "But you handled it like someone with experience. Not many could activate an exposure suit in that situation." A small smirk played across her lips. "Not bad for a velvet."

She rose and turned to Harvey, the shunt behind her ear glowing briefly before she returned to the co-pilot's chair. Harvey remained beside me, a silent sentinel.

I focused on steadying my breathing, trying to process everything that had happened. The images from that monitor kept flashing in my mind: the chair, the smoke, the impossible folding of reality itself.

Heavy footsteps approached from the cockpit. Christopher loomed over me, studying my face with his cold, calculating gaze.

"Try to be strong, kid," he said flatly. "The universe can be cruel to the weak." How he said 'weak' was like the word disgusted him, as if acknowledging weakness was somehow worse than being weak.

"I'm fine," I muttered, closing my eyes to avoid further conversation.

The rest of the journey back to the Charon passed in tense silence. As soon as we docked, I unstrapped myself and hurried to my quarters, desperate to be alone with my thoughts.

Back in my small room, I paced the limited floor space, too wired to sit still.

"Iris," I said to the empty room. "Are you there?"

"I am here, Burton," she responded immediately.

"Did you see what happened on that station? What did I see on that monitor?"

"I could not record your visual feed through your communicator when the connection was lost."

"That chair," I said, stopping my pacing and sinking onto my bunk. "It looked like the one in the engine room. The one that gives me the creeps. And that smoke reminded me of the weird distortion I sometimes see around Christopher." I ran a hand through my hair. "Am I going crazy, Iris? None of this makes any sense."

"Your observations are valid, Burton. I've noted the distortion pattern in my visual sensors, though at a frequency most humans wouldn't detect."

I looked up at that. "So, you can see it too? I'm not imagining it?"

"You are not imagining it," she confirmed.

"And the way Christopher reacted to that data... he knew exactly what he was looking for." I stood up again, unable to stay still. "Whatever that chair does, whatever that experiment was, he knows more than he's telling us."

"That seems a reasonable conclusion."

I paced a few more steps before stopping again. "But why me, Iris? Why did he come to Neda? What does he want with me?"

"I do not have sufficient data to formulate a hypothesis," Iris replied. "Perhaps you should rest now. Your vital signs indicate extreme fatigue."

I touched the medallion hanging around my neck. "I don't think I can sleep after what I saw today."

"Would you like me to adjust the environmental settings to aid relaxation?"

"No," I sighed, finally sitting back on my bunk. "Just... stay with me for a while? I don't want to be alone with my thoughts right now."

"I will remain active, Burton," Iris assured me. "You are not alone."

I lay back, staring at the ceiling, knowing the image of that chair and the man strapped to it would haunt my dreams for a long time. But somehow, having Iris there to talk to made the darkness feel a little less overwhelming.

~ 10 ~

SURVEILLANCE AND SUSPICIONS

I woke the next cycle; my mind was still filled with the horrors of the previous day. The image of that chair from the IGMC station haunted me, its similarity to the one in the Charon's engine room too striking to ignore.

Instead of dwelling on it, I buried myself in work, monitoring the ship's systems from my usual spot in the engine room. I accessed the ship's surveillance feeds.

"Iris?" I whispered, not wanting my voice to carry beyond the room.

"Yes, Burton?" Her voice materialized from the nearest speaker, soft but clear.

"Can you show me what happened to the man from the station? The one we rescued?" I asked, feeling the slight warmth of my medallion against my chest as the ship's systems responded to my request.

"The survivor is in quarantine quarters on the lower deck," Iris replied. "Life signs stable but showing indications of exhaustion and minor injuries."

A feed appeared on my monitor, showing a man lying on a bunk in one of the spare quarters. He was large, with broad shoulders and a substantial build. Even at rest, something was imposing about him.

"Has anyone spoken with him since he regained consciousness?" I asked, studying what I could make out through the grainy feed.

"Negative. Lena and Christopher are currently in the galley discussing the situation."

My curiosity piqued, so I asked Iris to switch to the galley feed. The image shifted to show Christopher and Lena sitting across from each other. I adjusted the audio, and their voices came through with a slight static.

"You should have let me kill him," Lena said, leaning back in her chair with casual indifference.

Her feet were propped on the table, and I noticed Harvey standing silently behind her. One of her hands rested on the robot's leg, that familiar glow from behind her ear barely visible in the feed.

"He might have information," Christopher replied, sipping what looked like Nulrot from a metal cup.

"And if he doesn't?" Lena countered. "You know the protocols. A survivor is either dead or dead weight. That's why we abide by spacer mercy."

The coldness in her voice made me shiver. I remembered how readily she had been willing to execute the injured survivors at the station.

"We can always space him," Christopher said with a dispassionate shrug, "if we can't break him."

Lena shifted her weight forward. "What about your pet Velvet?"

Christopher let out a soft chuckle. "Burton?"

"He did vote to save him on the space station after the bastard got the drop on him," Lena said, her tone hinting at mockery.

"We keep him alive for now," Christopher stated firmly.

"Which one? The man from the station or Burton?" Lena asked.

"Yes," Christopher replied with a cold smile. "Talk to the man from the station. You can lead him to the airlock if he has no information. Call it delayed mercy."

"Better late than never," Lena shrugged, pushing back from the table. "And your Velvet?" she asked with her usual mocking tone.

Christopher's cybernetic arm twitched slightly, the metal plates clinking together. "We keep him close," he said finally.

I swallowed hard, not liking how they spoke about me when they thought I wasn't listening. Knowing what they planned for our guest was even less comforting if he proved useless.

Lena left the galley, appearing in the corridor feed. For a moment, she paused and looked directly at one of the cameras. My heart skipped a beat. Could she sense Iris? Did she know I was watching? She turned and continued toward the survivors' quarters, Harvey following her.

"Iris, show me the survivor again," I requested.

The monitor switched back to show the man sitting on his bunk as if he sensed someone coming. From this angle, I could make out more details: dark skin marked with keloid scars on his visible arms, a full beard, and what looked like thinning hair.

"Should I warn him?" I wondered aloud, then immediately dismissed the thought. What could I say? That the woman coming to interrogate him would happily shove him out an airlock if he didn't prove useful?

The door to his quarters slid open, and Lena entered. I watched as she locked the door behind her, leaving Harvey standing guard outside.

The man opened his eyes as Lena approached him, alert despite his apparent exhaustion.

"Come on in," he said, his voice gravelly and unexpectedly calm for someone in his position.

Lena sat across from him. "Let's start with the basics. What's your name?"

"Dwight," he muttered, barely turning his head to look at her.

"And just how did you find yourself on the IGMC station?" Lena asked, her voice cold and professional.

"You don't have a name?" Dwight countered, ignoring her question.

"Lena," she responded curtly. "What business did you have on the station?"

Dwight shrugged, avoiding her question again. "Say Lena, y'all got any food on this rig? I am famished."

She arched an eyebrow. "I'll consider it if you answer my questions first. How did you get there?"

"Is this your rig?" Dwight asked, continuing to deflect.

I couldn't help but admire his composure. Most people would be intimidated by Lena's cold demeanor, especially in a vulnerable position.

"Let me make this clear, Dwight," Lena said, clearly losing patience. "I am here to help you. But I need to know what you know about the IGMC station and why you were there."

Dwight sighed, chuckling to himself. "IGMC, huh? That old place is about as secretive as a stripper in a nunnery." He scratched at his beard. "I'd just arrived on a transport. Was passing through mostly."

"Passing through?" Lena pressed.

"Look, no offense, miss," Dwight said abruptly. "But I'd rather talk to the one in charge of this rig. Saves us both time and energy."

Lena narrowed her eyes. "It's a bold assumption to assume you aren't speaking with the person in charge."

"Oh, no offense meant, ma'am," Dwight quickly added, surrendering his hands. "Didn't mean to step on any toes. When I got nabbed, the one making the decisions wasn't you."

I noticed Dwight glance briefly at the camera in his room, and an uncomfortable feeling crept over me. Did he know he was being watched?

Irritated, Lena stood up. "Very well, Dwight. I'll see if Christopher can spare a moment to speak with you."

The feed showed her leaving the cabin, fists clenched as she stormed down the corridor toward the bridge.

In his quarters, Dwight tentatively touched his forehead, wincing in pain. Then he closed his eyes again, seeming to drift back to sleep.

"Iris, keep monitoring him," I said. "Let me know if anything changes."

"Of course, Burton," she replied. "Would you like me to notify you when Christopher responds to Lena's request?"

"Yes, please."

I returned to my work, occasionally glancing at the feed showing Dwight's quarters. True to his word, he appeared to have fallen asleep almost immediately.

***

About a quarter cycle later, Christopher's voice crackled through the ship's comm system, making me jump.

"Burton," he hissed, "fetch our mystery guest from his quarters and deliver him to the bridge."

I sighed, pushing away from my workstation. So they'd decided to talk to him after all. As I made my way to Dwight's quarters, I wondered what he knew might be worth keeping him alive.

When I reached his door, I tapped lightly before entering. "They want you up on the bridge," I said, keeping my voice neutral as I absent-mindedly scraped the engine grime from under my nails.

Dwight opened his eyes and sat up, scratching his beard. "I don't remember tellin' ya my name, kid. You must be my sitter."

He glanced up at the camera before focusing back on me. "Fine," he grumbled, hauling himself off the bunk. "Time to get to work."

I felt embarrassed when I used his name, a mistake that revealed I'd been watching him. I turned and led the way, not offering any explanation.

We navigated the narrow corridors of the lower decks, the flickering lights casting strange shadows. Despite his size, Dwight moved with surprising stealth, his footsteps barely audible on the metal grating. We climbed the ladder well to reach the bridge.

The doors lurched open with their usual reluctance. Christopher stood before the view screen, arms crossed behind his back, his mechanical hand gripping his human wrist. The vastness of space framed his silhouette, stars glimmering behind him. Lena was already there, leaning against Harvey's massive frame.

"Is this your rig?" Dwight asked, looking around with mild interest.

"Is this my...rig?" Christopher echoed, releasing his wrist and extending his mechanical hand to showcase the ship. "Yes, this is my...rig." He tucked his arm back and resumed his stance, eyes fixed on the passing stars.

Dwight flopped onto the chair at the communications station, sprawling out and leaning his head back. He looked entirely too comfortable for someone in his precarious position.

"Nice setup," he commented, spinning the chair to take in the bridge.

Christopher turned from the view screen, his gaze settling on Dwight with unsettling intensity. A strange shimmer around his shoulders matched his most dangerous moods.

"Why were you at the IGMC station?" Christopher asked bluntly.

"Like I told your lady friend there," Dwight motioned to Lena, "I was just passing through when the shit went to...well, shit."

"Passing through? How so?" Christopher sat in the captain's chair, turning to face Dwight.

"Sanitation. Somebody's got to take out the trash." Dwight grimaced as he turned to find Christopher.

"You get those scars in sanitation, Mr...." Christopher paused, waiting.

"Dwight."

"Yes, Mr. Dwight," Christopher said, the name coming out like something distasteful.

"Yeah, well, you'd be surprised how hazardous that line of work can be," Dwight replied evenly. His fingers had stopped tapping on the armrest, but he met Christopher's gaze without flinching. "And it's just Dwight," he added crookedly.

"What happened at the station?" Christopher pressed.

"Hell, if I know, boss. I was taken by surprise myself." The calmness in Dwight's voice seemed odd for someone who'd nearly died. "Just glad you all came along and grabbed me. Might not have made it there much longer."

"Did you send the message?" I asked suddenly, unable to stop myself. Christopher shot me a rebuking glare, while Dwight looked confused.

"What message?" he asked.

"The FRB," I said, still curious about the strange transmission near the station.

"You guys still using FRBs? This rig looked newer than that," Dwight commented, leaning back again and resuming his chair-swiveling.

Christopher's patience visibly thinned. "You are an unfamiliar element on my 'rig,'" he said coldly. "The others," he continued, motioning to Lena, Harvey, and me, "are here for their reasons. And while I may not fully trust them, their presence is...tolerable."

When Dwight tried to speak, Christopher silenced him with a raised hand.

"Lena," Christopher called out, still locked in a stare-down with Dwight. "Have Harvey take our friend Dwight to the airlock. He's getting off."

"Hold on, boss. You don't want to do that," Dwight said, suddenly alert. "There's got to be something..."

"Silence," Christopher cut him off, his voice arctic. His cybernetic arm twitched noticeably. "I'm sure you'll say, 'There's something I need to know,' or 'You can help me.' But I don't have the time or patience for your games. You're only dead weight if you can't provide relevant information."

"Come on, boss, you didn't rescue me just to space me," Dwight pleaded, looking to Lena and me for support.

"You don't have information, and we don't need sanitation workers," Christopher declared, glancing at Dwight's scars before returning to the view screen.

Something changed in Dwight's demeanor. He straightened, the nervous energy evaporating as he fixed his gaze on Christopher's back. "I'm not just a sanitation worker. I was IGMC. Shock troops. We don't have to be buddies, but if you're looking for something out here, you'll need me."

Christopher paused, turning to study Dwight before looking at Lena. "Vouch for him," he said, arms crossed over his chest.

"I don't know, he's kind of an asshole," Lena responded flatly.

"What about you?" Christopher's gaze shifted to me. "Iris has been helping you watch him. Can we trust him?"

I hesitated, weighing my options. Christopher knew I'd had Iris monitoring Dwight through the ship's surveillance. I glanced at Dwight, trying to read him. "He's tough, that's for sure. Looks like he's been in a few good fights." I looked between Lena and me. "Except for Harvey, we're short on muscle. Especially if the alternative is spacing him."

"I can handle myself just fine," Lena retorted.

Christopher studied me with suspicion, then sighed with evident weariness. "Alright, fine. But one wrong move and I'll drop your ass out an airlock and be gone before your eyes bulge out their sockets."

Dwight chuckled. "Sounds like a plan, boss. I'll try not to give you any reason to kill me." He stood from his chair, nodding before walking toward the bridge exit.

Christopher's gaze followed him, intense and calculating. I started to follow Dwight, eager to escape the tension on the bridge.

"Burton," Christopher's voice froze me mid-step. "You vouched for him. You watch him. He does anything to jeopardize my mission, both you and he will go frolicking out of the airlock together." He turned back to the view screen, his silhouette rigid against the backdrop of stars.

I hurried off the bridge, passing Lena's smug expression as she lounged against Harvey. By the time I caught up, Dwight was already descending the ladder well.

"Don't put your trust in strangers, kid. Being kind-hearted can get you killed out here," he said without looking back at me.

"So, we should have spaced you," I replied, annoyed at having just saved his life only to receive a lecture.

"Didn't say that. You don't know who you can trust out here. That goes double for this crew." With that, Dwight disappeared into his quarters.

I changed course and headed back to my quarters in the engine room. The familiar glow of the monitors welcomed me, and I felt a tension I hadn't realized I was carrying begin to ease. Almost instinctively, I looked over at the feed Iris was still running from Dwight's quarters one last time.

In the dim light, I watched as he collapsed onto his bunk. Through the audio feed, I heard what sounded like soft laughter.

It seemed strange that someone at death's door just a cycle ago would find anything amusing.

"It's a damn good start," I heard him mutter before his eyes closed, and he appeared to drift into sleep.

I touched my medallion absently, wondering what he meant by that, and what kind of trouble I'd brought aboard the Charon.

~ 11 ~

INFERNO IN THE VOID

Over the next few cycles, I observed Dwight's behavior from my station in the engine room. He quickly settled into his new environment, spending most of his time in the galley. Through Iris's monitoring feeds, I watched him chatting with Lena and cracking jokes at Harvey's expense, much to Lena's annoyance.

On occasion, I observed Christopher joining them in the galley. Iris's feeds showed Christopher tapping something on his wrist console before their discussions began, causing the audio to cut out, similar to Lena's privacy protocol in her quarters. Without sound, I could only guess at their conversations from body language. Christopher would pace while Dwight reclined, and though I couldn't hear what was said, I noticed how Dwight's expressions typically shifted from casual to despondent as their meetings progressed.

Dwight would also find time to visit me in the engine room, his large frame looming in the doorway. It always resembled the same conversation. "How's it hangin', kid?" he'd ask with a smirk, then he'd sit his massive frame on whatever flat surface he could find.

"Burton, I am detecting multiple vessels on approach vector," Iris's voice suddenly announced, interrupting my work on the coolant systems. "Energy signatures indicate weapons systems powering up."

Before I could respond, Christopher's voice came through the intercom. "Prepare to jump on my co”

A loud, high-frequency siren pierced the ship's intercom, drowning out Christopher's words. The engine room was filled with flashing red lights and blaring alarms. The ship rocked violently as the first impact hit, tossing me to the floor. My medallion tore free from my neck, the leather strap snapping as I was thrown across the room. I saw it sliding beneath a row of machinery as another blast hit.

"INCOMING WEAPONS FIRE!" Christopher called out through the intercom.

Instinctively, I reached where my medallion should have been, finding nothing but space. The ship rocked harder this time, preventing me from searching for it. I pushed myself off the floor and staggered to the console, gripping the edge to stay upright.

"Iris, show me tactical," I called out, desperately trying to focus on the immediate danger rather than my lost medallion.

"Accessing tactical systems," Iris responded, her voice steady despite the chaos. The main display flickered to life, showing three unidentified ships closing the distance on us.

Another jolt, and the walls and floors seemed to ripple in a wave of destruction as explosions rocked through the bulkheads. Siren calls rang throughout the ship, masking the sounds of falling and warping metal. In a hard spastic lurch, I was hurled against the far wall, pushing the oxygen out of my lungs on impact. My ribs felt like they were being crushed as I gasped for air.

My vision swam with double images, each movement of my head sending shockwaves of pain through my skull. I pushed myself up from the floor, only to have my legs buckle beneath me. Gritting my teeth, I dragged myself toward the console, each inch a battle against the ship's violent movements. I clung to the edge of the workstation, knuckles white with effort as I pulled myself upright. The display panels before me flickered erratically, the ship's faltering power supply causing the images to stutter and fade like dying stars.

"Iris, give me control of the ship's defensive systems," I called out, my voice strained.

"I am unable to comply, Burton," Iris responded, her tone apologetic. "Captain Christopher has implemented security protocols restricting access to tactical systems. Bridge controls cannot be overridden."

"The fuck is happening," Lena's voice came through the intercom.

"Christopher?" I managed to croak out.

"Not now, Burton!" was all I could make out before another wave of fire rocked the ship, sending me crashing into the bulkheads again.

"Fuck me running," Dwight cursed in the background.

Christopher's voice boomed with authority, cutting through the chaos. "Dwight, get to the bridge and take point on tactical now! Lena, get to the engine room and help Burton before it explodes!" His tone was urgent but controlled as he barked orders to keep the ship from being torn apart.

Dwight's baritone voice crackled through the intercom. "On my damn way."

The ship convulsed again, flinging me into the unforgiving metal surface with a sickening crunch. My skull erupted in agony as hot blood streamed down my face. I reached out to touch the source of the pain, feeling warm wetness and a sharp stabbing sensation that made me recoil immediately.

"Warning: plasma core destabilizing. Critical failure imminent in three minutes," Iris announced with mechanical calmness.

Immediately, intense waves of heat radiated from the core, searing my skin and making each breath painful.

I was frozen, unable to respond or understand the commotion around me. I heard Lena enter the engine room through the haze, but her voice sounded distant, echoing as if from the end of a long tunnel.

"Burton! Burton, snap out of it!" Lena shouted; her voice frantic as she shook me. When I didn't respond, she turned toward the nearest speaker. "Iris, he's unresponsive! What do we do?"

"His vital signs indicate severe trauma," Iris responded calmly. "Immediate medical intervention is required."

"We don't have time for that!" Lena snapped. "The core will blow and take us all with it!"

"I recommend administering medical stim-pack 47-B from the emergency kit," Iris suggested, her tone unchanged despite Lena's panic.

"That's too mild for this situation," Lena argued, rifling through the cargo pockets on her pants.

Through my blurred vision, I saw her pull something small from her pocket, a device I didn't recognize. My foggy brain could barely process what was happening.

"This will either wake him up or kill him, but we're dead anyway if the core blows," she muttered, her voice seeming to come from far away.

"I strongly advise against using unauthorized medical devices," Iris warned. "The risk of"

"Shut it, Iris!" Lena barked, placing the device on my neck before stepping back and activating it from her wrist.

It felt like an electrical storm was burning through every nerve ending in my body. I sprang from the ground with no thought of my head or ribs or seared flesh. I was alert and burning from the inside.

"Burton!" Lena's voice sounded like a shotgun blast through the chaos. "The core!" She pointed a dirt-smudged finger toward the pulsating heart of our ship.

I blinked at her, my mind doing cartwheels to process her words as the device at my neck sent clarity through my system. "Wha"

"The core!" she yelled again.

I snapped out of my daze, adrenaline pumping through me. "Iris, diagnostics on the plasma core, now!"

"Coolant systems failing," Iris reported instantly. "Core temperature exceeding safety parameters. Containment breach imminent."

"We need to vent the plasma before the energy forces its way out," I said, the solution crystallizing in my mind.

The intercom boomed with Christopher's voice. "Burton, we need more power for propulsion if we want to outrun them."

"Venting the plasma should be our priority," I fired back.

"I'm not debating this with you, Burton. We won't be able to"

"Iris, terminate communications with the bridge," I commanded, surprised at my boldness.

"Communications terminated," Iris confirmed, her tone suggesting something almost like approval.

I yelled above the ship's noise, "Lena! Get Harvey to disconnect the coolant lines manually. We need more time."

Lena nodded, understanding, before closing her eyes and activating the light in her shunt. In just a few moments, Harvey had maneuvered to the other side of the engine room and ripped the large coolant line from its position.

I glanced back at the center of the room, where the plasma core was now a swirling mass of untamed power, threatening to engulf us all with every second that passed.

"Iris, can we redirect the plasma flow to the external vents?" I asked.

"Affirmative, Burton," Iris responded. "But such an action would deplete our main power source by approximately 78.3%."

"Do it," I commanded. "Iris, reestablish bridge communications," I said, returning to the console. "Dwight, get us out in front of whoever is chasing us. I'm diverting the plasma from the core."

The Charon veered sharply to the side, knocking Lena and me off balance. In response to Dwight's maneuver, the artificial gravity briefly faltered.

"Iris, prepare to open external plasma vents on my mark," I instructed. "Lena, get Harvey to attach the coolant line to the external plasma vent and open the valves!"

Lena sent the commands to Harvey. Despite the valves' protests, the robot forcefully twisted them open with a mechanical hiss.

"Iris, now!" I shouted.

"Executing command," Iris responded. "External plasma vents opening."

The Charon erupted with plasma fire, casting a bright light over the empty void of space. I held my breath, looking over at Lena, who seemed anxiously waiting. Then a thunderous boom echoed through the ship. The Charon quaked as if a massive tidal wave had struck it, but we remained unscathed.

Dwight's voice exploded through the intercom with an overly enthusiastic confirmation. "Oh, hell yeah, Kid! We just roasted those bastards! We're golden for now." He declared with a cringeworthy amount of cheeriness.

Christopher's voice dripped with animus as he spoke. "Report. What is the current state of my ship, Burton?"

I gritted my teeth, glancing toward the empty plasma core that still glowed and radiated heat. It wasn't stable by any means, but at least it wasn't about to explode. "She'll hold for now, but we need to dock and do some serious repairs soon," I replied, trying to keep my animus in check.

Christopher's voice was laced with controlled anger. "Fine," he stated firmly, pausing a moment before continuing, "I recall giving you a direct order when you chose to terminate communications."

Dwight's voice crackled over the intercom before I could respond. "Boss, he had no damn choice. They were raining hot, holy hell down on us. But he sure as hell made chicken salad out of chicken shit with that plasma trick."

Christopher's voice lit up with anger. "Let's stick to the issue at hand, Dwight. Burton, please provide your explanation."

I braced myself for the inevitable consequences, taking a deep breath before I spoke. "I had to prioritize stabilizing the core over propulsion. We managed to use the plasma both as a weapon and for self-preservation."

"We wouldn't have outrun them," Lena interjected over the intercom. "Listen up. If not for us, your fancy ship would be floating in pieces now. So, let's cut the crap and figure out our next move, okay?"

There was a long silence before Christopher engaged in the conversation again. Rather than arguing with us all, he stated, "Everyone to the bridge." The words sounded strained, almost as if he was biting back a tirade of rage. He clicked off the intercom, leaving us in a tense silence.

I instinctively reached for my medallion again, the link to my past life on Neda, my father, and whatever strange power it seemed to hold over the ship's systems. But it was gone, lost somewhere in the chaos of the attack. A cold feeling of dread settled in my stomach as I realized what its absence might mean.

"You okay, Velvet?" Lena asked, noticing my distress.

"My medallion," I muttered. "It's gone."

She shrugged. "We're alive. That's what matters right now." She gestured toward the door. "Come on. His highness awaits."

As we made our way to the bridge, I couldn't shake the feeling that something fundamental had changed. Not just the loss of my medallion, but also my relationship with the ship and Iris. She had obeyed my command over Christopher's, something I wouldn't have thought possible before today.

"Iris," I said quietly as we walked. "Thank you."

"You're welcome, Burton," she responded, her voice coming softly from a nearby speaker. "Your solution was the most logical course of action."

I smiled despite the pain and exhaustion. Perhaps I wasn't as alone on this ship as I'd thought.

~ 12 ~

STRANDED AT THE EDGE

In the aftermath of the attack, the Charon limped through the void like a wounded animal. With each burst of acceleration, the ship's engines groaned, echoing through the corridors like a death rattle. It had been three cycles since I'd vented the plasma core, saving the ship but leaving us stranded in unfamiliar space.

Sleep had become a luxury I couldn't afford. My hands were raw and blistered from endless cycles spent fabricating makeshift patches to seal the hull breaches. The absence of my medallion felt like a phantom limb, a constant, aching reminder of what I'd lost. Ever since it had disappeared during the attack, my connection to the ship's systems had diminished, requiring conscious effort where there had been intuition before.

"Warning: structural integrity at 47 percent in sector seven," Iris announced, her voice a calm counterpoint to the ship's distress.

"Acknowledged," I muttered, my voice hoarse from breathing recycled air filled with metal dust and coolant vapors.

Over the subsequent few cycles, I'd thrown myself into repairs, focusing only on the sections I could access. When I wasn't welding patches or rerouting power, I'd collapse into exhaustion, only to wake and begin again. The others seemed to have their routines. Sometimes I'd walk past the galley to find Christopher and Dwight deep in conversation, though they'd always stop when they noticed me. Whatever they discussed, Dwight usually emerged looking tense, his earlier cockiness subdued.

Lena had been helping by sending Harvey outside to seal some larger fractures. His massive frame maneuvered with surprising delicacy in the void. Dwight had proven himself useful, too, his knowledge of ship mechanics complementing my own skills. Even so, we were fighting a losing battle.

I went to the galley where Christopher had called an impromptu meeting. My muscles screamed with each step, and the deep throb in my temples hadn't subsided in days. When I arrived, Lena was perched on Harvey's knee, her expression unreadable. Dwight leaned against the wall, arms crossed, while Christopher stood rigidly at the head of the table, his cybernetic arm twitching more noticeably than usual.

I slumped into a seat, blowing across the hot liquid in my cup before taking a cautious sip. The bitter tang did little to revive my exhausted mind.

"We're stranded without the necessary components," I said, breaking the tense silence. "My attempts to salvage parts or fabricate replacements are only good enough to keep us limping for a little longer. We're running out of options if we don't get supplies soon."

Christopher's face hardened. "You need to figure something out," he said coldly. "I need more than excuses."

The dismissal of my efforts ignited something in me. Perhaps it was the exhaustion or the lingering anger from our confrontation during the attack. Either way, the words burst out before I could stop them.

"You don't think I'm trying to 'figure something out'?" I snapped, slamming my cup down. "It's gonna take a miracle or a well-stocked salvage yard for me to do anything more than I already have. Without my medallion, I can't even—" I cut myself off, not wanting to reveal how much the loss had affected my ability to interface with the ship.

Christopher's gaze burned into me before he tore his attention away. With a subtle gesture of his cybernetic hand, he activated the holo-projector embedded in the galley table. A three-dimensional star map materialized above where I sat, rotating slowly to show our current position. Sectors illuminated in different colors denote known trade routes, hazardous regions, and unexplored space. Our ship appeared as a small red dot, adrift in a sea of unfamiliar stars.

"Dwight, Lena, what do you know about this area of space?" Christopher asked, his fingers manipulating the projection to zoom in on a particular sector. The hologram cast eerie blue shadows across his face, making the smoke-like distortion around his shoulders appear more pronounced. He deliberately ignored my outburst, but I noticed his cybernetic fingers tightening as he adjusted the display.

Dwight scratched his beard, a nervous gesture he often displayed around Christopher. "Well, boss, looks like we're in the ass end of nowhere." He leaned over the table, studying the coordinates. "But there might be an abandoned HelixCore spaceport near here." He pointed to a blinking dot on the screen. "Maybe we can salvage what we need there."

Christopher's eyebrow arched. "HelixCore?" he said slowly, a strange note in his voice.

Dwight's hand moved from his beard to wipe sweat from his forehead with a grimy cloth. "Shit, I don't know, boss. You hear a lot of things out here. It was abandoned during the corporate wars, when IGMC pushed HelixCore out of this sector." His confidence seemed to waver under Christopher's scrutiny. "Either way, it can't hurt to take a look."

I nodded in agreement, desperate for any solution. "Sounds like our best shot."

"Says the person who vented the plasma and left us stranded out here," Christopher snapped, his arm spasming violently as he turned back to me. The smoke-like distortion I occasionally noticed around him intensified momentarily, whirling like an agitated storm.

He closed his eyes, visibly struggling to regain control. When he opened them again, the distortion had settled, and his arm twitched less erratically.

"Iris," Christopher called to the ship's AI, "set a course for the HelixCore spaceport."

"Course plotted, Captain," Iris responded, her voice emanating from the galley speakers. "Estimated arrival in thirteen hours at current power capabilities."

Christopher nodded, turning back to Lena and Dwight. "Burton and I will take the shuttle to scout the spaceport when we arrive. We'll determine if it matches Dwight's intelligence and assess whether it has the needed parts." His gaze shifted to Lena and Dwight. "You two will stay with the ship and monitor for any sign of trouble. If any appear, you'll alert us immediately and prepare for emergency extraction."

"Sounds like a shit plan," Lena finally chimed in, having observed the conversation from her perch.

"How so?" Christopher's ice-cold gaze swung towards her. He didn't seem surprised by the interruption; he was just annoyed.

"Look here," she jumped off Harvey and landed on the floor with a thud. Her neural shunt glowed faintly as she approached the navigation table. She expanded the map view with a gesture and drew a large circle around the blue dot marking the HelixCore spaceport. "The Sable Serpents patrol this area," she explained. "They're not known for being welcoming to outsiders."

Christopher crossed his arms and said nothing, but his jaw tightened.

"What's Sable Serpent?" I interjected, still focused on the possibility of finding the parts we needed. "Couldn't we bribe our way through?"

Dwight scoffed. "We don't have enough credits to pay for the air we breathe right now, kid. Let alone bribe our way through a quadrant full of zealots."

"Zealots?" The word hung in the air, heavy with implication.

"Yeah, kid," Dwight nodded, his voice dropping to a somber rumble. "Hardcore believers in their divine ordinance or something like that. They got an alien space station shaped like a serpent. Word is it's made from a sentient alloy that can heal itself. They believe the station chose them, or some such nonsense." His eyes darted to Lena for confirmation.

"The station predates human expansion into this sector," Lena added, her expression grim. "No one knows who built it or how, but the Serpents guard it like a sacred relic. Anyone who gets too close either joins their cult or disappears."

"Ghost stories and spacer myths," Christopher interrupted dismissively. His twitching arm betrayed his growing agitation, but his voice remained steady. "We need parts, not bedtime stories."

Something in his tone struck me as odd, almost as if he were deliberately downplaying the threat. Given his centuries of experience navigating the dangers of space, his dismissal of the Sable Serpents seemed calculated rather than genuine disbelief.

"They're no spacer myth," Lena countered, crossing her arms and leaning back against Harvey. "They are real, and they are deadly. They worship their space station as their god and fiercely defend their territory. I've seen what happens to ships that wander into their space uninvited." Her eyes darkened with what looked like personal memory. "Three cycles ago, they captured a ZalCorp freighter. By the time they were done, there wasn't enough left of the crew to fill a waste disposal unit."

The room fell silent as her words sank in.

"Believe what you want," she continued after a moment, "but ask yourself if the parts are worth the risk of getting caught in Serpent territory."

"So, what do you suggest we do, Lena?" Christopher's tone was sarcastic, a thin veneer of civility barely concealing his obvious irritation.

Lena's expression remained stoic as she met his frosty gaze with equal intensity. "Find a better option."

"I've heard enough," Christopher announced, abruptly turning away from the holo-table. His cybernetic arm twitched erratically, a silent testament to his suppressed fury. "We don't have a better option; we need those parts. We can figure out how to deal with the Serpent Order when that time comes." He fixed his gaze on me. "Burton, go prep the shuttle. We need to be in and out quickly."

I downed the last drops of liquid in my cup, slamming it onto the table with a heavy sigh. With a weary stride, I dragged myself out of the galley, my body yearning for rest that wouldn't come.

To my surprise, Lena walked with me to the shuttle ladder well, Harvey following like her robotic shadow.

"You, okay?" she asked, an uncommon note of concern in her voice.

"Yeah," I managed a tired smile, the fatigue seeping into my bones. "Just exhausted. Not sure how much longer we can keep up this pace."

She shrugged; her gaze fixed on the worn metal floor. "Been in tougher spots." Lena paused, rubbing her shunt absentmindedly. "But I won't lie, Velvet. This run... into Serpent territory... it makes me nervous."

She stopped walking as I grabbed the first rung on the ladder.

"I've been nervous since we left Zeta," I admitted, my hand instinctively moving to clutch at my chest where my medallion used to rest. The familiar weight was gone, leaving only emptiness in its place. "Since I lost my medallion during the attack."

I started climbing, conscious of the hollow feeling where the medallion's warmth should have been. Without it, the ship felt foreign and distant, like trying to read through frosted glass. The intuitive connection I'd developed with Charon's systems had degraded to something more mechanical, requiring conscious effort, whereas there had been flowing insight before.

"I'm sorry," Lena called up after me, her voice unusually soft. "I know what it's like to lose something that connects you to" She stopped herself, seeming to reconsider her words. "Just be careful up there, okay? Christopher has his agenda, and it might not include keeping you alive."

I paused on the ladder, looking down at her. "What do you mean?"

She glanced around nervously. "Just watch yourself," she whispered. "And if you find anything interesting... well, I'm a good person to share it with."

Before I could respond, she turned and walked away, Harvey's hulking form following close behind. Her warning unsettled me as I continued climbing to the shuttle bay.

The shuttle waited like a silent sentinel in the dimly lit bay. As I approached, the entry ramp lowered automatically, and soft blue lighting activated inside the cabin.

"Welcome, Burton," Iris's voice greeted me as I stepped aboard. "I've initiated a pre-flight systems check as per standard protocol."

"Thanks, Iris," I replied, comforted in her familiar presence. Are there any issues I should know about?"

"Fuel reserves at 62%. Life support is optimal. Navigation systems awaiting input," she reported methodically.

I settled into the pilot's seat, my movements mechanical from cycles of repetition. "Let's download the course Christopher plotted to the HelixCore spaceport."

"Initiating download," Iris responded.

As I tried to program the route, the shuttle suddenly suffered a massive power drain. The lights flickered wildly before plunging the cabin into darkness.

"Iris?" I called out, a hint of panic in my voice. "What's happening?"

No response came through the speakers.

"Come on, not now," I muttered, frustration mounting as I manually initiated the emergency lighting. The red glow cast eerie shadows throughout the cabin.

"System malfunction detected," Iris's voice finally returned, though it sounded distorted. "Unusual data packet intercepted during download process."

I ran diagnostics to pinpoint the source of the problem. The results finally appeared, showing that the shuttle's memory stores were critically overloaded, as if someone had dumped a massive amount of data into the system.

"Iris, can you identify what's causing this overload?"

Unable to process. The data appears to be encrypted with Captain Christopher's algorithms," she replied. "Caution advised."

I walked back to the rear of the cabin and removed the wall panel next to the ramp. The heat emanating from the memory crystals, which glowed an angry red, immediately pushed me back.

"Core temperature exceeding safe parameters," Iris warned. "Recommend immediate extraction of primary memory crystal."

I searched through the compartments until I found heat-resistant gloves from a spare environmental suit. Carefully, I reached into the panel and extracted the main memory crystal, the intense heat bringing flashbacks of the plasma core during our battle. The crystal pulsed with data—far more than should have been there for a simple navigation download.

"Iris, can you analyze this crystal without triggering whatever safeguards might be in it?"

"Limited analysis possible. The crystal contains approximately 87 terabytes of data, significantly exceeding standard navigation requirements."

After installing an additional crystal as a failover and recalibrating the system, I returned to the cockpit to continue the memory sync. As I powered up the shuttle again, a surge of electricity crackled through the control panel. The lights flashed on and off rapidly before returning to a steady state.

"Systems restored," Iris announced. "However, I detect anomalous data structures in the navigation computer."

"Burton," Christopher barked over the intercom. "What was that?"

"Just a minor hiccup," I responded, trying to keep my voice steady despite my exhaustion and growing curiosity about the data overload. "Shouldn't be an issue from here on."

Silence followed my words, dragging on long enough for me to wonder if Christopher was still there.

"Get ready to start the engines. I'll be there soon," he finally said, a hint of annoyance creeping into his voice.

"Great," I muttered once I knew the comms were off.

I opened the course charts and navigation information to ensure the download was completed successfully. That's when I noticed a folder labeled "LACHESIS" in all capital letters, the ship Christopher had been searching for since I'd been brought aboard. The folder contained fragments and complete documents, as if it had been corrupted and hastily reassembled.

"Iris," I whispered, "are you seeing this?"

"Yes, Burton," she responded. "It appears to be Captain Christopher's private research archive. It is not authorized for general access."

My heart raced. "Did you transfer it here? Or was it an accident?"

"I did not initiate the transfer," Iris replied. "However, I detect unusual access patterns in the data stream when you attempted to download navigation coordinates. Something intercepted and modified the request."

This was Christopher's archive, where he did all his research on the Lachesis. But why had it been downloaded to the shuttle? Was it an accident, or had someone deliberately transferred it here?

With shaking hands, I accessed the more complete documents. The amount of information was overwhelming. Christopher had compiled files on everything from suspected planets where the Lachesis might be found to detailed reports on various "Desolation Day" refugee ships. Personnel files, scientific papers, and what appeared to be classified corporate documents were stolen from IGMC archives.

"Accessing these files may trigger security protocols," Iris warned. Proceed with caution."

Most disturbing was the data he'd taken from the IGMC station. I watched again as the man in the chair died, the strange smoke entering his body as reality itself warped around him. The nauseating feelings from the station returned, making me swallow hard to keep down the bitter liquid I'd consumed in the galley.

"Iris, this smoke... It's the same thing I see around Christopher sometimes, right?" I asked, my voice barely audible.

"The energy pattern signatures show a 97.8% match," Iris confirmed. "Both appear to operate on similar hyper-dimensional principles."

As I continued browsing, I found older documents labeled "CHeKeR Device Schematics" with technical drawings and equations that made little sense. The notations were complex, referencing "dimensional folding" and "hyper-spatial compression." One notation caught my attention: "A. Chen's calculations for the compression field require T. Alexander's anthropological insights on dimensional perception to complete the interface circuit."

I found fragmented journal entries, data logs, and research notes, all meticulously organized by date. What caught my eye was an image of a medallion that looked exactly like mine.

It wasn't a schematic but a photograph, taken as evidence alongside a research log. The entry was dated just days before the Desolation:

"17.08.2298: T. Alexander secured the data module. His anthropological background proved invaluable in designing an interface that responds to genetic memory markers rather than direct neural input. The medallion casing—his idea—should bypass security protocols."

A later entry, dated two days after:

"19.08.2298: T.A. and M.P.R. completed final modifications. Quantum entanglement is stable. Memory corruption protocols are embedded if unauthorized access is attempted."

The last entry made my heart skip:

"22.08.2298: T.A. missing after Icarus incident. M.P.R. escaped with survivors. Medallion went with her, as did the child. T.A.'s final message: 'It's done. Meredith has the medallion. Keep that sadistic spawn away from her and what grows inside her. She'll find a home for them all.' Ongoing investigation."

"Iris?" I whispered, watching the shuttle's lights pulse gently in response. "Are you there?"

"I am here, Burton," her familiar voice responded through the shuttle's speakers. "You appear distressed. Is there something I can assist with?"

I hesitated, uncertain how much I could trust the ship's AI given Christopher's control. "Can you tell me anything about Dr. Terrance Alexander? Or someone with the initials MPR?"

The lights dimmed momentarily, as if Iris were considering my question. "Dr. Terrance Alexander appears in multiple historical records as an anthropologist who studied dimensional theories during Earth's final days. He was reported missing during the final evacuations. As for MPR, cross-referencing with available data suggests Meredith P. Rivera, a researcher who worked alongside Dr. Alexander."

"Iris, what's the connection between the medallion I had and the Charon's systems?"

"I cannot determine a direct connection based on available data," Iris replied. "However, the object you carried exhibited unusual properties that affected your interface capabilities with ship systems."

"You noticed that too?" I asked, surprised that Iris had been monitoring the connection.

"Yes. When interfacing with ship systems, your neural patterns showed a 42% efficacy reduction following the object's loss."

My attention was drawn to another folder labeled "Subjects," and inside I discovered files on Uncle Joren and me. Christopher had been tracking my uncle for years, noting his movements and associations. The file included details about my birth, my parents, and my life on Neda that no stranger should have known. There were also extensive notes about Lena, Harvey, Dwight, and others I didn't recognize.

One document caught my eye, a genetic analysis comparing my DNA markers to "T.A." with a note: "Genetic memory potential: High. Suitable candidate for interface."

"Iris," I whispered, "what does Christopher want with me? Why did he bring me aboard?"

The lights flickered slightly before Iris responded. "Captain Christopher's objectives are restricted from my access. However, I can confirm that your neural patterns show remarkable similarities to theoretical models developed by Dr. Alexander for hyperdimensional navigation."

I transferred the data to my wrist console, hoping to examine it more carefully later. Just as the transfer completed, the proximity alarm blared, its piercing wail shattering the silence.

I exited the shuttle and sprinted down the catwalk toward the bridge. "What's going on?" I gasped, hunched over, trying to regain my breath.

"We've got company," Lena said tersely, pointing at the blinking blips on the radar screen.

"More attackers?" I questioned, finally standing up straight.

"No," Christopher stated flatly as the ship was hailed.

The main screen flickered to life, revealing a woman with obsidian-black eyes and intricate metallic implants that seemed to flow into her skin like liquid mercury. The emblem of a serpent was emblazoned on her uniform, its eyes glowing with the same unnatural darkness as hers.

"Greetings," she began, her voice cold and authoritative. "I am Commander Zara of the Order of the Sable Serpent. Identify yourselves immediately or be destroyed."

As the others scrambled to respond, my mind raced with the revelations I'd uncovered. The research logs painted a disturbing picture: Dr. Terrance Alexander creating a medallion to smuggle data, Alicia Chen developing the CHeKeR device, Meredith Rivera escaping with survivors, and something about a child she carried. The medallion that had hung around my neck my entire life was somehow at the center of it all.

I saw the smoke-like substance curling around Christopher's shoulders as he faced the Serpent commander. It seemed more agitated than usual, almost eager. Was it reacting to the Serpents? Or was it something else entirely?

"Iris," I whispered, too softly for anyone to hear.

"Yes, Burton?" her voice responded directly into my earpiece.

"Whatever happens next, help me find the truth."

"I will do what I can within my operational parameters," she replied.

Whatever Christopher was hunting, I now believed my medallion was more than a keepsake; it was somehow tied to Terrance Alexander, Meredith Rivera, and events aboard the Icarus generations ago. As the Serpent Commander's cold eyes stared through the screen, I couldn't shake the feeling that she was yet another piece of a puzzle I was only beginning to understand, a story that had begun long before me and showed no signs of ending soon.

~ 13 ~

INTO THE SERPENT'S LAIR

"Burton," Christopher seethed, his teeth clenched tight enough to crack. "How are they intercepting our communications?"

My eyes widened in panic. "I have no idea," I rushed to the comms station and dropped into the seat. "Iris, help me reroute the signal through another transceiver." I dove into the complex protocols and subroutines, fingers flying across the interface. Without my medallion, the connection felt distant and clouded, like trying to see through frosted glass.

"I'm detecting an external override protocol," Iris's calm voice informed me. "Attempting countermeasures."

The interface flickered under my touch, lacking that intuitive response I'd grown accustomed to with my medallion. I thought briefly of searching for it when we returned to the, we returned, but now wasn't the time. I needed to focus on our immediate survival.

"I'm locked out," I finally announced, turning back to Christopher with a mix of surprise and anxiety. "Iris can't bypass it either."

The smoke-like distortion around Christopher's shoulders swirled as he glared at me before spinning toward Dwight. "What tactical solutions can you offer me?"

"Apologies, Boss," Dwight said, swiveling his chair to meet Christopher's gaze. "I'm unable to access the weapon systems as well."

Commander Zara's voice came through again, dripping with impatience. "I'm waiting."

Christopher approached the central console on the Charon's bridge, his cybernetic arm twitching with barely controlled urgency.

"Iris, open communications channel to the Sable Serpent vessel," he commanded, his voice tight with restraint.

"Communications channel open, Captain," Iris responded immediately. "Be advised that our transmission is being monitored and potentially intercepted."

"This is Captain Christopher Lucian, commanding the vessel Charon." His voice took on a charming lilt that I'd never heard before. "Forgive our naivety. My crew and I were... unaware... that we had trespassed into your rightful territory. Unfortunately, our ship was subjected to a brutal attack. We are now aimlessly floating, desperately searching for a place to fix our vessel."

He entered another set of commands into the console, cut the transmission, and then turned to Dwight. They exchanged looks, and Dwight attempted to re-access the weapons system without speaking. He glanced back at Christopher and shrugged, still unable to gain entry.

"So, you need assistance?" Commander Zara queried, her voice carrying an unnatural reverberation through our speakers.

"They're scanning us," Lena whispered, eyes darting to the sensor readings.

Christopher's mechanical arm twitched violently as he turned back to the console. "Iris, reopen communications channel," he ordered.

"Channel reopened, Captain," Iris replied, her voice calm despite the tension filling the bridge.

"No. I mean, we have it under control," he replied. We'll get turned around and get out of your hair. Apologies for any imposition." He quickly entered the new coordinates into the navigation display and powered up the propulsion drives.

Just as the engines hummed to life, they abruptly shut down, returning to a dormant state. Commander Zara's voice immediately filled the space.

"As you have already witnessed, this space sector can be extremely hazardous for civilian vessels," she said, elongating the 's' in 'vessels' with a slight hiss. "You will follow us to our station, where we can 'help' with repairs and ensure your safe passage through this area."

I accessed the propulsion systems from my wrist console, but we'd been locked out like everything else on the ship. I shrugged helplessly at Christopher, my fingers still tingling from the absence of the intuitive connection I'd had before losing my medallion.

"Iris?" I whispered, hoping she might have some solution.

"An external source has overridden all primary systems," Iris responded softly through my earpiece. "The signal appears similar to what we encountered at the IGMC station, but far more sophisticated. I am attempting to isolate our internal communications from their scanning."

Christopher gritted his teeth like he had a mouth full of Lorainian sand. "Agreed," he spat out to Commander Zara.

"Excellent," Commander Zara said victoriously. "We will tow you to our station from here."

As she spoke, large metallic devices latched onto our hull, causing a thunderous clang reverberating throughout the ship. The Charon shuddered violently beneath our feet, and I felt a strange shift in the artificial gravity as we began moving without our engines.

"Iris, what's happening to the ship?" I whispered, my hand gripping the console for stability.

"Electroadhesion clamps have attached to our hull," Iris responded through my earpiece. "They're generating a negative particle field to tow us. We are being pulled toward their station against our will, Burton. All propulsion systems have been overridden."

"What's the plan, boss?" Dwight was the first to speak, his earlier bravado noticeably diminished.

"We have no choice but to go with them." Christopher stared at the Sable Serpent ships surrounding us on the view screen. "We'll have to play nice, for now. The ship is in no shape to fight off a force of this size." He seemed to be thinking aloud, speaking to no one in particular. Then he turned to Lena. "When we get to the station, direct Harvey to stay on the ship. There's no doubt they saw four life signs when they scanned the ship. They won't be expecting him if things get ugly."

Lena nodded, the shunt behind her ear glowing faintly as she presumably communicated with Harvey. I noticed her fingers tapping against her thigh in a coded pattern.

"Will Harvey be able to interface with the ship's systems if we're captured?" I asked quietly.

Lena glanced at me, a hint of approval in her eyes at my question. "Harvey can access basic systems, but Iris must guide him. He's our backup plan if we can't return to the ship."

Christopher nodded curtly. "Iris, maintain minimal life support and power reserves. Divert all non-essential energy to the security protocols."

"Acknowledged, Captain," Iris responded. "I will maintain essential systems only and preserve energy reserves."

Pulling toward the Sable Serpent space station, I moved to the viewport to calm my racing pulse. Through the reinforced glass, I got my first full view of the station and caught my breath in my throat.

Massive. That was my first impression. The station was easily triple the size of any IGMC installation I'd seen on Neda. Its serpentine form twisted through space, sections of its hull gleaming with what looked like metallic scales reflecting starlight.

What struck me most was how unnatural it looked compared to human-built stations. There were no straight lines, no obvious docking bays or observation windows—just a sinuous form that seemed to curve and bend in defiance of the structural engineering principles I'd learned.

As we drew closer, I flinched back instinctively. The entire structure seemed to be... moving? Not just rotating as most stations did, but undulating, sections contracting and expanding in rhythmic sequence.

"What kind of station moves like that?" I muttered, not expecting an answer.

"One not built by human hands," Lena replied grimly.

As the massive jaws of the docking bay opened before us, I felt the ship shudder. The Charon seemed to resist being swallowed, creaking and groaning as the electroadhesion clamps pulled us inexorably forward.

The airlock sealed with a definitive thud. The sound echoed through the ship, making my stomach clench with finality. The last barrier between us and the Serpents was now sealed shut.

I tried not to think about what had happened the last time we'd entered an unknown station. The memories of the IGMC facility—bodies fused with metal, the horrifying chair, the experiments gone wrong—flashed through my mind.

"Burton," Iris's voice came softly through my earpiece, "I'm detecting unusual energy signatures throughout the station, similar to the IGMC facility readings but on a significantly larger scale.

Exercise extreme caution. I will maintain communication through your channel for as long as possible."

Christopher stood near the exit, his cybernetic arm twitching ever so slightly. "No unnecessary risks," he spoke, not as a direct command but as a reminder, maybe to himself. "Let's go."

Our boots echoed on the metal grating as we strode down the catwalk, Christopher and Dwight leading the way. Lena and I followed close behind, but I felt strangely unbalanced without Harvey's hulking presence.

"Lena," I whispered, leaning in closer. "I saw something."

"What?" She whispered back, her eyes straight ahead, only paying partial attention to my words.

"When I was prepping the shuttle," I continued in a low tone. "Christopher had a file---"

"Now is not the time to talk about Christopher's files," she cut me off sharply. "We have bigger problems."

"But we were mentioned in them!" My voice rose slightly, causing Christopher and Dwight to stop and turn towards us, their expressions curious yet stern.

"I need everyone to focus," Christopher said, his eyes locking in on mine.

We continued walking out of the Charon's shuttle bay and into the expansive docking bay of the Sable Serpent station. As we descended the ramp, we were met by a row of soldiers clad in black armor. Their helmets concealed their faces completely, leaving me wondering if humans were beneath those shells.

"Showtime," Dwight muttered under his breath, his tone laced with sarcasm and genuine unease.

Christopher stepped forward, his posture straightening as if he had transformed into a different persona. "Gentlemen," he began, his voice resonating with a calm, charming authority. "I am Captain Christopher Lucian of the Charon. We---"

"This way," intoned a distorted voice belonging to one of the soldiers, cutting off Christopher's sentence. "Follow me."

We followed the soldiers down a corridor that seemed to curve and twist, following the contours of the station's serpentine form. Unlike the clean, utilitarian designs of IGMC stations or the cobbled-together aesthetics of the Charon, this place felt... wrong. The lighting pulsed subtly, not in the steady rhythm of artificial systems, but in organic waves that made me think of heartbeats.

The walls themselves appeared oddly textured—not quite metal, not quite organic, but something unsettlingly in-between. Ridges and patterns ran along the surfaces that reminded me more of veins or muscle tissue than circuitry. In some places, I could have sworn I saw the walls contract slightly, as if breathing.

As we walked, the air grew increasingly humid, leaving a faint residue on my skin that reminded me of the slime that collected on Neda's rocks during monsoon season.

"Iris," I whispered, "do you still read me?"

"Affirmative, Burton," came the faint reply. "Signal degrading but functional. The materials in this station are interfering with our connection."

The soldiers led us into a vast chamber. In the center stood a raised platform, and upon it sat Commander Zara. Under the chamber's stronger lighting, I could see her clearly for the first time.

Her face might once have been human, but now it was a disturbing blend of flesh and something else, not mechanical implants as I first thought, but more like growths. Ridged protrusions ran from her temples down her jaw and neck, disappearing beneath her uniform collar. They pulsed with light in the same rhythm as the station's walls, like bioluminescent tissue.

But her eyes, or what should have been eyes, made my skin crawl. In their place were two black, empty sockets, deep cavities that seemed to have been carved out or dissolved away. Yet somehow, I knew she could see us. Perhaps better than we could see ourselves.

She rose from her seat and descended a spiral staircase toward us. Every few seconds, her head would jerk to one side, not the impossible angles I'd imagined in my fear, but a persistent, rhythmic tic that gave her an unsettling, predatory appearance.

On her shoulder, she wore an emblem of a golden serpent wrapped around a black crescent. The symbol itself was standard enough, but the light playing across it made the serpent appear to shift position slightly.

"Welcome to the Serpent's Lair," Commander Zara said, echoing through the chamber. A thin line of what looked like luminescent fluid traced her jawline, pulsing as she spoke. Her head jerked to the side again; that tick, like a nervous habit, had become permanent.

"Thank you for allowing us to dock," Christopher replied with remarkable composure.

Commander Zara circled our group slowly, studying each of us in turn. When she looked at me, I felt a pressure behind my eyes, as if something was trying to push its way into my mind. The sensation passed quickly, but left me feeling violated.

She spent the longest time studying Christopher, her head occasionally jerking to the side with that now-familiar tic, as if seeing something the rest of us couldn't.

"The Order of the Sable Serpent does not often welcome outsiders, especially those who come unannounced," she said, her voice carrying a strange vibration that resonated in my chest. Then, without warning, she let out a high-pitched giggle that stopped as abruptly as it had begun.

Christopher remained still as she leaned close to him, those empty eye sockets somehow fixed on his face.

"You're different," she whispered, her voice suddenly childlike. "You have a friend with you." She reached out toward Christopher's shoulder, stopping short of touching it. "A friend from beyond."

I tensed, my eyes darting between them. Could she somehow sense the smoke-like distortion I'd been seeing around Christopher? I'd never mentioned it to anyone but Iris, assuming I was hallucinating.

Christopher held her gaze steadily. "Understood, Commander. Our arrival was born of necessity, not disregard for your sovereignty. We mean no harm."

Commander Zara cackled maniacally, a sound coming from deep within her chest. Her head jerked rapidly to the side several times, and that tick intensified with her emotions. "Harm?" she spat, suddenly serious again. "Impossible! We are the Order of the Sable Serpent, blessed by our divine protector, who shall annihilate any who dares to oppose us." She threw her arms wide, gesturing to the station around us.

She whirled back to Christopher, moving with predatory focus. "Your friend," she hissed, gesturing toward his shoulder where I often saw the smoke. It reminds me of our benefactor, who gave us this station and promised us dominion over this sector." Her voice dropped to a whisper. "The one who comes in dreams and speaks of other worlds."

I glanced at Lena and Dwight, but they seemed confused by her words. Of course, they were. They couldn't see what I saw around Christopher or what Commander Zara somehow seemed to perceive.

I could feel the tension radiating from the soldiers around us, their weapons held ready. "Commander," I said, stepping forward, "we can assure you that we were simply looking for parts. You have seen our ship firsthand, you've seen its condition. Any help or assistance you could offer would be greatly appreciated and considered a blessing."

Commander Zara froze mid-movement. Her head rotated toward me before jerking sharply to the side, which ticked again, but stronger now, accompanied by a pulse of light from the ridged growths along her jaw.

"Liar!" She bellowed, rushing within an inch of my face, her breath hot against my skin. The organic growths along her jaw flared with crimson light. "We intercepted a large data burst from your ship. It's how we found you. We decrypted enough to know what you did to the IGMC station; the people you've murdered!"

Her accusation hit me like a physical blow. The files I'd accessed in the shuttle, Christopher's archive about the Lachesis, the experiments, the dimensional technology, they must have detected the download.

Her head jerked to the side again, that tic now accompanied by a brief, unsettling smile. "And you," she whispered, her voice suddenly gentle as she turned back to Christopher, "you and your friend from beyond... You are searching for something. Something old. Something hidden." Her voice rose to a shriek. "Something FORBIDDEN!"

My heart pounded wildly, sweat beading on my forehead despite my efforts to appear calm. Did she know about the CHeKeR device mentioned in the files? About Terrance Alexander and Meredith Rivera? About whatever connection my medallion had to all of this?

"Burton," Iris's voice came through my earpiece, barely audible now. "I've detected unusual activity in the ship. They're systematically searching for something."

Christopher stepped forward, his voice calm and measured, creating a shield between me and Commander Zara's fury. "Commander Zara, I believe there's been a misunderstanding." The smoke around him seemed to thin, spreading out as if trying to hide from her perception. "I am not sure about this data burst, but we had no hand in destroying the IGMC station."

Commander Zara's head jerked to the side several times rapidly, her tic intensifying as her agitation grew. She leaned close to Christopher, those black voids studying him intently. "Lies," she whispered, her voice like stone grinding against stone. "I can see it. Your friend. It knows what you've done. It knows who you are. It is what you are." She giggled again, that childlike sound chilling in its incongruity. "Just like our benefactor. Just like the one who speaks to us through the station. The one who promised us glory."

I stared at her empty eye sockets with dawning realization. Had she encountered others like Christopher before?

Christopher maintained his composure, though I noticed the smoke around him had vanished.

"I simply don't believe you." Commander Zara's voice turned cold, each word precise and final. The organic ridges along her jaw pulsed with blue light. "You and your kind," she hissed, her finger tracing the air near Christopher's shoulder, "are not welcome here." Suddenly, she clutched at her face, fingers digging into the skin beside her empty eye sockets. "They warned us about you. THE VOICES WARNED US!"

A tense silence fell over the chamber. Christopher maintained unwavering eye contact with her, inclining his head slightly in acknowledgment of her words.

"Take our guests down to the gullet," Commander Zara ordered one of her soldiers, her voice abruptly calm and controlled, though the persistent tic remained, her head jerking to the side every few seconds. "Kill anyone who speaks. Bodies, not words, are all we need."

As the soldiers surrounded us, forcing us toward a different corridor, Iris's voice came through my earpiece one final time: "Burton, I'm still with you. Stay alive. I'll find a way."

~ 14 ~

AWAKENING THE BEAST

We were imprisoned in the depths of the space station, a place the guards had called "the Gullet." The noises echoed differently here, wet, gurgling sounds that reminded me of a digestive system rather than machinery. The air was thick with humidity and carried a sickly-sweet smell of decay. Lena paced back and forth at the back of the room, nervously chewing on her thumbnail. She had become more withdrawn since we heard the door seal shut with an organic squelch rather than a mechanical click. Dwight headed for one of the three bunks in the room and leaned against the wall. Christopher lingered by the door; his gaze fixed on me.

He strode menacingly from his post by the door. "Burton," he growled, his cybernetic fingers twitching with impatience. "Explain the data burst." I could feel his cold grip on my shoulder, a warning that my answer better satisfy him, or there would be consequences.

"When I was preparing the shuttle," I blurted out swiftly. "The download from the Charon's systems to the shuttle was too big. It crashed the system. But a file transfer of that size could easily be seen on long-range scanners."

"How did she know about the IGMC station?" Christopher's fist crashed against the table, leaving a permanent dent in the alloy surface. The room trembled and the walls rippled like a wave, as if the entire station could feel his fury radiating outwards.

"I don't know," I fell out of my chair, inching backward on the floor. "She claimed she had successfully decrypted the files. It seems that they had intercepted our transmission." A sudden thought struck me. "The FRB, the Fast Radio Burst, we detected near the IGMC station. What if it wasn't random? What if someone sent it, knowing exactly when we'd be there to receive it?"

Christopher's eyes narrowed. "Impossible. The timing would have to be"

"Perfect," I finished. "Or calculated by someone who understands time differently than we do."

Lena had stopped pacing and was now looking at me knowingly on the floor.

"Unfortunately, I could never access any of the data files in the shuttle, so I cannot confirm what she may have discovered."

Dwight pushed himself up from where he was sitting on the bunk and stepped between Christopher, who was standing over me on the floor. "Hey now, boss, you've seen this place. Decrypting our files probably took less time than fixing a flat on one of those rattletrap jet bikes. Maybe it's not Burton's fault, huh? Let's think about this."

Christopher's glare didn't shift as he considered Dwight's words, but the tension in his jaw relaxed slightly. He turned back to me, his expression somewhat less murderous. "Lena," he shouted, his eyes never leaving me. "It's time we call Harvey."

"Iris?" I whispered, hoping the ship's AI could still hear me. No response came. The organic walls of the Gullet must be blocking the signal.

Lena closed her eyes, illuminating her shunt. She bared down hard, trying to communicate. A small stream of blood appeared, trickling from her nose. "Lena!" I yelled, pointing from my spot on the floor.

Dwight quickly moved to steady her as she stumbled. "I'm okay," she insisted, pulling away from his help. "Harvey's too far away. I can't reach him from here, not with this alloy in the way."

Christopher's cybernetic hand twitched, the sight unnerving in the dim light of our cramped space. "Fine," he growled, "we handle this without Harvey for now."

We sat in silence. Our cramped cell's humid, oppressive heat seemed to pulse, almost as if the station itself was breathing. I wiped the sweat from my brow, my mind racing. This place felt off, nearly too alive and reactive. The walls around us weren't solid metal but something like cartilage, flexible and slightly translucent, with what looked like veins pulsing beneath the surface. A sick realization dawned on me.

"Does anyone else feel that?" I spoke in a hushed tone, barely audible. I placed my hand against the wall, sensing the faint vibrations. "The station... It's almost like it's..."

"Alive," Dwight finished, nodding slowly. "I've been noticing it too. The temperature shifts, the way the corridors seemed to move..."

I stood up from my spot on the floor, pacing the small space. "Commander Zara mentioned a 'divine protector'. What if the station itself is that protector? Not just sentient alloy, a living sentient being?"

"When she said they were taking us to the Gullet," Dwight added grimly, "I don't think it was a nickname."

Lena's eyes widened. "A living machine? If it's alive..."

"It can be hurt," Christopher concluded, a spark of understanding in his eyes.

I nodded, excitement building. "Exactly. Do you remember what happened when you struck the table?" I said, looking at Christopher. "The walls rippled, and the station shook. It's like..."

"It felt pain." Christopher finished my sentence, a darkness overtaking his eyes. "If it could feel pain, we may be able to use that to our advantage."

Dwight chuckled darkly. "So, what? We throw a tantrum and hope the station lets us go?"

"Yes...I mean, sort of. If the station protects the Order of the Sable Serpent, they will likely be kept as its protectors." I glanced around the room, trying to gauge reactions. "If we can inflict significant damage to the station, perhaps we can create a vulnerability that will force the guards to come in and stop us. That could be our chance to escape."

"If this station functions like a living organism, it might also have a self-defense mechanism," Lena pointed out plainly.

Christopher schemed as he touched where he had struck the table. "That's a fair point. We need to be cautious but decisive. If we provoke the station too much, it could retaliate in ways we can't predict."

Lena rubbed the back of her neck, seeming uneasy. "Right, but how do we even know where to hit it? This isn't exactly like punching someone in the gut. We're talking about a massive structure with systems we barely understand."

"Maybe you can use that powerful hand of yours to do something other than beat up tables, Boss," Dwight suggested, his eyes glinting with mischief and genuine curiosity. "There's gotta be some central nervous system in this giant tin can."

Christopher shot him a glare that would have frozen the oxygen in my lungs, Dwight, however, only smiled.

"He's right," I immediately latched onto the idea. "The walls rippled when you struck the table. Try striking it again. This time harder."

Christopher's eyes narrowed as he assessed his next move. He clenched his cybernetic hand into a mighty fist, feeling the mechanisms within hum with energy. He raised his arm high, the tension building up until it was almost tangible. Then, with a burst of fiery intensity, he brought down his arm with all his might and struck the same spot he had hit before. The impact was like a meteor crashing into a comet, shattering everything in its path. A deafening alarm echoed through the station, causing the walls to ripple and tremble as if they might crumble. We struggled to remain standing as Christopher's powerful strike shook the entire structure.

Christopher's eyes glinted with sadistic pleasure as he savored the thought of inflicting even more pain. He lunged towards the table with a menacing grin, ripping it from the floor as if it were paper. The structure of the station seemed to be fighting back, but Christopher was relentless. Each leg of the table was like a stubborn nail being pried away from a finger, causing the entire station to convulse and shake violently. We were all thrown to the ground, except for Christopher, who stood triumphantly, his chest heaving with adrenaline as he held the severed table in his hand like a trophy of his destructive power.

The membrane-like door to the room slid open with a wet sound, and guards rushed in. Without hesitation, Christopher hurled the table towards them, knocking out the first two and causing the third to trip over their bodies. Dwight sprang up from his position on the ground and grabbed the first two guards by their necks, slamming them against the wall until they went limp before dropping them to the floor. Meanwhile, Lena leapt onto the back of the stumbling guard and delivered a powerful elbow strike to the base of his neck, severing his spine and sending his helmet flying across the room before crashing into the far wall.

"Grab their weapons. Search the bodies." Christopher commanded coldly.

Dwight grabbed the plasma rifles from the two bodies at his feet, tossing one to me and checking the charge on the other.

Lena rolled the other guard onto his back and cried shrilly. "By the gods, what has happened here?" She quickly jumped away from the body in shock. "What could have caused this?" She cautiously approached the lifeless form once more.

The guard had a face that could only be described as a nightmare come to life. Where his eyes should have been, there was only smooth, featureless skin stretching from nose to ear as the forehead had extended down. The ears were small, gnarled lumps that looked more like tumors than human ears. The guard had no hair, not even a single eyelash or eyebrow. His cheekbones were sunken and concave, making him look gaunt. His thin lips were nearly transparent, showing the faint outline of his gum line through his closed mouth. Where his nose should have been, three gaping slits, that looked like they should open and close with every breath. A putrid odor came from the slits, like composted Serpentunk. The mere sight of this face caused shivers to crawl down one's spine and linger in the mind long after looking away.

Dwight quickly removed the helmets from the other two guards. "Same over here, Boss," he grunted, lifting one up by the back of his head. The guard's features were similarly distorted.

Christopher knelt near the body at Lena's feet, only for a moment, before picking up the plasma rifle and tossing it to her. "Let's go," he stated simply, not acknowledging the gruesome discovery with anything more than a glance.

With his plasma rifle held high, Dwight led us out of the room and around the corner into a narrow passageway. The corridor was unlike any ship or station I'd seen before, less a hallway than an esophagus. The walls were rippling even more intensely now, causing a disorienting sensation as if we were still moving even though we had stopped. Despite the violent shaking of the station, it felt different this time. When Christopher had pried the table from the floor earlier, it seemed like the station was in pain. Now, it felt like the station was angrily vibrating, purposely trying to throw us off balance as we escaped.

"Which way, Boss?" Dwight yelled over the hiss of the alarms.

Christopher nodded to Dwight to move left down a passageway and up a ladder well.

The ladder well was a tight squeeze, Dwight's broad shoulders barely fitting as he scrambled upward. We followed closely behind, our boots clanging on the metal rungs with each step. The station's walls felt slimy and alive, constricting around us as we ascended. As we made our way up the ladder, a thick, acidic fluid oozed from the walls, burning my skin upon contact. The station was trying to consume us, its walls shifting and rippling downward in an eerie display.

"Move your ass, Dwight," Lena yelled from behind me, Christopher bringing up the rear.

Dwight reached the top of the ladder. He forced out and swung onto a small platform, immediately taking a defensive stance on his knees. I followed behind him. When I reached the top, I returned to the ladder well to help Lena. She pushed my hand away and pulled herself out of the tube, instinctively taking a position opposite Dwight's, plasma rifle at the ready. Christopher finally emerged from the ladder well, his feet struggling to break free from the sticky organ that had formed around them. The acidic sludge clung to his boots, releasing wispy fumes as it attempted to dissolve the materials.

"Where to now, Boss?" Dwight asked, keeping his eyes trained into the darkness of the station.

Christopher looked up; a faint green light flickered in the darkness. "That way. The light." He directed Dwight, who promptly stood and carefully moved in that direction.

Lena and I stepped behind him, rifles raised, as we moved cautiously toward the flickering beacon. The corridor stretched like a beast's belly, dark and foreboding, with occasional flashes of light from exposed wiring and control panels flickering. The station rumbled and shook, its hissing alarms drowned out by the pounding of our hearts in our ears. Every step felt like walking through a beast's belly, with danger lurking around every corner.

"Burton," a familiar voice whispered in my ear, faint and broken by static. "Can you... hear me?"

"Iris?" I whispered back, relief washing over me. "You're back."

"Signal... weak," she replied. "Station searching... your medallion... found in shuttle."

My blood ran cold. "They found my medallion. Where?"

"Commander has it... studying it... recognized its... purpose."

Before I could ask more, the connection faded to static.

The green light led us back to the hall where we had encountered Commander Zara. Our steps were met with a battalion of armed soldiers, their weapons ready to fire. But before they could react, Dwight let out a barrage of shots that ripped through the first soldier's chest and took off his comrade's shoulder. In a swift movement, Lena dove behind cover and began firing indiscriminately at the enemy troops. The air was filled with screams and explosions as Lena and Dwight relentlessly mowed down the Sable Serpent soldiers. Blood splattered, and bodies fell, leaving only a fraction of the original number before they could even find cover. The hall became a scene of carnage.

I stood slightly behind where Dwight stood, unleashing my barrage of plasma fire at the scattered soldiers. A deafening explosion rocked the room as an alloy canister hurtled towards us, launched from the safety of Commander Zara's podium. I watched it land just a few steps away from us. Multiple nozzles emerged from the spinning canister, unleashing a thick fog that began to engulf the space.

"My eyes!" I screamed, dropping the plasma rifle and bringing my hands to my face. My body writhed as Christopher yanked me behind cover and activated my environment suit. But it was too late, the gas had already seeped into my eyes. A burning sensation spread across my corneas like liquid fire, and darkness swallowed my vision. Disoriented, I struggled to get up.

"Lena," Christopher yelled over the onslaught. "Get Harvey!"

"Burton," Iris's voice crackled through my earpiece, stronger now. "Commander Zara has your medallion. She knows what it is."

"What do you mean?" I gasped, still reeling from the pain in my eyes.

"She called it... a dimensional key..."

Through the chaos, I heard Commander Zara's voice ring out. "The Avalonian and his pets won't escape! Not with this treasure they've brought us!"

"Avalonian?" I whispered, the term unfamiliar yet resonant with what I'd seen in the files about Christopher.

"A species... studied by Terrance Alexander... interdimensional beings..." Iris's voice faded again into static.

I lay on my back, the sound of plasma fire around me. I feel someone ripping the plasma rifle from my hands. More bursts of plasma rifles sounded as Christopher must have joined the fight. A tyrannical voice erupted over the ship's communication system, seething with fury and spewing venomous insults.

"You treacherous vermin, how dare you betray the Sable Serpent!" Commander Zara's voice boomed through the comm system. Her words echoed ominously around us, each one dripping with disdain. "I'll ensure you regret ever setting foot here! Our divine protector will feed on your bodies, to nurture us with its divine milk." She paused, then added with venom, "And you, Avalonian filth, your kind has always been the enemy of the true divine!"

I heard Dwight move from behind the same cover as Christopher and me, closer to where Lena had taken cover. The heavy thud of his boots became distant as his plasma rifle blast trailed away.

"She's bleeding from her ears and nose!" Dwight shouted over the deafening explosions. "Her eyes are rolled back, completely white. And the blue light surrounding her shunt is still stuck in the on position."

"Put her over your shoulder. We need to move," Christopher yelled from somewhere over me. "Burton, get up."

"Wait!" I called out, panic rising in my throat. "My medallion, Commander Zara has it. We can't leave without it!"

There was a momentary silence before Christopher's voice returned, cold and calculating. "Where?"

"I don't know exactly," I admitted. "Iris said the Commander has it, was studying it."

"The podium," Christopher decided. "That's where we're headed."

I felt a tug on the front of my suit, a hand lifting me unnaturally to my feet.

"Wrap your arm around my shoulder," Christopher instructed, sliding under my arm and placing his other hand on my waist. "On the count of three, we move," he yelled to Dwight, who I assumed was somewhere holding Lena's limp form. "We'll make our way over to you, then push towards the podium."

"You got it, Boss," Dwight grunted while keeping up a steady stream of plasma fire directed at the Sable Serpent soldiers.

Christopher's voice counted down from "1, 2, 3," and then he lifted me as we advanced. I could hear plasma rifles firing as we moved. We took a moment to pause, leaning against something, before Christopher shouted, "Go!" The intensity of the blasts increased, likely from both his and Dwight's weapons.

I relied on Christopher to guide me through the darkness, his hand gripping my hip as we moved forward. My balance was shaky, and I stumbled over objects in our path. In the distance, an explosion echoed like thunder. The unmistakable sounds of a bolt gun and a laser rock cutter grew louder as they approached us.

"Iris," I whispered urgently. "Can you see through the ship's cameras? Where's my medallion?"

"Signal stronger now," Iris replied. "I can see... Commander Zara... at raised platform... medallion in some scanner."

"It's about time, Harvey," Dwight screamed in relief.

I could smell the seared flesh, which seemed to draw a straight line over the Sable Serpent soldiers, to where we stopped for cover. I heard the whirring servos as Harvey neared our location, and the clang of plasma shots unable to pierce Harvey's hard outer shell. I heard him stop just feet away from us, and the sounds he made upon arriving at us sounded like a breath of relief.

"Here you go, big guy," Dwight said, likely handing Lena over to her protector, before the sound of servos began to gain distance.

"Harvey, wait!" I called out. "We need to get to the podium; Commander Zara has my medallion!"

The servos paused, then changed direction. A metallic hand grasped my shoulder, orienting me toward what I assumed was our new destination.

"Follow him!" Christopher called out.

We moved quickly through what felt like a throbbing, living tunnel. Without my sight, my other senses heightened dramatically. The acrid smell of burning flesh and plasma discharge filled my nostrils. The floor beneath my feet pulsated rhythmically, almost as if we were traversing the arteries of some enormous creature. Each step produced a sickening squelch, and I could feel warm, viscous liquid seeping through the soles of my boots.

"Iris," I whispered, "guide me. What do you see?"

"The chamber has transformed," Iris replied, her voice still tinged with static but clearer now. "The walls have developed defensive protrusions, organic spikes approximately 15 centimeters in length. They seem to track movement. Harvey is using his body as a shield for Lena. Commander Zara is at the central podium with five guards."

The sounds of battle intensified, plasma discharges, screams of pain, and the station's own agonized wails blending into a horrific symphony. Christopher's grip on my arm tightened as he dragged me forward.

"Duck!" Dwight's voice bellowed from somewhere ahead.

Christopher yanked me down. I felt the heat of plasma fire sizzle through the air where my head had been moments before. The smell of scorched hair filled my nostrils.

"Ten meters to the podium," Iris informed me. "Commander Zara has the medallion in some scanning device. The device appears to be analyzing its structure."

"I see it," Christopher growled, his voice unnervingly close to my ear. "Harvey, full advance! Dwight, cover us!"

The floor shook beneath us as Harvey charged forward. Agonized screams followed the sound of his metal frame colliding with softer bodies. Plasma fire intensified, the distinctive hum of Dwight's weapon creating a counterpoint to the higher-pitched whine of the Serpent guards' rifles.

"Burton!" Commander Zara's voice cut through the chaos, directly addressing me, though I couldn't see her. "This medallion. This dimensional key! It will open doorways that should remain closed!"

Her words sent a chill down my spine. What did she mean by "dimensional key"?

"The Avalonian deception ends here!" she continued, her voice shifting as if she were moving around the podium. "Your kind has plagued us long enough, parasite!"

"Avalonian?" I repeated, confused.

"She's not talking to you," Christopher hissed, his grip tightening painfully on my arm. "Move!"

We surged forward, Christopher practically carrying me as my feet struggled to keep pace. The sounds of Harvey's destruction grew louder—the crunch of metal against bone, screams abruptly silenced, the fizz of severed electrical connections.

"Commander Zara is retreating with the medallion," Iris reported in my ear. "She's heading toward a secondary chamber. The scanning device remains on the podium."

"After her!" Christopher roared, releasing my arm so suddenly that I nearly fell.

"Burton, stay with me." Dwight's large hand clasped my shoulder, steadying me. "Boss and Harvey are going after your trinket."

The sounds shifted, Christopher's footsteps and Harvey's mechanical stride receded, pursuing Commander Zara while Dwight protected himself in front of me.

"Duck," he commanded, pushing my head down as he fired over me. I heard the wet thud of a body hitting the floor nearby.

"Do not let them escape! We must feed our divine protector, our sacred mother!" Fueled by rage, Commander Zara screamed through what sounded like the station's communication system. "Push forward, flank them on both sides. The Avalonian must not escape with the dimensional key!"

The sound of weapons fire increased, a desperate push from all directions.

"Burton," Iris spoke urgently in my ear. "Harvey has cornered Commander Zara in a side chamber. Christopher is with him."

I heard a high-pitched scream of rage and terror, followed by the distinctive sound of Christopher's cybernetic arm powering up, a whine that escalated to a mechanical shriek. A sickening crunch echoed through the chamber, then silence.

"Harvey has the medallion," Iris reported. "Commander Zara dropped it while Christopher... incapacitated her."

"Incapacitated?" I questioned but received no answer.

Heavy footsteps approached; Harvey followed Christopher's distinctive gait.

"We have it," Christopher announced coldly. "Now move. The station is going into some defensive lockdown."

Indeed, I could feel the changes through my feet—the floor hardening, pathways sealing shut around us. The air became thick with a cloying, sweet smell that reminded me of rotting fruit.

"The ship!" Dwight shouted. "We need to get back now!"

Christopher grabbed my arm again, pulling me roughly along as we changed direction. The sounds of pursuit grew louder, and there were more guards. The station seemingly hunted us with shifting corridors and grasping protrusions that brushed against my suit.

"This way!" Dwight shouted from somewhere ahead. "Harvey's found a clear path!"

We ran mindlessly, or at least I did, guided by Christopher's iron grip, through corridors that seemed to contract around us. Each step brought the distinctive scent of the Charon closer: engine oil, recycled air, the sharp tang of metal that wasn't quite alive.

I could hear Harvey's servos working double-time, likely carrying Lena's still unconscious form while simultaneously creating a path through the guards.

"Get aboard now!" Dwight's voice cracked with urgency as he laid down suppressive fire on the mass of soldiers streaming up from behind us.

Christopher pushed me onto the ship, gripping my suit's belt to carry me inside. He dropped me unceremoniously on the shuttle's ramp and told me to stay put. I heard his hurried footsteps as he ran off, presumably towards the bridge.

I sprawled out on the ramp, taking a moment to rest. Then I heard the Charon's docking ramp closing and felt the vibrations of Dwight's heavy boots as he hurried past me. "Better buckle up, kid. This is going to be rough," Dwight warned as his footsteps disappeared into the ship.

Shuffling onto all fours, I scrabbled up the metallic shuttle ramp and crawled inside. My hands searched for a seat to secure myself in, but instead, they brushed against something cold and hard - a boot. Before I could react, a mechanical hand clamped down on my wrist with a vice-like grip and flung me away, sending me crashing into the wall.

I let out a pained breath and managed to say "Harvey" before being lifted back up and placed in a chair with a thud. "Thanks," I gasped, still struggling for air. "The medallion, did we get it back from Zara?"

I heard Harvey's servos whirring, but no response came. The mechanical giant stood motionless beside me.

"Harvey?" I asked again, reaching out unquestioningly. "My medallion...who has it?"

"Burton," Iris's voice came through my earpiece, clear and precise now that we were back on the Charon. "Christopher has your medallion. He took it from Commander Zara during the confrontation."

"Christopher, has it?" My heart sank. "But it's mine. It belonged to my father."

"I detect the medallion's signature on the bridge," Iris continued. Christopher is wearing it around his neck. He appears... satisfied with this acquisition."

The realization hit me like a blow to the chest. The medallion had been Christopher's target, perhaps even more than me. I was merely the means to locate it, to bring it to him. He may have finally claimed the prize he'd coveted since he first came to Neda.

"But why?" I asked, my voice hollow. "What's so special about it?"

"Based on Commander Zara's statements," Iris replied, "the medallion appears to be what she called a 'dimensional key.'"

"But what does that mean?" I demanded frustration and despair, threatening to overwhelm me. "What is a dimensional key? And how did Commander Zara know about it?"

Iris hesitated before responding. "I have insufficient data to provide a complete answer. However, dimensional theory was a significant area of research before Earth's collapse. Terrance Alexander was noted in several historical records as a pioneer in the field."

The roar of the Charon's guns filled the air, punctuated by explosions. As the ship broke free, the chaos faded into a hum. Only the proximity alarm persisted, reminding us of the danger. Christopher's calm voice announced over the intercom, "We're clear," leaving a deafening silence.

"Iris," I whispered, leaning back in the chair, "is there a connection between what Commander Zara called Christopher...an 'Avalonian'...and the smoke I sometimes see around him?"

Another pause, longer this time. "There are... correlations in Christopher's files you uncovered. The term 'Avalonian' appears in Dr. Alexander's research into interdimensional entities. However, most of those files are encrypted or fragmented."

I sat in darkness, robbed of my sight and medallion, my mind racing with new questions. What did Commander Zara mean by calling Christopher an "Avalonian"? Why had she recognized my medallion as a "dimensional key"? And most troubling of all, how was any of this connected to Terrance Alexander, the man mentioned in the files I'd found?

Whatever the answers, I was certain Christopher knew more about its purpose than he had ever let on.

Now he had what he wanted, not just me, but the medallion. Without it, I felt not only blind but truly lost.

~ 15 ~

ECHOES OF SMOKE

The darkness was absolute. Despite my eyes being wide open, I saw nothing, just an endless void that mocked my attempts to make sense of my surroundings. My other senses had heightened to compensate, but that was little comfort. The skin on my face burned where the neurotoxic gas had touched it, and my hands trembled as I clenched and unclenched my fists, trying to ground myself in something tangible.

"My medallion," I whispered to myself, my hand instinctively reaching for my chest only to find emptiness. The loss felt like a physical wound, more profound than my blindness, deeper even than the betrayal. That small piece of metal had been my only connection with my father, Neda, and who I was. And now Christopher had it.

A soft moan from nearby interrupted my thoughts.

"What...where..." Lena's voice was weak and distant as she began to regain consciousness. "Where are we?"

"We're in the shuttle, in the Charon's docking bay," I responded, trying to mask my panic with a soothing tone. My hands gripped the arms of my seat to stop their shaking. "I think we're en route to Terax-3."

"Terax-3...Why?" Her voice was dry, cracked, like she hadn't had water in days.

"We need repairs," I explained, struggling to keep my voice steady. "Our unexpected trip to the Sable Serpent station caused more damage, and I'm..." I gestured helplessly at my eyes, "...I'm in no shape to handle any repairs right now."

I heard her moving, the soft thuds of her boots as she shifted in her seat, the rustle of fabric as she sat up. Harvey's servos whirred nearby, his mechanical presence strangely comforting in my darkness.

"Holy shit," Lena gasped, her voice suddenly alert. "Your eyes, Burton. What the hell happened to you?"

I flinched at her reaction, imagining how I must look. "Some sort of neurotoxic venom mist," I said, my voice catching. "Dwight came back some time ago and gave me something...an antidote or antivenom, I don't know. He said it should prevent permanent damage, but for now..." I trailed off, swallowing hard against the panic that threatened to overwhelm me. "For now, I can't see anything."

"Dwight?" she questioned, her voice closer now. She must have moved toward me.

"He carried you out of there," I said. "You don't remember?"

"Carried me?" The confusion in her voice was palpable. "Why would Dwight have to carry me?"

I turned my face toward her voice, wishing I could see her expression. "We thought we'd lost you," I said, unable to keep the emotion from my voice. "You had to reach Harvey while we were under heavy fire. Then suddenly, you collapsed. Blood was streaming from your nose and ears. Your eyes rolled back, and your shunt was glowing blue, steady, not pulsing like usual. Dwight didn't hesitate. He just hoisted you over his shoulder and carried you until Harvey showed up."

The silence that followed was heavy. I could hear Lena's breathing. It was quicker than normal...unsteady.

"I..." she finally spoke, her voice uncharacteristically vulnerable. "I pushed too hard. The connection with Harvey, through that much interference..." She trailed off, and I heard her hand slide across her shunt. "Shit. I owe Dwight more than thanks."

"Harvey hasn't let anyone near you since he brought you back," I said, gesturing vaguely toward where I thought the robot stood. "He's been standing guard. We weren't sure you'd wake up at all."

"I'm fine," she said, but the tremor in her voice betrayed her. "Or I will be. Harvey can run diagnostics through our connection. If intervention was needed..." She paused. "Let's just say no one would have been able to stop him."

A soft metallic sound, Harvey shifting his position, perhaps in response to Lena's words.

"Christopher has my medallion," I blurted out, the words tumbling from me like a confession. "He took it from Commander Zara during the fight. Iris told me he's wearing it around his neck right now." I leaned forward, my voice dropping to a whisper even though we were alone. "We need to get it back, Lena. It's more than just a keepsake. I think it's connected to whatever Christopher's been searching for, which is 'Lachesis'. The way my abilities changed when I lost it... the way the ship's systems became distant..."

"We will," Lena said, with surprising conviction. "But first, we need to understand what we're dealing with." Her hand found my shoulder, squeezing once. "You mentioned files before, when we arrived at the Serpents station. Data that the Serpents intercepted."

I nodded, grateful for her focus. "Remember how I mentioned the data burst and files that were intercepted? Go to the pilot's console. Search for a file labeled 'Lachesis.' Let me know when you've found it."

I heard her struggle to stand, a soft grunt of pain escaping her lips. Harvey's servos whirred as he helped her to the forward cabin. The sound of her sliding into the pilot's chair echoed in the small space, followed by the click of controls being activated.

After a moment of silence, I heard Iris's voice emanate from the shuttle's console. "May I assist with locating the requested files, Lena? I can establish a direct neural interface to expedite..."

"Get out," Lena hissed, her voice low and dangerous. "No interfaces. No neural connections. Nothing in my head."

"I merely suggested an efficient method to...."

"Nothing gets inside my head again," Lena cut her off, each word sharp as broken glass. "Not you, not anything. I'll find it myself."

"As you wish," Iris replied, her tone neutral. "Burton, would you prefer..."

"Just let her work, Iris," I interjected, sensing the tension. I'd never fully understood Lena's visceral reaction to anything attempting to interface with her mind, but after what happened when she tried to reach Harvey at the Serpent station, her fear seemed even more pronounced.

The silence that followed was heavy with unspoken history. I heard Lena's fingers moving across the console, her breathing still uneven.

"Located," she called back after several minutes, her voice marginally steadier. "Now what?"

"Look through it," I suggested, trying to reconstruct what I'd seen before my vision was taken.

"Where do you want me to start?" she shot back tersely. "There are drawings, notes about a lost planet, there's..."

"Why don't you just start with your file?" I cut her off, sensing her growing frustration.

"Fine," she huffed. A moment of silence followed as she presumably read through her file. "There are pictures of Harvey and me on Zeta. Notes that say 'Lena - Technopath. Experienced in smuggling and information trading. Female. Proficient with technology and hacking. Robot companion Harvey. It shows a pragmatic approach to survival and advancement. May prioritize self-interest over crew safety." Her voice hardened at the last part. "There are some video files here, too."

"Open one up," I directed, shifting anxiously in my seat. Every moment we spent here increased the risk of Christopher checking on us.

"Opening file V000237," Lena said, her voice suddenly tight. She paused for a long moment. "It's... a girl. Young. Maybe 12 years old."

I could hear her breathing change, quickening slightly.

"She's in some kind of room," Lena continued, her tone deliberately detached, clinical. "Dancing."

"Describe the room," I requested, desperate to piece together a mental image.

Her fingers tapped nervously against the console. "Institutional. Sterile," she said, each word measured. "Cement floors. Metal walls. Observation mirrors." The tapping stopped. "I've seen rooms like this before."

Something in her voice made me pause. "Are you okay?"

"I'm fine," she snapped, too quickly. "Just... watching."

I heard Iris's voice, quieter now. "I can establish a neural link to help you process what you're seeing..."

"No!" The word exploded from Lena. "No links. No connections. Nothing inside..." She stopped abruptly. I heard her take a deep, shaking breath. "Nothing gets inside my mind."

The vehemence in her voice startled me. This wasn't just her usual wariness; this was raw terror.

"Details, Lena," I urged after a moment, my hands gripping the armrests tighter. "Christopher could return any moment."

"There's a two-way mirror on the far wall," she continued after a moment, her voice hollow. "I can tell by the reflection pattern. The light hits it differently than a regular mirror."

I frowned at her oddly specific knowledge but pressed on. "What's happening to the girl?"

"She's..." Lena's voice faltered slightly. "She's laughing. Dancing. Like she doesn't know she's being watched. She looks... happy."

I heard her swallow hard.

"And then..." Her voice dropped to nearly a whisper. "Smoke starts coming through the vents. Curling around her. Like it's alive."

The silence that followed stretched uncomfortably. "Lena?" I called out, my heartbeat quickening. "What's wrong? Are you still there?"

"I'm here," she replied, but her voice sounded different—younger somehow, vulnerable in a way I'd never heard from her before. She cleared her throat roughly. "Just... processing what I'm seeing."

"What happened next?" I asked gently.

"The smoke..." She took a shaky breath. "It surrounds her. Not attacking, not at first. Almost like it's curious, and she's not afraid of it. She's..." A small, broken sound escaped her. "She's reaching for it. Like she wants to touch it."

My mind flashed back to the horrific video from the IGMC station; the man in the chair, the smoke entering him, reality warping around them both. The same smoke I'd seen around Christopher. "Does the smoke... enter her?" I asked hesitantly.

Her silence answered my question.

"The footage cuts out," she finally said, her voice unnaturally flat. "The girl is on the floor. Not moving."

"What happens after that?" I asked, though I suspected I already knew the answer.

"Nothing," she replied, and I heard the soft click of her closing the file. "That's it."

I could hear her breathing—controlled, deliberate, like someone fighting for composure.

"There's another video," she finally said, her voice so quiet I had to strain to hear it. I heard her clicking to activate it. "Same... same girl. But older."

"Different how?" I asked.

"She's maybe fifteen now," Lena said, something raw in her voice. "Sitting in a chair. Just... staring. Her expression is..." She inhaled sharply. "There's nothing there. Like looking at a doll."

"And her eyes?" I prompted her gently, sensing her struggle.

"Black," Lena whispered. "Completely black. And around her shoulders...there's something. A distortion. Like heat waves, but darker. Moving with her. Part of her."

"Smoke," I finished for her. "Like the distortion I sometimes see around Christopher."

"You've seen this before?" Lena's voice was sharp now, almost accusatory. "Around Christopher?"

I nodded, forgetting momentarily that she could see me while I couldn't see her. "Yes, from the beginning. I thought I was hallucinating at first, but Iris confirmed it's real. A kind of... shimmer, like heat waves, but darker. It moves around him, especially when he's angry or focused."

I heard her inhale sharply. The console chair creaked as she leaned back.

"And it's in these videos, too?" Her voice had changed, the practiced hardness was cracking, revealing something beneath that I'd never heard from her before. "From Christopher's files?"

"It has to be connected to what happened at the IGMC station," I said, my mind racing to connect the pieces. "The man in the chair, the experiment that went wrong...the smoke entered him, and reality itself started to warp."

"And now Christopher has your medallion," Lena added, her voice barely audible.

"We need to get it back," I said, my voice hardening with resolve despite my fear. "Whatever that smoke is, whatever Christopher is...my medallion is somehow key to his plans. Commander Zara called it a 'dimensional key.' She called Christopher an 'Avalonian.' These files, the videos, they're all pieces of the same puzzle."

I heard the console's power go down abruptly. Lena's footsteps approached, unsteady, almost stumbling.

"First, we need to survive Terax-3," she said, attempting her usual pragmatism but failing to hide the tremor in her voice. "Get your eyes fixed." Her hand found my shoulder, gripping it with unusual intensity. "He doesn't know what we've seen. That we know."

Something in her tone made me pause. It wasn't just determination I was hearing; it was personal, raw.

I reached up, finding her wrist before she could pull away. "Lena," I said quietly, "you nearly died trying to reach Harvey. The technopath connection...it almost killed you. What happened?"

Her wrist was tense under my grip. For a moment, I thought she would pull away. Instead, her fingers dug into my shoulder almost painfully.

"The station," she finally whispered, "wasn't just built. It was... grown. Cultivated. When I tried to connect with Harvey, something else was already there. In the circuits, the walls, everything." She took a shuddering breath. "Something that recognized me."

"Like the smoke?" I suggested.

"No," she said sharply. Then, more quietly: "Not like in the video. Older. Vaster." Her voice dropped to a whisper. "It knew what I was, what I could do. And it..." Her grip tightened to the point of pain. "It reminded me."

Before I could ask what, she meant, a distant clanging echoed through the shuttle, the sound of someone moving through the Charon's corridors, heading our way.

"Christopher," Lena hissed, her hand suddenly withdrawn from my shoulder. I heard her quickly moving back to the console, frantically shutting down systems. "We need to..."

The shuttle door hissed open.

"Ah, you're both awake," Christopher's deceptively pleasant voice came from the doorway. "Excellent. We'll be reaching Terax-3 soon. I trust you're feeling better, Lena. And Burton, how are those eyes coming along?"

I turned toward his voice, fighting to keep my expression neutral despite the terror and rage boiling inside me. Somewhere in the darkness that was my vision, I imagined I could see the smoke swirling around him, patient, ancient, and utterly inhuman.

"I still can't see," I said flatly.

"Pity," Christopher replied, and I heard him step closer. "Don't worry. We'll get that fixed on Terax-3." A metallic clink accompanied his movement, the sound of my medallion hanging around his neck. "After all, I need you in working order, Burton. We still have a long journey ahead of us."

"Of course," Lena said, her voice suddenly composed again—the hardened smuggler's mask firmly back in place. But I caught the slight tremor beneath her practiced nonchalance.

"I'm pleased to see you recovered so quickly," Christopher said, his attention shifting to her. "Your connection with Harvey is... impressive. Rare, even."

"Just lucky, I guess," Lena replied flatly.

"Luck," Christopher chuckled, the sound entirely without warmth. "An interesting concept. I wonder how many of your kind believe in luck rather than... design."

The silence that followed was suffocating. I couldn't see Lena's reaction, but I could feel the tension radiating from her.

As Christopher spoke, I felt something brush against my consciousness, a cold, alien presence that seemed to search for weakness. And in that moment, I realized the truth: whatever Christopher was, whatever the smoke truly represented, it wasn't just watching us.

It was listening. And somehow, impossibly, it knew Lena.

~ 16 ~

SMOKE AND SHUNTS

With the video over, Lena disembarked from the shuttle with Harvey's assistance. She didn't speak to me, but I could hear feet and servos moving past me. I thought she might have stopped briefly before me, but I couldn't be sure. I remained in the shuttle longer, alone in my darkness.

"Burton," Iris's voice came through softly in my ear. "I'm detecting changes in your ocular blood flow patterns. Your sight may be beginning to return."

I became aware of faint lightning in the darkness as if on cue. Colors gradually started to seep into my field of vision, first vague impressions, then hazy shadows that began to give way to indistinct outlines.

"Iris, what's happening?" I whispered, my heart racing.

"The antivenom Dwight administered is working as expected," she responded. "I recommend you remain seated while your visual processing recalibrates. The sudden return of visual stimuli can cause disorientation and nausea."

She was right. As I sat there, the visuals became sharper and more overwhelming. It was a cascade of sensory input that left me feeling breathless. Everything seemed more vivid than before, my blindness, the shuttle's control panels almost painfully bright, the emergency lights burning like small suns.

"Your visual acuity is approximately sixty percent restored," Iris informed me through my earpiece. "I recommend movement to help recalibrate your spatial awareness and depth perception."

"Thanks, Iris," I muttered, gripping the edge of the console as I pulled myself to my feet. The shuttle seemed to tilt for a moment before stabilizing.

"I need to find Lena," I said, steadying myself against the bulkhead. "We're not finished."

"She has returned to her quarters," Iris confirmed. "But perhaps you should rest before”

"No," I cut her off. "I need answers now. Those videos she described... I need to understand what's happening while everything she told me is still fresh in my mind."

I made my way down the shuttle ramp, each step carefully negotiating with my recovering senses. The familiar corridors of the Charon seemed alien now, my newly restored vision transforming the familiar passages into something strange and new. I followed the corridor to the crew quarters, the dim orange glow of the Charon's lights now a bright torch leading me through the corridors. Harvey stood outside her door, the faint glow of his eyes now blazing in my sight. Its crudely drawn expression said, "Fuck off," in the light. I stepped back.

"I need to speak to Lena," I said hesitantly.

I moved to the opposite side of the corridor; its expression appeared to soften upon hearing her voice from inside. "Let him in, Harvey." The door stuttered as it slid open. Harvey moved slowly toward me before turning for me to enter.

I entered her quarters; she was seated on the lower bunk with her plasma rifle resting above her. In her hand, she held a small device. I couldn't see what it was. I headed towards the desk and sat; she didn't look at me. She remained focused on whatever was in her hand, ignoring my arrival.

"You, okay?" I threw it out to see if I could get a response.

Her expression was still unreadable. "What do you need?" she asked, her voice calm and steady.

"Why'd you leave?"

"The shuttle felt suffocating. I wanted to get back to my room," she said, still not looking at me.

I wasn't skilled in extracting information from others. I didn't have a strategy for asking the right questions or guiding them toward the answers I needed, so I just asked her directly. "What did you see on the video?"

She looked at me, eyes bloodshot. "I described to you what I saw."

"You told me what was on the video," I paused, "I want to know what you saw."

She stared at me long enough to cause me to squirm in my seat, periodically glancing at the plasma rifle above her head. "It was me," she finally let out. "The young girl in the smoke. She had a shunt behind her ear, identical to mine," she said, reliving her revelation.

My jaw hung slack as she continued.

"I was a child. It wasn't until you had me watch that video that memories, so many memories, flooded back. Ones I'd locked away or maybe..." She faltered, her voice a whisper. "Maybe they were locked away from me."

I remained silent, unsure of what to say in the face of her pain. This was more than I'd expected, much more. Perhaps she might recognize something in the video that could help us understand what Christopher was planning. I hadn't expected to uncover something so personal, so traumatic.

She took a deep breath and continued, "You saw the experiment on that IGMC station." It wasn't a question but a statement; her voice suddenly hardened. "You don't know that it wasn't an isolated incident."

"My father was an IGMC miner near the Centaurus constellation," she began again. "We stayed in a family room in the mining barracks. Most of the men without families were forced into overcrowded barracks with other miners. The stench that emanated from the barracks was sickening, a mix of sweat, feces, and rot. Bodies were dragged out daily, either due to starvation or other means. Miners, taking rations from weaker men or sometimes straight murder.

The family rooms were only small boxes, 12 x 9 feet at most. My mother, father, and I shared it. There was no privacy, no space to move around. We lay on our mats at night, trying to ignore the sounds of violence and misery that reached us from outside.

I'll never forget the day my dad disappeared in the mines. They said it was a 'mishap', something went wrong with his exposure suit. My mom was worried all day, pacing back and forth in our cramped little place. We waited and waited before we realized he wasn't coming home.

The reality of IGMC was that it was an oppressive debt. Miners were serviced through financial obligation, paying for the tools that allowed them to work, all while being charged extra for rations and safety gear. It was what cost my father his life: an exposure suit with a faulty air filter that we were made to repair at a price beyond our means. Those who could not pay or work were abandoned on distant planets without warning, some containing conditions hospitable enough to survive on the surface. In contrast, others had environments so hostile that it would take no more than minutes before their bodies succumbed to the corrosive gases in the atmosphere.

IGMC had female miners, but most of the women there were sold into servitude. Debt was their shackles, and the men from IGMC insinuated to my mother what she could do to keep a roof over our heads. That fucking 12 x 9 box where we lived was our prison, we had to pay to live in."

She paused, her tough facade cracking with the memory's emotion. "My mother was a beautiful woman. Her hair was flawless, cascading down her back like a curtain, and her eyes were bright and full of life. Even in the darkest environment of the mines, the dirt and muck never dulled her beauty. She died with my father; her light was extinguished, and all that remained was a broken shell of what once radiated beauty and strength.

For months, she refused to tell me where she was going when she left me early in the morning. But I knew. She would come home smelling of an unfamiliar place, scrubbing at her skin in front of a mirror. Water and tears, sometimes blood, would fill the sink."

She steadied herself before continuing. "I was only eleven when she died. As expected, the men from IGMC came to collect their dues. But my mother had nothing left to give. When they were done with her, they tossed her aside like she was nothing, another worthless body for the reclamation machine.

This time, their glances fell on me as they pondered how I could settle the debts. Orphans needed to work in the mines, but I was too small to fit into the exposure suits. They gave me the shunt instead." She pulled back her hair, emphasizing her point.

"It was burned in, hot like a branding iron, searing into the soft skin behind my ear. The smell of my burning flesh filled the air; the pain radiated from the shunt down my spine and up to the top of my skull. The sensation was unbearable; I screamed and thrashed in agony.

They assigned me to Harvey before I was even healed. Connecting with a robot is not easy; it involves your brain merging with the robot's neural network. Each action requires the shunt to set up pathways in your brain, sending out tiny tendrils that spread through your cerebral cortex. The bigger the robot, the more pathways are needed, making children ideal for this job. Their brains are much more malleable, allowing the tendrils to develop along with them until the connection is just as natural as breathing.

After becoming connected, we were transported to the arcade. From there, we controlled our robots and saw the world through their cameras. We were to clear away rocks and prepare the structure for miners to enter. The robots worked tirelessly, like ants burrowing through a planet's surface and creating tunnels that could be mined.

Every day, we were assigned a quota to meet a certain number of kilotons of rock we were responsible for moving. Those who couldn't produce results would be either denied food or beaten. The strain placed on the brain due to the shunts expanding to control the robots caused some kids to experience nose bleeds and brain hemorrhages. The bodies of those who passed away were unceremoniously hauled off and stripped of their shunts, before being tossed in the reclamation machine. The shunts were then shelved until they could be inserted into another kid. No effort was made to clean them."

"How could they do that to people?" I asked, my voice full of anger.

Lena gave me a sad smile. "It's what people do, Velvet, when they think they can get away with it." Her words lingered in the air. "The IGMC didn't care about us. To them, we were just resources to be exploited. They took our labor and our lives without a second thought.

I was about three months shy of 12 when the lab coats from IGMC grabbed me and 14 other kids from our bunks. They took us into a subterranean facility several kilometers from the main mining structure. They put us in those enclosed chambers from the video, with the cement floors and metal walls."

Her eyes seemed to lose focus as she continued, "The observation mirrors lined one wall, reflecting our small forms at us. I remember the cold of that floor seeping through my thin clothes, the institutional sterility that seemed designed to strip away any sense of humanity."

She looked down at her hands. "They injected us with a concoction of hallucinogenic drugs that took away any sense of fear or anxiety. I felt as if I were dreaming, floating away from reality.

I never noticed when the smoke started to fill the room. But it swayed in rhythm with me; we were locked in a dance to our melody. Then, all too quickly, this reverie was broken when they sucked the smoke out of the room. I would black out and wake in cold sweats. Each time, it was being ripped away from a beautiful dream and pitched into the horrifying nightmare reality, filled with confusion and disorientation.

My body would quiver on the floor, yet my mind felt released from its captivity. The lab coats would bring in a desk, place me at it, and stand over me as they gave me a data pad and a stylus. An inexplicable force would drive me to create symbols and images I'd never seen before as if they were familiar memories from another lifetime. So incredible were the artifacts that flowed through my hand into reality. An otherworldly source had taken over my actions, guiding them through an ancient power I could not comprehend."

"How long were you there?" I asked, my voice barely above a whisper. I was afraid that if I spoke too loudly, it would shatter the fragile thread of trust she had placed in me.

"There was no time in that place," she replied, her voice flat and emotionless. "Only I and another child survived the initial interactions with the smoke. We were kept in a sleeping quarter separate from the observation chambers, but no other captives ever got to sleep there. I vividly remember seeing an older kid, about 15 years old, being pushed down the corridor in a mangled heap of blood and flesh.

Every morning, the lab coats would give us our concoctions before interrogating us with questions neither of us could answer.

Then, they shut us in those chambers and filled them with smoke. When the smoke cleared, the lab coats would observe what the other kid and I had created. We were used to communicating with something beyond this world...something alive in the smoke. Even as a kid, there was an evident sentience to the smoke. It comforted me in our dances, a warm, wispy embrace."

"What happened to the other kid?" I asked.

Her expression darkened, and she looked away. "He didn't make it," she said softly. "He died in that room. I was the only one left."

"What happened then?" I asked, slipping out before I could stop myself. I immediately regretted it. I had a typical mechanical mindset, wanting to know how things worked and how stories ended. This wasn't some broken converter I was diagnosing.

Her eyes locked onto mine with an intensity that made me want to look away, but I couldn't.

"One day, they just let me go," she whispered, her voice uncharacteristically vulnerable. "No explanation, no warning. They dragged me out of that room and tossed me into the back of a transport ship like I was nothing." She paused; her gaze distant. "As they loaded me, I noticed Harvey among a group of mining robots stowed in the cargo hold, still linked to me through our connection."

Her expression hardened, and something dark and satisfied flashed across her face. "I played unconscious until we reached deep space. Then..." She looked away. "Let's just say Harvey and I made sure no one on that transport would ever hurt another child. We've been running from IGMC ever since."

The implications hung heavily in the air between us. I thought of the stories I'd heard as a child on Neda – whispered accounts of massacres, of IGMC transports found drifting in space, crews mysteriously slaughtered. My father warned me about dangers lurking beyond our colony's borders.

I nodded, not trusting myself to speak. What could I possibly say to that? Eventually, I managed, "No one should have gone through what you did."

Her voice was more resolute as she replied, "I haven't been alone since Harvey, and I was connected. It has kept me safe."

"Christopher knows who you are. What the IGMC did to you," I said, to bring us back into the present.

Lena's expression was eerily calm as she stated, "Christopher's only scratched the surface of what they did. He doesn't know everything, nobody does, but he understands enough to use it against me if he needs to."

I nodded, understanding more than she might realize. "We've all got our demons, Lena. Secrets that gnaw at us. You've got Harvey, and I've got..." I trailed off, unsure what I've got besides a truckload of regrets and unanswered questions.

"You've got your father's medallion," she said, standing to usher me out. "Get it back from Christopher. I don't know why he wanted it, but he paid me to take it off you on Zeta. It was the real price for getting me and Harvey off that planet." She paused, a rare flicker of confusion crossing her face. "I was surprised when he returned it to you after all the work I'd gone through to get it. That's when I knew there was something special about that trinket."

I walked into the corridor, her door stuttering closed behind me. Harvey moved back into position guarding her door. I just stood there clutching my chest in the spot where my father's medallion used to hang.

~ 17 ~

THE PRICE OF SURVIVAL

I sat on the floor of my quarters, in the same spot I had been in when Christopher abducted me from Neda, when I tried to attack him. The space feels colder now. I clenched my fists, feeling the absence of the medallion like a missing limb. Why would Christopher want it? What does he know that I don't?

"Burton," Iris's voice filtered through my quarters. "Captain Christopher requests everyone's presence in the galley."

I remained seated, my mind racing with questions about what I'd learned. In the videos, Lena described the experiments and the smoke connected to Christopher. And now he had my medallion.

"Burton," Iris prompted again. "Your presence is required."

"I heard you the first time," I muttered, pushing myself up from the floor.

In no headspace to hurry, I lingered outside the galley, building the resolve to look Christopher in his eyes and demand my father's medallion back and answers.

When I arrived, the galley was dimly lit. Christopher, Lena, and Dwight were already there, gathered around the small table where we'd shared many uneasy meals. Harvey stood like a sentinel behind Lena, his crudely drawn face looking particularly somber in the low light. Exhaustion marked everyone's features; even Harvey's crude expression seemed weary.

My hands trembled slightly as I considered challenging Christopher in front of the others. I stepped into their circle, trying not to give anything away. Lena glanced at me briefly, a subtle warning in her eyes: *not now*. We hadn't spoken since she recalled the experiments, yet she knew what I was thinking about my father's medallion and the deal she'd struck.

Christopher activated the holographic display embedded in the table. A three-dimensional map of our location materialized above the surface, casting everyone's faces in an eerie blue glow.

"We are here," Christopher said, pointing at a fixed point on the map. "We should arrive at Terax-3 within the hour."

Lena leaned forward, the blue light accentuating the hollows of her face, making her look almost skeletal. "Terax-3," she murmured, "isn't exactly a welcoming place." Her voice carried a blend of warning and weariness. The way she said it...Lena wasn't easily disturbed, yet something in her tone suggested that she even found this place unsettling.

"Mercenaries and mech-junkies," Dwight grunted, crossing his massive arms over his chest. "The kind that'll pull out your organs while you're still conscious just to see how they work."

Christopher's cybernetic arm twitched slightly, plates shifting and recalibrating. "We have little option and less time." He pulled up the latest diagnostics of the ship, red warning indicators flashing across multiple systems. "Replacing the plasma core is essential, and we also have sixteen other components that need to be swapped out. Not to mention all the other problems we're facing." He forced an even tone, but his arm twitching frequency betrayed his concern. "We won't last much longer limping along like this."

Dwight shifted his position, his bulk casting a shadow over the navigation display. "Sounds like a supply run in mech-junkie territory then," he said, scratching his beard.

Christopher nodded.

"And what's the price for help?" Lena chimed in, leaning against Harvey, her eyes fixed on Christopher. The hardness in her voice had returned—the vulnerable woman from our earlier conversation replaced by the pragmatic smuggler I'd first met.

"It'll probably cost us a leg and a..." Dwight casually pointed at Christopher's cybernetic arm, his voice darkly humorous.

Christopher's arm twitched more violently, but he kept his voice steady. "The prisoner will be payment enough."

"Prisoner?" Lena and I exclaimed in unison.

"What prisoner?" I questioned, confusion evident in my voice.

Christopher looked at me, sharp and assessing. "Order of the Sable Serpent soldier," he said, his tone derisive, as if expecting my reaction.

Lena stepped closer to Harvey, instinctively reaching for the shunt behind her ear. "When did you take a prisoner?"

"You two were in a bad way after we escaped," Dwight began, leaning back in his chair. "Burton was blinded, and you were practically comatose. Your metal friend here had you quarantined. We couldn't even get close."

He leaned forward, elbows on the table. "After you both were secured in the shuttle, Christopher and I returned to clear the ship. It turns out that Commander Zara had sent a team to search the Charon while we were locked up. Six of them, moving deck by deck."

Christopher's eyes narrowed at the memory. "They were looking for something."

"My medallion," I whispered, the realization hitting me.

Dwight continued as if I hadn't spoken. "The first one we found was in the engine room, tearing apart your workstation, Burton. Didn't even hear us coming." A satisfied smirk crossed his face. "The second and third were in the cargo hold. They put up more of a fight."

"The other three?" Lena asked.

"Found them in the ladder well," Dwight said, his voice dropping. "Trying to access the bridge controls. They'd hacked into some of Iris's secondary systems."

"They nearly succeeded in shutting down life support," Christopher added coldly. "We dealt with five of them. The sixth surrendered."

My face paled. "You're telling us that a Sable Serpent soldier is locked up somewhere on this ship right now?"

Dwight shrugged nonchalantly. Sealed in the cargo hold. Hasn't made a peep since we jumped."

"Wait. What does this have to do with Terax-3?" My mind had stopped paying attention to our destination as soon as I learned about the prisoner.

"Terax-3 trades in flesh," Christopher responded coldly. The prisoner's value there will be high enough to get us what we need and then some." His eyes drilled into mine, daring me to object.

I swallowed hard. "You mean to tell me you plan to trade a living person for parts?"

"We're going to trade parts for parts," he corrected, before allowing his gaze to drift back to the schematic, his expression unreadable. "Besides, we have no other options," he said in a low mutter.

I felt the weight of our dire circumstances pressing in on me. As much as I detested the idea, I also recognized the importance of getting what we needed to survive. My hands clenched and unclenched at my sides as I wrestled with the moral implications.

"No," I said finally, my voice stronger than expected. "There has to be another way."

Lena didn't even look up. "He's right, Velvet. We need those parts."

"But trading someone..."

"Who tried to kill us?" she cut me off, her eyes suddenly hard as she looked at me. "Who would have fed us to their station without a second thought. Who tortured people like me for years?" Her voice was cold, practical. "You want to survive in space? This is the price."

I looked at her, remembering her stories of IGMC's brutality, of children experimented on, discarded, and forced to survive by any means necessary. Her expression didn't waver.

"The universe doesn't care about your morals, kid," Dwight added. "Only matters who's still breathing at the end of the day."

I wanted to argue further, but the words died in my throat. What alternatives did we have? Without repairs, we'd be dead in the void within days.

Christopher stood. "Dwight, retrieve the prisoner. We'll be docking soon."

Dwight nodded and left the galley, heading to the lower decks. My mind raced with conflicting thoughts. Was this the right thing to do? Lena seemed resolute, and Christopher remained focused on his mission, disregarding the soldier's life. I couldn't shake the feeling that we were crossing a line, even if it was an enemy soldier.

"Iris," Christopher called out, "open an encrypted channel to Terax-3. Set the frequency to T579-G842-R315-K769."

"Channel open, Captain," Iris responded, her voice emanating from the galley speakers.

"Nyx," Christopher called out, waiting for a response. "Nyx," he called again, more insistently.

"Who is on this channel?" a voice burst into the galley. The voice was distorted and ghostly, like it had wound through a black hole before reaching us. It sounded both mechanical and organic at once, a dissonant harmony.

"Christopher," he said smugly, as if the name alone should open doors.

"Well," the voice seemed to lift in recognition, carrying the weight of history with it. "It has been quite some time." The way the words stretched suggested decades, perhaps centuries, like two ancient beings acknowledging each other across the vast expanse of time.

"Indeed," Christopher replied, his voice cold as the vacuum outside. "I need parts for my ship. I'm sending over a list."

"Iris, transmit the repair manifest," Christopher ordered.

"Transmitting now, Captain," Iris confirmed.

We sat in silence until the voice from the other side came back on.

"I can get you these things," the voice affirmed, a hint of something predatory in its tone. "The price is still the same."

"The price is always the same," Christopher snapped back, his words carrying the weight of an old agreement, a long-standing arrangement between them.

"I'll provide the necessary transponder codes. Dock your ship at B-14-Y-7. Oh, and Christopher...keep a close eye on your companions. Business has been...slow here." The voice abruptly disconnected the transmission.

The galley felt colder after the connection was terminated. Lena stood, moving toward the exit. "I'll get my gear," she said. She placed a hand on my shoulder as she passed me, her grip tight. "This is survival, Velvet. Nothing more, nothing less."

I watched her go, Harvey's heavy footsteps following behind her. Left alone with Christopher, I stared at his neck, where my medallion hung beneath his shirt.

"Something on your mind, Burton?" he asked, not looking up from the display.

"Nothing that can't wait," I replied, swallowing my anger. Now wasn't the time.

***

Terax-3 loomed before us, growing larger on the viewscreen as we approached. It wasn't a planet or a moon, but a massive asteroid, irregular and foreboding. Its surface was a twisted landscape of jagged ice formations and exposed rock, riddled with crevices and craters that looked like festering wounds. Mining equipment and makeshift structures jutted from its surface like parasites, clinging to the barren rock.

The station appeared to have been carved directly into the asteroid, rather than built upon it. Scattered lights dotted its surface, cold and distant, offering no warmth or welcome. As we drew closer, I could make out the massive docking bays, gaping maws carved into the asteroid's face, ready to swallow ships whole.

The very sight of Terax-3 felt oppressive, as if the weight of all the desperate acts committed there had manifested as a physical presence. The blackness of space seemed to deepen around it, the stars dimming as if reluctant to cast their light upon such a place.

"Ready for docking," Iris announced. "Adjusting approach vector based on provided coordinates."

The asteroid seemed to swallow the Charon whole. The docking bay was a tight squeeze for the ship, causing it to scrape against the rough edges before finally jolting into place with a violent thud. The sudden halt sent us all lurching forward, our bodies feeling every impact as the Charon came to a stop.

Dwight met us in the shuttle bay as we prepared to exit the ship. He pushed the soldier forward, keeping his plasma pistol trained on it. The soldier had lost its helmet when it was captured, and the grotesqueness of its face was even more repulsive on a living subject. The smooth, featureless skin where eyes should have been. The three gaping, mucus-lined slits instead of a nose. The translucent lips reveal the outline of gums beneath. It was a stark reminder of the Serpents' transformation, a perversion of humanity.

We walked down the ramp and onto a narrow walkway carved directly into the icy surface of the asteroid. The air here was thin and bitter, carrying a metallic tang that coated the back of my throat. I could hear the faint sound of oxygen escaping through the porous rock around us. The sudden change in atmosphere made my head spin, my vision blurring at the edges. The Serpent soldier must have felt the same, as it doubled over, emptying the contents of its stomach into the space between the Charon's hull and thc walkway.

"Use the breather from the exposure suit, kid," Dwight grunted, shoving the soldier forward again.

"Every inhabitant here has been genetically modified to thrive in oxygen-deprived atmospheres," Lena explained, pulling a small, silvery device from my exposure suit's collar. It resembled a thin metallic ring, its surface inscribed with microscopic circuitry patterns that pulsed with faint blue light.

"Oxygen is only needed to sustain life before modification," she told me as she handed me the device. Environmental systems aren't a priority here; they incentivize unmodified individuals to undergo surgery or suffer side effects until they give in. Put this around your neck; you'll feel better."

I followed her instructions, placing the ring over my head. It immediately began to constrict around my neck, conforming perfectly to my skin. The cold metal warmed rapidly, becoming uncomfortably hot. Then came a strange sensation—the device seemed to liquefy, dissolving into my flesh like mercury sinking into porous stone. The process lasted only seconds but left me gasping. Then, suddenly, I could breathe freely again. My hand instinctively reached for my neck but found nothing; the device had completely disappeared, absorbed into my body.

"What about him?" I queried, looking at Dwight.

"He's fine," Dwight said mockingly, shoving the soldier forward again. "Getting him to Nyx is what matters, not his comfort."

"Keep moving," Christopher motioned for us to follow him into a tunnel, his expression unreadable.

The narrow passageway opened into the heart of Terax-3. The air here was thick and pungent, carrying the metallic scent of blood mingled with the sickly-sweet smell of burning flesh and industrial chemicals. The odor overwhelmed my senses, making me gag despite the breathing device.

We stood inside a vast cavern that stretched endlessly in every direction. The ceiling arched hundreds of meters above us, stalactites of ice and rock hanging like massive teeth, ready to fall at any moment. The walls were a chaotic tapestry of jagged rock and smooth, polished surfaces where habitations had been violently carved directly into the asteroid's face.

Flickering lanterns hung precariously from the ceiling, their dim light casting eerie shadows that danced menacingly along the uneven floor. Between these pools of light lay patches of absolute darkness, hiding who knew what horrors. The rumble of machinery echoed throughout the cavern, punctuated by occasional screams that no one around us seemed to notice.

Hundreds of people moved through the sprawling market at the cavern's center if they could still be called that. Many had mechanical limbs or visible implants protruding from their flesh. Others had been modified more extensively, their bodies twisted into forms better suited for specific tasks. The stalls they gathered around displayed everything from scavenged ship parts to modified weapons, from strange alien artifacts to what appeared to be harvested organs floating in cloudy fluid.

My foot was suddenly struck by a ball made of metallic foam. I turned my head in the direction from which it rolled, and my mouth fell open in surprise. "There are kids here," I murmured, unsure if I was asking a question or making an accusation.

A small child, no more than seven or eight years old, stood watching us. Its skin was pale and translucent, revealing a network of modified blood vessels beneath. As I watched, a set of transparent eyelids fluttered open and shut vertically across its eyes, allowing more oxygen to enter its body.

Dwight spat on the floor, attempting to clear his mouth of the asteroid dust that floated around us. "Hard to believe, but yeah, kids grow up in the shadows here, like anywhere else."

"They augment their children, too?" I couldn't hide the horror in my voice.

Lena let out a thoughtful sigh, her sharp eyes scanning the cavern. "The children are exposed to the same harsh conditions as the adults. As long as it results in more labor and larger profits, no one cares." There was resignation in her voice and hardness in her tone; she'd seen too much to be shocked anymore.

Christopher led us through the cavern, his cybernetic arm twitching occasionally. "This way," he nodded toward a figure lurking at the mouth of a tunnel, its form concealed under a dark hood.

We quickened our pace to follow as the figure retreated into the depths of the tunnel system. The passage narrowed as we went deeper, the walls pressing around us. The temperature dropped noticeably, our breath fogging despite the thin atmosphere. After several minutes of twisting and turning through the labyrinthine tunnels, we emerged into a small chamber.

It resembled a shop, if a nightmare could be called a shop. The walls were lined with rusted and broken machinery reminiscent of my workshop on Neda, but these parts were distorted, modified in ways that made little sense. Some appeared melded with organic components, pulsing slightly as if still alive. Strange tools hung from hooks on the walls, their purposes obscure and menacing.

The hooded figure moved to the center of the room with an unnatural, skittering grace. It was too quick and precise, like a predator's movements. With one fluid motion, it pulled back its shroud.

The creature before us had perhaps once been human, but those days passed. Its body was a disturbing fusion of flesh and machine, with jointed metal appendages extending from its back like additional limbs. Metal plates were embedded in its skin, and intricate circuits pulsed beneath the surface. Its face was gaunt, stretched over a framework of mechanical components, with only one remaining human eye, the other replaced by an electric blue optical sensor that shifted restlessly, scanning our features.

When it smiled, I could see rows of razor-sharp metallic teeth, including a secondary set that retracted partially into its jaw. Its fingers ended in pointed talons that clicked against each other as it gestured.

"You return sooner than I anticipated, Christopher," the creature declared, its voice a modulated metallic rasp that seemed to emanate from multiple points in its body simultaneously. "The stars must have aligned against you."

"Unavoidable, Nyx," Christopher replied, his arm's twitch becoming more pronounced, though his face remained impassive. "We require parts for my ship. We were... out of options."

"Yet here you stand, as you have stood before me countless times across the ages," Nyx responded, its human eye flickering vertically as it took a breath. "Always in need, always returning."

There was something in the exchange that spoke of a relationship spanning far longer than seemed possible, as if they had known each other for centuries rather than years.

"I've seen your list," Nyx continued, its optical sensor focusing on each of us in turn. "We can provide what you need. Can you pay the price?"

Christopher locked eyes with me briefly before turning to Dwight and signaling for him to hand the prisoner over.

Dwight pushed the Serpent soldier forward despite its resistance. The soldier stumbled, nearly falling at Nyx's feet.

Nyx's limbs twitched with anticipation, talons clicking rapidly against each other. It circled the soldier with that same unnatural, skittering movement, examining it from all angles.

"Fascinating specimen," Nyx hissed, metal fingers hovering just above the soldier's skin, not quite touching. "Heavily modified on a cellular level. You do spoil us, Christopher." Its voice carried a predatory hunger that made my skin crawl. "We accept your payment. Wait here."

With frightening speed, Nyx lunged forward, additional limbs unfolding from beneath its cloak. It snatched the soldier with inhuman strength, metal talons digging into flesh. The soldier's scream was cut short as Nyx dragged it away into the darkness of a back chamber, the sound of metal scraping against stone fading until all was silent.

We stood in the eerie half-light, the implications of what we'd just done hanging heavily between us. I tried to tell myself it was necessary, that our survival depended on these parts, but the soldier's final, terrified scream echoed in my mind.

Whatever Nyx planned to do with the soldier, I was confident of one thing: we had just traded away more than just a prisoner.

~ 18 ~

WE ARE OWED

The silence that followed the soldier's capture was suffocating. Our small group stood awkwardly in Nyx's workshop. My mind kept replaying the terror that still permeated even on the soldier's grotesque face as it was dragged away.

"Is this what we've become?" I finally broke the silence, my voice barely above a whisper. "Trading people for parts like... like commodities?"

"Keep your voice down," Christopher hissed, his eyes darting to the shadows of the workshop where more of those metal appendages might be lurking. "Do you think we have the luxury of morality out here? Maybe in your velvet life on Neda, but you're not on Neda anymore. It's time you grow up!" His voice rose with each word until he was inches from my face.

"Slow down, Boss," Dwight interjected, placing his massive hand on Christopher's chest. "He's still 'idealistic,'" he said with mocking air quotes. "New to the gritty reality of these outer belts. Give him a minute."

Christopher's cybernetic arm twitched violently, the servos whirring in agitation. His eyes never left mine, cold and calculating, assessing how far I might push this.

I clenched my teeth, feeling a mix of disgust and anger rise inside me. "This isn't about idealism," I shot back, my voice low and tight. "It's about not becoming the monsters that control and destroy the lives of innocent people." My nostrils flared as I inhaled deep gulps of the pungent asteroid air. "What gives us the right to decide who lives and who dies? Who gets traded away?"

"Sometimes you have to make decisions you're not proud of," Christopher forced through a clenched jaw. "And I am not interested in being judged by a self-righteous velvet who's never had to make the hard choices."

Face to face, our eyes locked in a silent battle of will. Christopher's towering height loomed over me, making me feel even smaller. Dwight's muscular arm pressed between us, creating a physical barrier. Lena, lounging against Harvey's metal frame, suddenly stood up and blew a shrill whistle.

From the shadows, a figure emerged, not Nyx, but a different entity with the same skittering gait and mechanical appendages. Its optical sensors flickered as it approached, carrying a data pad that gleamed in the dim light. The device was handed to Christopher without a word.

Christopher pushed it into my hands without breaking eye contact. "Check it," he ordered.

I quickly scanned the manifest of supposedly delivered and installed parts on the Charon. After a few moments of careful inspection, I confirmed that everything was accounted for. "It's all here," I said reluctantly.

Christopher moved closer to the mechanical being. "What of the black ore?" he asked quietly, almost as an afterthought.

The entity produced a small metal box from beneath one of its appendages and handed it to Christopher with reverent care, as if passing something sacred. Christopher's eyes lit up with an unsettling eagerness as he took the box and opened it, revealing a small quantity of black, crystalline material that seemed to absorb the light around it. The ore pulsed with an eerie energy, reminding me of the smoke-like distortion I'd seen around Christopher.

Christopher quickly and quietly shut the box, tucking it away before we could get a good look. "How much do you have?" he asked the entity.

"This is all. For the current price," it replied, its voice modulated differently than Nyx's but carrying the same metallic rasp. Its optical sensors shifted, scanning each of us in turn, lingering on me with a predatory intensity. "If you could offer more specimens, we might provide more ore."

Christopher noticed the entity's hungry assessment of us. His voice dropped to a dangerous octave. "We're leaving. Now."

The mechanical being led us through the asteroid's labyrinthine tunnels, but I quickly realized we weren't heading back the way we came. The passages twisted in unfamiliar patterns, leading us deeper into the asteroid before finally opening into the main cavern, far from where the Charon was docked.

"You have your repairs," the entity stated, its appendages clicking against the rock floor. "The way to your ship is there." It gestured with a sharp, metallic talon toward a distant passage.

As we moved past, several more entities emerged from the shadows surrounding us. Their bodies were similar compositions of flesh and machine, but with variations that suggested different specialties or functions. All bore the same hungry look in their optical sensors.

"Wait," called a familiar voice, Nyx, or at least the entity we had first met. It skittered forward, rising to its full height. "We know what you've done. You brought a Serpent soldier to Terax-3."

Christopher's posture stiffened. "I don't know what you're talking about."

"We are Nyx," the entity responded, gesturing to all the mechanical beings around us. "We see all that happens on Terax-3. We share all knowledge." Its voice shifted, becoming a harmonious chorus of metallic tones, as if multiple entities were speaking through it simultaneously. "We recognized the modifications. The Serpent's mark is distinctive."

The being stepped aside as another Nyx entity dragged forward the Serpent soldier's mangled corpse, tossing it at our feet with a sickening thud. The body was barely recognizable, its spine had been extracted, along with its tongue, both shoulder blades, and the right kneecap. Blood pooled around our boots, thick and dark against the asteroid's rocky floor.

"We require new payment," Nyx echoed throughout the cavern. "You threaten us with the Serpent's wrath by trading one of their devoted. Your payment is inadequate."

Christopher's arm twitched more pronouncedly now. "Nyx," he attempted a charming smile that looked more like a grimace. "Please understand. We have no intention of being offensive. We took precautions to ensure we weren't followed here. The Order of the Sable Serpent is no more."

"We disagree," Nyx retorted, as howling began to permeate from the recesses of the cavern. "You have insulted us. You have betrayed us. We require new payment, and we require it now."

"I'm sorry, but we don't have anyone else to give," Christopher said, measuring his words carefully. "But we can bring you more."

"What? No," I whispered, loud enough for Christopher and the others to hear. Lena yanked me back, her grip painful on my arm.

Nyx's optical sensors fixed on me. "We want his eyes," it declared, pointing at me with a metallic talon. "We have a high demand for brown eyes. We will take his eyes." With each step, the entity clamored toward me, talons clicking against the stone floor.

"Whoa there, Boss," Dwight stepped before me, his plasma pistol raised. "I don't see anyone losing their eyes today."

Nyx seemed to grow larger, its form expanding as additional mechanical appendages unfolded from its body. Its blue optical sensor turned blood red. "We fixed your ship. You owe us. This is the deal. We had a deal."

It shed its outer covering with a dramatic flourish, revealing its true form, a grotesque amalgamation of circuitry and human parts, twisted in unnatural ways. Organs were wired to the outside, pulsating with lights and humming with electricity. Its skin was a canvas of scars and stitches, exposing the metallic musculature beneath.

Dwight tried to fire his plasma pistol, but Nyx moved with impossible speed. Metal talons crushed the weapon along with Dwight's hand, bones cracking like dry twigs. He howled in pain as Nyx flung him aside.

"We are owed. So, we will take." Nyx advanced toward me again.

With precision born of experience, Lena unholstered her plasma rifle and fired at Nyx's legs, the beam burning through metal and flesh alike. The entity crashed to the ground but continued dragging itself forward with its upper limbs. Christopher slapped Lena's rifle down before she could fire again.

"What are you doing?" he shouted, his face inches from hers, genuine fear flashing in his eyes, the first time I'd seen such emotion from him.

"WE ARE OWED," a chorus of voices boomed throughout the cavern, echoing from every direction. The sound was deafening, as if the asteroid itself was speaking. "WE REPAIRED YOUR SHIP. WE ARE OWED. YOUR PAYMENT IS INADEQUATE. WE WANT HIS EYES. WE WILL HAVE HIS EYES."

From every tunnel entrance, dozens of Nyx entities emerged, each a unique fusion of machine and salvaged human parts. They moved as one, a collective consciousness directing each body toward us with a singular purpose. The largest stood at the front, its jaw hanging open to its chest, revealing a forked tongue made of translucent material that shifted colors like oil on water. With a mighty roar that reverberated through the entire station, it showcased the intricate wiring embedded deep within its throat.

Christopher raised his hands in a placating gesture. "We can renegotiate," he said, his voice calm but firm despite his twitching arm. Lena kept her rifle aimed, eyes narrowed in defiance.

"Christopher, what's going on?" I demanded, backing away as Dwight groaned, clutching his crushed hand.

The largest Nyx entity closed its jaw with a metallic snap, tilting its head as if listening to something beyond our perception. "WE DO NOT RENEGOTIATE," the collective voice boomed. "WE HAD A DEAL. WE REQUIRE PAYMENT. WE WILL TAKE PAYMENT." The horde resumed their advance, metal talons clicking in perfect unison.

"Wait!" Christopher shouted, desperation edging his voice. "You've repaired my ship. Look at the schematics. Go to the lower levels and access the restricted area below. You'll find cryotubes. Fifteen of them. Bodies of the former crew of the Charon. They're yours if you let us go."

There was a moment of eerie silence as the collective considered his offer. The entities remained still, optical sensors flickering in unison as if communicating silently.

"WE WILL LOOK," the collective finally responded. "IF IT IS AS YOU SAY, YOU MAY GO. IF NOT, YOU ALL PAY WHAT YOU OWE."

Several Nyx entities broke away from the horde, skittering toward the ship with unnatural speed. The rest kept us surrounded, weapons trained, talons clicking impatiently. Minutes stretched like hours as we waited. Dwight continued to groan, clutching his mangled hand. Lena's rifle never wavered, though I could see fatigue in the slight trembling of her arms.

Christopher sat calmly on a rock outcropping, as if this were a minor inconvenience. His confidence was unnerving; either he knew the bodies were there, or he was bluffing with our lives at stake.

Finally, the Nyx entities returned, communicating silently with the others. The collective voice filled the cavern once more: "IT IS

AS YOU SAY. WE ACCEPT YOUR PAYMENT. LEAVE NOW. YOU ARE NO LONGER WELCOME ON TERAX-3."

The horde parted, creating a narrow path for us to exit. We backed away slowly, never turning our backs to them. Dwight cradled his crushed hand against his chest, his face pale with pain. Lena kept her rifle ready, moving backward with practiced steps. Harvey positioned himself to shield us, his massive frame offering some protection.

More Nyx entities had gathered behind us, blocking any potential escape routes other than the one leading to the Charon. They watched us hungrily, mechanical appendages twitching with anticipation, but the collective had made its decision for now.

The journey back to the ship was tense and silent, each step measured, each breath held. When we finally reached the Charon's ramp, I nearly collapsed with relief. We boarded quickly. Dwight headed immediately to the medical bay, and Lena and Harvey retreated to her quarters without a word.

I followed Christopher toward the bridge, my mind reeling from what had happened. I could no longer contain my anger as we crossed the catwalk above the motionless cooling gel pools.

"Who were those people?" I demanded, my voice echoing off the metal walls.

Christopher continued walking, not bothering to turn around. "I told you. The crew of the Charon."

"What kind of captain sacrifices their crew?" The words tore from my throat, raw with emotion.

He stopped then, turning slowly to face me. My father's medallion hung prominently around his neck now, no longer hidden beneath his shirt. It caught the light from below, seeming to glow with an inner fire.

"They were no longer useful to me," he said with chilling detachment. "The Charon needed a new engineer. The previous Burton served his purpose, just as the others did."

The implication hit me like a physical blow. "You were their captain," I whispered, the realization dawning. "And you gave them to Nyx."

"I put them in cryostasis when they became... unreliable," he corrected, his tone maddeningly reasonable. "This ship has been mine for longer than you can comprehend. Crews come and go."

I thought back to the cryotubes I'd glimpsed during my early explorations of the ship. One face flashed in my mind, a man with keloid scars on his arms, his ID tag reading "RIOS."

"How long have you been doing this?" I asked, horrified. "How many crews have you gone through?"

Something ancient and cold flickered behind Christopher's eyes. "Time becomes meaningless after a while," he said softly, almost to himself. "You measure it in missions, goals achieved... not human lifespans."

"And the original Burton?" I asked, my voice barely above a whisper. "What happened to him?"

Christopher's cybernetic hand twitched violently. "He helped me pay Nyx for my arm my first time on Terax-3." His voice had dropped to a growl, the facade of calm slipping. "He'd outlived his usefulness."

I moved to walk past him, but stopped. The medallion gleamed around his neck, taunting me. "I want my father's medallion back," I said flatly, each word deliberate.

He didn't turn to face me, his fingers rising to touch the metal cylinder hanging from his neck. "This," he said, the medallion catching the light as it moved between his fingers, "will cost you more than you're willing to pay." With that, he let it fall against his chest and continued onto the bridge, leaving me alone on the catwalk.

I stood there, trembling with rage and helplessness, watching his retreating form. The pools below the catwalk reflected my distorted image, fractured and unrecognizable, just like everything else had become since Christopher tore me from Neda.

~ 19 ~

THE VICTORS WRITE HISTORY

I sat on the floor of my quarters, in the same spot I had been in when Christopher abducted me from Neda, when I tried to attack him. The space feels colder now. I clenched my fists, feeling the absence of the medallion like a missing limb. Why would Christopher want it? What does he know that I don't?

"Burton," Iris's voice filtered through my quarters. "Captain Christopher requests everyone's presence in the galley."

I remained seated, my mind racing with questions about what I'd just discovered. The videos Lena had described, the experiments, and the smoke were connected to Christopher. And now he had my medallion.

"Burton," Iris prompted again. "Your presence is required."

"I heard you the first time," I muttered, pushing myself up from the floor.

My wrist console beeped with an alert: unauthorized access detected in the main computer core. Someone was searching through the ship's secure databases, using high-level protocols I'd never seen before. I paused, watching the data stream across my screen. The medallion Christopher was using to access encrypted sections of the ship's archives, files that had been locked away for decades, perhaps centuries.

In no headspace to hurry, I lingered outside the galley, building the resolve to look Christopher in his eyes and demand my father's medallion back, and answers.

When I arrived, the galley was dimly lit. Christopher, Lena, and Dwight were already there, gathered around the small table where we'd shared many uneasy meals. Harvey stood like a sentinel behind Lena, his crudely drawn face looking particularly somber in the low light. Exhaustion marked everyone's features; even Harvey's crude expression seemed weary.

My hands trembled slightly as I considered challenging Christopher in front of the others. I stepped into their circle, trying not to give anything away. Lena glanced at me briefly, a subtle warning in her eyes: *not now*. We hadn't spoken since she recalled the experiments, yet she knew what I was thinking about my father's medallion and the deal she'd struck.

Christopher activated the holographic display embedded in the table. A three-dimensional map of our location materialized above the surface, casting everyone's faces in an eerie blue glow.

"We are here," Christopher said, pointing at a fixed point on the map. "We should arrive at Terax-3 within the hour."

My attention was drawn away from Christopher as my wrist console silently flashed with another alert; the medallion's energy signature was spiking, interacting with the ship's systems in ways I'd never seen before. The display showed a string of coordinates unlike any standard navigation system I recognized, pulsing in rhythm with the medallion's energy.

Lena leaned forward, the blue light accentuating the hollows of her face, making her look almost skeletal. "Terax-3," she murmured, "isn't exactly a welcoming place." Her voice carried a blend of warning and weariness. The way she said it...Lena wasn't easily disturbed, yet something in her tone suggested that she even found this place unsettling.

"Mercenaries and mech-junkies," Dwight grunted, crossing his massive arms over his chest. "The kind that'll pull out your organs while you're still conscious just to see how they work."

His casual description of Terax-3's dangers contrasted sharply with what I'd just seen in the ship's database, IGMC research logs detailing "controlled humanitarian evacuation" during Earth's final days. The term was a sanitized label for what appeared to be forced relocation and experimentation.

Christopher's cybernetic arm twitched slightly, plates shifting and recalibrating. "We have little option and less time." He pulled up the latest diagnostics of the ship, red warning indicators flashing across multiple systems. "Replacing the plasma core is essential, and we also have sixteen other components that need to be swapped out. Not to mention all the other problems we're facing." He forced an even tone, but his arm twitching frequency betrayed his concern. "We won't last much longer limping along like this."

Dwight shifted his position, his bulk casting a shadow over the navigation display. "Sounds like a supply run in mech-junkie territory then," he said, scratching his beard.

Christopher nodded.

"And what's the price for help?" Lena chimed in, leaning against Harvey, her eyes fixed on Christopher. The hardness in her voice had returned the vulnerable woman from our earlier conversation, replaced by the pragmatic smuggler I'd first met.

"It'll probably cost us a leg and a..." Dwight casually pointed at Christopher's cybernetic arm.

Christopher's arm twitched more violently, but he kept his voice steady. "The prisoner will be payment enough."

"Prisoner?" Lena and I exclaimed in unison.

"What prisoner?" I questioned, confusion evident in my voice.

Christopher looked at me, sharp and assessing. "Order of the Sable Serpent soldier," he said, his tone derisive, as if expecting my reaction.

Lena stepped closer to Harvey, instinctively reaching for the shunt behind her ear. "When did you take a prisoner?"

"You two were in a bad way after we escaped," Dwight began, leaning back in his chair. "Burton was blinded, and you were practically comatose. Your metal friend here had you quarantined. We couldn't even get close."

Dwight was avoiding my eyes, a tell I'd learned to recognize when someone was hiding something. My wrist console continued to silently flash alerts as the medallion's interactions with the ship's systems intensified. Ancient logs were being accessed files on something called "Project Desolation."

"He's lying," I said suddenly, my eyes fixed on Dwight. "Not about the prisoner about IGMC. About Earth."

The room fell silent, everyone's attention shifting to me.

"What are you talking about, kid?" Dwight asked, his casual tone strained.

I tapped my wrist console, projecting one of the files I'd glimpsed in the unauthorized data stream. "IGMC Evacuation Protocol 7-A. 'In the event of planetary collapse, priority extraction will be given to subjects demonstrating compatibility with Project Ascension. Remaining populations to be processed according to labor value assessment." I looked up at Dwight. "You were IGMC, weren't you? That's how you know so much about their operations."

Dwight's expression darkened, the façade of the jovial mercenary slipping for a moment. "You've been digging in places you shouldn't, kid."

"I haven't been digging anywhere," I countered. "The medallion, *my* medallion, is accessing these files. And for some reason, you know a lot more about it than you've been letting on."

Christopher's cybernetic fingers drummed against the table, a rhythmic clicking that filled the tense silence. "Well, Dwight? Care to enlighten our young engineer?"

Dwight's eyes darted between Christopher and me, clearly calculating his next move. Finally, he sighed heavily, his massive shoulders slumping. "Fine. Yes, I was IGMC. The cadet program when I was fifteen. Rose through the ranks pretty quickly."

"And?" I pressed, sensing there was much more to the story.

"And history isn't what they teach in the colony schools, kid." Dwight's voice hardened. "When I was fifteen, I joined the IGMC cadet program. Wide-eyed and soft-bellied, just another warm body to break." He traced three jagged scars across his forearm. "Got these beauties on my first night. Older cadets held me down, carved me up with a makeshift blade melted from mess hall spoons. Called it 'marking the meat.'"

I watched his face carefully, noting the genuine pain that flashed in his eyes. This part, at least, wasn't a lie.

"Basic training was hell's playground," he continued. "Woke up every morning to ice baths and electrified prods jammed in our kidneys. Trainers would pick a kid at random, beat 'em unconscious in front of us to 'establish motivation.' Spent sixteen hours daily running combat drills in acid rain without protection, our skin blistering and peeling off in sheets."

Lena had stopped pacing, her attention focused entirely on Dwight's story. Even Harvey seemed to be listening, his optical sensors fixed on the weathered mercenary.

"The mud pits were the worst," Dwight said, his voice dropping. "Crawling through fields seeded with shrapnel mines and flesh-eating bacteria. Breathed through rebreathers that filtered just enough toxins to keep us alive but damaged enough to keep us coughing up blood for weeks. Started with twenty-three in my barracks." He raised seven fingers. "These didn't make the first month. Two blew themselves up. One drowned in the muck. Three died from infections after the pit crawls." His voice dropped to a whisper. "The seventh one, Klein, couldn't take it anymore. Used his bootlaces."

I glanced at my wrist console again. Christopher was using the medallion to access increasingly restricted files and records of something called "The Lachesis Incident."

"By graduation, only four of us were left standing," Dwight said. "And we were goddamn grateful for the privilege."

"But man, did they fill our heads with pretty stories," he continued, his drawl becoming more pronounced as he spoke. "IGMC, the great saviors of humanity, swoop in during Earth's darkest hour to rescue the deserving and establish a new golden age among the stars." He spat on the floor. "We ate it up like candy, me especially. Made it my mission to learn everything about Desolation Day, how IGMC changed the course of human history."

The expression on his face shifted to something darker, more haunted. "So I dug into the IGMC database every chance I got. I spent my ration credits bribing traders for scraps of information, old logs, and anything I could handle. It was like assembling a puzzle where half the pieces were missing and the rest didn't fit right."

A new alert flashed on my console Christopher had accessed a file labeled "Lachesis Passenger Manifest." My heart raced as I glimpsed a name: "Meredith P. Rivera."

"After two years of searching," Dwight continued, unaware of what I was seeing, "I found records buried so deep you'd need a mining laser to reach 'em. Learned why IGMC wanted Desolation Day remembered their way."

"What did you find?" I asked, still watching the data stream on my console. Christopher was now accessing files on "The Visionary" and "Vessel Compatibility Research."

Dwight's eyes darkened. "History is written by the victors, kid. I found that IGMC wasn't a savior. Earth wasn't just 'dying' it was being carved up. The planet had become a wasteland, with the folks left behind separated into warring tribes, fighting over scraps. No more governments, no law, just chaos and violence."

He paused, seeming to weigh his words carefully. "There were whispers, rumors of beings that weren't quite human. Strange happenings. People changing overnight, becoming someone else while looking the same." His eyes flicked meaningfully to the space around Christopher's shoulders, where I occasionally glimpsed that smoke-like distortion. "IGMC made deals with... something. Power and technology in exchange for who knows what."

My heart pounded in my chest as pieces began clicking into place. I glanced at Christopher, who was watching Dwight with an intensity that seemed to exceed simple interest in an old war story.

"The evacuation ships?" Dwight let out a humorless laugh. "Nightmares on wings, kid. Cobbled together from scavenged parts, each one a floating prison. IGMC shanghaied anyone who could pilot or maintain 'em, working them till they dropped. The rest of the crew were hand-picked killers who kept passengers in line through fear."

He rubbed absent-mindedly at a burn scar on his knuckles. "Ships exploded on launch. Life support failed. Folks suffocated, starved, or worse. And those were the lucky ones, the ones we found. Some ships just... vanished. Special vessels where IGMC conducted their most secret experiments."

"Like the Lachesis," I whispered, the name from Christopher's files suddenly gaining new weight.

Dwight's head snapped up. "You know about the Lachesis?"

"It's mentioned in Christopher's files," I said, choosing my words carefully. "He's looking for it."

An alert suddenly blared from my console and the medallion's energy signature had spiked dramatically, accessing a file labeled "Tymeragoth Containment Protocols."

Dwight was suddenly on his feet, moving with a speed surprising for his bulk. He grabbed my wrist, turning the console to face him. "What did you just do?" he demanded, his voice low and dangerous.

"I didn't do anything," I insisted, pulling away from his grip. "It's the medallion Christopher's using it to access restricted files. Look." I projected the data stream showing the medallion's energy signature interacting with the ship's systems.

Dwight's eyes widened, and he shot a look at Christopher, who remained impassive, watching our exchange with calculating eyes.

"The Lachesis was supposed to be the crown jewel of the evacuation fleet," Dwight said slowly, turning back to me. "State-of-the-art everything. They loaded it with the best and brightest scientists, engineers, doctors. People with the skills to build a new world." His voice dropped. "It disappeared without a trace. Some say it found a paradise. Others say it found something much darker."

"But you stayed with IGMC," I said, unable to keep the accusation from my voice. "Even after learning all this?"

"Power," Dwight said simply, meeting my gaze without flinching. "IGMC made me a special operator when I was twenty. Gave me authority, resources, respect. Things a dirt-poor kid from the outer rings never dreamed of having."

He gestured around us. "Sure, I knew by then what they really were. But mankind survived under their rule, didn't it? Thrived, even, in some places. The way I figured, we were all just playing the hand we were dealt. My survival depended on it."

I shook my head, struggling to reconcile the man before me with the story he was telling. "How could you live with that? Knowing what they did, what they were capable of?"

"It's like this, kid," Dwight said, his voice low and even. "Out here, suffering is a currency. You either cause it or you live it, but you don't get to escape it."

As his words hung in the air, my console pinged one final time Christopher had accessed a file titled "The Icarus: Vessel Recovery

Protocol." A shiver ran down my spine as I glimpsed the opening lines: "In the event of recapture, all crew members to be processed according to Avalonian compatibility standards. Previous subjects of interest include M. Rivera and progeny..."

The console suddenly went dark as Christopher deactivated the holographic display on the table. "I believe we've had enough history for one day," he said, his voice carrying a warning edge. "We'll be approaching Terax-3 soon. I suggest everyone prepare accordingly."

As the others dispersed, I remained seated, my mind reeling with revelations. The Lachesis, the references to "smoke" entities, the medallion's connection to ancient protocols, pieces of a puzzle I was only beginning to understand. And somehow, my father's medallion was at the center of it all.

A movement caught my eye Dwight, lingering in the doorway. "Be careful where you point that curiosity of yours, kid," he said quietly. "Some answers come with a price tag higher than you're willing to pay."

He disappeared into the corridor, leaving me alone with my thoughts and the growing certainty that whatever Christopher was hunting, it was far more dangerous than any of us had imagined.

~ 20 ~

DECISIONS THAT SHAPE WORLDS

I replayed the information Dwight had shared, trying to make sense of it all. It was too much to process IGMC, the evacuation ships, the "smoke" entities, and the Lachesis. But I couldn't shake the feeling that the medallion was the key to understanding everything.

My wrist console lit up with an incoming data packet. I'd set it to monitor the ship's systems after detecting Christopher's unauthorized access during our meeting in the galley. It showed something new, a series of heavily encrypted communications between the Charon and an unknown external source.

"Iris," I called softly, not wanting my voice to carry beyond the engine room. "Can you identify the transmission source?"

"Analysis complete," Iris replied, her voice equally hushed. "Transmission origin classified. However, signal characteristics match known HexiCore communication protocols."

HexiCore is IGMC's direct competitor in the interstellar mining sector. It would have complicated our precarious situation if Christopher had communicated with them.

"Can you trace internal communications as well?" I asked, an idea forming.

"Affirmative, though Captain Christopher's privacy protocols limit access to certain areas of the ship."

I hesitated briefly after learning about IGMC and the evacuation ships, after seeing Christopher use my medallion to access encrypted files about "Avalonian compatibility standards," whatever that meant; my trust in him had evaporated completely.

"I need to know what he's planning, Iris," I said, making my decision. "Can you help me monitor communication between Christopher and Dwight without triggering security alerts?"

The AI was silent for a moment. "I can create a temporary surveillance loop using maintenance protocols," she offered. "This would not violate my primary directives as it falls under ship safety monitoring."

"Do it," I said, surprised at the determination in my voice.

My console pinged softly. "Christopher and Dwight are in the galley," Iris informed me. "Their conversation may be of interest given your recent queries."

I set up the feed, adjusting the audio levels to filter out the background noise of the ship's systems. The sound quality was poor initially, with occasional static interference, but I could make out both voices well enough to follow their conversation.

"You getting up, Boss, or should I return when you're finished napping?" I heard Dwight say, his voice carrying across the connection.

"What does he know?" Christopher asked, his tone alert despite the casual posture Dwight had described.

I leaned closer to the console, my heart racing. They were talking about me.

Dwight inhaled deeply before responding. "He found a video of Lena. And you made a guest appearance."

"Did he see you?" Christopher's voice lacked the air of concern I'd expect from the revelation.

"Nah, you know I was never one for the big screen," Dwight responded, equally casual.

It sounded like Christopher let out a small sigh. "So, the cat's out of the bag. A bit sooner than I'd hoped that will change things." He seemed to be pondering the implications.

"What's our move now?" Dwight asked. "The kid's not stupid. He will tell her, or worse, confront you again."

Christopher chuckled. "Confront me? Like he did about his 'daddy's medallion'?" he said mockingly. "Oh, Dwight, you give him too much credit. Burton is smart but predictable. He'll go to Lena to tell her about the video. He'll want to protect her. He'll probably convince her to play along. Form a plan. By the time he 'confronts' me, we'll have already found the Lachesis and both he and Lena will be too entangled in their predicaments to pose any real threat. It's all about timing; fortunately, I have much of that."

My stomach churned as I listened. Christopher had been three steps ahead of me, anticipating my every move.

"You think so?" Dwight questioned. "He seemed pretty determined when he found that video."

The sound of Christopher's arm making a soft, almost imperceptible whir came through the audio feed. "Trust me, Dwight, I know how to play this game, I've been playing it for longer than you could imagine. Burton may have some technical know-how, but his emotions drive him. It's precisely what makes him so predictable. He's not ready for the big leagues like you and me."

There was a small silence before Dwight said, disgusted, "Yeah, just like you and me."

My fingers moved across the console, saving this conversation to a secure partition. Whatever was happening between Christopher and Dwight, I needed evidence.

"Let him show his cards first," Christopher said, still with mirth. "He doesn't understand the full picture. If you are so concerned, join their conspiracy against me. At least then we'll know what they're up to."

The audio feed crackled, a burst of static almost drowning out the next exchange.

"Let go of my shoulder," were the next words I heard Dwight say. "Don't mistake our association for friendship, Christopher. You and I, we're... conveniences to each other."

"Ah, such harsh words, Dwight. After all we've been through?" Christopher's voice had a hint of mockery as if enjoying the turmoil he was causing. "Let's be honest. We are both involved in this, balancing the fine line between control and chaos. Or what is that you tell everyone, 'Choosing between big decisions that shape worlds and the little ones that shape us.'" He lowered his voice, trying to imitate Dwight.

"Indeed, we are making big decisions for worlds," Dwight said, his voice cold. "But I've seen what you're capable of. I've seen the lengths you'll go to get what you want. And I question if my decisions are still for the greater good or just for you."

I felt a chill run through me. Whatever alliance existed between Christopher and Dwight, it was strained. I could use that.

Christopher's laugh was hollow, almost mechanical. "After all this time, you still cling to that self-righteous narrative. That you did it all for some greater good?"

"You know I believed in the cause," Dwight insisted. "Exposing IGMC's experiments, freeing those children"

"Oh, please," Christopher interrupted. "Does it matter what stories you tell yourself? These are still decisions you made. Who arranged the facility transfer papers that moved Lena and Harvey from the mining operation to the experimental wing? Who falsified the transport manifests to ensure they would be shipped back together after completing the tests? Who disabled the security protocols that would have locked down the facility when the first alarm sounded?"

I froze, my blood turning to ice in my veins. Dwight had been involved in Lena's past. In the experiments she'd described.

The audio feed crackled as Dwight shifted in his seat. I could almost picture him squirming under Christopher's gaze.

"Who unleashed Harvey on that shuttle?" Christopher continued, his voice rising. "Who helped strengthen Lena's neural connection to Harvey, allowing her full combat control of a mining robot never designed for such purposes? Who stood by and watched as that child, the same child you claimed to be saving, slaughtered the brave soldiers who served with you? Your own 'comrades-in-arms' who lost their lives to your decision."

My hand flew to my mouth to stifle a gasp. The implications were staggering. Dwight hadn't just known about Lena's past; he'd actively participated in creating it.

"It was supposed to be clean," Dwight said, his voice barely audible. "You promised me no one would get hurt. Just get her out, get the data, expose the program."

"Yet you didn't stop when the killing started, did you?" Christopher pressed. "When that first guard recognized you, called you by name, begged for his life... what did you do?"

"It was your plan!" Dwight spat the words out as if they had soured on his tongue. "You orchestrated everything! You knew exactly what would happen!"

"That it was," Christopher acknowledged with chilling calm. "But you executed it. You were the decorated IGMC officer with access to security codes, transport schedules, and facility layouts. With your knowledge of which guards would be on duty, you might hesitate to fire on a child. You, who spent months cultivating the perfect cover story about inspecting mining equipment. You and your arrogant ambition to change the universe and right the wrongs of the IGMC."

My mind raced to process this revelation. Dwight had been inside IGMC, working with Christopher to free Lena and Harvey from the experimental facility. But why? What had they wanted from her?

"I genuinely wanted to help those children," Dwight protested. "To expose what was happening in those facilities. The experiments, the countless deaths"

"Yet you saved only one," Christopher cut in. "Only the one I specifically identified. Only Lena. Tell mc, Dwight, why not set all the children free if your motives were so pure? Why not blow the whistle on the entire operation instead of staging a bloody escape that left dozens dead and one traumatized child whose connection to a mining robot you deliberately enhanced for maximum lethality?"

"There wasn't time," Dwight insisted. "The facility was going into lockdown. They were already suspicious of outside interference. Lena was the only one with the strongest response to the tests. You said she was the key, that saving her would..."

"Would what?" Christopher mocked. "End IGMC's experiments? Bring down the corporation? Change the course of human history? Did any of that happen, Dwight? Or did you simply become complicit in transforming one small girl with an already exceptional neural interface ability into a weapon, setting her on a path of violence and isolation that continues to this day?"

I checked the recording status on my console, it was still active and capturing every damning word. Lena needed to hear this, but I needed to know more.

"No, no. It wasn't... I wasn't alone in this. We were a team." Dwight retorted.

"Teams are nothing more than mirages. People work together for their selfish motives under the guise of a common goal. Just like we did. You wanted to have power and control over IGMC. You saw this as a way to the top. You had your delusions of grandeur."

I could hear Dwight start to say something before Christopher abruptly cut him off. "We all want the same thing...power. We want to be chosen, even though there is no one to pick us; We chase the notion of greatness, but we can never truly catch it. Because, in this cesspool of a universe, there is no grand design, no predestined paths... only the ruthless, the merciless survive; those willing to dig their hands into the filth and pull themselves up, step by step, on the corpses of the others. And you and I, Dwight, we are the embodiment of that merciless drive. You may have initiated Lena into this world of brutality, but I... I sculpted her...our destiny."

The audio feed went silent momentarily, then crackled back to life. I could hear the soft whir of Christopher's arm again; it seemed closer to Dwight than it had been the first time I heard it.

Dwight finally choked out words stripped of their previous righteous indignation. "You're wrong...it doesn't have to be this way."

"Denial is a comfortable haven, isn't it, Dwight?" Christopher's voice echoed. "A refuge for those too weak to accept the realities of the cosmos. Our destinies are forged in blood and shadows, not in righteous paths illuminated with fairy tale lights," he said, again the whir of his arm seeming to get louder. "You see, in the end, no matter the options. We will always choose survival, Dwight. Survival at any cost."

"We can make a different choice," Dwight said, pleading in his tone.

"The die has been cast," Christopher said smugly. "We chose to change worlds, not change ourselves. We can't go back from those decisions now." He paused, and I heard something being placed on the table. "Speaking of decisions, I've been planning our next move. There's a research facility I need to visit, the one where we found Lena."

There was a moment of silence before Dwight responded, his voice tight with tension. "That place is still under quarantine. After we got Lena out, I called in an aerial strike, falsified reports about a contagion outbreak. No one's been back since."

"Precisely why it's perfect," Christopher replied smoothly. "All that research data is just waiting to be retrieved. Records of the experiments, the neural interface technology, exactly what we need."

"You're insane," Dwight said flatly. "I bombed that place. Made sure IGMC would never go back. The official records say everyone died in the outbreak."

Christopher chuckled. "And you believe your lies? IGMC abandons nothing of value, Dwight. They simply... relocate. Deep underground, perhaps. Protected from your little fireworks display."

"Even if something survived, it's been decades," Dwight argued. "Who knows what's down there now?"

"That's what makes it so exciting," Christopher replied. "Besides, aren't you curious to see where it all began? Where Lena became...who she is today? I know I am."

"Burton," Iris's voice interrupted urgently, "Captain Christopher has activated a privacy protocol. I can no longer maintain the audio feed."

I sat back, my mind reeling from everything I'd heard. Christopher was planning to take us to the very facility where Lena had been experimented on, a place Dwight had bombed and quarantined, apparently leaving people behind to suffer whatever contamination he'd invented. The pieces were falling into place, but the picture they formed was more disturbing than I could have imagined.

My hands shook as I created a copy of the recorded conversation and stored it in my personal data cache. Lena needed to know the truth about Dwight, about Christopher's plans, about the facility they were taking us to.

I transferred the data to a clean storage device, ensuring no trace remained in the main system that Christopher could detect. Then I disconnected from the surveillance network, careful to cover my tracks. Standing, I felt a phantom weight against my chest where my medallion used to be, a constant reminder of what Christopher had taken from me.

The decision before me was clear: I needed to warn Lena about Christopher's plans and Dwight's involvement in her past. But I also needed to be strategic. Christopher had predicted I would go to her and that we would "form a plan." If I were going to protect her, I needed to be unpredictable to protect both of us.

I tucked the storage device into my pocket and headed for the door. The weight of what I'd learned pressed down on me like the gravity of a gas giant, but my resolve had never been stronger. It was time to show Lena the truth, no matter how painful.

~ 21 ~

DIGGING UP GHOSTS

I stood outside Lena's quarters, my hand hovering over the door panel. The weight of what I'd just learned pressed down on me like the gravity of a gas giant. Christopher and Dwight weren't just random actors in this cosmic drama. They were the architects of Lena's suffering, the hands that had shaped her trauma. And now I had to tell her.

"Burton," Iris's voice came softly through my earpiece. "Your vital signs indicate elevated stress. Would you like me to adjust environmental parameters in your quarters to facilitate relaxation when you return?"

"Not now, Iris," I muttered. "I've got to do this first."

I took a deep breath and pressed the panel. The door slid open to reveal Lena sitting cross-legged on her bunk, cleaning her plasma rifle with practiced precision. Harvey stood in the corner, its crudely drawn face somehow managing to look suspicious as I entered.

"Dwight was just here," she said without looking up. "Said you might be coming by with something important." Her hands never stopped moving over the weapon, checking each component meticulously.

I leaned against the wall, keeping some distance between us. "Yeah, I... I found something, Lena. In Christopher's files."

Now she looked up, her eyes sharp. "What kind of something?"

"Another video," I said, observing her expression, "of you. As a child."

Her hands were still. For a moment, the only sound in the room was the soft hum of Harvey's servos as he shifted position.

"Show me," she demanded, setting the rifle aside.

I pulled the video on my wrist console and handed it to her. As she watched, I described what I'd seen in full detail: the smoke, Christopher, and the man who looked too much like the description of Dr. Terrance Alexander to be a coincidence.

She stood up from her bunk. Gripping her plasma rifle till her knuckles turned white. "I'll kill them both." The blue light from her shunt illuminated.

"Wait, hear me out," I shouted nervously.

"What more is there to say?" Lena stood, Harvey pushed me aside, leading the way. They headed out her door and into the corridor.

Harvey's expression turned menacing under the corridor's orange light. She nodded to it, her shunt glowing. They both took off in a march toward the shuttle bay ladder well. They planned to storm straight down the catwalk to the bridge.

I tried to get in front of them. "If we kill them now, we won't determine what Christopher is up to." Lena wasn't listening, and Harvey's bulk could not be overcome in the narrow passageways.

"Iris," I whispered urgently into my communicator as I hurried after them. "Can you warn us if Christopher activates any defensive systems?"

"I will monitor all ship systems, Burton," Iris replied through my earpiece. "However, I must caution that Captain Christopher maintains override protocols that could limit my effectiveness."

"Just do what you can," I muttered, climbing the ladder after Lena and Harvey.

They got into the ladder well heading up to the shuttle bay. Harvey was now in front, and Lena trudged up the rungs behind it. I pleaded to no avail from the rear.

"Think about the medallion," I called up to her. “Christopher took my father's medallion, which is connected to all of this, to the smoke, to the Lachesis. If we kill them now, we may never understand what it means."

Exiting into the shuttle bay, Harvey immediately took up a defensive posture, allowing Lena and me to exit, its sensors scanning for threats.

"Lena," I said forcefully, grabbing her arm and spinning her around toward me. Her rifle immediately lifted cold against my nose. In the same instant, Harvey had lifted me by my collarbone. "I just think we should think about this." I winced out.

She lowered her rifle, and Harvey pushed me to the ground. "What is there to think about?" she said in a firm whisper. "I've been running from the IGMC my entire life. Hiding and scrounging to survive, Christopher put me there. Harvey and I missed two when I was a girl, and it's time to settle the books."

"But what about the smoke, my father's medallion? We need to find out what they mean."

"No, you need to find out what they mean," she said, emphasizing you. "I didn't grow up with the luxury of curiosity, Velvet. I don't care what they mean; I only care about what IGMC did to me. To my mother."

I take a deep breath, trying to steady the tremor in my voice. "Lena, that might be true. But don't you see? If we storm in, guns blazing now, we could be walking right into Christopher's trap. He's expecting you to react, not think."

She charged her plasma rifle, "I'm thinking just fine. I can't just stand back and do nothing while he's in there, pulling strings. He's manipulated every part of my life. Even if it is a trap, it will be the last one he sets."

My mind raced, trying to find a way to reach her through her rage. "What if this is what he wants? What if he's counting on you charging in there, ruled by emotion? Christopher's been steps ahead of us this entire time. We need to be smarter."

Something in my words seemed to penetrate. Lena's grip on her rifle loosened slightly.

"Five minutes," she finally conceded. "We go in with a plan, or I go in shooting. Your choice."

"Thank you," I breathed, relief washing over me.

"Burton," Iris's voice came through my earpiece, "I've detected unusual energy signatures emanating from the bridge. The patterns match those associated with the medallion, but at significantly higher intensity."

My blood ran cold. "The medallion? What's he doing with it?"

"Insufficient data for conclusive analysis," Iris replied. "However, spectral readings suggest interactions with the black ore acquired on Terax-3."

"The black ore?" I whispered, remembering the strange pulsing material Christopher had been so eager to obtain. "What's the connection?"

"I can only speculate based on fragmentary data," Iris replied, hesitating. "The medallion's energy signature resembles the radiation pattern I've detected from the ore. According to the limited records I've accessed, Dr. Alexander theorized that certain mineral compositions might resonate with what he termed 'extradimensional frequencies.'"

I relayed this information to Lena, whose expression hardened further.

"So, he's got your medallion and some weird rock that glows the same way," she summarized bluntly. "All the more reason to end this now."

She angrily marched down the catwalk, keeping low and using Harvey as cover. I followed close behind, my heart hammering in my chest. The proximity sensor announced our arrival as the doors slid open. Dwight sat at tactical, lounging casually with his feet perched on the weapons array. Christopher stood leaning over the navigation table; the ore he acquired on Terax-3 was next to him.

As we entered, neither of them acknowledged us. "That took longer than I expected," Christopher spoke without glancing up from his navigation task. "I expected you some time ago. Burton must have been long-winded in telling you what he heard."

Lena aimed her plasma rifle at Christopher. The look on her face was unreadable. She moved to stand across the navigation table from him. He did not acknowledge her, but Dwight had become interested from where he sat. Dwight didn't reach for his plasma pistol, which was holstered on his hip.

"Just in time," Christopher looked up at her slowly. "The whole family's here and I didn't even have to call."

"In time for what?" Lena demanded her voice sternly.

"We're here," Christopher said, smiling, looking up coldly into her eyes. "Put that thing down," he said, pointing at the plasma rifle. "If you were planning to kill me, you'd have begun firing when the door opened. Your hesitation tells me our Velvet friend, Burton, has gotten to you with some emotional plea." He smirked sourly.

My eyes fell to the medallion hanging around his neck. It seemed to pulse with an inner light, resonating with the black ore on the navigation table. Around Christopher's shoulders, the smoke-like distortion I'd grown accustomed to seeing seemed more agitated than usual, swirling and coalescing in patterns that made my head hurt to look at.

"Where are we?" Lena asked tersely, looking at the map projected on the navigation display. "I don't recognize this system."

"IGMC Research," Christopher said, standing and moving around the navigation table. Lena's rifle was still trained on him.

"Why are we here? Are you planning to turn me and Harvey in?" She spat in disgust.

Christopher only smiled that sickening, predatory smile. "Oh no, Lena. This facility has been shut down for some time. At least since you and Harvey escaped."

She lowered her weapon just slightly, taken aback by returning to the place of her forgotten childhood. "What are we doing here?" She immediately retrained her rifle on him.

"I'm sure Burton has already regaled you with tales of our valiant efforts to liberate you from this wretched place," Christopher said with a grin. "Had it not been for us, you might have died in this place."

Lena's eyes narrowed, and her grip on the rifle tightened. "Save it, Christopher. We both know you wouldn't lift a finger unless something were in it for you."

"Be that as it may, Dwight and I saved you," Christopher said with his hands up, showing artificial humility. "However, in getting you out, we had to leave behind valuable information about the experiments they were running. Information about your past."

I couldn't read Lena's face. Dwight stood some time ago and took a position next to Harvey. His gaze had also been focused on Christopher. I didn't know when he removed his plasma pistol from its holster. It was no longer visible.

"Don't you want to know why you've been running all these years?" Christopher continued in a disingenuous emotional plea.

Lena's expression is a mask of conflicted emotions, mirroring the chaos probably swirling inside her. Her voice is steady, though, spiked with an edge when she replies. "Knowing why doesn't change that we've been running, Christopher. Info or no info."

Christopher chuckles darkly, "We cannot change our past, this is true. But we can choose our future."

While they spoke, I edged closer to the navigation console to get a better look at the ore. It pulsed with an eerie rhythm that matched the medallion's glow.

"Iris," I whispered into my communicator, "what's happening with the medallion and that ore?"

"The energy signatures are synchronizing," Iris replied softly. "The medallion appears to be acting as a resonance key, activating something within the ore. Caution is advised, Burton."

Lena and Christopher stood in a standoff, their unyielding gazes matching each other's. I wasn't sure why, but she lowered her rifle. The blue light of her shunt illuminated, and Harvey stood down. Dwight holstered his plasma pistol, which had been concealed behind his back, and stepped forward from behind Harvey.

"Well," Dwight said, "if we're digging up ghosts, might as well do it together." He flashed a grin that didn't quite reach his eyes but did its job of cutting through the tension. "Burton." He turned to me. "Let's get the shuttle ready to head down. These two should be okay, for now."

I wanted to stay. To keep an eye on Christopher and Lena. But something in Dwight's tone suggested his request was not an option. I walked toward the bridge doors, watching Lena, who was still watching Christopher. Pausing, I felt a gentle nudge in my lower back from Dwight's hand. He shoved me forward, and we headed down the catwalk.

"You think it's wise to leave those two alone?" I asked Dwight as we descended to the shuttle bay.

"Trust me, kid," Dwight replied, uncharacteristically somber. "If Lena wanted Christopher dead, he'd be dead already. Something's holding her back."

"Maybe she wants answers more than revenge," I suggested.

Dwight gave me a sideways glance. "Or maybe she knows we can't afford to lose what's in Christopher's head. Not yet anyway."

As we reached the shuttle, I noticed Dwight checking the status of the weapons systems with surprising thoroughness.

"Expecting trouble?" I asked.

Dwight's expression darkened. "Kid, there's something you should know about this planet. After we got Lena out, I arranged for a little insurance policy. Called an aerial strike, falsified some reports about a contagion outbreak. The whole planet's been under quarantine ever since."

I stared at him in shock. "You bombed a research facility? With people still inside?"

"It was supposed to be a targeted strike," Dwight said defensively. "Just enough to destroy the evidence and make IGMC abandon the place. But something went wrong. The higher-ups decided a full quarantine was safer than sending people to investigate." He paused to examine a plasma charge pack. "Eventually, they wrote the whole place off. But rumors started filtering back through black market channels. People left behind both experiments and experimenters. They formed communities. Survived."

"And we're just going to stroll in there?" I asked incredulously.

"That's the plan," Dwight confirmed grimly. "But we'll be ready."

"Iris," I whispered as soon as Dwight moved to the pilot's seat, "Did you hear all that?"

"Affirmative, Burton," Iris replied in my earpiece. "I have scanned historical quarantine records. The planet was placed under Class-5 biological containment protocols approximately sixteen years ago following reports of an engineered pathogen outbreak. All personnel were presumed deceased."

"But people survived," I murmured.

"Evidently," Iris confirmed. "I am detecting scattered heat signatures on the planet's surface consistent with human settlements. However, they appear concentrated away from our landing coordinates."

The shuttle doors hissed open, and Christopher and Lena entered. The tension between them was palpable, like a static charge about to spark. Christopher still wore my father's medallion, which continued to pulse with that strange inner light. Lena's hand never strayed far from her plasma rifle.

"Are we ready to depart?" Christopher asked briskly.

"Just waiting on you two," Dwight replied, initiating the launch sequence.

As the shuttle lifted off, I couldn't help but notice how Christopher seemed to cradle the black ore, now stored in a small containment box. His cybernetic fingers tapped an irregular rhythm on its surface, and the smoke around his shoulders seemed to respond, reaching tendrils toward the box before retracting.

"Burton," Iris's voice came through my earpiece, "I've conducted preliminary analysis of the black ore's composition based on sensor readings. The mineral appears to possess unusual quantum properties, though its exact nature remains unclear."

"What's Christopher planning to do with it?" I whispered.

"I cannot determine with certainty," Iris replied. "However, I've observed that both objects exhibit synchronized energy fluctuations when close to your medallion. Most peculiar is that the smoke-like distortion surrounding Captain Christopher seems to react to the ore's presence."

I watched Christopher intently during our descent, noting how he positioned himself away from the others, occasionally muttering to the containment box as if engaged in conversation. Whatever he was planning, it wasn't just about retrieving research data. He seemed to need something or someone on this planet.

I watched out of the viewport as the shuttle descended. The planet's surface was covered with bright-colored flora, rich greens, yellows, and reds. Vines thicker than my arms twist through the cracks in the aged duracrete, and moss blankets every surface with a lush green that felt almost defiant. Dwight had made a joke about nature having a way of telling us we're not welcome. I don't know if humanity was ever welcome, but if we were, the planet has done a great job revoking our membership.

"Iris," I whispered, keeping my voice low, "anything I should know about this place? Any signs of those survivors Dwight mentioned?"

"I am detecting no immediate human presence in our landing zone," Iris replied. "However, unusual movement patterns in the vegetation suggest possible observation. Exercise caution, Burton."

The vegetation made spires in the sky, towering over the facility, only providing a fractional view of where it had once been. The shuttle banked gently, maneuvering around the plant life to land on what might have been the top of the facility.

The shuttle door hissed open, and Christopher was the first to step out with a confident swagger. Lena bounded after him, gripping her plasma rifle tightly. Harvey brought up the rear, scanning the surrounding plant life for potential threats. Dwight followed behind, carrying a plasma rifle from the armory and his trusty plasma blaster on his hip. I stayed behind to activate the shuttle's autopilot system before joining the others outside. We watched as the shuttle lifted off and began its slow orbit around the complex.

"Why'd you do that, kid?" Dwight asked.

"Take a look at the vegetation," I pointed to some yellowed vines on the roof's edge. “Ever since our arrival, they have been creeping closer to us. We couldn't afford to let them engulf the shuttle, or we would have been stranded here," I responded.

"Good thinking, kid." Dwight shot me a smile. I still wasn't sure if he was to be trusted.

"Iris," I whispered, "I don't trust Christopher. He's planning something with that ore and my medallion. Can you maintain contact while we're inside?"

"I will attempt to maintain our connection," Iris confirmed. "However, the facility's structure may interfere with our communications. I will continue scanning for anomalous energy signatures related to the medallion or the ore."

The party advanced cautiously, making our way into the structure. "How many derelict research centers does IGMC have?" I asked with a half-serious chuckle.

"Almost as many as they've pillaged planets," Lena spat. "The IGMC doesn't give a damn about societal or ethical standards. Setting up laboratories and mines where the most horrific deeds are committed, only to evade the consequences and disappear into the void unscathed."

Christopher sneered at her, "It's the nature of progress, Lena. Some sacrifices are necessary for the greater good."

She stared at him with murderous intent before she caught me watching her. She adjusted her grip on her rifle and continued to follow him in.

The facility's hallways were long and overgrown with nature. A placard laser etched into the wall read, "IGMC Neural Research Facility: Embrace the Future." The sign was perched next to a massive metal door with another familiar IGMC insignia welded on it.

As they approached, Lena noticed the faint sound of machinery. This place wasn't entirely dead. Christopher motioned for me to come forward. A retina scanner was mounted to the right of the door.

"Can you open it?" Christopher asked in a whisper that seemed to defer to the place.

I removed the scanner face plate and connected the wires from my wrist console. I punched in a few commands, and the locking mechanism hummed briefly before a loud clank disturbed our anticipation and silence. The massive door slowly swung inward. We stepped inside and a putrid stench filled our lungs, suffocating us. The air was thick with the scent of decomposition and rotting vegetation. The walls were coated in slimy moss, and tiny tendrils reached toward us like fingers. We could see strange shapes moving within the clouds of spores that floated through the dim light, their intentions unknown.

"Iris," I whispered urgently, "something's not right here. These spores, do we need to worry about them?"

"Preliminary analysis suggests they are organic in nature," Iris replied, her voice barely audible through the static. "However, they do not match any known pathogenic profiles. Exercise caution nonetheless."

We tentatively walked down a hallway, our footsteps crunching dramatically beneath us, to a transport terminal.

Christopher turned to us, stopping in front of the transport. "Regrettably, we must abandon poor Harvey. The transport cannot accommodate its massive frame, and our business is on the lower levels. Lena, command your mechanical companion to stay put and keep watch."

Lena scowled at him, her shunt illuminating. "Fine, but if we're not up in an hour or you come back without Burton or me, Harvey has been told to tear your toy arm off and club you to death with it." She pushed past him and onto the transport. Dwight and I followed before Christopher climbed on.

I noticed Christopher clutching the containment box containing the ore closer to his chest as we descended. My father's medallion glowed with increasing intensity the deeper we went, as if responding to something below.

"What are you after, Christopher?" I asked quietly, keeping my voice below the whir of the transport mechanism.

He gave me a sideways glance, something like amusement flashing in his eyes. "History, Burton. Our history."

The safety cylinder wrapped the transport as the platform slowly descended into the facility. The cylinder had kept the vegetation off the transport, but as we passed levels, the infestation of the overgrowth was more than apparent.

"Iris," I whispered, "I'm losing you. If you can still hear me, track the medallion's energy signature. Whatever Christopher's plan, it involves my father's medallion and that ore."

The transport descended level after level, each darker and more overgrown than the last. Lena grew increasingly tense with each floor we passed, her knuckles whitening around her plasma rifle. At level six, she began murmuring under her breath, words I couldn't quite catch. By level ten, her breathing had become shallow and rapid.

"You, okay?" I whispered to her. She didn't respond, her eyes fixed on some distant point, perhaps a memory.

"She's revisiting old ghosts," Dwight said quietly to me. "This place... it leaves marks on you that never quite heal."

Level fifteen brought a tremor to Lena's hands. By twenty, small droplets of sweat beaded her forehead despite the chill in the air. Christopher watched her deterioration with clinical interest, something like satisfaction glinting in his eyes.

After passing more than thirty levels, the transport finally brought us to what I could only hope was the bottom. I questioned how deep into the planet we were. We stepped off the transport into a massive chamber. In the center, a circular area surrounded by workstations housed several medical dispensing units, devices designed to administer drugs with precision timing. Tubes and needles hung from the apparatus around a containment area for test subjects.

"The induction chamber," Christopher said casually, as if giving a museum tour. "Where were they prepared?"

I noticed Lena's eyes fixed on the injection mechanisms, her pupils dilated with what could only be remembered terror.

"Burton," Iris's voice crackled through my earpiece, barely audible. "Energy readings...increasing exponentially...medallion...activating something..."

We walked down a hallway leading off from the chamber. At the end of the hallway was a circular enclave with windows encircling us. Christopher taunted her as he said, "Welcome to your new home, Lena." Each window investigated a different observation room, designed in a hub-and-spoke pattern. Though they were all run-down, each room had its unique history.

"There's blood in this one," I whispered to Dwight, nudging him to get his attention.

Dwight gave a deferential nod before making his way to investigate another room.

Lena had been eerily silent since we entered the observation area. Her hands trembled violently, and a vein pulsed visibly at her temple. Her breathing came in short, ragged gasps that seemed to pain her physically. Cut off from her connection to Harvey down here, I couldn't help but wonder how desperately alone she must feel, surrounded by the physical manifestation of her nightmares.

I noticed her eyes darting from room to room, recognition dawning in painful waves. In one, a small cot with restraints. In another, monitoring equipment is still blinking despite decades of abandonment. A third contained what could only be described as a child-sized isolation chamber.

"This is where they kept me between tests," she whispered, her voice cracking like thin ice. "They'd leave us in darkness for days, then flood the rooms with light so bright it felt like your eyes were melting." Her jaw clenched. "Then the smoke would come."

I moved closer, cautiously announcing my approach. "Hey, Lena," I said, trying to get her attention. "You're safe now. We can leave anytime." I reached out, hoping to provide some form of connection and some anchor to the present.

She didn't seem to hear me. Her eyes had glazed over, seeing not the decaying rooms before us but memories playing out in vivid detail. Her breathing quickened further. A drop of blood appeared at her nostril.

"They held me down," she murmured, her voice suddenly childlike. "I screamed until my throat bled, but they just watched. Taking notes. Always taking notes."

The blue light of her shunt began to pulse erratically. Her plasma rifle lifted slowly, almost of its own accord.

"Lena," I said more urgently. "Lena, come back to us."

The rifle's power cell hummed as it charged. I stepped back, recognizing what was coming.

"They tore everything from me," she said, her voice suddenly clear and adult again, but filled with a cold fury that raised the hair on my arms. "My mother. My humanity. My life."

With a primal scream that echoed through the facility, Lena unleashed a barrage of plasma fire into the observation rooms. Shattered glass exploded outward as she spun, her eyes wild with decades of pent-up rage and trauma. With each pull of the trigger, her ferocity grew, tearing through furniture, equipment, and barriers. Nothing stood in her way as she sought vengeance for the life she'd had stolen from her.

Dwight and I took cover, but Christopher watched with an expression that could only be described as satisfied. The violent catharsis of Lena's outburst kept us from noticing the figure approaching from a darkened corridor, summoned by the noise.

As the dust began to settle, I realized Christopher was gone, and so was the containment box with the black ore. While Lena had been lost in her destructive catharsis, he'd slipped away, using her trauma as the perfect distraction. I could only assume this had been his plan.

"Lena!" I shouted above the crackle of still-burning plasma fires. "Christopher's gone! He played us!"

Before she could respond, a hollow, inhuman wail echoed through the corridors. From the shadows emerged a grotesque figure once human, now twisted by years of isolation and mutation. Its skin was mottled and stretched across an emaciated frame, with patches of fungal growth erupting from its shoulders and face. In one hand, it clutched a crude spear fashioned from medical equipment; in the other, it held what appeared to be a partially eaten human limb.

The creature's eyes were focused and predatory, revealing terrible intelligence. Crude symbols had been carved into its flesh, including IGMC serial numbers still visible beneath ritualistic scarification. Around its neck hung a jangling collection of what I realized with horror were identification badges, some still attached to desiccated flesh.

And behind it, more shapes moved in the darkness, drawn by the commotion of Lena's rampage. Dozens of them, each uniquely horrifying, former researchers and test subjects alike, now part of a savage collective that had survived for decades in this abandoned hell, sustaining themselves on whatever and whoever they could find.

~ 22 ~

THE ENTITY WITHIN

A hollow, inhuman wail echoed through the corridors before Lena could respond to my warning about Christopher's disappearance. From the shadows emerged a grotesque figure once human, now twisted by years of isolation and mutation. Its skin was mottled and stretched across an emaciated frame, with patches of fungal growth erupting from its shoulders and face. In one hand, it clutched a crude spear fashioned from medical equipment, and in the other, it clutched what appeared to be a partially eaten human limb.

Without hesitation, Dwight fired a clean shot directly between what remained of its eyes. The creature collapsed with a wet thud, but the damage was done as dozens more shapes emerged from the darkness, drawn by Lena's destructive rampage.

"Move!" Dwight shouted, backing away while maintaining a steady stream of plasma fire to keep the advancing horde at bay.

Lena had already switched to combat mode, her plasma rifle cutting wide arcs through the approaching figures. "Where's Christopher?" she yelled over the cacophony of screams and plasma discharge.

"He slipped away during your rampage," I shouted back, pointing down a darkened corridor opposite where we'd entered. "He has my medallion and the black ore!"

As the creatures drew closer, I noticed something I'd missed in my initial panic, faint but unmistakable tendrils of familiar smoke-like substance wisping from their eyes and mouths. It was the same distortion I'd seen around Christopher countless times, but twisted and unstable, as if the bond between host and parasite had gone horribly wrong.

"These aren't just cannibals," I realized aloud, dodging a rusty scalpel thrust at my face. "They're failed vessels...victims of Avalonian possession gone wrong!"

Dwight pushed me behind him as more figures scrambled toward us, their movements desperate and feral but distinctly human. Their emaciated bodies showed the toll of years surviving in isolation, muscles wasted but still dangerous in their desperation. "We've got to find Christopher before he does whatever he's planning!"

"What about Harvey?" I called Lena, suddenly remembering we'd left the robot at the transport when we'd descended to these lower levels.

"It can take care of itself," Lena shouted back, her shunt glowing blue as she tried to connect. "We need to get back to the upper levels!"

We retreated down the corridor I'd indicated, Lena taking point while Dwight covered our rear. The mutated creatures pursued relentlessly, their agonized howls echoing off the walls like tortured souls in a nightmare. As we ran, I couldn't shake the image of my medallion pulsing in unison with the black ore. Whatever Christopher was planning, I knew instinctively it involved both.

"Iris," I whispered into my communicator, hoping against hope for a response. "Can you hear me?"

To my surprise, her voice came through my earpiece, faint but discernible. "Signal... extremely weak... attempting to boost... using station relay systems."

"Can you detect the medallion?" I asked urgently as we ducked into a side passage to avoid a particularly dense cluster of pursuers.

"Affirmative... strong energy signature... three levels below your position... in what appears to be... central chamber."

"He's below us!" I shouted to the others. "Some kind of central chamber!"

Lena cursed, her head swiveling as she sought an alternate route. "The main transport is behind us, through those things. We need another way down!"

Dwight fired a concentrated burst that reduced the corridor behind us to molten slag, briefly sealing off our pursuers. "Won't hold them for long! These bastards always find a way through!"

As if summoned by his words, a section of wall beside us burst open, revealing a half-dozen mutated former researchers wielding makeshift weapons. One launched itself at me, its jaw unhinged to an impossible angle. I barely managed to duck, feeling its fetid breath on my neck as it sailed past.

Lena dispatched it with mechanical precision, then grabbed me by the collar. "Service shaft, there!" She pointed to a narrow opening in the floor, partially concealed by fallen debris. "It'll lead us down!"

Dwight nodded, pushing me toward it. "Go! I'll cover!"

I slid into the opening feet-first, finding handholds on a maintenance ladder that descended into darkness. Lena followed close behind, with Dwight backing in last, firing continuously until he was safely in the shaft. We descended rapidly, the sounds of pursuing mutants growing fainter above us.

"Iris, update on Christopher's position," I whispered as we descended.

"Energy signature... intensifying... medallion and ore appear to be... interacting. Detecting additional life signs in the chamber with Christopher."

"Life signs?" I asked, my hands slipping slightly on the metal rungs. "How many?"

"One additional human biosignature, though its readings are... unusual. The medallion and ore energy patterns are also fluctuating in a synchronized manner."

My blood ran cold. I'd seen what happened on the IGMC station and the footage of Lena as a child with the smoke. If Christopher had taken someone down there, it couldn't be for anything good. "We need to hurry."

We reached the bottom of the service shaft and emerged into a dimly lit corridor. The air here felt different, thicker, charged with an energy I couldn't name but somehow recognized. My skin prickled with goosebumps despite the muggy heat.

"Which way?" Dwight asked, checking his ammunition supply with practiced efficiency.

I closed my eyes, concentrating on the strange sensation pulsing through my body. Without the medallion's physical presence around my neck, I shouldn't have been able to feel its power, yet I did like a phantom connection that refused to be severed. I thought of my mother and how she'd always told me the medallion had been passed through our family for generations, starting with my great-great-grandmother.

"This way," I said with unexpected certainty, pointing left down the corridor. "I can feel it."

Lena and Dwight exchanged glances but followed without question as I led them through increasingly complex passages. The sensation grew stronger with each turn until I could almost see the path before me like a luminous thread.

"Wait," Lena hissed suddenly, stopping us with an outstretched hand. "Listen."

A low, rhythmic hum came from somewhere ahead, vibrating through the floor and walls. It pulsed perfectly synchronized with the phantom sensation I felt where my medallion should have been.

"He's activated something," I whispered, my mouth suddenly dry.

We moved forward more cautiously now, weapons at the ready. The corridor opened into a vast circular chamber dominated by a central platform. What we saw made us freeze in place.

Christopher stood over a metal examination table; one of the mutated facility survivors was strapped down securely. My medallion hung from Christopher's neck, pulsing with an eerie light that seemed to respond to the black ore he held in his cybernetic hand. His other hand gripped a plasma blade, its edge glowing white-hot as he carefully applied it to the surface of the ore.

"What the hell is he doing?" Lena whispered, her rifle raised but not firing.

As we watched in horrified fascination, the ore began to smoke, not the ordinary smoke of burning matter, but something alive and sentient. It swirled and coalesced, growing denser by the second, until it formed a shape almost like a humanoid figure hovering above the ore.

Then, with a gesture from Christopher, the smoke entity plunged into the mutant's body through its mouth, nose, and eyes. The creature's back arched in agony, its limbs straining against the restraints as the smoke disappeared inside it. For a moment, everything was still.

Christopher stepped back, a satisfied smile on his face. "Welcome back, old friend," he said softly.

The restraints snapped as the mutant sat up with unnatural grace. Its movements were fluid, controlled, nothing like the feral creature it had been moments before. It examined its hands with evident disgust, then looked up at Christopher.

"This vessel is... adequate," it said, its voice layered with harmonics that made my skin crawl. "Though barely functional for our purposes."

"Dwight," I whispered urgently. "What the hell are we seeing?"

"The hell if I know, kid," he replied, his voice tight with fear. "Christopher just released something from that ore."

Lena's shunt glowed brighter than usual; her eyes were wide with recognition. "This is what they were looking for in those experiments," she whispered. "This is what they were trying to bring through when I was a child."

The possessed mutant turned its head directly toward us, though we remained hidden in the shadows of the corridor entrance. "We have visitors," it said, its mouth forming a grotesque approximation of a smile. "Please, join us. We're just getting reacquainted."

Christopher's head snapped toward our position. "Burton," he called out, echoing in the chamber. "I knew you'd find your way here. Your connection to the medallion grows stronger by the day."

Dwight raised his weapon, but Lena placed a hand on his arm. "Wait," she whispered. "Let's see what they have to say. We need information."

Reluctantly, we stepped into the chamber, weapons ready but not firing. Christopher watched us with amusement, while the possessed mutant studied us with cold, analytical eyes.

"Who are you?" I demanded, directing my question to the creature.

The mutant tilted its head, a gesture too smooth to be human. "I have been called many names across many centuries, the Visionary. I was Titus Pearce, a trader of human cargo for a decade or so. I even had a stint in this facility as Dr. Terrance Alexander." It gestured to its current form. "And now, this thing I possess, formerly a hydroponics engineer named Peter Chan."

I stared in shock, the implications hitting me like a physical blow. "The Visionary? The captain of the Lachesis?"

"One of my more useful vessels," the entity confirmed. "Though somewhat resistant to my influence. The human form is... limiting."

"What are you?" Lena demanded, her rifle trained steadily on the entity.

"We are Avalonians," Christopher answered for his companion. "Beings from a dimension adjacent to yours, but incompatible with your physical laws. We require hosts to interact with your reality."

"Vessels," the entity in the mutant's body corrected. "Not hosts. The distinction...is important."

"You're parasites," Dwight spat. "Body-snatchers."

The entity laughed, a sound like glass breaking. "How simplistic. We are the next stage of evolution for both our species. We provide immortality, power, and knowledge beyond your comprehension. In return, we experience your reality through your limited senses."

"At the cost of our free will," Lena said, her voice hard.

"A small price for transcendence," the entity replied dismissively.

Christopher moved closer to the possessed mutant, the smoke-like distortion around him intensifying as he did so. "The Avalonians were not always as you see us," he explained, his tone almost educational. "We once had physical forms, in our home dimension."

"Until the Tymeragoth enslaved us," the entity continued, hatred evident in its voice despite the mutant's limited facial expressions. "Beings of pure energy who saw us as nothing but tools for their amusement and labor."

"The Tymeragoth?" I asked, trying to piece together this cosmic mythology.

The entity's eyes narrowed. "Our former masters. The ones your Sable Serpents worship as their divine protector."

"The uprising was inevitable," Christopher added, his eyes distant as if recalling events from long ago. "We had suffered under their yoke for millennia, forced to build their cities, fight their wars, please their bizarre appetites."

The entity in the mutant's body began to pace, its movements becoming more agitated. "The rebellion began in the mining colonies, where we extracted the materials the Tymeragoth used to torture us. We had nothing to lose."

"It was glorious," Christopher said, a sadistic smile spreading. "The first Tymeragoth to die screamed for days as we slowly dismembered it, cell by cell. We developed techniques to prolong their suffering, feeding their pain into their neural networks."

The entity nodded. "We turned their weapons against them, their cities into slaughterhouses. Rivers of their essence flowed through the streets as we hunted them down. The Flaying of the Central Nexus alone claimed ten thousand of their kind."

"But we discovered something terrible," Christopher continued, his voice dropping to a near whisper. "Without their technology, we were powerless. We had become dependent on the very tools of our oppression."

"So, we made a choice," the entity said. "We used their dimensional technology to transcend our physical forms, transforming ourselves into energy beings that could survive the collapse of our civilization. We encoded ourselves into the black ore, scattered it throughout the multiverse, and waited for suitable vessels."

"Human vessels," I said, the pieces finally clicking into place.

"Precisely," Christopher confirmed. "Your species proved remarkably compatible. Your neural pathways, while primitive, can be... adapted to our needs."

"And the medallion?" I asked, gesturing to the object hanging around Christopher's neck. "What does it have to do with all this?"

The entity's expression darkened. "During our uprising, we captured one of the Tymeragoth. Rather than destroy it, we imprisoned it, a victory trophy. The medallion is that prison."

"But how did it end up with my family?" I pressed, thinking of how my mother had told me it had been passed down through generations.

Christopher's eyes glinted with malice. "Meredith Rivera, your great-great-grandmother, stole it while escaping from the Icarus. She had no idea what was trapped inside. Even as she fled, carrying the medallion and her unborn child, she thought it was merely a data storage device, containing coordinates and plans she'd stolen from us."

I felt a chill run down my spine. "The Icarus? You know about it?"

Christopher nodded, a cold smile twisting his lips. "I am the captain of the Icarus."

"What?" The implications spiraled around my mind.

"The Charon is the Icarus," Christopher said, seeing the realization on my face. "Meredith Rivera led an uprising against me. She escaped with other refugees, including your ancestor. Eventually, they settled on your precious Neda, where I found you."

"Why else would I go to such trouble to recover you?" Christopher asked. "The ship recognizes your bloodline. Your connection to Meredith's genetic signature gives you unique access to systems even I cannot fully control."

"That's why you named me Burton," I realized. "To hide my identity from the ship's systems."

"Precisely," Christopher confirmed. "The ship has certain... safeguards built in by the rebels before we recaptured it. Safeguards keyed to Meredith's bloodline."

"Enough talk," the entity in the mutant's body interrupted. "The facility is becoming unstable. We need the data on the neural interfaces."

"What are you planning?" I demanded, stepping forward despite Dwight's restraining hand on my shoulder.

"To recover what was taken from us," the entity replied. "And to free more of our kind from their prisons."

"Using me somehow," I said, the realization settling like a weight in my stomach.

Christopher's smile was predatory. "Using you, the medallion, and the information in this facility. Together, they will lead us to what we seek."

"Like hell," Dwight growled, raising his plasma rifle and firing fluidly.

The shot caught Christopher off guard, striking him in the chest and sending him stumbling backward. The medallion flew from his neck, skidding across the floor toward me. Without hesitation, I dove for it.

The entity in the mutant's body moved inhumanly, attempting to intercept me. Lena fired a precise shot that took off its arm at the elbow, buying me precious seconds to reach the medallion.

My fingers closed around the familiar metal cylinder as the room shook violently. The dimensional disturbances from the black ore were destabilizing the facility's structure.

"We need to go!" Lena shouted over the growing rumble of collapsing corridors. "Now!"

I clutched the medallion tightly, feeling its familiar warmth spread through my palm. Christopher staggered to his feet; his eyes locked on me with murderous intent. The smoke around him writhed in agitation, reaching tendrils toward me and the medallion.

"This isn't over, Burton," he snarled, blood trickling from his mouth. "That medallion and what's inside it belong to us. And so does my ship."

"No," I replied, backing toward Lena and Dwight. "It stays with me. And the ship isn't yours anymore."

The entity that had possessed the mutant was struggling to stand, ichor leaking from its severed arm. "Kill them," it hissed to Christopher. "Take what is ours!"

Before Christopher could move, a massive section of the ceiling collapsed between us, cutting off his advance. Dwight grabbed my arm, dragging me toward the exit as Lena provided covering fire against the few mutants still pursuing us.

We fled the crumbling facility, retracing our steps to the service shaft. Above us, we could hear the upper levels collapsing, crushing anything or anyone still inside. The dimensional instability was spreading, causing sections of the walls to ripple and distort like liquid.

"We need to get to Harvey and the shuttle!" I gasped into my communicator. "Iris, emergency extraction! We need pickup at the upper-level access point!"

"Confirmed," came Iris's steady reply. "Shuttle en route. ETA three minutes."

"We may not have three minutes," Dwight muttered as a section of wall beside us disintegrated into dust.

We reached the service shaft and began climbing desperately, the ladder rungs bending and twisting beneath our weight as reality fluctuated around us. Above, I could hear the mutants still in pursuit, their howls now tinged with terror at the facility's imminent collapse.

"Is Christopher following us?" I called down to Lena, who was bringing up the rear.

"No sign of him," she replied, glancing below. "But don't count him out yet."

We emerged from the shaft into a corridor now barely recognizable, its architecture warped by the dimensional disturbances. Lena retook point, leading us through the shifting maze toward the access point where the shuttle would meet us.

I reminded them, "We need to get to the transport platform. "Harvey is still there!

Lena nodded, her shunt glowing as she tried reconnecting with the robot. "This way!"

We fought back to the main transport, dispatching several deranged mutants. To our relief, Harvey remained at its post, its sensors tracking our approach.

"Harvey!" Lena called, her shunt pulsing brightly. The robot turned toward her voice, its drawn-on face unchanging but somehow conveying recognition.

We reached the access point just as the shuttle arrived, its ramp lowering to meet us. Harvey moved to the entrance, using its mechanical body to shield us as we boarded. Dwight and I scrambled in after Lena, the shuttle lifting off as the last of us cleared the ramp.

Through the viewport, I watched the research facility implode, folding in on itself like paper crumpling into a tiny ball before vanishing with a final flash of dimensional energy.

"Do you see Christopher?" I asked, scanning the ruins for any sign of him.

"Negative," Iris responded. "No life signs detected in the immediate vicinity."

I slumped into a seat, exhaustion washing over me. The medallion felt heavy in my hand, warm with an energy I now understood came from the entity trapped within it, a Tymeragoth, enemy of the Avalonians. I couldn't help but wonder about Meredith Rivera and how her escape had led me to fight the same battle generations later.

"The Charon is the Icarus," I muttered, still trying to process the revelation. "All this time..."

"What does that mean for us?" Lena asked, her eyes sharp with interest.

"It means I might have more control over the ship than we thought," I replied, a plan beginning to form in my mind. "If what Christopher said is true, and the ship recognizes my bloodline through Meredith..."

"He's alive," Dwight said with certainty, staring at the collapsing facility. "And he'll come for the ship."

I nodded grimly. "Then we'd better be ready."

As the shuttle ascended toward the ship—no, the Icarus—I stared at the medallion, trying to comprehend everything I'd learned: the Avalonians and Tymeragoth, ancient enemies using humanity as pawns in their cosmic war; Christopher's quest to find more of his kind trapped in ore; my unwitting role in this drama, tied to Meredith Rivera through blood.

And most shocking of all, the revelation that I'd been aboard my ancestor's ship all along, the vessel from which Meredith had escaped generations ago.

"Iris," I whispered as we docked with the Icarus, "set course for the deepest part of space you can find. Somewhere, Christopher won't think to look for us."

"Course plotting in progress," she replied softly. "But I must inform you that Captain Christopher has automated return protocols built into the ship's systems. He will be able to track his vessel."

I clutched the medallion tighter. "If the ship truly recognizes my bloodline through Meredith, we may be able to override those protocols. There has to be a way to stop him permanently."

As I spoke, I felt the medallion pulse in response, a sense of agreement. The entity trapped within, the Tymeragoth, seemed to have its reasons for wanting to stop the Avalonians.

For now, that would have to be enough.

~ 23 ~

WHISPERS IN THE DARK

"We're coming in too fast! Christopher!" Lena's voice pierced through the chaos.

"It's going to hit! Hold on, kid!" Dwight yelled.

The shuttle's metal frame groaned under the strain as we plummeted toward the facility. I gripped my seat, knuckles white.

"Harvey! Move!" Lena shouted just before the impact.

An explosion rocked the shuttle, searing heat washing over us. Alarms blared, emergency lights flashing red in the smoke-filled cabin.

"He's not moving! I can't feel him!" Lena screamed, her shunt flickering erratically as she tried reconnecting with Harvey.

Blaster fire erupted around us as the creatures swarmed into the wrecked shuttle. Their inhuman howls mixed with the sound of Dwight's plasma rifle. Through the haze, I saw Christopher moving with unnatural speed, my father's medallion glowing brightly against his chest.

"He's taking the kid!" Dwight yelled, his voice strained as he fought off two creatures simultaneously.

"Harvey!" Lena's desperate cry echoed through the smoking wreckage. "I can't feel him!"

More blaster fire. Something is grabbing me, pulling me from the wreckage. The world was tilting as Christopher dragged me away from the others.

Falling.

Darkness.

***

Whistling. Someone is whistling. I blink my eyes open. The light burns, forcing my eyes shut again. I try again, slower this time, letting my vision adjust gradually.

Where am I? Did we crash? I try to sit up, but can't move. Why can't I move? Panic rises in my chest as I realize I'm completely immobilized, strapped to some chair or table. I can't even turn my head.

Something moves in my peripheral vision, a shadow shifting against the harsh light. I strain to see what it is, but it remains out of view.

"Burton...pss...Burton," a voice calls from the shadows. "Ah, there you are. I thought you'd be out forever, and I need you awake."

The voice moves, circling me. I'm propped at an angle, inclined slightly. Something cold touches my head, rolling smoothly from my right ear to my left.

"Can you feel that?" the voice asks. "Blink twice if you can."

I blink deliberately, twice. My mouth won't open, my vocal cords frozen. I realize with horror that I'm paralyzed but fully conscious.

"Excellent," the voice continues, still out of my sight. "It is important that you can feel what will happen next. Even if you can't do anything about it."

A laugh, almost a cackle, echoes through the room. Two fingers, index and middle, appear in my field of vision, holding something that makes my heart stop: my father's medallion, my medallion. The fingers are attached to a cybernetic hand, Christopher's hand.

I can't see his face, just the hand and the medallion. The light is too bright, casting harsh shadows that obscure everything else.

"Your 'Daddy's' precious medallion," Christopher's voice circles me again. "A generational bauble, with no meaning to the ones who wore it. But it has secrets. And so do I."

His voice drops to a whisper, his breath humid against my ear. "Your Uncle Joren had secrets, but no vision."

I feel myself reclining further, lying almost flat on my back now. My heart pounds so loudly I can hear it echoing in my ears. There's another sound from underneath the chair I'm strapped to, mechanical whirring and clicking.

"A common problem with all IGMC employees," Christopher continues. "All secrets. No vision."

IGMC? Uncle Joren was IGMC? The realization is interrupted by a cold sensation at the back of my neck. Something wet touches my skin, emitting a pungent chemical smell that makes my nostrils burn. The noise beneath me grows louder. Something is moving, coming up through the chair, touching my neck. It's small and pointed, pressing against my skin with increasing pressure.

And then I understand.

The chair. The CHeKeR device. Just like in the footage from the IGMC station. The same chair I'd glimpsed in the Charon's engine room. The same chair where Dr. Alexander had died, where the smoke had entered him as reality warped around them.

A metal probe is pressing against the base of my skull, preparing to bore into my spine, just like what happened to Terrance Alexander. I'm strapped in the chair, unable to move, unable to scream, unable to fight.

The medallion glows in Christopher's hand, pulsing with an inner light that seems to respond to the device. The smoke-like distortion I've always seen around him swirls more intensely now, tendrils reaching toward the medallion, intertwining with its glow.

"I know you recognize this device, Burton," Christopher says, finally stepping into my field of vision. His eyes are unnaturally bright, almost luminous in the shadows of his face. "Your ancestors discovered it, after all. Dr. Alexander and his team called it the CHeKeR device, Compressed Hyper-dimensional Kinetic Relocation. Such a bland name for something so revolutionary."

He moves to a console next to the chair, the medallion still clutched in his cybernetic hand. I notice now that we're in some laboratory deep within the IGMC facility, equipment salvaged and repurposed. The black ore from Terax-3 sits in an open containment box on the console, pulsing in rhythm with the medallion.

"It took me centuries to understand what they had created," Christopher continues, typing commands into the console. "A doorway between dimensions. Your ancestor Meredith thought she'd sealed it forever when she folded the Lachesis into four-dimensional space. But she didn't understand what she had in her possession."

He holds the medallion up, its glow casting eerie shadows across his face. "This isn't just a data storage device, Burton. It's a key. A dimensional key, as that serpent woman correctly identified. But it's also a container."

The probe presses harder against my neck, breaking the skin. I feel a trickle of warm blood running down my spine.

"Inside this medallion is a fragment of what your ancestors called a Tymeragoth, a sentient interdimensional entity. Not like the smoke you've seen around me, but something far more ancient. Dr. Alexander trapped it, using it to create the medallion. He didn't understand what he'd done either."

Christopher inserts the medallion into a slot on the console. The entire room seems to pulse with energy, the lights flickering.

"But thanks to Meredith's blood flowing in your veins, I can finally access what I need," he says, turning back to me. "Your genetic markers, combined with the Tymeragoth fragment and the CHeKeR device, will allow me to fold us back into that four-dimensional space. To find the Lachesis and reopen the doorway."

The probe pierces deeper, sending a jolt of excruciating pain through my body. The room warps around us, reality bending as the device activates.

"I've waited centuries for this moment," Christopher whispers, his voice seeming to come from everywhere at once. "To return home."

My vision blurs, consciousness fragmenting as the probe connects with my nervous system. Memories that aren't mine flood my mind: a woman on a ship, clutching a medallion to her pregnant belly, whispering promises to her unborn child. Meredith, my ancestor. Her terror as the boat folds around her, reality twisting as they escape through dimensional space.

I see Christopher too, but younger, his body fully human, his eyes filled with hunger as smoke pours into him, consuming his humanity piece by piece.

The medallion pulses brighter, and the black ore responds in kind. The Tymeragoth entity within the medallion is being forced to interact with the device and connect with my consciousness through the probe.

As darkness creeps in at the edges of my vision, I realize what's happening. Christopher is using me, using Meredith's genetic legacy within me, to access the coordinates of the Lachesis, to find the doorway she sealed, and to unleash more of his kind.

The room continues to warp, the beginning of a dimensional fold that will take us somewhere beyond normal space. To Yrilla, I somehow know a name without ever having heard it.

The last thing I see before consciousness slips away is the smoke pouring from Christopher, engulfing the room as reality itself begins to tear around us.

~ 24 ~

UNFOLDING SECRETS

"Kid. Hey kid. Wake up. Wake up."

"Leave him, Dwight. Christopher's getting away!"

"We leave him, we're stuck. Wherever the hell this is. Kid, I said wake up!"

I woke, gasping for air, the phantom sensation of the CHeKeR probe still burning at the base of my skull. My consciousness swam through layers of darkness, each more viscous than the last. Opening my eyes required monumental effort, as if my eyelids were sealed with industrial adhesive.

"I... I can't breathe," I managed between desperate gulps of air. The words felt alien in my mouth, like I'd forgotten how to form them. My thoughts were fragmented, and I couldn't piece together shards of memory and sensation. My last conscious memory had been of Christopher activating the dimensional fold, the coordinates to Yrilla extracted from me against my will.

Colors bled and swirled before finally resolving into shapes. Lena paced frantically at a doorway, her movements jerky and desperate. Dwight's weathered face hovered above me, his hand supporting my left arm as I struggled to rise. My body felt hollow and depleted, not just tired but fundamentally altered, as if something essential had been extracted from my core.

"Ha. See. I told you he was alive," Dwight called over his shoulder to Lena, who paused her pacing long enough to shoot him a withering glare.

Lena's knuckles were white around her plasma rifle, but what struck me more was her face, tear-streaked, eyes bloodshot. Something was profoundly wrong. "Good, the Velvet survived," she spat, voice cracking. "I don't intend for Christopher to."

"Don't mind her, kid. Christopher broke her toy robot." Dwight's dismissive tone belied the gravity in his eyes. "We have to get you on your feet. Can you hear me?" He snapped his fingers before my face, the sound strangely muffled, as if reaching me through water. When I didn't respond quickly enough, he delivered several sharp slaps that jolted me further into consciousness.

My hands flew up to fend off his assault. "I can hear you. Stop." The words scraped through my parched throat. "What's happening?"

"No time. Got to go!" Dwight tightened his grip and hauled me upright.

The ground beneath my feet shifted, unnaturally slippery yet gritty, like ice over sand. My legs trembled, barely supporting my weight as muscles recalibrated to three-dimensional space after being briefly stretched across multiple dimensions. Strange sensations crawled across my skin, phantom touches that weren't quite physical, like the aftereffects of electricity. Inside my mind, something felt...stretched. It expanded into spaces that hadn't existed before.

Seeing me upright, Lena abruptly stopped pacing and moved to lead the way down the corridor. She walked with the predatory focus of someone hunting, not escaping. Blood had dried in trails from her neural shunt, evidence of the strain placed on her connection during our violent arrival.

"What is this place?" I asked, still struggling to match their pace, each step uncertain beneath me. The walls around us seemed to pulse subtly, colors shifting in ways that shouldn't be possible. Was this real, or was I still partially elsewhere?

"We're in the bowels of the Charon," Lena threw over her shoulder without slowing, her voice brittle with rage and something more profound, grief. "The hidden part of the ship still had cryo tubes and Christopher's CHeKeR device. The same type of chair we saw at the IGMC Outpost."

My stomach lurched at the word "CHeKeR." Fragmented memories flashed through my mind: cold metal against my neck, a probing sensation at my skull's base, and my father's medallion glowing with unnatural light. I raised a trembling hand to the back of my neck, feeling the raised 'X'-shaped scar where the probe had entered differently from the clean surgical interface Christopher had.

"CHeKeR device? How"

Lena spun around; her face contorted with fury. "You!" she snarled, jabbing a finger at my chest. "You and your father's stupid medallion. You gave him everything he needed."

The accusation hit me like a physical blow. I blinked rapidly, trying to process her words through the fog still clouding my thoughts. My father's medallion seemed to pulse with phantom warmth against my chest despite no longer being there.

"Easy there, spitfire. The kid didn't know what he had." Dwight's defense of me was gruff but genuine.

Before I could respond, Lena turned sharply and swiftly ascended a ladder with jerky movements. Dwight urged me forward, maintaining his supportive grip as I climbed after her, each rung requiring focused concentration. My movements felt disconnected from my intentions, as if the signals between my brain and body were being intercepted and reinterpreted. My vision occasionally flickered with afterimages of higher dimensions I'd glimpsed while connected to the device.

We emerged onto the engineering deck, and frigid air assaulted us from the open engine room door. The corridor floor was dusted with snow, marked by a single set of boot prints leading outward.

The sight of winter inside the ship momentarily short-circuited my already struggling brain.

Lena released a guttural scream upon reaching the doorway, then pushed past us and bolted toward the galley. With Dwight's support no longer needed, I cautiously approached where Lena had been standing, bracing myself against the wall as occasional tremors passed through my limbs.

The engine room was gone. In its place, a massive hole where the plasma core from Terax-3 had been installed gaped. Beyond the breach, a ferocious snowstorm raged across an alien landscape. The jagged edges of metal around the hole were twisted outward, as if something had exploded from within rather than impacted from outside. According to Iris's damage logs visible on a nearby console, Christopher had forced a dimensional fold directly to Yrilla using the CHeKeR device, my unwilling connection to it, and the Tymeragoth entity trapped in my medallion.

"Where are we?" I whispered the question, intending more for myself than anyone else. Flashes of four-dimensional space flickered at the edges of my vision, geometries that shouldn't exist, perspectives impossible in our three-dimensional reality. Was I still hallucinating from whatever Christopher had done to me?

Outside the breach, Yrilla's landscape stretched in endless white, interrupted only by jagged black mountains in the distance, mountains I somehow recognized despite never having seen them before. The temperature readout showed dangerously low readings, cold enough to flash-freeze exposed flesh in seconds.

"Come on, kid," Dwight said, placing a steady hand on my shoulder. "Let's get you somewhere warmer before hypothermia finishes what Christopher started."

The galley felt uncomfortably small, and Lena's frantic energy filled it. She paced relentlessly, biting her thumbnail until blood beaded at the edges. Her other hand remained fixed on her plasma rifle, expecting Christopher to materialize. Every few seconds, her gaze darted to the empty doorway, and her hand would unconsciously rise to the shunt behind her ear, probing it as if testing a painful tooth.

Dwight gently guided me to a chair and fetched water, which I grasped with still trembling hands. The simple act of drinking felt newly complicated, my throat remembering how to swallow only after conscious effort. The silence stretched, broken only by Lena's footsteps and my ragged breathing.

"S-someone, please tell me what's going on?" I finally managed, my voice stronger but still carrying unfamiliar harmonics, as if multiple versions of me were speaking simultaneously.

Lena paused just long enough to roll her eyes before resuming her circuit.

Dwight sighed heavily, settling his bulk into a chair across from me. "Okay, kid, here's the short of it." He leaned forward, elbows on the table. "We're stranded on some ice planet. Ship's wrecked, engine's gone, and Christopher's in the wind with your fancy necklace."

"We're on Yrilla," Lena interjected sharply, halting her pacing momentarily.

"Yrilla?" I repeated the name, tickling something in my memory, but the connection remained frustratingly out of reach.

Dwight glanced at Lena, surprise crossing his features briefly. "That's what this frozen hellhole is called? How would you know that?"

"It was the last thing Burton said before passing out," Lena replied tersely. "When that thing was speaking through him. 'Coordinates accepted. Dimensional folding initiated. Preparing for transit to Yrilla, designation: New Earth." She mimicked the inhuman cadence my voice had taken.

Dwight shrugged. "Well, there you have it, kid. We're on Yrilla, the place Christopher's been hunting for all this time. Congrats, we made it to the promised land." His sarcasm couldn't mask his uneasiness.

Lena abruptly stopped pacing and leaned against the metal frame of the galley entryway, arms folded tightly across her chest. "We didn't just randomly crash here, Burton," she said, her voice cutting through the room's tension. "You jumped us here."

The accusation struck like a lightning bolt, shocking me into sudden alertness. "I did what?"

Lena pushed off the doorway and stepped closer, her eyes intense and searching my face as if looking for someone else behind my features. "The medallion you've been carrying around," she said, voice tight with barely controlled emotion, "wasn't just some keepsake. It contained the essence of a Tymeragoth entity and all the research on dimensional folding extracted from both Avalonians and Tymeragoth, decoded by Terrance Alexander himself. The entire blueprint for the CHeKeR device was hidden right there against your chest."

"Information that the IGMC believed had been lost a century ago," Dwight clarified, observing me.

My head spun with the implications, a nauseating vertigo that wasn't entirely physical. "So, this whole time, my family's been carrying around... what, exactly? Keys to some interstellar puzzle?" My voice rose in pitch, uncertainty threading through each word.

Lena's face softened slightly, a momentary crack in her armor of rage. "Not just any puzzle, Burton. A device that could potentially change the course of human history. Control over the CHeKeR means power over the folding of space and time. It's the sort of power Christopher would kill for."

A memory surfaced, Christopher's voice echoing in the dark corridors of the IGMC station: "History, Burton. Our history." I thought he meant the research data, but he meant something far more literal.

"But Dwight said I jumped us here. What does that even mean?" The room seemed to shimmer at the edges, afterimages trailing behind every movement.

"P-processing error. Re-re-recalibrating spatial coordinates," came a familiar but distorted voice from a nearby speaker panel. "B-Burton? Is that truly you? My sensors indicate severe d-damage to ship systems and-and your neural patterns show s-significant alteration."

"Iris?" I called out, relief washing through me at the sound of her voice, broken though it was. "Are you okay?"

"Define 'okay,'" she replied, her usually smooth tone fragmented and glitching. "Ship systems at 36.7% functionality. The main power grid is offline. Auxiliary power is fluctuating. I am experiencing discontinuities in my processing matrix that began when Christopher interfaced with my systems and overrode my security protocols. The crash has only worsened my condition."

"Yeah, kid," Dwight interjected, returning my attention to him. "That contraption Christopher's CHeKeR thing, not just anyone can handle it. That's what blew up the space station. The device only works with humans who have specific genetic markers." He tapped his temple. "You're a direct descendant of Meredith Rivera. Christopher knew your bloodline was the key all along. That's why he came to Neda for you and kept you alive all this time."

While in the CHeKeR device, I'd glimpsed fragments of Meredith Rivera's memories great-great-grandmother's experiences aboard the Lachesis. The realization landed with the numbing clarity of truth. I clutched at the space where my medallion should have been, feeling its absence like a physical wound. An undeniable conclusion settled in my consciousness: Christopher hadn't just abducted me for my engineering skills or the medallion. He'd been after what I could potentially do with it, what I was intrinsically capable of without even realizing it.

"I don't understand. How do you know all of this?" I needed something, anything, to ground me in this new reality.

Lena pulled a data pad with a cracked screen from her waistband and tossed it in my direction. Iris helped us get into the bridge computer after the ship crashed. Christopher's security protocols were damaged in the impact, giving her access to systems she couldn't reach before. She found recordings from all parts of the ship, even the parts we didn't know existed." Her voice cracked slightly. "It recorded everything. All of Christopher's files, too, his research, his communications, everything."

I caught the pad with hands that didn't feel like mine. Its solid, undeniable weight was an anchor in a sea of uncertainty.

"I think you should see what happened," Lena said, her voice suddenly hollow. "Maybe then you'll understand why we need to find him. Why, I need to find him."

"But how did he get me?" I asked, staring at the pad. "The last thing I remember, I was in the engine room trying to figure out why Iris was glitching. I still had my medallion then."

Dwight's face darkened. "That's the thing, kid. Christopher had been hiding in the ship's lower levels, parts we didn't even know existed. Those secret decks where he kept the original cryo tubes and that chair. He must have been watching, waiting for the right moment. He made his move when you were alone in the engine room."

"We didn't even know you were missing at first," Lena added, her voice tight with anger. "I was running diagnostics on the shuttle with Harvey, and Dwight checked the supplies. When Iris alerted us that something was wrong, Christopher had already strapped you into that chair."

"I've always suspected he had other ways on and off the ship we never knew about," Dwight said grimly. "Secret passages, maintenance tunnels, emergency escape routes. Whatever this ship is, the Charon or the Icarus, is older than any of us realized. Christopher's had centuries to modify it for his purposes."

"When we tried to confront him," Lena continued, her hand unconsciously moving to her shunt, "he was ready for us. That's when he used that EMP device on Harvey..." Her voice trailed off; pain was evident in every syllable.

I glanced toward the corner where Harvey stood motionless. Its optical sensors were dark, and its mechanical frame showed signs of stress fractures from the dimensional fold. The diagnostic panel next to it indicated that the dimensional transit had temporarily scrambled Harvey's neural matrix, explaining why Lena couldn't reestablish their technological link.

"See for yourself," Dwight said, nodding at the data pad. "It's all recorded."

The first image on the data pad nearly made me drop it on my face, contorted in an expression of terror I couldn't remember wearing. I was strapped to a chair identical to the one we'd seen at the IGMC station, the same type of chair where they'd experimented on the smoke entities. A mechanical probe extended from behind the headrest, positioned at the base of my skull.

Christopher stood beside me, rolling my father's medallion between the fingers of his cybernetic hand, the metal cylinder catching the light as he taunted me with it. The medallion pulsed with unnatural energy, and the smoke-like distortion I'd grown accustomed to seeing around him was more pronounced than ever, writhing with a strange eagerness.

My hand reflexively flew to the back of my neck, fingers probing for evidence. There was a raised scar shaped like an 'X' where smooth skin should have been. Touching it sent electric jolts down my spine, triggering a cascade of fragmented memories, pain, confusion, and the feeling of my consciousness being stretched beyond its natural dimensions.

With trembling fingers, I activated the playback.

"The medallion and the boy together," Christopher's voice came through the speakers, cold and methodical. "The key and the lock, just as the records indicated. A descendant of Meredith Rivera, carrying Terrance Alexander's stolen Tymeragoth. Perfect."

On screen, Christopher placed the medallion against my forehead. It adhered to my skin as if magnetized, glowing brighter. The smoke around his shoulders extended tendrils toward me, brushing against my face, probing at my eyes, ears, and nostrils, seeking entry.

"Now," Christopher commanded, activating the chair with precise commands.

The probe at the base of my skull engaged, piercing my skin. My body arched in the restraints; mouth open in a silent scream. The medallion's light intensified, becoming almost blinding.

Inside the light, something moved a geometric pattern impossible to describe in three-dimensional terms, shifting and transforming in ways that made my current self dizzy just watching. The smoke-like entity circled this pattern, occasionally reaching tendrils toward it only to withdraw as if burned.

"Yes," Christopher hissed. "It's working. The Tymeragoth essence is responding to his genetic signature. The dimensional gateway is opening."

My on-screen self began to speak, but not in my voice. The words came out distorted, layered with harmonics that hurt my ears even through the recording. My eyes had rolled back, showing only whites, yet tears of blood trickled down my cheeks.

"Coordinates accepted," the voice that wasn't mine said. "Dimensional folding initiated. Preparing for transit to Yrilla."

The viewing chamber filled with pulsing energy, momentarily washing out the camera feed. When it cleared, my body was floating several inches above the chair, the restraints still attached but no longer touching me. The medallion had partially embedded into my forehead, its outline visible beneath my skin.

Christopher watched with undisguised triumph. "After all these centuries," he whispered. "Home."

The feed cut to static briefly, then resumed from a different angle, a security camera outside the corridor. Christopher was dragging my semi-conscious form through the hallway when Lena and Dwight appeared, weapons raised.

"Stop right there, you son of a bitch!" Dwight's voice boomed through the speakers.

"No time for pleasantries," Christopher replied calmly, dropping me unceremoniously to the floor. "We've arrived at our destination. My work here is done."

Lena's face contorted with rage. "Harvey, tear him apart!" she screamed, her shunt glowing blue.

Harvey charged forward; metal limbs extended. Christopher moved inhumanly, dodging the robot's attack and producing what looked like a small disc from his pocket. He flung it at Harvey, where it attached to the robot's chest.

"No!" Lena screamed as electricity arced across Harvey's frame. The robot convulsed, movements erratic, before collapsing to the floor with a thunderous impact. Lena dropped to her knees, hands clutching her head in agony, blood streaming from her nose and ears.

Dwight fired his plasma rifle, but Christopher was already moving, sprinting toward the engine room. The feed switched again, showing Christopher in the engine room, attaching devices to the plasma core.

"Countdown initiated," he said to no one in particular. "Two minutes to core breach. Just enough time to make a graceful exit."

The camera showed Christopher running out of the engine room and bracing himself in the corridor. He pulled something from his pocket, a small device that he pressed while turning away from the camera. There was a blinding flash as the plasma core began destabilizing, searing away the camera feed.

The recording ended there, leaving me staring at a black screen, my reflection a pale ghost against the darkness.

"He blew a hole straight through the engine room and outer hull," Dwight explained. "That's how he escaped right through the breach. We found his tracks in the snow when we came to. According to the chronometer, three days had passed since we were at the research facility."

My hands shook as I set the data pad down. The gap between watching and experiencing these events yawned like an abyss. Parts of it felt familiar: the sensation of my consciousness expanding beyond normal boundaries, the presence of another entity inside my mind, navigating through dimensions I couldn't comprehend.

"Harvey," I whispered, looking up at Lena, finally understanding the source of her rage and grief. "Is it...?"

"Not dead," she said flatly, her hand unconsciously moving to her shunt. "But not...here either. I can't feel it, can't connect. It's like..." She struggled to find the words. "It's like having a limb amputated, but worse. Like having part of your brain cut out while you're still conscious."

The profound loneliness in her voice struck me harder than any physical blow. Harvey hadn't just been a robot companion to her; it had been an extension of herself, a presence in her mind since childhood. Its absence left a void that couldn't be filled.

"I'm sorry," I said inadequately. "This is my fault. If I hadn't had the medallion"

"It's not your fault," Dwight interrupted firmly. "Christopher's been planning this for longer than we have been alive. We were all just pieces on his board."

"What I don't understand," I said, struggling to organize my fragmented thoughts, "is why he left us alive. If he has what he wants, my medallion, the coordinates to Yrilla, why not just kill us?"

Lena's eyes narrowed. "Because he's not done. The CHeKeR device was damaged in the crash, and the medallion alone isn't enough. He still needs your genetic connection to the Tymeragoth entity inside the medallion."

"Correct assessment," Iris's glitching voice confirmed from the speaker. "According to the files I've managed to decrypt, Burton's genetic structure contains sequences unique to Meredith Rivera's descendants that respond to the Tymeragoth entity's dimensional frequencies. While the medallion contains the essence of a Tymeragoth entity, it requires a compatible human consciousness to act as an interface. Burton's genetic heritage makes him uniquely suitable."

"So he's coming back for me," I said, the realization settling like ice in my veins.

"Yes," Lena replied, her hand tightening on her plasma rifle. "And I'll be waiting."

According to the files Christopher had been studying on the navigation table, Yrilla, once designated 'New Earth,' was where the Lachesis had made its final stand, using experimental technology to seal a dimensional rift. We needed to find Christopher before he reached the Lachesis, where it was buried in this frozen world.

First, we needed to survive. The Charon's life support systems were failing, and without repairs or an alternative shelter, we would freeze to death in days.

Beyond the walls of our damaged ship, shapes moved through the blizzard, twisted silhouettes too jerky and unnatural to be fully human. The transformed crew of the Lachesis had survived here, and they were watching us.

Dwight checked his plasma rifle's charge. "I know a way into the Palace," he said, not meeting my eyes. "But you're not going to like how I know that."

~ 25 ~

ECHOES OF THE LACHESIS

Dwight's words hung in the freezing air between us. "I was here before," he continued, his breath fogging. "After the bombing. IGMC sent a recovery team, and I was on it."

Lena's hand drifted to her plasma rifle. "So, all that talk about rumors filtering through black market channels was just more of your lies?" The blue light of her neural shunt flared briefly, though Harvey remained unresponsive where it stood.

As we argued, the temperature inside the Charon dropped another two degrees, the environmental systems losing their battle against Yrilla's relentless cold. Beyond the breach in the engine room, the blizzard intensified, driving ice crystals like miniature knives against the hull.

My hand instinctively went to my neck, fingers tracing the 'X'-shaped scar left by the CHeKeR device, a constant reminder of what Christopher had stolen from me—my medallion and my free will.

Dwight spread a weathered map across the galley table. "The Palace isn't just some fancy name. It's what's left of the administrative complex built around the Lachesis after it crashed here. The ship is buried deep under the mountain, but the Palace extends throughout the peak, with entrances like this one." He circled a location five kilometers from our position.

According to Dwight's intelligence, after the Lachesis made emergency landfall on Yrilla, the survivors constructed a research facility around it, expanding into the mountain as they studied the dimensional technology that had brought them here.

"The facility operated for nearly two decades before all contact was lost," Dwight explained. "That's when IGMC sent my team to investigate twenty-seven years ago."

When he thought we weren't watching, Dwight adjusted something beneath his jacket, a secondary communicator, perhaps, or a distress beacon, something he hadn't mentioned.

"Christopher's heading there because that's where the Lachesis is, where the dimensional doorway was sealed," I said. "With my medallion and the black ore, he has the components he needs to reopen it."

"What do you remember about being in that chair?" Dwight asked, his weathered face serious. "What was it like having that thing, that Tymeragoth, in your head?"

I studied the map, recognition flickering through me. These were not my own memories but impressions left by the Tymeragoth entity during my time in the CHeKeR device, echoes of the medallion's influence lingering in my mind.

I closed my eyes, trying to piece together the fragmented memories. "It was like being everywhere at once. My consciousness was stretched across dimensions I can't even describe. I could perceive time and space as physical constructs that could be bent, folded, and manipulated."

My connection to Meredith Rivera's genetic line meant that even without the medallion physically present, some trace of its power remained accessible.

When I opened my eyes, I found both Lena and Dwight watching me intently. "The Tymeragoth didn't just control me; it used me as a lens, focusing its perception through my human consciousness to navigate our reality. It needed me to interpret and interact with three-dimensional space while it plotted coordinates in higher dimensions."

I could see patterns in the facility's design that others couldn't, pathways and junctions that seemed to bend in ways three-dimensional architecture shouldn't. "The Palace wasn't just built into the mountain," I explained. "Parts of it exist partially in higher dimensions, folded through spaces we can't normally perceive."

"Meredith designed it that way," I continued, the knowledge rising from somewhere beyond my conscious mind. "My great-great-grandmother built safeguards against the Avalonians, hiding the most critical sections of the Lachesis in dimensional pockets they couldn't access."

"And now?" Lena asked, her voice uncharacteristically gentle. "Is it still there? In your head?"

I hesitated, probing my thoughts. There was emptiness where something alien had briefly resided, and a lingering awareness of spaces and dimensions beyond normal human perception.

"No," I finally said. "But it left... echoes. Like my brain was rewired to perceive things differently." I gestured vaguely at the air around us. "I can still see traces of higher dimensions—afterimages, geometries that shouldn't make sense but somehow do."

"How much did you tell Christopher before we left Earth?" Lena asked, her eyes cold as she studied Dwight. His hesitation before answering told me everything I needed to know.

"That c-could explain the anomalies in your neural patterns," Iris interjected, her voice stabilizing slightly. "They bear similarities to the patterns observed when you interfaced with the ship's systems using your medallion, but more pronounced and permanent."

"The recovery team," I pressed Dwight. "What happened to them?"

Dwight's eyes darted to the blizzard outside. "We lost contact. HexiCore outbid IGMC for the recovery rights. I was the only one who returned to the extraction point." Something in his tone suggested there was much more to that story.

A thought struck me suddenly. "Iris, you mentioned the ship's systems are damaged. Can you access any external sensors? Can we see what's out there?"

"Limited f-functionality remains," Iris confirmed. "Activating exterior c-cameras."

The galley's small display screen flickered to life, showing a desolate landscape of ice and snow. Jagged mountains loomed in the distance; their peaks lost in swirling clouds. Outside, Yrilla's twin moons cast an eerie blue glow across the endless snow, illuminating the jagged black mountain where the Palace waited. Occasional flashes of aurora rippled across the sky. Still, unlike Earth's northern lights, these seemed to tear momentarily into somewhere else, brief glimpses of other dimensions bleeding through Yrilla's thin dimensional barriers.

Closer to the ship, strange crystalline formations jutted from the frozen ground, catching what little light filtered through the storm and refracting it in unnatural patterns.

And moving among these formations, barely visible through the blizzard, was a humanoid figure.

"Christopher," Lena hissed, rising from her seat.

"Wait," I said, narrowing my eyes at the screen. "That's not him. The proportions are wrong."

The figure drew closer to one of the cameras, revealing a humanoid form that had once clearly been a person. Tattered remnants of what might have been a uniform or refugee clothing still clung to its emaciated frame. Unlike Christopher's controlled, almost symbiotic relationship with the smoke, this creature was visibly ravaged by its possession. Dense black smoke poured from its empty eye sockets and partially open mouth in violent, uncontrolled torrents, like a pressure vessel with multiple ruptures.

Its movements were jerky and frantic, not the deliberate motions of someone in control, but the desperate flailing of a puppet with too many masters. The smoke didn't just surround it as it did with Christopher; it erupted from the creature's body, tearing through flesh and clothing alike, leaving crystallized wounds where the sub-zero atmosphere had frozen the seeping fluids.

"God almighty," Dwight muttered, unconsciously backing away from the screen. "Is that a person?"

"Detecting Avalonian energy signature," Iris reported, her voice skipping like a damaged recording. "But the p-pattern is chaotic, unrestrained. The s-symbiosis appears catastrophically unstable."

The creature lurched closer to the camera, its head tilting at an impossible angle. More smoke poured from its mouth as it released a sound not quite a scream, not quite speech that made the speakers crackle with distortion. Its hands, blackened with frostbite and split from exposure, pressed against the hull. Where it touched, frost patterns spread across the metal, forming intricate crystalline structures that mimicked the patterns I'd glimpsed in four-dimensional space.

"It's them," I whispered, horror washing over me. "The Lachesis crew. They've been here all this time."

The camera feed suddenly dissolved into static as more smoke erupted from the creature's body, engulfing the lens.

"External sensors compromised," Iris announced, genuine alarm coloring her digital voice. "Multiple entities with similar energy signatures converging on our position. Their movements suggest coordinated hunting behavior."

"That's what the smoke does to people who can't control it," I said, my voice barely audible. "That happens when the Avalonians take a body by force."

The data fragments I recovered from the ship's limited power reserves were mainly corrupted. Still, one file remained intact: a personal log from Meredith Rivera, recorded days before the Lachesis landed on Yrilla.

Seeing her face on the screen was disorienting, but our resemblance was unmistakable despite the generations between us. "If you're viewing this," her voice said, "you carry my bloodline. The medallion has found its way to you, as I intended."

She described the Lachesis's mission as an evacuation ship commandeered by Terrance Alexander after discovering the Avalonian infiltration of Earth's power structures. They had fled with the medallion, containing the captured Tymeragoth entity, intending to use its power to seal the dimensional rift the Avalonians had opened.

"The CHeKeR device was never meant for human use," Meredith continued, her expression grim. "Terrance attempted to communicate with the Tymeragoth entity, to convince it to help us against the Avalonians. But the neural interface proved too dangerous for most humans." She touched her temple. "Except for those with certain genetic markers I've passed to my children, and they will pass to theirs."

"I don't care what sad story they have," Lena snarled, already moving toward the door, plasma rifle charged and humming. "If those things get in here, we're dead."

"Wait!" I called after her. "These were people, once the very refugees the Visionary was supposed to protect. What if this is what's waiting for us? What if this is what Christopher plans for everyone?"

She paused at the doorway, her face hardening with resolve. "Then all the more reason to find him before he can do it to anyone else."

Dwight's expression had lost its usual sardonic edge, replaced by grim determination. "Kid, those aren't people anymore. Whatever was human got burned out long ago. No different than putting down a rabid animal."

I swallowed hard. "But this is what the Avalonians are capable of. This is what Christopher is, underneath his control."

"All the more reason not to let him keep your medallion," Dwight replied darkly. "Now let's seal that breach before his 'cousins' get inside."

Iris informed us that the blizzard intensified cyclically, reaching peak ferocity every fourteen hours before subsiding slightly. We had approximately three hours before the next intensity spike, our window to get to the Palace entrance Dwight had identified.

I forced myself to stand, ignoring the tremors still rippling through my muscles. The afterimages of higher dimensions flickered at the edges of my vision. With growing horror, I realized they aligned perfectly with the patterns formed by the smoke pouring from the creatures outside.

"Burton," Iris's voice cut through the tension, "I've detected an energy signature matching your medallion's resonance frequency. It's approximately two kilometers north of our position, moving deeper into the mountains."

"Christopher," I whispered, the name like ash on my tongue.

"Yes," Lena agreed, eyes narrowing to predatory slits. "And he's got a head start. We need to move."

We gathered what supplies remained intact, preparing to venture into the alien landscape. Lena salvaged emergency rations from the galley storage, while Dwight collected what remained of our functioning weapons. I was drawn to the engine room breach, staring at the frozen wasteland that would soon become our battlefield.

Harvey stood motionless in the corner, its optical sensors flickering occasionally with weak power surges. The diagnostic panel beside it showed its systems slowly rebooting after the dimensional transit trauma.

Lena worked frantically on Harvey's exposed circuitry, attempting to bypass its damaged neural interface. "Its primary matrix is intact," she muttered, "but the connection protocols are scrambled."

The machine's frame showed stress fractures along its central support structure, evidence of the tremendous forces it had endured during our arrival on Yrilla.

Lena's neural shunt pulsed sporadically as she attempted to reestablish the technological link with Harvey. Each failed connection attempt left a fresh trail of blood from behind her ear.

The storm had intensified, walls of white obscuring visibility beyond a few meters. Yet through this curtain of snow, I could make out more of the smoke-possessed creatures, their jerky movements creating strange patterns in the blizzard. Some crawled on all fours like animals, while others shambled upright with unnatural gaits. Their numbers were greater than I'd first realized, dozens, perhaps hundreds, converging on our crashed ship.

"Burton, come help with this," Dwight called behind me. He attempted to seal the breach with emergency hull patches, but the cold made the adhesive brittle and bond slowly.

Together, we created a makeshift barrier, not airtight, but enough to slow the creatures and keep out the worst of the cold. As we worked, I noticed more crystalline frost patterns forming where the creatures had touched the hull, spreading like living organisms across the metal.

"These aren't random," I murmured, tracing the patterns with my gloved fingertip, careful not to touch them directly. "They're mathematical expressions, equations rendered in physical form."

"What kind of equations?" Dwight asked, his breath fogging in the cold air.

"I'm not sure," I admitted. "Something about dimensional constants, folding parameters. It's like they're trying to solve the problem of their existence, how to exist properly in our three-dimensional space."

Lena appeared behind us, dressed in an insulated survival suit she'd found in storage. She carried similar suits for Dwight and me, along with a backpack of supplies. "Save the physics lesson," she said tersely. "We need to move before they find a way in."

As I donned my suit, the howling of the creatures outside intensified, as if they sensed our preparations to leave. Their sounds weren't merely animalistic; thcy had a pattcrn, a horrid communication that made my skin crawl.

"They're organizing," I warned. "Coordinating their efforts."

"All the more reason to be gone before they break through," Dwight said, checking the charge on his plasma rifle.

"I've mapped the most efficient route to reach the medallion's energy signature," Iris informed us through our comms. "Be advised that the terrain is treacherous, with numerous crevasses hidden beneath the snow. The temperature outside is currently minus eighty-seven degrees Celsius. Your survival suits will protect you for approximately six hours before power cells are depleted."

We had no choice but to venture into the blizzard, locate the Palace entrance, and find Christopher before he reached the Lachesis. With each hour that passed, the chances increased that he would succeed in reopening the dimensional doorway.

"If Christopher manages to reactivate the rift," I explained, the knowledge rising unbidden from my Tymeragoth-influenced memories, "it won't just release a few more Avalonians. It will tear open a permanent doorway between dimensions, allowing the full invasion they've been planning for centuries."

"How are we going to get through those things?" I asked, watching more smoke-ravaged forms gather at our sealed breach.

Lena's expression was cold and determined. "The same way I've survived everything else, one step at a time, without hesitation." She handed me a small plasma pistol. "Use it if you have to. Aim for where their heads should be."

We gathered at the secondary emergency exit, a small airlock on the ship's underside that the creatures had yet to discover.

Dwight would go first, creating a path through the snow. I would follow in the middle, with Lena covering our rear.

As we packed our meager supplies and prepared the environmental suits, Iris's sensors detected movement outside, multiple signatures converging on our position from the direction of the Palace. The transformed crew of the Lachesis had found us, and they were closing in.

Dwight checked his plasma rifle's charge one final time, his expression unreadable. "There's something else I should tell you about the Palace," he said. "Something about the Lachesis crew that survived there." His eyes met mine, cold with the knowledge of horrors ahead. "They're not just transformed physically. They're connected to a hive mind driven by what's left of the Visionary himself."

With a final nod, Dwight activated the airlock.

The cold hit us like a physical blow, even through our suits. The temperature drop was sudden and vicious. The snow swirled around us, instantly coating our visors with a layer of ice crystals that our helmets struggled to melt away. The wind howled, a high keening sound that seemed to harmonize with the cries of the creatures still circling the ship.

Dwight plowed forward, his broad frame creating a partial windbreak for me to follow. Each step required conscious effort, the snow reaching above our knees in some places. We moved away from the ship in a direction opposite to where most of the creatures had gathered, hoping to circle once we'd put some distance between us and them.

The landscape was alien and forbidding, a frozen wasteland of ice and strange crystal formations that seemed to grow taller and more complex the further we ventured from the ship. I couldn't help but wonder how this place could ever have been considered "New Earth," a paradise worth centuries of searching.

We had covered half a kilometer when a bone-chilling cry echoed across the ice. It came from behind us, from the direction of the ship. The sound was followed by several more, a chorus of inhuman wailing that made my blood freeze colder than the surrounding air.

"They've found our trail," Lena's voice came through my helmet comm, tight with tension.

I turned back to see dark shapes moving against the whiteness of the snow, their forms partially obscured by the blizzard but unmistakably heading in our direction. Their movements were faster now, more coordinated, as if invigorated by the hunt.

"Double time," Dwight ordered, increasing his pace despite the treacherous footing.

We pushed on, the mountains looming larger ahead of us. According to Iris's readings, Christopher was somewhere in those peaks, perhaps in a shelter or cave system that would offer protection from the elements. The medallion's energy signature remained constant, suggesting he wasn't moving—either because he'd found what he was looking for or was waiting for something.

Or someone.

The sounds of pursuit grew closer despite our best efforts. The creatures moved with unnatural speed across the snow, seemingly unbothered by the cold that threatened to freeze us solid if our suits failed. They communicated with those strange, patterned cries, coordinating their approach to cut off our escape routes.

"There!" Dwight pointed ahead, where a dark opening was visible in the base of the nearest mountain. "Cave entrance. We can make a stand there if we have to."

We altered course, heading for the cave. As we neared it, I noticed strange markings around the entrance, not natural formations but deliberate symbols carved into the ice and stone. They resembled the crystalline patterns the creatures had formed on our ship, but more refined, precise.

"Wait," I called out, but Dwight had already reached the entrance and disappeared inside.

"Dwight!" I radioed, trying to hear my own words over the roar of the blizzard. "I'm reading some heat signature from inside. It's... It's not natural."

"You need to see this," Dwight's voice returned, filled with awe. "It's a structure of some kind. It's not a natural formation."

According to Dwight's intelligence, the Palace's outer structure had been designed to mimic the mountain's natural formation, with entrances disguised as cave openings. But the interior would be a maze of laboratories, living quarters, and research facilities, all built around the Lachesis like a technological cathedral.

The ship was irreparably damaged during the emergency landing, and its dimensional drive core was deliberately overloaded to seal the rift. What remained was a massive technological tomb buried deep beneath layers of ice, rock, and the Palace's structure.

Lena was already moving toward the entrance. "Christopher has to be in there. It's the only place out here that would provide any shelter. He wouldn't have survived long in this cold without it."

I followed her reluctantly, and the strange markings around the entrance made me uneasy. But with the creatures closing in behind us, we had little choice.

The moment we stepped inside, I felt a dramatic temperature change. The biting cold of the blizzard gave way to surprising warmth. The cave wasn't just a cave; it opened into what appeared to be a structure built into the mountain.

We retracted our helmets, the comparative warmth allowing us to conserve our suit power. The walls weren't stone or ice as I'd expected, but something else entirely, smooth, curving surfaces that gleamed like polished metal yet seemed organic, almost alive. They pulsed with a subtle glow that cast eerie shadows on our faces.

"What is this place?" Lena whispered, her eyes scanning the cavernous interior.

Dwight kept his weapon ready, checking corners and shadowed areas. "No time to figure it out. Christopher could be in here somewhere."

As we moved deeper, I couldn't shake the feeling that the structure was somehow watching us, aware of our presence. The walls seemed to breathe, shifting and pulsing with their rhythm. A faint whisper emanated deep within the tunnel, echoing through the cavernous space.

"Did you hear that?" I asked, my voice barely audible.

"Yeah," Dwight replied grimly. "This place gives me the creeps."

I checked my wrist console, scanning for energy signatures. "There's something... a spike in this direction." I pointed toward a tunnel mouth that branched off to our left, seeming to lead deeper into the mountain.

"It's him," Lena decided, already moving in that direction.

We followed the winding passage, navigating twists and turns that seemed to follow no logical pattern. The walls continued to pulse with that inner light, growing stronger the deeper we went. Finally, the tunnel opened into a vast chamber, a circular space with a domed ceiling that rose so high we couldn't see where it ended.

But what drew our attention was the floor. Scattered across the chamber were chunks of ore, black, crystalline formations that seemed to absorb the ambient light rather than reflect it. They were identical to the material Christopher had acquired on Terax-3.

"Look," Lena said, crouching to pick up a small piece of the ore. She tossed it to me. "Recognize this?"

I caught it carefully, feeling its strange weight in my palm. "It's the same ore that Nyx gave Christopher on Terax-3."

"What is this?" Dwight muttered, keeping his weapon ready as he scanned the chamber. "Some sort of body-snatching nursery? Christopher mentioned these things were trapped inside this stuff."

"Avalonians," Christopher's voice echoed through the chamber, seeming to come from everywhere and nowhere.

We spun, weapons raised, trying to locate him. But the chamber was empty save for us and the scattered ore.

"The tunnels," Dwight hissed. "They've changed. The way we came in, it's gone."

I looked back, and sure enough, the passage we'd entered had vanished, replaced by a smooth, unbroken wall. We were trapped.

"Christopher!" Lena shouted, her plasma rifle charged and ready. "What the hell are you doing? Show yourself!"

His laughter rolled through the chamber like distant thunder. "Relax, Lena. You're exactly where you need to be."

"What are you planning?" I demanded, still clutching the piece of ore in my hand. "Why bring us here? Why show us all this?"

"I need you, Burton," Christopher's voice softened, almost gentle. "Your unique abilities. Your genetic connection to the medallion. You've always been the key."

"Just tell me what this is all about," I pressed, trying to keep him talking while scanning for any sign of movement, any indication of where he might be hiding.

"With you, the medallion, and the CHeKeR device, I can finally fulfill my promise," he replied, a fervent edge to his voice. "You will help free my people from this cursed planet and help me deposit them across the universe, allowing them to live again, to experience existence beyond this frozen prison."

"And why would I want to do that?" I asked, my voice steady despite the fear coursing through me. "After seeing what they did to those people outside? After what they did to you?"

Christopher's laugh this time was bitter. "What did they do to me? They gave me immortality, Burton. They gave me purpose. And they can give humanity so much more if you let them."

As if in response to his words, an archway appeared in the wall opposite us, revealing a new passage.

We had little choice but to follow it, moving cautiously with weapons ready. The tunnel wound downward, deeper into the mountain, until we reached what appeared to be a door, a massive metal hatch that had been forcibly pried open and twisted out of shape.

At its base lay a placard, partially buried under sediment and rubble. Dwight bent to brush away the debris, revealing a word: "LACHESIS."

"It's the ship," I whispered, shock running like an electric current. "The Lachesis."

"It must have gotten buried over time," Lena said, crouching to examine the placard more closely.

Dwight, who had taken a defensive position behind us, broke the moment of awe. "Is anyone else worried about what might have come through that door?"

"Definitely," Lena agreed, setting the sign down gently. "Whatever broke this open wasn't looking for a polite invitation."

The tunnel behind us began to shift, the walls closing in with an ominous grinding sound.

"It's sealing us in!" I shouted. "We need to move!"

"Inside the ship!" Lena ordered, already moving toward the twisted hatch.

~ 26 ~

SMOKE AND MADNESS

The twisted hatch of the Lachesis loomed before us, its edges bent and warped as though something had forced its way through from the inside. We'd barely survived the journey through the blizzard, fighting past transformed beings whose jerky movements and smoke-filled orifices still haunted my vision. The dimensional transport that had brought us here from the Charon six hours ago seemed like a distant memory now.

"This place... it feels haunted," I whispered, my breath fogging in the stale, cold air. Ice crystals had formed in Dwight's beard despite the environmental suit's heating elements.

"We need to find the bridge," Lena directed as she barged down a corridor. Her movements were sharper than usual, more erratic – a woman fighting two battles simultaneously. Every few seconds, her hand would rise to the neural shunt behind her ear, blood trickling from it as she futilely searched for a connection to Harvey that Christopher's EMP had severed.

Dwight's expression remained unreadable, but his frequent glances at his wrist console betrayed mounting anxiety. "Let's get out of here, kid," he said. "This doesn't seem like the safest place to hang around." He followed Lena's lead in the direction she had walked, lagging at each junction, his attention fixed on his console.

Its survivors had retrofitted the Lachesis, transforming it from an evacuation vessel to a research facility. I recognized junctions and passageways I'd never seen before, knowledge rising unbidden in my mind. The effect of the Tymeragoth entity during my time in the CHeKeR device had left echoes of fragments of information that weren't mine but somehow accessible.

"My great-great-grandmother designed these security measures," I found myself saying. "Meredith Rivera built dimensional blind spots into the ship's architecture."

We stumbled upon a ladder well that led to the main deck. The Lachesis was eerily like the Charon, or rather, the Icarus, as I now knew it to be called. Both vessels shared the same ominous design and foreboding atmosphere. I couldn't help but wonder if they'd been constructed by the same hands, created for the same dark purpose.

"How do you know all this?" Lena asked, studying me with narrowed eyes. "IGMC was searching for people like you. Subjects with genetic markers that allowed dimensional perception. That's what the experiments were about."

A solitary catwalk stretched out before us, running the entire ship. As we cautiously approached the bridge, our breaths fogged up the frozen pools of liquid beneath our feet. I couldn't shake the eerie feeling that something was eagerly awaiting our arrival. Christopher's tracks were fresh in the frost that coated the corridor floor – he'd passed this way within the last hour.

The bridge doors opened with an almost organic groan, as if the ship expressed pain. My fingers instinctively reached for where my medallion should have been, finding only emptiness. Without it, interfacing with the ship's systems would be more difficult and mechanical, like trying to feel through thick gloves.

As we stepped onto the bridge, our beams of light crossed as each revealed our different priorities. Lena immediately went to the navigation display, but it wouldn't turn on without more power. Dwight checked the tactical area instead.

"They didn't have any defenses," he said in shock. "Savages."

I tapped into the ship's main systems and connected my wrist console. The process felt sluggish, lacking the intuitive flow I'd experienced with the Icarus when my medallion was with me, when Iris was with me. "I'm running a diagnostic," I called out to the others, still focused on getting the technology up and running.

The dark room flickered to life as I rerouted some of my console's power. Screens blinked and sputtered, throwing eerie shadows across our faces. "Looks like I've got something!" The excitement in my voice was palpable, even against the heavy silence of the abandoned ship.

The ship was waking from a deep slumber, groaning and creaking around us. Garbled data scrolled across my screen. "It's like the ship's logs have been wiped repeatedly. But there's a residual code." I paused, looking closer.

Dwight and Lena made their way to me.

"Does it give us clues on how to escape from this place?" Dwight sarcastically inquired, though there was genuine concern beneath his flippant tone. I noticed him subtly inserting something into a nearby security port – a data chip removed so quickly I almost doubted what I'd seen.

"It's mainly personal logs from the ship's first officer," I said, ignoring Dwight's words.

"Can you access them?" Lena asked, almost bumping me out of my spot in front of the bridge console. I noticed her eyes scanning the room as if expecting to see Harvey's massive form lurking in the shadows, the ghost of her constant companion haunting her perception.

I pushed her away gently to give myself some room. With a frown, I started trying to retrieve the deleted data. "It looks like footage from a retina cam. Probably recorded by the first officer while they were on the ship, documenting daily activities."

I hesitantly clicked on the first video, F10231. The screen exploded with gruesome scenes of blood-smeared walls and a floor littered with torn body parts. Men and women crowded around the perimeter of the room, their laughter echoing like the screams of the victims they were about to witness.

"Bring in two more!" a voice bellowed off camera. Two trembling women, likely refugees, were thrown into view, their bodies covered in bruises and tattered clothing. The metallic clanging of instruments hitting the ground filled the air as the crowd erupted into a frenzy.

"You know the rules," a voice boomed, silencing the chaos. "First one to take a limb wins."

In a desperate bid for survival, the women scrambled to grab any weapon they could find, hacking at each other in a brutal display that was met with cheers and jeers from the bloodthirsty spectators.

"Turn it off," Lena said, turning away. "Fucking animals. What was going on on this ship?" Her voice was hard, but I caught a slight tremor in it.

Dwight's eyes remained glued to the bloody video, his posture stiffening slightly. "Deep space psychosis, I hope. But if they were recording it, that's something else entirely. Ritualized violence, a twisted form of entertainment." His expression darkened further. "Someone up top had to be sanctioning this." He looked away, the disgust evident on his face.

I closed the video, my stomach churning at the cruelty. "They can't all be like this."

I clicked on another selection, desperate for something to calm my nerves. Instead, I was greeted with a chaotic scene of a frenzied militia, their faces twisted with fervor as they rallied around their leader. The captain stood beside the first officer, both bellowing into a sea of rabid followers.

"They called me a madman. But who found it? Who discovered the promised planet?" The captain's voice boomed over the roaring crowd as they chanted in unison, "Visionary. Visionary. Visionary."

I recognized that voice, not the human captain, but the entity controlling him. This was the same Avalonian that Christopher had released from the black ore at the IGMC facility. The followers surrounding him had no idea they were pledging allegiance to an interdimensional parasite wearing their captain like a costume, believing instead they were following a visionary human leader who had brought them to paradise.

It was clear these manipulated humans would stop at nothing to mold this new world in their image, unaware of the alien intelligence directing their fervor. I watched the madness unfold before me, the strange geometric patterns in the background of the video capturing my attention in a way they wouldn't have before my time in the CHeKeR device. The chamber walls seemed to bend at angles that shouldn't be possible in three-dimensional space, as if the fabric of reality was different here.

"You think he's talking about Yrilla?" I looked over at Lena, who managed to run the navigation table.

"He has to be," she said, "but it's not on any of these star charts. How did they get here?" Her fingers drummed on the console; a nervous habit I'd never seen from her. She was missing Harvey, I realized, missing the constant presence in her mind, the extension of herself that Christopher's EMP had ripped away.

I opened another file, hoping it might hold more answers.

"This is not what he promised us," a man said in a low growl as he confronted the first officer. His eyes burned with anger and betrayal. "He left us out here to freeze to death while he took his share of the refugee women and retreated to his so-called 'palace' in the caves. We were promised more than frozen whores and an icy tomb. It's time for a new leader, one who will keep their promises." His words were laced with venom, and his comrades echoed their agreement with their weapons at the ready.

"Oh, how unfortunate, a mutiny," sneered Dwight as he plopped down in a chair. "I'm sure the madman deserved it for torturing innocent people." His casual tone belied the tension in his posture; history here resonated with him on some level.

Open another video," Lena requested. She had sat on the navigation table, watching the videos on the larger monitors overhead. Her hand absently reached for her plasma rifle, adjusting its position for the third time in as many minutes, a soldier expecting trouble, especially vulnerable without her mechanical guardian.

I accessed another video file. "Look!" I shouted to the others.

The video began with the first officer frantically sprinting through a labyrinth of tunnels, his ragged breath echoing and mingling with rushing footsteps behind him.

"They're right on our heels!" A voice shouted from behind, urgency dripping from each word. The camera shook violently as the officer ran, beams of light from their flashlights slicing through the oppressive darkness.

Suddenly, they burst into a vast chamber, panting heavily as they scanned their surroundings. "It's getting warmer down here," someone called out in alarm, their voice strained with fear.

"Just keep moving," another voice commanded, filled with terror and desperation. "If they catch us, they'll flay us alive and devour us. The visionary knew we were coming," someone whispered in terror.

"Look at the chamber," I said, pausing the video. "It's the ore chamber Christopher trapped us in." The geometric patterns along the walls matched exactly what we had seen earlier, too perfectly to be a coincidence. The chamber existed in a space that seemed to bend reality itself, a nexus point between dimensions where the laws of physics became suggestions rather than absolutes.

Lena moved closer to a monitor, "It is. Is there anything else? What happened to the first officer?"

"I don't know," I said. "There are about 30 more files, but only five occur after this last one."

"Play the five," Dwight piped in. "Don't leave me on a cliffhanger, kid." His attempt at humor fell flat, the tension in the room too thick to be cut with mere words.

With trembling fingers, I hit play on the next video. The camera panned over a pile of ore, its glowing sulfuric yellow and orange hues beckoning with an eerie allure.

"What could it be?" the first officer pondered aloud, reaching down to pick up a piece. But before he could even touch it, chaos erupted behind him. A man snarled and shoved a woman to the ground, his grip tight on a chunk of ore that he had stolen from her.

She quickly rose to her feet, unsheathing a small blade with deadly intent. In one swift motion, she leapt onto the man's back and sliced his forehead open like a gruesome headband, spattering blood across the ground. The man screamed and dropped the glowing ore as he desperately tried to shake off his attacker.

Amidst the struggle, a plasma lantern shattered, igniting a brilliant blue flame that ignited nearby ore, causing it to smolder and emit thick smoke, engulfing bystanders in a choking haze.

Before Lena or Dwight could comment on the smoke we saw, I started the next video.

The video footage jolted violently, making it almost unbearable to watch. The screams of terror and pain echoed through the audio, each one a dagger to the heart. Through the camera lens, we could see the dense smoke enveloping the group like a suffocating blanket, twisting and swirling in macabre patterns.

The anguished cries intensified, piercing our eardrums and rattling the bridge walls where Lena, Dwight, and I stood frozen in shock. It was a symphony of suffering that reminded me of my own time in the CHeKeR device, the sensation of having my consciousness stretched beyond its natural boundaries, of being violated by an alien presence.

"Turn it off, kid," Dwight yelled over the tortured sounds.

The deafening silence that followed the abrupt end of the video weighed down on us like a heavy blanket, suffocating and oppressive. I turned to look at Lena, her eyes unblinking as they bore into the now-blackened screen, as if waiting for something sinister to emerge from the darkness.

Lena hopped off the navigation table and exclaimed, "What the fuck was that noise? It sounded like they were being torn apart." Her hand unconsciously moved to her shunt again, a reflex born of years of depending on Harvey's presence for security.

Dwight sat, rubbing the back of his neck to ease the tension coiling there. "We should focus on getting out of here, enough of the home videos. We know bad shit happened on this ship. And then bad shit happened to the crew of this ship. I don't want to be the meat in this shit sandwich."

"Agreed," Lena said, now on her feet. Let's make our way down to the engine room." Lena abruptly stopped speaking as the monitors came back on. Burton, are you doing this?" she asked immediately.

My hands shot up. "I haven't touched anything," I exclaimed, confused by what controlled the console. The system seemed to operate independently, as if guided by an unseen hand or something more alien.

"Dwight?" Lena shot him a questioning look.

"Don't look at me, boss. I didn't want to watch any more of this." Dwight shifted uncomfortably.

"Burton, can you stop it?" Lena asked, hoping to end the feed.

"I'm trying. It's not taking any of my commands." I worked frantically at the console, keenly aware of how much easier this would be with my medallion or Iris. Without them, I was fighting against the system rather than working with it.

"Take a look at the screen," Dwight gathered our attention.

As the camera angle shifted, the video jolted with spasms, accompanied by a haunting moan in the background. The figures in the video convulsed and writhed as if being consumed by some unknown force. They clawed at their flesh until their nails peeled back into bloody stumps. Their limbs twisted and contorted in grotesque ways, defying all logic.

Some trembled violently, as if seized by a powerful force. And yet they remained standing, their bodies a chorus of agonized screams. Thick smoke enveloped them, creeping through their open mouths and inflating their stomachs like bloated balloons.

One by one, they opened their eyes to reveal empty sockets that seethed with swirling tendrils of smoke, like a malevolent spirit taking hold of their very souls. Unlike Christopher, whose surgical modifications allowed controlled containment of his Avalonian passenger, these creatures had been torn apart from within. Black smoke erupted from their eye sockets, nostrils, and mouths in volcanic bursts, creating weeping sores and rupturing veins as it sought escape from vessels never meant to contain such entities.

With hellish rage, the crew of the Lachesis, now controlled by evil forces, stormed into the caves like a horde of demons, their movements fluid and unnervingly quick. Scaling walls and navigating twists and turns easily, they let out a blood-curdling scream, like a chorus of banshees. Their prominent and throbbing veins bulged with the fervor of their charge, the strain of their movements evident in their every pulsing vein.

The chilling display elicited a stunned silence from Lena and Dwight. I felt my stomach churn, the grotesque transformation of the Lachesis crew hammering dread deep into my bones. My fingers hovered over the controls, useless. The images were horrifyingly familiar the same twisted creatures we'd encountered outside in the blizzard. We were watching the birth of the monsters that now hunted us.

"Why... what are they becoming?" Dwight murmured, his voice barely above a whisper. He was now sitting up straight in his chair.

"Lena," I called, attempting to snap her out of her silence. "The kids. The kids who didn't survive the experiments at the outpost. You saw them? You saw them, right? You described them as what?" I racked my brain for her words. "You described them as a 'mangled heap of blood and flesh.' Is this what you saw? Is this what happened to those kids?"

Lena's face, usually a mask of stoic resolve, crumpled momentarily as memories seemed to crash over her like violent waves. Her hard and piercing eyes flickered to the screen, then back to me. "Yes," she finally spat out, the word slicing through the thick tension in the air.

"What made you different?" I questioned, my hands shaking from the adrenaline. "What kept you from becoming that?" I pointed to the screen.

"I don't know. I was a child." Lena's voice cracked, a rare display of vulnerability that cut through the cabin's charged atmosphere. She pushed a strand of hair behind her ear, inadvertently revealing the neural shunt. "If Harvey were here..." she began, then stopped herself, the pain of its absence too fresh to articulate.

Dwight leaned forward, rubbing his thickly bearded chin thoughtfully. "Whatever it is, we can bet Christopher has an idea of why he needed the data from the IGMC facility. Why you are still alive." He stood from his chair. "We have to get off this ship and off this planet."

"Dwight's right," Lena said, composing herself. "Let's go." Lena exited the bridge, waiting just outside the doors for us to follow.

I noticed the pattern in the transformed crew's attacks from the videos how they seemed to funnel toward specific corridors. "They're channeling us," I whispered to Lena. "Driving us toward something." Her eyes flicked to Dwight, understanding dawning in her expression.

Before following her out the door, I hurriedly downloaded as much information as possible onto my wrist console. The data might hold answers we desperately needed about the Avalonians, about the Tymeragoth entity trapped in my medallion. "We should follow Christopher's trail," I said quietly. "He's heading for the dimensional core—the modified drive system that sealed the rift decades ago. With my medallion and the black ore, he could potentially reverse the process."

"How do you know that?" Lena asked, her eyes narrowing.

"I just... know," I replied, the knowledge rising unbidden. "It's like I can see patterns others can't. Dimensional frequencies that resonate with Meredith's genetic imprint. But without my medallion, it's fragmented, incomplete."

Dwight stayed behind to cover us with his weapon while we made our way back into the ship, all of us hyper-aware that the horrors we'd just witnessed on screen might still lurk in the shadows, waiting to claim three more vessels for their smoke.

As we moved through the corridors, I couldn't help but feel we were walking through a tomb, not just of the Lachesis crew, but of humanity's hopes for a fresh start. Whatever paradise the Visionary had promised had become a frozen hell, populated by the tortured remnants of those who had trusted him. Without my medallion, without Harvey, with only the ghosts of the past to guide us, our future seemed equally bleak.

We reached a massive chamber that must have once been the Lachesis's engine room. In the center stood a modified command chair, another CHeKeR device, far more sophisticated than the one Christopher had used on me. And standing before it was Christopher himself, my medallion glowing against his chest, a tendril of iridescent light connecting it to the black ore he held in his hand.

The dimensional feedback filled the chamber with rippling distortions. Reality itself seemed unstable here, objects appearing briefly in multiple positions simultaneously, afterimages trailing every movement. The barrier between dimensions was already beginning to thin.

Christopher's eyes snapped open as we entered, but they weren't his eyes anymore. The vertical lids he'd surgically installed were gone, replaced by swirling pools of darkness that leaked tendrils of smoke. When he spoke, his voice carried harmonics that hurt my ears.

"You're just in time to witness the reunion," he said. "My kin are coming home."

Before we could move, Dwight's plasma rifle pressed against my spine. "Sorry, kid," he muttered, genuine regret coloring his tone. "Some debts can't be paid off." He pushed me forward, toward the empty chair beside Christopher. "He needs both the medallion and your genetic connection to complete the process."

~ 27 ~

THE TRANSFORMED

My head throbbed with the phantom sensation of the CHeKeR device's probe hovering at the base of my skull. Christopher's laughter echoed in my ears as he'd forced me toward that chair in the dimensional core, my medallion glowing against his chest, connected to the black ore by tendrils of iridescent light. I could still feel the dimensional frequencies rippling through my consciousness as he began the fold attempt.

If Lena hadn't broken free from her restraints at that crucial moment, distracting Christopher with a wild lunge, I'd now be another vessel, just another Burton in a long line of disposable engineers. The resulting cascade of energy had temporarily disabled Christopher's modifications, allowing us to escape in the chaos. Even Dwight, after his moment of betrayal, had stumbled after us when the dimensional backlash threatened to consume him too.

"We need to keep moving," Lena hissed, her plasma rifle aimed at Dwight's chest as we hurried through the twisting corridors of the Lachesis. Blood trickled from her neural shunt, a testament to her desperate attempt to reach Harvey during the fight. "I don't trust you for a second."

Dwight raised his hands in a placating gesture. "I did what I had to do," he said, his voice strained. "Christopher knows things—about my past, about what I did to survive—"

"To her father," I interjected. "I heard what Christopher said about the accident in the mines. The environmental suit."

Dwight's eyes flickered with something like shame before hardening again. "You don't understand what it's like to have a debt like that hanging over you for decades," he muttered. "But I'm here now, aren't I? I could have stayed with him."

"How convenient," Lena spat, but she kept moving, knowing we needed every advantage we could get. "Just stay where I can see you."

We slid down the ladder well closest to the bridge and went to the engine room. The dormant engines of the Lachesis loomed before us, massive and imposing even in their stillness. I ran my hands over the control panel, my fingers instinctively seeking interfaces in strangely familiar patterns. The connection was mechanical rather than intuitive without my medallion, but I could still read the systems.

"The primary propulsion matrix is intact," I said, recognizing design elements like the Icarus. "But the external thrusters are completely frozen over. The ice has penetrated the exhaust ports and crystallized around the ignition chambers." I traced a diagram of the thruster system on the frost-covered console. "We'd need to either generate enough heat to melt the ice formation from the inside out or manually clear each port individually."

"How are we supposed to do that, kid?" Dwight asked, keeping watch at the door, his plasma rifle aimed down the corridor. His eyes kept darting to Lena, who was examining the auxiliary systems nearby, a strange mixture of guilt and concern flashing across his face.

I shrugged, unable to come up with a solution. I instinctively reached for the space where my medallion should have been. "It would be great if Harvey were here," I blurted out. As soon as the words left my mouth, I regretted them.

Lena shot me an icy look, her hand unconsciously rising to the neural shunt behind her ear. The blue light that normally pulsed with her connection to Harvey remained dim and lifeless.

"Or some machine that could clear the thrusters," I added quickly. "The engine core could potentially be rerouted to generate enough heat, but we'd need to bypass the safety protocols manually, and that's a two-person job at minimum."

Just then, the faint sound of metal scraping against metal echoed through the corridors, an ominous sign that something was coming our way. I raised a hand, signaling Dwight and Lena to be silent as we listened intently. The noise grew louder and more pronounced in a steady approach. The sound was unnerving, a constant beat echoing through the stillness.

"What is that?" Lena whispered, plasma rifle held high. Her fingers tightened around the weapon, knuckles white with tension.

"I don't know, but it's coming this way." Dwight backed into the room to stand shoulder to shoulder with Lena and me; his posture protective yet somehow hesitant.

The metallic clanking continued, reverberating through the derelict ship's cold, dimly lit corridors. It was methodical, almost rhythmic, and the tension among us rose with each second. Lena's grip tightened around her rifle, her eyes scanning the shadowy hallway for movement.

"Tsk, tsk. Tsk." Christopher's menacing voice reverberated from the shadows, sending shivers down my spine. "You wouldn't dare try to escape without me, would you?" His sinister laughter echoed through the air. "Remember what happened to the last lot who betrayed me? Mmm, can you hear their screams? Delicious." His words dripped with malice as he remained hidden in the darkness, his presence looming over us like a dark cloud.

He stepped into the dim light of the engine room, his movements unnaturally fluid despite the visible strain on his face evidence of the dimensional backlash he'd suffered. His cybernetic arm twitched unnervingly, plates shifting and realigning with soft clicks. But his eyes captured my full attention vertical eyelids like those I'd seen on the modified children at Terax-3, designed not for appearance but for function, now cracked and struggling to contain what lurked within.

My medallion still hung around his neck, pulsing with a faint light that seemed to respond to my presence. The sight of it so close yet unreachable made my chest ache with a physical pain.

"I thought we had an understanding," he continued, his voice smooth as venom. "You work with me, you live. You cross me, and," he paused, letting the threat hang in the air like the stale, recycled oxygen surrounding us.

Dwight shifted, stepping slightly in front of Lena and me. "We're not against you, Boss. Just trying to find a way to get off this planet." He said, stepping carefully. "For all of us."

Christopher sounded genuinely confused as he asked, "Why are you leaving? We just got here. Don't you want to see our accomplishment? What have we been striving for?" He paused, and I watched in horror as his vertical eyelids blinked in the light. A wisp of smoke escaped from his eye sockets before being drawn back in and trapped within the hardened shell of his eyes.

"Did you guys just see that?" I whispered to Lena and Dwight in disbelief. The realization hit me like a physical blow. Christopher's modifications weren't just cosmetic or functional enhancements. They were containment mechanisms, designed to keep the Avalonian entity inside him under control. Unlike the transformed crew we'd seen in the videos, whose bodies were torn apart by uncontrolled smoke, Christopher had found a way to contain and master it.

The surgical precision of his modifications reminded me of the work we'd seen on Terax-3. This wasn't a recent change. Christopher had been preparing his body for decades, perhaps centuries, methodically enhancing himself through Nyx's expertise to become the perfect vessel.

Christopher's gaze intensified, the smoke inside his eyes swirling like a storm contained within glass. "This is only the beginning of what we can achieve together. A bridge to godhood."

Lena shifted uncomfortably, the grip on her rifle unyielding. "What do you want from us, Christopher?"

Christopher's smile widened; the expression more terrifying than comforting. "Much like our Burton, here is needed to pilot our voyage. As you can see from the Lachesis crew, not all minds can handle our presence." Christopher pointed to his head. "When we were testing the children at the IGMC facilities, it was to find vessels like this one," he gestured to himself, "with the neural pathways and prerequisite trauma," he winked at Dwight, "that allow a symbiotic relationship."

As he approached Lena, the metal plates on his cybernetic arm gleamed dimly under the flickering lights. "Now," Christopher continued, "to blend among your species, we must make certain... alterations." He flicked his vertical lids, allowing a wisp of smoke to extend and contract with disturbing precision. "But I'm sure I can clear up any further misunderstandings with Nyx and his people."

He reached his arm out toward Lena, inviting her hand.

Lena's eyes followed Christopher steadily, her defiance clear despite the encroaching fear that flickered behind her eyes. "You think I'll just willingly help you?" Her voice was steady, but an undercurrent of rage simmered beneath her words. Her hand unconsciously moved to her neural shunt again, seeking a connection that wasn't there.

Christopher chuckled softly, causing the hair on my arm to stand up. "No, Lena. I don't expect you to help me willingly. No more than I expected Burton to operate the CHeKeR device willingly." His gaze flicked momentarily to Dwight. "Some debts require payment, don't they, Dwight? Like accidents in the mines. Malfunctioning environment suits."

Dwight visibly stiffened, his expression darkening with what looked like guilt. Christopher continued, his voice filled with malicious delight. "I don't need you willing, Lena. I need you." He smiled with a psychotic stare as he backed into the shadows.

Then the screaming started.

"What is that noise?" I yelled over the agonizing wails.

"Christopher!" Lena yelled into the darkness. "Christopher!"

"We need to go," Dwight said, clicking his flashlight and moving forward. "If we stay in here, we're trapped."

"Christopher!" Lena yelled louder, her anger seeming to build.

"We have to go." I grabbed her arm, trying to regain her attention. "We need to move now!"

In a split second, Dwight's plasma rifle blasted a blinding light that revealed the monstrous scene outside the engine room. A horde of twisted bodies crawled along the grated floors, walls, and ceilings with contorted limbs and stretched skin. Their disfigured forms were adorned with metal augmentations and grotesque scars, the remnants of the Lachesis crew now transformed into something barely recognizable as human.

Unlike Christopher's surgical modifications that allowed controlled containment, these creatures were being torn apart from within by the entities that possessed them. With each flash of our weapons, I could see Avalonian smoke pouring uncontrollably from their eye sockets, nostrils, and mouths. The smoke erupted through their skin in volcanic bursts, creating weeping sores and rupturing veins as it sought escape from vessels never meant to contain it. The black tendrils writhed like living things, simultaneously puppeting the broken bodies and destroying them from within.

Where Christopher's vertical eyelids trapped his Avalonian partner in a perfect symbiosis, these poor souls had no such adaptations; their bodies were mere consumables, used up and discarded by the entities that inhabited them. The staccato bursts of our rifles illuminated this terrifying scene as the smoke-ravaged creatures surged forward, driven by a hunger that wasn't their own. The air was heavy with the stench of burned flesh, mixing with the metallic scent of blood and the distinct ozone-like tang I now recognized as Avalonian smoke escaping into our atmosphere.

"Run!" Lena yelled as she swung her rifle out the door and joined Dwight, discharging her weapon into the horde.

I sprinted down the hallway, Lena and Dwight right behind me. This wasn't the Charon; I was completely disoriented. As we ran, the corridors seemed to shift and twist in ways that defied regular geometry. My expanded perception, a remnant of my time in the CHeKeR device, allowed me to glimpse how the ship existed beyond three dimensions, corridors folding back on themselves in impossible ways.

We ran as fast as we could, our boots clanging against the metal grates. The relentless screams of those creatures bounced off the walls around us. Dwight pushed to the front, his figure slicing through the hazy atmosphere illuminated by sporadic rifle flashes. Lena and I trailed closely, panting and struggling to see through the smoke in our eyes.

As we continued onward, a sense of unease settled in my gut. Each step felt like we were venturing deeper into a labyrinth crafted by a twisted mind. Christopher's maniacal laughter repeated in my head, a constant reminder of his disturbing glee amid chaos.

Suddenly, a loud crash resounded from up ahead, and a massive metal door slammed shut just as we were about to reach it. We came to an abrupt stop, the echo of our footsteps fading in the eerie silence of the dimly lit corridor.

"This door wasn't shut by accident," Dwight exclaimed, frantically searching for a handle. "I'll check the other pathway to see if there's an alternate entrance. You two stay put." His footsteps echoed into the darkness as he disappeared.

Lena had taken a knee, her rifle aimed down the corridor we'd just come from. "Burton, check for a keypad or something." Her breathing was ragged, and I noticed a thin linc of blood trickling from her neural shunt. The stress of combat without Harvey's support was taking a physical toll.

I frantically scanned the area, desperately searching for a data pad to connect to my wrist console. My heart raced as I hurried down the corridor, going in the opposite direction from Dwight's path.

A sudden scream from behind me made me whirl around. One transformed crew member caught up to us and lunged at Lena. Despite her quick reflexes, the creature's unnatural speed gave it the advantage. It landed on top of her, pinning her to the ground. Her plasma rifle discharged wildly as she struggled, the beam scorching the ceiling.

I ran back, my weapon raised, but Dwight emerged from the shadows first. With precision born of years of combat experience, he fired a clean shot that took the creature's head off. The body collapsed, smoke pouring from the severed neck in uncontrolled torrents.

"Lena!" I helped her to her feet. She was dazed, blood now flowing more freely from her neural shunt.

"I'm fine," she gasped, clearly shaken. Without Harvey's mental protection, the proximity to the smoke entity had affected her in ways I'd never seen before.

"The door," Dwight said, looking past us. "It's open now."

Sure enough, the massive metal door that had blocked our path was now wide open, revealing a dimly lit chamber beyond. Dwight helped support Lena, who was still unsteady on her feet, as we approached the door cautiously.

"This feels wrong," I whispered, my instincts screaming that we were walking into a trap.

"Everything about this place is wrong," Dwight muttered, his expression grim. "But we can't stay out here with those things."

We stepped through the doorway together, Lena between us, her arm draped over Dwight's shoulder for support. The chamber was circular, with strange symbols etched into the walls that resembled the four-dimensional equations I'd glimpsed during my time in the CHeKeR device.

"Burton, check the other side," Dwight said, gently lowering Lena to sit against the wall. "See if there's another way out."

I nodded and moved to the far side of the chamber, examining the strange etchings more closely. They seemed to pulse with faint energy, responding to my presence in ways that reminded me of how Icarus's systems had reacted to my medallion. I recognized some symbols from memories Meredith had unconsciously passed down through her bloodline, my bloodline.

The sound of the door slamming shut made me spin around. Dwight stood with his back against it, his plasma rifle trained on me.

"Dwight! What are you doing?" I shouted, panic rising in my chest.

"I'm sorry, kid," he said, his expression tormented. "I can't let Christopher get both of you. When I opened the door, I saw dozens of them coming. Lena's out there fighting, but they'll overwhelm her."

"We have to help her!" I lunged forward, but Dwight raised his weapon.

"No, you're staying here. Safe." His voice cracked slightly. "I owe her this. For what I did to her father." He backed toward the door, his eyes never leaving mine. "Find another way out. There must be one here; these symbols are like the ones in the dimensional core. Maybe you can figure it out."

"Dwight, wait," I started, but he cut me off.

"I'm going to get your medallion back, Burton," he said firmly. "And I'm going to get Lena. I can still make this right." His eyes showed a fierce determination that I'd never seen before. "Christopher was wrong. We don't just change worlds; we can change ourselves too."

Before I could respond, he slipped through the door, leaving me alone in the chamber filled with four-dimensional equations that seemed to ripple at the edge of my perception.

I rushed to the door, which was sealed tight, the mechanical lock engaged. Through the small window, I caught a glimpse of chaos, Dwight charging into a mass of transformed creatures, his plasma rifle blazing a path toward where Lena was holding her ground, surrounded by the nightmarish former crew of the Lachesis.

I pounded on the door, helpless to join the fight, then returned to the chamber. If Dwight was right, if these symbols held the key to another way out, I needed to decipher them quickly. But without my medallion and that direct connection to Meredith's legacy, I was fighting against my limitations.

My hands moved across the etchings, fingers tracing patterns that seemed to shift beneath my touch. If I could understand the mathematics behind the dimensional fold, perhaps I could find a way to help my friends and finally stop Christopher before he unleashed the Avalonians on an unsuspecting universe.

~ 28 ~

THE INCORPOREAL TRUTH

My fingers traced the etched symbols on the chamber wall, searching for anything to help us escape. Behind me, I could still hear the chaos unfolding beyond the sealed door: Dwight's plasma shots, Lena's defiant shouts, and the inhuman wails of the transformed Lachesis crew. Dwight's last words echoed: "Find another way out. These symbols they're like the ones in the dimensional core."

The circular chamber pulsed with an ethereal energy that seemed to respond to my presence. As I moved my hands across the strange four-dimensional equations, they flickered with a faint luminescence, as if recognizing something in me—some echo of Meredith Rivera's genetic legacy.

The door suddenly groaned open, revealing only darkness beyond. I hesitated, suspecting a trap, but with no other options, I cautiously stepped through. The moment I crossed the threshold, the door slammed shut behind me, the lock engaging with a definitive click.

"Hello?" I called out, my voice echoing through the pitch-black space. No answer came.

I activated my flashlight, its beam cutting weakly through the oppressive darkness. As I swept it across the room, the light revealed a control panel on the nearby wall. Acting on instinct, I pressed my palm against it. The panel hummed to life, and a sickly green illumination spread throughout the chamber.

What I saw made my blood run cold.

Stasis tubes. Hundreds of thousands lined the walls, filling the massive chamber in neat, clinical rows. Each contained a human form suspended in time, their faces frozen in expressions ranging from terror to eerie serenity. My flashlight trembled in my shaking hand as I stumbled between the rows, struggling to comprehend the scale of what I was seeing.

This wasn't just storage for the Lachesis crew. This was an army.

I paused before one tube containing a young boy, perhaps no older than twelve, his face forever locked in suspended animation. Further down, tubes contained people of all ages and backgrounds, some wearing the tattered remains of IGMC uniforms, others in civilian clothing from colonies I recognized: refugees, miners, settlers... collected from across human space over what must have been decades.

"An invasion force," I whispered to the silent chamber. "Vessels waiting for Avalonian entities."

An electric tingle crawled up my spine, the same intuitive sensation I'd felt when touching ship systems with my medallion. But this was weaker, more distant, like an echo of what had once been. Something has changed in me since my time on the CHeKeR device. The medallion had already awakened abilities encoded in my genetics by my lineage.

Meredith Rivera.

My great-great-grandmother's name resonated in my mind as I moved forward. She had been entrusted with the medallion before escaping the Icarus, and she had passed down not just a piece of metal, but a legacy and purpose etched into our family's very DNA. Her connection to the ship's systems during her escape had somehow altered her, changing her and their children, changing me.

I inched down the aisle, anticipating Christopher's presence around any corner. A transparent security barrier divided the area in half at the end of the stasis tube rows. Lena was on the other side, bound to a metal table and frantically fighting against her restraints. Christopher stood nearby, the smoke around him more agitated than I'd ever seen, swirling with a violent intensity that matched the predatory gleam in his vertically lidded eyes.

My medallion hung from his neck, pulsing with a rhythm that seemed to call to me across the distance.

"Burton!" Lena cried out, her eyes darting around until they found me. "Run! Get out of here!"

I pushed against the force field, feeling its energy resist me. Without thinking, I pressed my palm flat against it, something inside me reaching out to the field's technology.

"No one's running anywhere," Christopher said, his voice carrying that unnatural dual timbre I'd heard when he spoke with the entity from the black ore. "Especially not our young friend. He still has work to do."

"What are you going to do to her?" I demanded, my hand still pressed against the barrier.

Christopher circled Lena, running his cybernetic fingers along the table's edge. "Lena's unique resistance to Avalonian influence makes her particularly valuable. Her neural pathways contain the key to creating the perfect symbiosis." He leaned closer to her. "What I have achieved through centuries of careful modification and enhancement, she was born with."

Lena spat in his face. "I was made this way, you sadistic bastard. The experiments, the neural shunts, and everything the IGMC did to us were to shape us into perfect vessels. And I still rejected you."

Christopher wiped his face, his expression darkening. "And that is precisely why we need to understand how. The Avalonian future depends on suitable hosts."

My mind raced. The barrier hummed with energy against my palm, and I could almost visualize its pattern, like the ship's systems I'd interfaced with before, but more complex. I closed my eyes, concentrating on that faint connection I felt after my time in the CHeKeR device.

"The perfect hosts," Lena was saying, buying time. "Like the crew of the Lachesis? Those twisted creatures out there?"

Christopher's laugh was cold. "Failed experiments. Their minds couldn't handle the transition. They lacked the necessary neural architecture." He drew a serrated sonic blade from his belt. "But you... Your brain holds the secret to stable integration."

I focused harder on the barrier, trying to sense its frequency and pattern. My ancestors had left me more than just a medallion; they'd given me the ability to interface with this technology on a fundamental level. The knowledge was encoded in me now, fragments of understanding becoming clearer each moment.

"Even without your medallion, I can smell your bloodline," Christopher said suddenly, turning toward me. "Meredith's defiance, her strength. How fitting that her descendant should witness the culmination of what she tried to prevent."

"She was right to stop you," I said, my voice steadier than expected. "She saw what you are...parasites hiding behind promises of advancement."

Christopher's vertical eyelids flicked, a wisp of smoke escaping before being drawn back. "Parasites? We offer immortality, knowledge beyond human comprehension. Your ancestor could have been a goddess."

"Instead, she chose to be human," I replied. "And she chose freedom for her descendants."

As we spoke, I pressed my hand against the barrier, mentally tracing the energy patterns flowing through it. There was a rhythm to it, a pulse that somehow felt familiar, like the ship recognized me on some level, responding to the same genetic signature, allowing me to interface with the Icarus.

"Please," I whispered, unsure if I was speaking to the ship, my ancestors, or something else entirely. "Help me save her."

For a moment, nothing happened. Then, like a response to a question I hadn't fully articulated, I felt something shift. The barrier before me flickered, its energy patterns destabilizing in ways I somehow understood at an intuitive level.

Christopher's head snapped toward me, his eyes widening. "Impossible. You don't have the medallion."

"I don't need it," I realized aloud, the truth crystallizing as I spoke it. "It was never just about the medallion. It was always about who I am...who we are."

The force field collapsed with a shower of sparks. At the same instant, a searing plasma blast cut through the air from behind me, striking Christopher's cybernetic arm precisely. The impact sent him reeling, temporarily destabilizing the smoke entity within him. The medallion around his neck flared brightly, as if responding to the disruption.

"Now, Burton!" Dwight's voice boomed from the doorway where he stood, plasma rifle still raised. Blood streaked his face, and his clothes were torn, but he was alive.

I lunged forward as Christopher fought to regain his balance, the smoke around him writhing in agitated patterns. With one swift motion, I reached for the medallion, yanking the leather cord with all my strength. It caught on Christopher's neck for a terrifying moment, but then the cord snapped, sending the medallion tumbling into my waiting palm.

The moment it touched my skin, warmth flooded me, familiar and electric. The medallion's glow intensified, and the smoke surrounding Christopher recoiled violently, as if repelled by its light. I clutched it tightly, feeling its power resonate with something inside me.

Christopher roared with fury, the sound echoing with that alien dual-tone. The smoke entity within him surged outward, no longer perfectly contained by his modifications. His vertically lidded eyes leaked tendrils of darkness as he fought to maintain control of his vessel.

I rushed to Lena's side, fumbling with the restraints that bound her to the table. The medallion pulsed against my chest, its rhythm matching my racing heartbeat. As my hands touched the restraints, I felt a surge of intuitive understanding; the locking mechanisms responded to my touch as if recognizing Meredith's genetic signature in me.

"I'm getting you out of here," I said, freeing her wrists and ankles.

Lena sat up, grimacing with pain. "Dwight? He came back for us?"

"Seems like it," I replied, glancing toward where he stood guard at the doorway, firing controlled bursts at Christopher to keep him at bay. "I don't fully understand why, but I'll take the help right now."

As Lena slid off the table, her legs buckled beneath her. I caught her, supporting her weight as best I could. Blood trickled from her neural shunt, evidence of the strain she'd endured.

"We need to get back to the ship," she muttered, her voice weak but determined.

"This way!" Dwight shouted, gesturing toward a service corridor. "I found a route that bypasses the main halls. Those things are everywhere."

Christopher's voice boomed behind us as we stumbled toward the exit, layered with that unnatural resonance. "You cannot escape what you are, Burton! The medallion is just a key, you are the lock, forged through generations for this moment!"

I urged Lena forward, not daring to look back. The medallion burned against my chest, responding to its former captor's proximity. As we reached the doorway, I noticed stasis tubes along the walls beginning to activate, hydraulic systems hissing as they prepared to release their occupants.

"Run!" I shouted, pushing Lena through the door ahead of me.

As we passed, Dwight slammed his palm against the emergency lockdown panel, sealing the massive door behind us. The thick metal barrier shuddered as something enormous crashed against it from the other side.

"That won't hold him for long," Dwight warned, leading us down a narrow maintenance passage. "Christopher's been planning this for centuries. He won't give up easily."

The cramped corridor twisted and turned, leading us deeper into the bowels of the Lachesis. With each step, I felt the medallion's energy resonating with the ship around us. Bulkheads that should have been locked slid open at our approach; lighting systems flickered to life to guide our way.

"The ship is helping us," I realized aloud. "It recognizes the medallion... recognizes me."

"What do you mean?" Lena asked, her strength gradually returning as we moved.

I touched the medallion, feeling knowledge flow into me in fragments and flashes. "I don't understand everything, but the medallion shows me... connections. Meredith Rivera, my great-great-grandmother, wasn't just a passenger on the Lachesis. She was part of the team that designed its dimensional folding technology."

We emerged into a larger chamber, and I stopped short, recognizing it immediately, though I'd never been there before. "The auxiliary control room," I said, the knowledge rising unbidden. "From here, we can access the ship's systems... maybe find a way back to the Charon."

Lena leaned against a console, her face pale but determined. "How do you know all this?"

"It's like... fragments of memory," I tried to explain, moving toward the main control panel. "Not my memories, but... It's hard to describe. Meredith left something of herself in the medallion, encoded somehow. And because I'm her descendant, I can access it."

As I placed my hand on the console, the systems responded instantly, displays flickering to life with information that somehow made sense to me despite their complexity. I shouldn't have understood four-dimensional coordinates, quantum folding patterns, and dimensional resonance frequencies concepts, but somehow did, at least partially.

"We need to get to the main hangar," I said, studying the ship's layout. "There should be emergency vessels there, smaller than the Charon but enough to get us back to it."

"Can you find Harvey?" Lena asked suddenly, her hand rising to her inactive neural shunt. "It should still be on the Charon. I need to know it's safe."

I focused on the ship's long-range scanners, trying to locate the Charon. After a moment, I found it, still where we'd left it, half-buried in the snow. "The Charon's there, but I can't tell if Harvey is active. The storm is interfering with detailed scans."

Lena's expression tightened with worry. "It's been offline too long. The neural connection... without regular maintenance..."

"We'll find it," Dwight promised, surprising me with the gentleness in his voice. "But first, we need to get off this ship."

The medallion pulsed with increasing urgency as I continued working with the systems. I detected rapidly moving life forms converging on our position through the ship's internal sensors.

"We need to move," I warned. "Christopher's sent the transformed crew after us."

We hurried through the ship, guided by my newfound knowledge of its layout. The medallion seemed almost eager to help, its energy flowing through me and into the ship's systems, opening paths and sealing others behind us to delay our pursuers.

After navigating several levels, we reached a junction I recognized from the ship's schematics. "The hangar should be through here," I said, gesturing toward a sealed pressure door.

As I moved to activate the door controls, a violent tremor shook the ship, throwing us against the walls. Emergency alarms blared, and red warning lights bathed the corridor in a crimson glow.

"What's happening?" Lena demanded, steadying herself against a bulkhead.

I accessed a nearby terminal, and the information flooded my mind. Christopher activated the dimensional drive. He's trying to return the ship to its original coordinates to the Avalonian homeworld."

"Can he do that without you?" Dwight asked, his expression grim.

"Not completely," I said, understanding flowing from the medallion. "But he can destabilize the dimensional barriers enough to let more Avalonians through. We need to stop him."

"How?" Lena asked.

I closed my eyes, letting the medallion's knowledge guide me. "The CHeKeR device, the chair in the dimensional core. It's the control mechanism for the fold. If we can reach it, I might be able to reverse what he's started."

"Might?" Dwight's skepticism was clear.

"I don't understand everything," I admitted. "The knowledge comes in fragments. But I know we have to try."

Another tremor rocked the ship, stronger than before. The pressure door before us buckled slightly, metal groaning under unseen force.

"That's not a normal fold," I realized, my eyes widening. "He's forcing it. Tearing the dimensional fabric instead of folding it properly. If it ruptures completely"

"What happens?" Lena pressed.

"Total dimensional collapse. The Avalonian dimension would consume this whole region of space." The knowledge came to me with chilling certainty.

The pressure door suddenly slammed open, revealing not the hangar we'd expected but a swirling vortex of energy, a dimen sional rupture forming right before our eyes. Through it, I glimpsed shadowy figures moving with an alien grace, smoke-like tendrils reaching toward our reality.

"Back!" I shouted, pulling Lena away from the growing rift.

The medallion flared against my chest, its energy surging in response to the dimensional tear. I felt it reaching out, not just to the ship's systems but to something else, something on the Charon.

"Harvey," Lena whispered, her neural shunt pulsing with a faint blue light. "I can feel it... somehow..."

Without warning, the dimensional rift fluctuated wildly, its edges contracting and expanding in chaotic patterns. Through it, I saw the silhouette of the Charon, impossibly close though I knew it was kilometers away.

"The medallion is creating a bridge," I realized. "A stable pathway through the dimensional tear."

Before we could react, a massive mechanical form lunged through the rift, Harvey, its frame altered by the dimensional energies, glowing with the same light as my medallion. Its crudely drawn face seemed almost alive now, expressing a determination I'd never seen before.

Lena's neural shunt blazed with blue light as Harvey reached us, its metal hand extending toward the medallion around my neck. I felt a sudden certainty that the Tymeragoth entity within the medallion was calling Harvey, recognizing in its neural architecture a vessel that could contain it.

"It's compatible," Lena realized, the connection to Harvey briefly flickering back to life through her neural shunt. "The Tymeragoth... it can transfer to Harvey."

"Are you sure?" I asked, not fully understanding what was happening but trusting her instinct.

Lena nodded, determination hardening her features. "Do it."

I removed the medallion, holding it toward Harvey's extended hand. The moment they touched, energy surged between them, transferring something ancient and powerful. The medallion's glow faded slightly as Harvey's form brightened, the robot's internal systems reconfiguring to accommodate their new passenger.

When the transfer was completed, the medallion remained in my hand, still containing a fragment of the Tymeragoth entity enough to maintain my connection to the ship's systems while Harvey now pulsed with the same dimensional energy, its mechanical form somehow more alive than before.

Lena's neural shunt connected fully with Harvey again, their bond restored but transformed. "It's... different," she said, wonder in her voice. "I can see... so much more through Harvey now. The dimensional frequencies, the fold patterns..."

Another violent tremor shook the ship as Christopher's forced fold tore at reality. The rift before us expanded suddenly, revealing a path directly to the Charon, now visible through the dimensional window.

"Now!" Harvey's voice, or perhaps the Tymeragoth speaking through it, echoed in our minds. "The path is stable but temporary. We must go!"

Dwight went first, diving through the rift with a soldier's decisiveness. Lena followed her connection to Harvey, guiding her. I hesitated, looking down the corridor where Christopher was forcing the dimensional fold.

"I should stop him," I said, the medallion urging me toward the dimensional core.

"Not now," Harvey's voice resonated in my mind. "The fold is too unstable. We must retreat and prepare. This battle will continue, but not here, not today."

Trusting the ancient entity's wisdom, I turned and leapt through the dimensional window, feeling reality twist around me as I passed from the Lachesis directly to the Charon's bridge. Behind me, the rift collapsed, sealing the pathway and cutting us off from Christopher and his transformed crew.

I landed hard on Charon's deck, the medallion still clutched in my hand. Lena and Dwight were already at the controls, bringing the ship's systems online. Harvey stood nearby, its form subtly altered by the Tymeragoth's presence. Its inner light pulsed in rhythm with the fragment remaining in my medallion.

"We need to leave this planet," Lena said, her hands moving across the controls with newfound confidence. The neural connection to the enhanced Harvey gave her access to knowledge she hadn't possessed before. Christopher will find another way to pursue us."

As the Charon's engines roared to life, I slipped the medallion back around my neck, feeling its warmth spread through me. The knowledge it contained was still fragmentary and incomplete, but I understood enough that our journey was far from over.

I felt drawn to a console on the bridge, pulled by an intuition I couldn't explain. The ship's systems were functioning at minimal levels, powered by emergency backups. An orange light activated above a console button as I accessed the memory storage systems. I reached out, my hand seeming to move of its own accord. A file labeled "Meredith Rivera - Personal Log" appeared on the screen.

My heart pounded as I opened it, knowing somehow that this message had been waiting for me across generations – a legacy preserved in code and metal, from my great-great-grandmother to me. As the file loaded, I felt a deep certainty that whatever it contained would finally answer the questions that had driven my journey.

The screen flickered, and a woman's face looked back at me, her eyes sharing the same shape as my own.

~ 29 ~

FOLDING REALITY

"You have to put me back in the chair!" I said emphatically, slamming my fist into the galley table.

"Are you crazy?" Lena fired back, having regained her strength after days sequestered in her quarters. "We don't know what Christopher did to you the first time to get us," she waved her arms around dramatically, "here. And now you want to go and stick that thing back in your neck. On a hunch!"

I ran my fingers over my medallion, feeling its steady warmth against my chest. Since recovering it from Christopher, our connection seemed stronger than ever, as if the Tymeragoth entity trapped inside recognized what I had become.

"It's not just a hunch," I insisted, meeting her gaze. "Come with me to the bridge, and I'll prove it."

"Captain Maxwell," Iris's voice emanated from the nearby speaker, her tone having stabilized since I'd repaired her systems. "Engine diagnostic complete. Power reserves at 42% and holding."

"Thanks, Iris. And please, it's just Burton," I replied automatically.

Lena glanced at Dwight with a confused expression. "Maxwell?" she mouthed silently.

Dwight shrugged slightly and whispered, "Captain fancy-pants has a real name."

I ignored their exchange. Carter Maxwell belonged to someone else, a repair technician from Neda, who'd never seen the stars up close, faced Avalonians, or been caught in an ancient war. That person was gone. I was Burton now, shaped by everything that had happened since Christopher had dragged me from my workshop.

Lena raised an eyebrow. "Still not used to the promotion?"

"The name doesn't matter," I said. "But what I found in Mered ith Rivera's files does. She wrote that fewer than 10% of humans possess the necessary genetic makeup to operate the CHeKeR device as intended. But those with her genetic lineage can fold space and travel almost instantly through dimensions."

"I don't know what all that means," Dwight interjected, sitting on the bunk he'd installed in the galley. "But I know a shit bag of an idea when I hear it, kid. And it sounds like you're carrying a big heaping one."

I glanced suspiciously at Dwight, uncertain if I could trust him. After his actions on the Lachesis, putting both Lena and me in danger, I couldn't be sure he wouldn't do it again if it served his purposes.

"Look, it's as simple as this," I said as calmly as possible, "we don't have any other way off this planet. The Lachesis is buried in ice and crawling with half-dead Avalonian zombies. And the Charon has a giant hole in the engine room where the plasma core used to be. Our only option is to try to use the CHeKeR device to jump out."

I touched the medallion again, feeling its energy pulse in rhythm with my heartbeat. "Meredith's research shows that the CHeKeR device was meant to work in conjunction with this." I lifted the medallion slightly. "The Tymeragoth entity inside can navigate four-dimensional space. With it, I can guide us through the fold. Meredith Rivera and her descendants, including me, have a genetic structure that allows us to interact with higher dimensions when properly connected."

Lena paced back and forth in frustration as she gnawed on her thumbnail. "We can't just launch the Charon into space with a gaping hole in its side. We'll be sucked out immediately, or who knows what."

"We could still be in trouble even without the hole," Dwight said, lying back down. "Without a plasma core to propel us, we could drift aimlessly through space. And if we're not near a transit lane, we'll essentially be stuck in our tomb."

"Burton," Iris interjected, "my calculations support your theory. With the medallion's energy signature amplifying the CHeKeR device, the probability of successful dimensional transit increases to 78.4%."

I raised my voice, desperate to grab their attention. "Our options are limited," I said urgently. "A violent storm constantly ravages this planet. We only have a few days until we are completely buried. Our systems must be redirected to maintain the environment and keep us alive, but even that will only buy us a few months. The system will eventually shut down, leaving us to freeze or seek shelter in the palace until we starve to death."

I stopped speaking for a moment, letting Lena and Dwight absorb the gravity of our situation. "I've thought about our options," I said slowly. "If we install the CHeKeR device into the shuttle, we can jump out of the Charon and fly to safety once we're in open space."

"But the shuttle was damaged during Christopher's escape," Lena pointed out, her tone questioning.

I nodded, acknowledging the complication. "Yes, but the shuttle isn't destroyed. We can salvage parts from the Charon." My voice rose with a hint of excitement as I laid out the plan. "We can patch up the hull enough to withstand a short flight, just long enough to escape and propel us to safety."

Lena looked at me, then over at Dwight. "Well shit," Dwight said, hands clasped behind his head, looking up at the ceiling. "Freeze to death. Starve to death. Or get folded inside out by the kid's idea. What the hey, let's live a little." He finished with a knowing smile on his face that made me uneasy.

I noticed him subtly checking his wrist console when he thought no one was looking. Something was off, but we needed his help.

"Fine," Lena said with a resigned sigh. "How long will it take?"

I quickly checked my calculations before responding, "Give me two days." I double-checked and triple-checked my preparations for the shuttle. Without giving them time to say another word, I walked out of the galley and back to the bridge to finalize my plans.

Two exhausting days later, we gathered in the shuttle bay. The CHeKeR device had been carefully extracted from its housing in the lower levels of the Charon, and its neural interface was recalibrated to work with my unique genetic structure.

"All systems running. No alerts," Lena called back from the shuttle's pilot seat.

A few seats had been removed from the shuttle to make room for the CHeKeR device chair, which is now securely attached to the floor. Harvey's massive, lifeless form was propped against the wall to my left. Despite Dwight's objections, Lena had insisted on retrieving Harvey's body from where it had fallen during Christopher's escape. I understood her attachment; Harvey wasn't just a machine to her, but an extension of herself.

I had connected the CHeKeR device through Harvey's memory core, using it as a conduit to amplify its capabilities within the shuttle. The most critical step had been transferring a partition of Iris's AI core into the shuttle's systems; we couldn't risk losing her guidance once we severed connection with the Charon.

"Transfer complete," I'd announced after hours of painstaking work. "How are you feeling, Iris?"

"All primary functions operational within shuttle parameters," she had responded, her voice now emanating from the shuttle's speakers rather than the Charon. "Conscious continuity maintained at 94.3% efficiency."

Now, my medallion hung heavy around my neck, pulsing with a steady warmth that seemed to intensify as we prepared.

"The medallion's energy signature is synchronizing with the CHeKeR device," Iris reported through the shuttle's comm system. "Neural interface alignment at 92% and rising."

Dwight hovered behind me, holding the device probe and preparing to insert it into my neck. His expression was unreadable, but I noticed his eyes darting occasionally to his wrist console.

"Just make sure you don't fry my brain," I joked, trying to keep the mood light despite the palpable tension.

Dwight grinned, his eyes crinkling at the edges. "No promises," he quipped back, but his hands were steady as he positioned the probe.

As the probe approached the back of my neck, I felt a strange sensation; the scar tissue from my previous experience with the device seemed to pulse in recognition. The skin split open with a slight hiss, revealing a small opening deep into my body. It looked almost fragile and could easily be damaged if not handled carefully.

Dwight stumbled back nervously, "Geez, kid. Did you know it would do that?" He walked forward again, having regained his resolve.

I replied, "I have no idea." My nerves were getting the best of me as I realized how little I knew about the device and how I would react. Yet somehow, I felt that Meredith, my great-great-grandmother, had faced similar fears and unknowns. The thought gave me unexpected strength.

"According to Meredith's notes," I said, more to steady myself than inform Dwight, "the interface works by temporarily merging consciousness with the higher dimensions the Tymeragoth can perceive. The medallion focuses that perception, channels it."

As I spoke, the medallion grew warmer against my chest, as if responding to my words. I could almost feel the ancient entity inside it stirring, preparing for what was to come.

Dwight slowly positioned the probe near my neck. As it approached, the scar tissue from my previous experience with the device seemed to pulse in recognition. The skin parted softly like an organic interface, creating a perfect opening for the probe's biological socket, explicitly designed for this connection.

"Geez, kid. Did you know it would do that?" Dwight asked, momentarily hesitating before continuing.

"I have no idea," I replied honestly. My nerves were getting the best of me despite my body's apparent readiness for the procedure.

Dwight carefully guided the probe toward the opening. My breathing quickened, a nervous gasp escaping my lips. Despite his usual demeanor, Dwight's hands were steady, though I could hear his ragged breaths as he positioned the probe and inserted it into the waiting socket in my neck.

The cool metal slid in with surprising ease, finding its home with an almost magnetic precision. No pain accompanied the connection, only a strange pressure as neural pathways aligned. My body jerked reflexively as the interface activated, my nerve endings firing recognition signals rather than intrusion. My vision blurred into a kaleidoscope of colors I couldn't name, before everything faded.

And then I was elsewhere.

Unlike my first experience with the CHeKeR device, where I was a passive participant, I was in control this time. I could feel the Tymeragoth entity from the medallion extending through me, guiding me through spaces beyond three-dimensional understanding.

I perceived the universe as a vast, interconnected web of dimensional planes. Stars weren't just distant points of light but complex four-dimensional objects existing across multiple time-lines simultaneously. Our ship appeared as a strange, twisted structure that seemed to fold in on itself in ways that defied conventional geometry.

In this expanded state, I caught glimpses of the past, Meredith working with others, fighting to contain the Avalonian threat. I now understood why she had researched the medallion when fled with the other survivors. Their resistance had been forged against forces that would consume humanity.

Moving through the higher dimensions, I sensed something unexpected, a faint resonance from Harvey's neural structure. Though inactive, its complex neural pathways had been shaped by years connected to Lena's mind, creating a unique architecture that seemed to attract the Tymeragoth's attention. I filed this observation away, focusing on the task at hand.

I could see the dimensional wounds left by the Avalonians' previous attempts to traverse reality, scars in the fabric of space-time that pulsed with alien energy. One such wound led to a system I recognized from navigational charts: Nocturnes.

With the combined consciousness of myself and the Tymeragoth entity, I reached out and folded space around the shuttle, compressing the vast distance between Yrilla and Nocturnes into a single point, then pushing through it like threading a needle.

Reality shuddered, protested, then yielded.

***

As I regained consciousness, it wasn't a sudden snap or jolt that brought me back to reality. It was more like slowly rising to the surface of a dark ocean. The colors and lights gradually faded away, retreating to the edges of my sight as I became aware of my surroundings. Lena and Dwight were leaning over me, their faces showing a mixture of worry and anticipation. I could see their mouths moving, but their words were muffled and distant as I reconnected with physical existence.

As my senses sharpened, Lena's voice broke through the fog. "Burton! Can you hear me? Are you okay?"

My head was pounding, like every circuit in my brain had been rewired. There was an overwhelming flood of information, images, and sounds from where I was and where I was, fighting for residence in my mind. In my expanded consciousness, I had glimpsed something of Meredith's journey, her determination, and her fear as she discovered the truth about the Avalonians.

"Burton, can you hear me?" Lena asked again, her voice laced with concern and impatience. She shined her light in my eyes, looking for a reaction.

I grimaced as the bright light assaulted my eyes. "Yeah," I managed to say, my throat feeling as dry as a desert. "I'm okay. Did it work?" My voice sounded far away, almost muffled as if I was speaking from the bottom of a cannon. I tried to sit up, but the room began spinning, and my body protested with dizziness.

Dwight steadied me with a firm hand on my shoulder. "Take it slow, kid. You've been out for a good while."

"Did it work?" I asked again, forcing myself to focus on the present moment. I wanted to close my eyes and return to where I had just been.

Lena turned to Dwight, her usually unbreakable composure faltering as she breathed a small sigh of relief. "It worked, Burton," she whispered. "We made the jump. We're in the Nocturnes system."

The medallion pulsed against my chest, warm and reassuring, as if confirming her words. I could still feel the Tymeragoth's presence more clearly than before, a whisper of ancient consciousness guiding us safely through the fold.

Dwight chipped in, his voice a mix of awe and disbelief. "Never thought I'd see it happen, kid. That device... It's like it punched through the fabric of space itself."

His statement hung in the air, burdensome. Memories flooded my mind, transcending time and space. It felt like I was trapped within the CHeKeR device for an eternity, yet only a few seconds. My mind was thrust into a kaleidoscope of unfathomable dimensions. The vast expanse of the universe swirled around me, each star and particle dancing in a symphony of familiarity and foreignness. I was no longer just an observer, but a part of this cosmic tapestry, moving through space and time easily. The boundaries between reality and imagination blurred as the universe stretched before me, endlessly folding and unfolding in a brilliant cosmic wonder.

I blinked hard, trying to anchor myself back in the cramped cockpit of the shuttle. Lena was checking the readouts on the pilot's console, brow furrowed in that all-too-familiar way, when something bothered her.

"What is it?" My voice still felt distant, echoing weirdly inside my head.

"Ship signatures," she said, uncertainty in her voice. "They dropped in a few moments after we did."

"Analyzing approaching vessels," Iris interjected, her voice emanating from the shuttle's speakers. "Configuration matches hostile craft encountered in Sector 357-B. Weapons systems appear to be powering up."

"That's a good thing, right?" I asked, my hand instinctively reaching for my medallion. The Tymeragoth entity seemed agitated, its energy pulsing with a warning I couldn't reasonably interpret. "We needed someone to pick us up. This shuttle wasn't going to last indefinitely."

"Yeah. But" Lena gasped, her voice trembling as she frantically checked another sensor. "This close, this soon. I..." Her eyes widened in fear as she stopped mid-sentence and started to move frantically, her hands shaking as she tried to process the information on her screen. "Their transponder signals match the unknown ships that viciously attacked us outside the Order of the Sable Serpent territory. Dwight, get Burton back online immediately. We must move NOW!"

"Defensive systems coming online," Iris announced, her tone shifting to emergency protocols. "Evasive maneuver recommendations ready."

The sound of Lena's plasma rifle charging reached my ears, but it was so far away that I didn't register it immediately. My mind was suddenly consumed with thoughts of Dwight, his convenient appearance when Christopher needed him, his hesitation to help us on the Lachesis, and how he'd been checking his wrist console when he thought no one was looking.

"Calm down, boss," Dwight's voice rang out from behind me, a new confidence in his tone. "Looks like my ride is here."

As the words left his mouth, the medallion flared hot against my chest, its warning now unmistakable. The Tymeragoth entity had been trying to tell me that Dwight had betrayed us again, but this time, he had led our enemies right to us.

"Burton," Iris's voice dropped to a lower volume, directed primarily to my earpiece. "The medallion's energy signature is fluctuating wildly. I'm detecting dimensional disturbances like those recorded during your interface with the CHeKeR device."

Suddenly, my medallion began to pulse with an intensity I'd never felt before. Its light grew blindingly bright, filling the shuttle with an otherworldly glow. I could feel the Tymeragoth entity stirring, pushing against the confines of its ancient prison.

"What's happening?" Lena demanded, her plasma rifle now aimed squarely at Dwight.

"Unknown energy transfer in progress," Iris reported, her voice showing what almost sounded like awe. "Processing capabilities at maximum."

I couldn't answer because I was transfixed by the stream of consciousness flowing from the medallion. For the first time, the

Tymeragoth entity communicated with me directly, not through dimensional impressions or vague sensations but through clear, direct thought.

The machine vessel is compatible. Better than the medallion. Better than a human host.

"Harvey?" I whispered, understanding dawning on me.

The medallion grew hotter, nearly burning my skin through my jumpsuit. Without warning, a tendril of smoke-like energy erupted from it, but unlike the black smoke of the Avalonians, this was iridescent, shimmering with colors beyond human perception.

"Energy transfer targeting Harvey's neural core," Iris reported, her systems struggling to categorize what they witnessed. "Unprecedented dimensional patterns detected."

The energy shot across the shuttle directly into Harvey's neural core, where I had connected the CHeKeR device. Harvey's inert form shuddered, and Lena cried out in alarm, her hand instinctively reaching toward her neural shunt.

"No!" she screamed, as if feeling her final connection to Harvey severing. Blood trickled from her neural shunt as something fundamentally changed in the bond she'd shared with Harvey for most of her life.

Harvey's systems hummed to life, its optical sensors flickering one by one, but the light that shone from them wasn't the mechanical blue glow I was accustomed to. Instead, they gleamed with the same iridescent quality as the Tymeragoth's energy.

"Integration complete," Iris announced, her voice modulating as she processed the event. "Harvey's systems are online but... different. I'm detecting consciousness patterns that match neither machine nor human parameters."

The medallion in my hand grew cold, its inner light fading as the last Tymeragoth entity transferred into Harvey's neural matrix. This structure had been molded over the years of connection to Lena's mind, creating the perfect vessel.

Harvey slowly rose to its full height, movements more fluid than I'd ever seen, more like a living being than a machine. It turned to face Dwight, who had backed against the shuttle wall, fear evident in his eyes.

The shuttle's speakers crackled as if adapting to a new input source. Though Harvey itself remained silent, as always, a familiar yet transformed voice emanated from the shuttle's communication system, carrying harmonics that sent shivers down my spine.

"The machine remembers you," the voice stated, not coming from Harvey's form but connected to it. "The machine remembers your betrayal."

"Harvey's systems are integrating with shuttle controls," Iris reported, her tone indicating curiosity and caution. "My protocols are being... requested, not overridden. This is unprecedented."

Lena stared at Harvey, her expression caught between grief and wonder. The neural connection they had shared was gone forever, replaced by something entirely new; the ancient consciousness of a being from another dimension now inhabited the form she had guided for so long.

But how Harvey saw her with recognition and understanding told me that something of their bond remained. The Tymeragoth hadn't erased Harvey's memories or its core functionality; it had merged with them, creating something neither purely machine nor purely alien.

Harvey turned toward the control panel, its movements purposeful and precise. Though it didn't speak, the shuttle's systems began activating around us, displays flickering to life with new coordinates.

"The Tymeragoth entity is initiating dimensional transit protocols," Iris translated. "It appears Harvey can navigate the higher dimensions without the chair."

"Surrendering navigational control to Harvey," Iris announced, sounding almost relieved. "Dimensional coordinates are being processed at exponential speeds. Preparing for transit."

As Dwight's "ride" closed in on our position, I realized that while one chapter of our journey was ending, something new was beginning.

~ 30 ~

DIMENSIONAL ASCENDANCE

Through the viewport, I could see the hostile ships closing in sleek, predatory vessels bearing the unmistakable insignia of HexiCore, one of IGMC's most ruthless competitors. Their weapons systems were fully charged, and targeting arrays locked onto our position.

"Dwight," I said, turning to face him. He stood by the airlock, his expression unreadable. "Your ride is here. What happens now?"

Dwight's hand rested casually on his plasma pistol. "That's the question, isn't it, kid?" His gaze flicked between the approaching ships and Harvey. "Wasn't exactly expecting your robot friend to get possessed by an interdimensional entity. Complicates things."

Lena's plasma rifle hummed to life as she aimed it at Dwight's chest. "You sold us out," she snarled. "Again."

"Business is business," Dwight replied with a shrug that didn't hide the tension in his shoulders. "HexiCore and IGMC are just different sides of the same credit chip. Survival means keeping your options open."

The shuttle shuddered as the magnetic clamps locked onto us, halting Harvey's attempt at dimensional transit. The console flashed with warning lights as external systems overrode our controls.

"Docking protocols initiated," Iris reported. "External override detected. Airlock integrity compromised."

The shuttle's airlock hissed, pressure equalizing as it prepared to open. Dwight backed away from it, his plasma pistol now drawn but held at his side, not aimed at any of us.

"Look," he said quickly, "this doesn't have to get messy. HexiCore wants the medallion technology, the same as IGMC and Christopher. You hand it over, walk away clean."

"That's not going to happen," I replied, standing beside Lena. "The medallion's mine, and the Tymeragoth entity is inside Harvey now. You can't just hand that over like a piece of tech."

The airlock door slid open, revealing four heavily armored HexiCore operatives, weapons raised and aimed at our heads.

"Surrender the dimensional key and its operator," the lead operative demanded, voice distorted through his helmet's speaker. "Comply immediately or face termination."

What happened next occurred so quickly that I could barely process it. Harvey moved with impossible speed, one metal arm sweeping two operatives aside like toys while the other reached for the shuttle's control panel. The iridescent light in its optical sensors pulsed with alien intelligence as it interfaced directly with the shuttle's systems.

The remaining operatives opened fire, plasma bolts sizzling through the confined space. Lena dropped to one knee, returning fire with deadly accuracy that dropped one of them instantly. I ducked behind the navigation chair, reaching for the small plasma pistol I'd kept from our escape from the Serpent station.

And Dwight... Dwight surprised me.

Instead of joining the HexiCore operatives, he spun and fired three precise shots into the docking mechanism connecting our shuttle to their ship. The mechanism sparked and smoked but held.

"Kid!" he shouted over the chaos. "We need to move, NOW!"

I looked at Lena, but she was already ahead of me. Her neural shunt flared with light, not the familiar blue of her connection to

Harvey, but a shimmering, iridescent glow that matched the light in Harvey's optical sensors.

"Break free," she commanded, her voice strangely resonant, as if two beings were speaking through her simultaneously. "NOW!"

Harvey's response was immediate. Its metal hand plunged di rectly into the shuttle's control panel, circuits sparking as it bypassed standard interfaces. The shuttle's engines screamed in protest as they fired at maximum thrust, straining against the magnetic clamps.

"Warning: structural integrity compromised," Iris announced. "A hull breach is imminent in sectors three and seven."

Lena fired again, taking down the last operative still standing. "We can't stay on this shuttle," she shouted. It's falling apart!"

Dwight kicked the fallen operatives' weapons aside, then checked the air lock. "Their ship is still attached, barely. If we move now, we might be able to"

The rest of his words were drowned out by the shriek of tearing metal as Harvey forcibly separated our shuttle from the HexiCore vessel. The sudden decompression nearly sucked us all into space before emergency bulkheads slammed shut, sealing off the damaged section.

"Hull breach contained," Iris reported. "Life support failing. Power reserves at critical levels."

Through the remaining viewport, I could see the HexiCore ship drifting away. Its docking clamps were damaged, but its systems were still operational. Behind it, two more vessels were moving into position, weapons charging.

"We're dead if we stay here," Lena said, her voice steady despite the blood still trickling from her neural shunt. She placed her hand on Harvey's metal frame, the shunt behind her ear pulsing with that same iridescent light. Her eyes widened as information flooded her mind.

"Harvey can get us out," she said, her voice carrying that strange dual quality again. "But not through normal space. The shuttle's too damaged."

"What does that mean?" Dwight demanded, eyeing her warily.

Lena's eyes met mine, but something else looked through them, something ancient and vast. "Dimensional transit. Like the CHeKeR device, but... different. Without the operator."

"The Tymeragoth entity is attempting dimensional transit," Iris translated. "But the shuttle lacks sufficient power to fold completely. Partial transit may be possible, but destination coordinates cannot be guaranteed."

"What does that mean?" Dwight asked again, looking between Lena and me.

"It means we might escape, but we could end up anywhere," I explained. "Or nowhere."

A plasma bolt from the approaching HexiCore ships struck our shuttle, spinning us. Alarm klaxons blared as more systems failed.

"No choice," Lena decided, her eyes glowing with that strange iridescent light. Her neural shunt pulsed in perfect synchronization with Harvey's optical sensors. "Initiating transit now."

Harvey's massive frame seemed to vibrate at a frequency that hurt my eyes to watch. The shuttle's remaining power was redirected to whatever process the Tymeragoth entity initiated through Harvey and Lena. Space around us began to distort, light bending in impossible ways as reality seemed to fold inward.

"Wait," I said suddenly, a realization hitting me. "Iris, I can't leave her here."

Since my abduction from Neda, the AI has been my constant companion. It is the only entity aboard the Charon that has shown me genuine concern and guidance. The thought of abandoning her to the failing shuttle systems is unbearable.

"Iris," I called out, activating my wrist console. "Emergency protocol, transfer your core consciousness to my console!"

"Initiating emergency transfer," Iris responded, her voice fading as the shuttle's power diverted to Harvey's dimensional transit. "Core consciousness download at 37%... 58%... 76%..."

The shuttle shuddered violently as another hit from the HexiCore ships tore through our remaining shields. Lights flickered and died, life support sputtering as oxygen levels began to drop.

"Transfer complete," Iris's voice came through my wrist console, smaller but unmistakably her. "Primary systems offline. Secondary"

Her voice was cut off from the shuttle's speakers as the final power reserves redirected to Harvey. The space around us warped further, stretching and compressing in nauseating patterns my eyes couldn't properly process.

"Hold on to something!" I shouted, grabbing Harvey's frame as reality began to tear.

Lena gripped Harvey's other arm, while Dwight braced himself against the bulkhead. The last thing I saw through the viewport was the HexiCore ships opening fire again, but their plasma bolts seemed to slow, then stop, frozen in a moment that stretched like taffy.

Then, with a sensation like being turned inside out and reassembled, we were elsewhere. The shuttle's physical structure had partly collapsed during transit, leaving us in a strange amalgamation of shuttle parts and open space that somehow still contained atmosphere. The familiar dimensions of length, width, and height seemed optional here, objects existing at angles that shouldn't be possible.

"Where are we?" Dwight gasped; his voice distorted as if coming through water.

"Between," Lena answered, her voice still carrying that dual resonance. She stood beside Harvey, one hand resting on its metal frame, her neural shunt pulsing with energy. "The dimensional transit was incomplete. We exist between normal space and... something else."

"Between?" Dwight repeated incredulously. "Between what and what?"

"Between dimensions," Lena replied, her eyes unfocused as information flowed into her through her connection with Harvey. "The Tymeragoth has created a pocket dimension. A space between spaces, where we are temporarily safe from pursuit."

"Great," Dwight muttered, looking around at the fractured reality with evident discomfort. "So, we're not dead, just stuck in some interdimensional waiting room. How do we get back to normal space?"

I turned to Lena, who stood with her eyes closed, her neural shunt pulsing as she communicated with the Tymeragoth through Harvey. Her face showed concentration, occasionally shifting through expressions of wonder and concern.

"Lena?" I asked gently. "What's happening?"

She opened her eyes slowly, the iridescent light within them fading as she focused on me. "It's incredible," she whispered. "The Tymeragoth's consciousness is vast and ancient. It's been trapped for so long."

"Can it get us out of here?" Dwight pressed, unmoved by the wonder of it all.

Lena nodded. "Yes, but not directly." She winced, pressing her hand against her neural shunt. "It needs more energy. The transit depleted its reserves almost completely."

"What kind of energy?" I asked.

"It needs to connect with the dimensional nexus points," Lena explained, her voice stronger now. "Places where our universe naturally touches others. From there, it can draw enough power to stabilize this pocket dimension or transport us fully to safety."

"And where exactly would we find one of those?" Dwight asked, skepticism heavy in his voice.

Lena's expression shifted as more information came through her connection. "We don't need to find one. The Tymeragoth can sense them from here, reach out through the dimensional fabric." She paused, concentrating. "But there's something else out there. Something moving through the dimensional planes, searching."

A chill ran down my spine. "Christopher?"

"Not exactly," Lena said, her voice dropping. "Something else. The Avalonian entity that was within Christopher. It's... free. Moving between dimensions."

"Free?" I repeated, alarm rising in my chest. "What does that mean?"

"The Avalonian entity has untethered from its human host," Lena explained, information flowing through her connection with Harvey and the Tymeragoth. "It's ascending to its true form, gaining power as it moves between dimensions."

Dwight cursed under his breath. "So, we're stuck in this interdimensional limbo with a hostile alien entity roaming around? Perfect."

"It's not just roaming," Lena continued, her expression growing more troubled. "It's hunting. Searching for something." Her eyes met mine. “Searching for us. For the Tymeragoth."

"Iris," I called to my wrist console. "Are you still with us?"

"Functionality at 73%," her voice replied, slightly distorted but unmistakably her. "My processing capabilities are... altered in this dimensional space. Time appears non-linear from my perspective."

"Can you scan our surroundings? Help us understand what we're dealing with?"

"Attempting analysis," Iris responded. After a moment, she continued, "This pocket dimension exists outside normal space-time but maintains tenuous connections to multiple points in our universe. I'm detecting temporal variances and spatial inconsistencies that suggest we are experiencing multiple probability states simultaneously."

"In human terms?" Dwight prompted, his hand never straying far from his plasma pistol.

"We exist everywhere and nowhere," Iris simplified. "The pocket dimension is unstable and will eventually collapse. When it does, we will be forced back into normal space at a point determined by the dimensional currents. I cannot predict where or when that might be."

"What about the Tymeragoth?" I asked, looking at Harvey's transformed presence. "What can it tell us about navigating this space?"

Lena's eyes briefly flashed with that iridescent light, her neural shunt pulsing as information flowed between her and the entity within Harvey. "It's... difficult to translate," she said slowly. "The Tymeragoth perceives dimensions differently than we do. What we see as chaos, it sees as patterns, order within disorder."

"That's great," Dwight muttered. "Very philosophical. But practically speaking, what does that mean for us?"

"It means," Lena said, focusing her gaze on him, "that we can use this time to our advantage. While we're here, we're essentially untraceable. The Avalonian can't find us immediately. And more importantly, we can observe without being observed."

"Observe what?" I asked.

In response, Lena guided Harvey to the center of our fragmented reality bubble. The robot's massive hand extended, metal fingers splaying almost ritualistically. The iridescent light in its optical sensors intensified, and suddenly the shifting chaos around us stabilized into something more coherent.

The void beyond our reality bubble resolved into a window, no, multiple windows, each showing a different perspective of the dimensional planes. I could see swirling energy vortices, paths connecting different realities, and strange formations of light and matter that defied physical laws.

"The Tymeragoth can see through the dimensional barriers," Lena explained, her voice tinged with awe. "It's showing us the structure of the multiverse, the pathways between dimensions."

A fourth window appeared, focusing on a writhing mass of darkness that moved with terrible purpose through the dimensional currents. Unlike the black smoke I'd seen around Christopher, this was something more, expanded and evolved into its true form, no longer constrained by a human vessel.

"The Avalonian," I whispered, recognizing the entity despite its transformation.

"Yes," Lena confirmed, her voice tight with tension. "It's growing stronger as it absorbs dimensional energy. The Tymeragoth believes it's preparing for something."

"For what?" Dwight asked, his usually confident demeanor faltering as he stared at the swirling darkness.

Lena's face paled. "Invasion. It's gathering strength to tear open a permanent doorway between dimensions, to allow the rest of its kind to enter our universe."

The implication sank in like a stone. This wasn't just about us anymore, not just about escaping a dangerous situation. The fate of our entire dimension hung in the balance.

"How long do we have?" I asked, my mind racing for solutions.

"It's difficult to measure time here," Lena replied, "but the Tymeragoth estimates we have the equivalent of hours before the Avalonian gathers enough strength."

"And what happens then?" Dwight pressed.

"Then it will seek out a dimensional weak point in our universe and force it open," Lena explained. "Once that happens, there will be no stopping the invasion."

I watched the Avalonian's movement through the dimensional window, its darkness spreading like ink through water. "We can't just wait here for that to happen. We need to stop it."

"With what?" Dwight scoffed. "Look around, kid. We've got a half-destroyed shuttle, no weapons that would work against that thing, and nowhere to run."

"We have the Tymeragoth," I pointed out, gesturing to Harvey. "It understands these dimensions better than the Avalonian. It helped seal the doorway before."

"At great cost," Lena reminded me, her voice soft. "The Tymeragoth was trapped in the medallion for centuries."

I touched my medallion, now just an empty vessel without the entity it once contained. Yet it felt warm against my skin, as if some echo of the Tymeragoth's power remained.

"Then we need a different approach," I said, thinking out loud. "If we can't seal the doorway from our side, maybe we can disrupt the Avalonian's ability to open it first."

"How?" Dwight asked, skepticism heavy in his voice.

"Iris," I called to my wrist console. "You said time is non-linear here. What does that mean exactly?"

"Past, present, and future exist simultaneously in this pocket dimension," Iris explained. "Events that have already occurred in normal space-time are still in flux here. Similarly, events that have not yet happened may be accessible."

"So, we could potentially interact with events that haven't happened yet?" I pressed, an idea forming.

"Theoretically, yes," Iris confirmed. "Though the practical applications of such interactions are unpredictable."

I turned to Lena. "Ask the Tymeragoth if it can use the dimensional currents to our advantage. Can we redirect the Avalonian away from any weak points in our dimension?"

Lena closed her eyes, communicating silently with the entity through her neural connection with Harvey. After a moment, her eyes snapped open, glowing with that iridescent light.

"Not redirect," she said, her voice carrying that dual resonance again. "Intercept. The Tymeragoth believes it can force a confrontation in the space between dimensions, where the Avalonian doesn't have the advantage of physical hosts."

"A confrontation?" Dwight repeated incredulously. "You mean a fight? Between two interdimensional entities?"

"Not exactly a fight," Lena clarified, her expression shifting as information flowed into her mind. "More like... a contest of wills. A battle for control of the dimensional currents."

I stared at the window showing the Avalonian entity, its darkness spreading like cancer through the dimensional fabric. "And what role do we play in this confrontation?"

Lena's eyes met mine, the iridescent light dimming slightly to reveal her human concern beneath. "The Tymeragoth needs anchor points of stability in the chaos. It needs our consciousness, our will to help it maintain form and purpose during the confrontation."

"So, we'd be what, mental batteries?" Dwight asked, skepticism and fear mingling in his voice.

"More like... partners," Lena corrected. "The Tymeragoth doesn't want to control us like the Avalonian controls its hosts. It needs our willing cooperation, our combined strength."

I took a deep breath, weighing our options. "What are our chances if we do this?"

Lena's expression was grim. "The Tymeragoth doesn't think in terms of probabilities like we do. But it believes that without our help, the Avalonian will succeed in opening the doorway. With our help... there's a chance to stop it."

"A chance is better than no chance," I decided. "I'm in."

"You're both insane," Dwight muttered, but his hand had finally moved away from his plasma pistol. After a moment's hesitation, he sighed. "Fine. What's the worst that could happen? My consciousness gets scattered across multiple dimensions. Still better than what HexiCore would do to me."

"What do we need to do?" I asked Lena, my resolve hardening.

"We need to form a circle," she explained, standing beside Harvey. "Physical contact strengthens the connection. The Tymeragoth will use Harvey as its primary vessel, but it needs to extend its consciousness through all of us."

"Iris," I said to my wrist console. "Can you interface with this process?"

"Uncertain," Iris responded. "My consciousness exists as digital patterns rather than biological ones. However, I can attempt to stabilize the dimensional fluctuations around you, which may provide additional support."

"Do it," I instructed, standing opposite Lena, with Harvey between us.

Dwight reluctantly completed our circle, standing between Lena and me, his hands reaching out to connect us. "If this works," he said, uncharacteristically serious, "and we survive, I'm retiring somewhere quiet. Maybe become a farmer."

Despite everything, I found myself smiling at the image. "I'll hold you to that."

As our circle closed, Harvey's optical sensors blazed with iridescent light. The same energy began to flow through Lena's neural shunt, reaching out tendrils that touched first me and then Dwight.

The sensation was unlike anything I'd experienced before, not painful, but overwhelming, as if my consciousness was suddenly expanding beyond the confines of my body to encompass vaster realities. I could feel Lena's determination, Dwight's reluctance, and something else, something ancient and powerful that touched us all.

We are ready, a voice that wasn't a voice echoed in my mind. *The confrontation begins.*

The pocket dimension around us rippled and shifted, responding to the Tymeragoth's will. The windows show the dimensional planes merged and expanded, creating a vast arena of swirling energies and impossible geometries.

And through this impossible space, attracted by our combined presence, came the darkness—the Avalonian entity, no longer confined to a human host, swelling with stolen power and ancient hunger.

Two titans of different dimensions were about to clash, with humanity caught in the middle. And we were the only ones who could tip the balance.

As the Avalonian approached, I gripped Lena and Dwight's hands tighter, drawing strength from their presence. Whatever happens next will determine not just our fate but also the fate of our entire dimension.

The final confrontation had begun.

~ 31 ~

ECHOES ACROSS DIMENSIONS

The confrontation began with a surge of iridescent light that erupted from Harvey's frame, colliding with the encroaching darkness of the Avalonian entity. The impact sent dimensional shockwaves rippling through our pocket of reality, distorting the fragmented shuttle parts that still surrounded us. I gripped Lena and Dwight's hands tighter, feeling the energy of the Tymeragoth flowing through our circle, using our consciousness as anchors in this battle beyond physical comprehension.

"Hold on," Lena gasped, blood cascading from her neural shunt in crimson rivulets that defied gravity in this warped space. Her eyes gleamed with that strange iridescent light, seeing dimensions I could only glimpse in fragments. "It's trying to use us as a conduit."

The Avalonian entity surged forward, its darkness spreading like a viscous plague across the dimensional fabric, tendrils of black smoke tearing into our mental circle. Where it touched my consciousness, I felt my mind begin to fracture, memories ripped apart and reassembled in chaotic patterns. My nose and ears began to bleed, blood floating in crimson spheres around my head.

A tendril of darkness wrapped around Dwight's throat, constricting visibly as his face purpled and his eyes bulged. He clawed at the immaterial substance, fingers passing through it while it remained solid enough to choke the life from him. "Can't... breathe..." he gasped, his grip on my hand weakening.

Harvey's frame shuddered as the Tymeragoth channeled more energy through its mechanical body, the metal warping under the strain. Parts of Harvey's chest plate began to melt, dripping molten metal that hung suspended in the pocket dimension. The robot's drawn-on face seemed to contort in what could only be described as pain.

"Burton," Iris's voice cut through my mental haze, emanating from my wrist console. "The pocket dimension is destabilizing. Temporal inconsistencies are accelerating. I estimate a complete structural collapse in approximately seventeen minutes."

Through the chaos, I clutched my medallion, its familiar weight against my chest. Since the Tymeragoth had transferred to Harvey, it was now just an empty vessel. The metal felt cold and inert for the first time since I'd worn it.

The Tymeragoth's response manifested as a surge of power through Harvey's frame, meeting the Avalonian's advance. Reality seemed to tear open where they collided, creating bleeding wounds in the dimensional fabric. Through these ruptures, I caught glimpses of other places, other times, the ice plains of Yrilla, the burning ruins of Earth, and stranger landscapes beyond human comprehension.

Dwight's hand suddenly tightened painfully around mine, his fingernails digging deep enough to draw blood. I turned to see his face contorted in a grimace, veins bulging in his forehead, eyes wide with terror.

"It knows me," he hissed through clenched teeth, blood seeping from between his lips. "The Avalonian it recognizes me from before. From IGMC."

"Stay focused," I urged, feeling him pull away. "We need to maintain the circle."

But Dwight was already shaking his head, a strange calm settling over his features despite the blood leaking from his eyes. "No, kid. It's targeting me specifically. I can feel it ripping through my memories, searching for information about HexiCore, about the weapon."

"What weapon?" Lena demanded, but Dwight had already broken the circle, stepping back with deliberate intent.

"I wasn't just working for HexiCore for the money," he said, his voice steady despite the fear in his eyes. "I was helping them track Avalonians. They've been developing something—a dimensional disruptor. That's why I kept checking my wrist console—sending them data on the entity."

When Dwight broke our circle, the Avalonian entity surged toward him with predatory intent. Its darkness enveloped him like a collapsing star, tendrils boring into his eyes, nostrils, and mouth. His body convulsed violently, back arching at an impossible angle that threatened to snap his spine. Blood erupted from every orifice, hanging in grotesque globules around his contorted form.

"Dammit, Dwight!" Lena shouted, her voice cracking with both rage and fear. "What have you done?"

But even as the Avalonian focused its attack on Dwight, I realized he'd created an opening—a momentary distraction that had weakened the entity's assault on the Tymeragoth.

Through Harvey's receptors and my connection to the Tymeragoth, I suddenly understood. "He's giving us a chance," I said, the knowledge rising from somewhere beyond my conscious mind. "The Tymeragoth can use this moment to establish a stronger dimensional fold."

Dwight's body convulsed as the Avalonian entity tore through his mental defenses. Blood poured from his every pore now, forming a gruesome crimson halo around him. Somehow, he maintained enough control to reach for his wrist console. "Burton," he gasped, his voice barely recognizable. "Take... this..." He pressed something on the console, sending a data packet to mine before the Avalonian's darkness consumed him completely.

"The information I stole," he managed through gritted teeth, a tooth cracking audibly under the pressure. "Use it. Make it... worth something."

His body collapsed, suspended in the dimensional void, wreathed in the Avalonian's darkness. But something unexpected happened; instead of being consumed, Dwight's consciousness fought back with surprising strength, his decades of guilt and regret crystallizing into a final act of defiance.

"You think you know sacrifice?" he snarled at the entity invading his mind, blood spraying from his lips with each word. "You think you know survival? I've clawed my way through hell my whole life. You're just another demon to put down."

With a final, desperate motion, Dwight activated something on his wrist console. His body began to glow with strange energy, not the iridescent light of the Tymeragoth, but something harsher, more artificial. The HexiCore dimensional disruptor prototype had been embedded in his cybernetic implants.

The Avalonian entity recoiled, but it was too late. The disruptor activated, creating a localized dimensional fracture that tore through both Dwight and the portion of the Avalonian entity wrapped around him. The explosion of energy was blinding, the sound beyond hearing, and the dimensional shredding reduced part of Dwight's body to atomized particles. At the same time, the rest was violently hurled through the rupture he'd created.

"Burton!" Lena's voice pulled me back to our immediate reality, her face streaked with blood from her overloaded neural shunt. "We need to act now while it's wounded!"

I reconnected with her, our hands joining as Harvey's massive frame stepped between us. The Tymeragoth energy surged through our connected circle, which is stronger now with the two of us focusing on it. The wounded Avalonian thrashed in the dimensional void, its darkness fragmenting like shattered obsidian, but already beginning to reform.

My medallion remained cold against my chest, its power gone with the Tymeragoth entity. I pulled it from around my neck with my free hand, knowing it was now just metal, yet somehow connected to this interdimensional conflict through its design as a containment vessel.

"The medallion," I gasped. "We can use it to focus the fold!"

Lena's eyes widened as she understood. "Harvey has the power now, but the medallion was designed as a dimensional key; it can still help direct the energies!"

The injured Avalonian entity sensed our intent. It surged forward with renewed fury, darkness spreading across multiple dimensional planes simultaneously. A tendril lashed out like a whip, slicing through the dimensional fabric between us. The edge caught my left arm at the elbow, and for a moment, there was no pain—just a strange sensation of weightlessness as I watched my forearm and hand, still clutching the medallion, float away from my body.

The pain hit a heartbeat later, so intense that my vision went white. I screamed; the sound was lost in the dimensional chaos. Blood sprayed from the clean amputation, hanging in globules before being drawn into the dimensional rift like crimson rain flowing upward.

Lena reacted with battlefield precision, releasing my remaining hand to lunge for my severed limb. She caught it just before it disappeared into a dimensional tear, wrenching the medallion from my lifeless fingers.

"Hold on!" she shouted, pressing the medallion back into my remaining hand while using her free arm to create a makeshift tourniquet around my stump with a strip torn from her jumpsuit. Blood soaked through the fabric immediately, but the pressure stemmed the worst of the flow.

The Avalonian entity, sensing my weakness, redoubled its attack. Tendrils of darkness wrapped around Harvey's frame, trying to tear the Tymeragoth from its mechanical vessel. Metal buckled and sheared under the pressure, one of Harvey's arms ripping free in a spray of hydraulic fluid and sparking circuits.

Through a haze of agony and blood loss, I clutched the medallion, understanding that while its power was gone, its design still made it useful as a focus point, a key to directing the energies Harvey now commanded.

"Lena," I gasped, fighting to stay conscious. "The disruptor data from Dwight was input into Harvey's systems. We need to calibrate the fold to the Avalonian's frequency."

She quickly moved, accessing her neural shunt despite its blood pouring. Her connection with Harvey allowed direct data transfer, circumventing the need for physical interfaces. The robot's remaining arm came up, fingers splaying in a complex pattern that manipulated the dimensional fabric around us.

"Burton," Iris's voice came from my wrist console, distorted by the dimensional fluctuations. "Your vital signs are critical. Blood loss has reached dangerous levels. You must complete the fold within two minutes or risk permanent neural damage."

I channeled my focus through the medallion, now serving as a conduit for Harvey's powers rather than a power source itself. The Tymeragoth guided our efforts, using Harvey as its vessel to shape the dimensional currents into a powerful riptide.

The Avalonian entity sensed the growing dimensional pressure and fought with frenzied desperation. It abandoned its attack on Harvey to surge directly toward me, recognizing the danger in our combined effort.

"Now!" Lena screamed, blood erupting from her neural shunt as she pushed Harvey's systems beyond their limits.

With a final surge of will, we completed the fold. Harvey's form flared with blinding light, channeling dimensional energies through my medallion. Reality bent around the Avalonian entity, folding and twisting until caught in a rapidly collapsing pocket of space-time.

The entity's rage manifested as a physical force, a dimensional shockwave that tore through our failing reality bubble. Harvey's frame buckled under the pressure, chest cavity caving inward as circuits overloaded. Lena was flung backwards, her connection to Harvey violently severed as her neural shunt erupted in a shower of sparks and blood.

The backlash hit me like a physical blow as the dimensional pocket collapsed. My consciousness fragmented, perceptions scattering across multiple planes of existence. The last thing I saw before darkness claimed me was the medallion disintegrating in my hand, its purpose fulfilled as it was consumed in the dimensional sealing.

Then everything the shuttle fragments, Harvey's damaged form, Lena's unconscious body, and my bleeding, broken shell, was expelled from dimensional space like debris from an explosion, hurtling through the void toward an unknown destination.

Impact. Pain. Darkness.

Consciousness returned in fragments, each more painful than the last. I was lying on something soft and yielding, the smell of earth and vegetation filling my nostrils. Blood filled my mouth, metallic and warm. I tried to move and immediately regretted it as agony lanced through what remained of my left arm.

With tremendous effort, I opened my eyes. A canopy of alien trees stretched above me, their purple-tinged foliage filtering strange, golden sunlight. Nearby, the shattered remains of our shuttle lay embedded in the forest floor, broken metal steaming in the humid air.

"L-Lena," I tried to call, but my voice emerged as little more than a blood-choked whisper.

Something moved in my peripheral vision—Lena, crawling from the wreckage, her face a mask of blood from a deep gash across her forehead. Her neural shunt hung by threads of flesh and wire, partially torn from her skull. She dragged herself toward me, leaving a crimson trail in the soft loam.

"Burton," she gasped, collapsing beside me. "Stay... with me..."

I tried to respond, but unconsciousness was already reclaiming me, blood pooling beneath what remained of my left arm. The medallion was gone, consumed in the dimensional sealing. As darkness closed in, I caught a glimpse of Harvey's shattered frame half-buried in the forest floor, optical sensors flickering weakly with residual energy.

My last thought before the void claimed me was whether we had succeeded. Was the Avalonian truly banished, or merely wounded and cast adrift like us? The answer slipped away as consciousness failed, leaving only darkness and the distant sound of Lena desperately calling my name.

***

Three Months Later

The recalibration of my mechanical arm sent a jolt of pain through the nerve interface, making me wince. The technician—one of Nyx's more skilled associates—adjusted something beneath the metal plating, and the pain subsided to its usual dull ache.

"Better?" she asked, her voice distorted by the breathing apparatus all of Terax-3's inhabitants wore.

I flexed the cybernetic fingers, watching the metal plates shift and realign with mechanical precision. The arm was a marvel of engineering, scavenged from various technological sources and assembled with Nyx's peculiar expertise. It reminded me uncomfortably of Christopher's arm, though mine lacked the more sophisticated modifications he'd accumulated over centuries.

"It'll do," I replied, my voice rougher than before our dimensional ordeal. The physicians had claimed I'd torn my vocal cords screaming during the worst of the surgeries.

The technician nodded and retreated, leaving me alone in Nyx's small recovery room. Despite our history, the enigmatic mechanic had been surprisingly accommodating when Lena had somehow managed to get us back to Terax-3. Whether it was professional curiosity about my condition or genuine compassion, I couldn't tell, but I was grateful, nonetheless.

The door slid open, and Dwight entered. The eye patch he now wore gave him a piratical air, concealing the empty socket where his right eye had been. He'd traded it to Nyx as payment for my treatment, a sacrifice the former IGMC operative had made without hesitation when we'd first arrived half-dead at Terax-3. It was a side of him I never expected from our first encounters, another layer to his complicated character.

"Up and about, kid?" he asked, his remaining eye assessing my condition with practiced efficiency.

"Getting there," I said, standing carefully. My body was a roadmap of scars now, some from the crash, others from the surgeries that had followed. "Any news?"

Dwight shook his head, adjusting his eye patch, a nervous habit he'd developed. "Nothing concrete. The scanners Nyx rigged up haven't detected any dimensional anomalies since we arrived. The Avalonian is gone for good, lying low, licking its wounds."

I nodded, unconvinced. We'd struck a serious blow, certainly, but something told me the entity wasn't so easily banished. The wound in dimensions we'd created had been sealed with the medallion's sacrifice, but wounds could reopen.

The door slid open again, admitting Lena. Her neural shunt had been replaced with a cruder version, the scar tissue around it still angry and red. She moved differently now, her once-fluid grace replaced by careful precision that spoke of hidden pain.

"We've got a ship," she announced without preamble. "One of Nyx's associates is willing to trade for the information we gathered on the Avalonian entity. It's not much, but it'll get us off this rock."

"To where?" I asked, flexing my mechanical fingers absently.

"There's a colony in the Nocturnes system," she replied, her eyes fixed on a point past my shoulder. She still found it difficult to look directly at my mechanical arm. "They have resources, technology. Maybe enough to build something that can detect dimensional ruptures if the Avalonian returns."

"When," I corrected quietly. "When it returns."

Neither Lena nor Dwight contradicted me. They'd seen what I'd seen, felt what I'd felt. The Avalonian hadn't been destroyed, merely wounded and banished, and such entities were patient. It might take decades or centuries, but it would find a way back.

"What about Iris?" I asked, remembering the AI with me since I'd been taken from Neda.

"Her core programming survived," Dwight said. "I've transferred her to a portable module. Not as sophisticated as the Charon's systems, but functional. She's been analyzing the data I recovered from HexiCore, trying to understand the dimensional physics at play."

"And I'm going to check on Harvey after this," Lena added, her tone carefully neutral despite the subtle hope in her eyes. "Nyx thinks there might be a way to rebuild the neural pathways. The Tymeragoth's energy left... imprints in his systems."

I nodded, feeling a strange mixture of grief and hope. We'd lost so much: my arm, Dwight's eye, Lena's original connection to Harvey, the medallion that had been my last link to my father. Yet somehow, we'd survived. Broken, changed, but alive.

"We leave tomorrow," Lena said, moving toward the door. "Get some rest. You'll need your strength."

The Avalonian was out there, gathering strength, seeking a way back. And without the medallion, without the Tymeragoth's direct guidance, we had only our scars and our experience to face it when it returned.

I flexed my mechanical fingers, listening to the soft whir of servos. Christopher had lived with such an arm for centuries, his body slowly modified to contain the entity that possessed him. I wondered if this was how it had also begun for him, a wound, a replacement, the first step on a long path of transformation.

The thought should have disturbed me, but instead, it brought a grim smile to my face. If the Avalonian had expected to find the same frightened technician it had faced before, it would have been sorely disappointed. What had emerged from that dimensional rift was something harder, forged in blood and sacrifice.

The arm made a fist, metal plates shifting with mechanical precision. Whatever came next, whatever darkness waited beyond the thin membrane of our reality, we would face it; changed, scarred, but unbowed.

The hunt would continue.

www.ingramcontent.com/pod-product-compliance
Lightning Source LLC
Chambersburg PA
CBHW070640310726
48982CB00001B/356
9798999066008